THE HEART
KNOWS THE WAY
HOME

THE HEART KNOWS THE WAY HOME

CHRISTY DISTLER

AVODAH BOOKS

Published by Avodah Books
www.avodahbooks.com

Library of Congress Cataloging-in-Publication Data

Names: Distler, Christy, author.
Title: The heart knows the way home / Christy Distler.
Description: Warminster, PA: Avodah Books, 2021
Identifiers: LCCN 2020923640 | ISBN: 978-1-7347789-2-2 (paperback) | 978-1-7347789-5-3 (casebound) | 978-1-7347789-3-9 (ebook)
Subjects: LCSH Lancaster County (Pa.)--Fiction. | Mennonites--Fiction. | Family life--Pennsylvania--Fiction. | Love stories. | BISAC FICTION / Amish & Mennonite | FICTION / Christian / Romance / General
Classification: LCC PS3604.I78 H43 2021 | DDC 813.6--dc23

Unless otherwise indicated, Scripture quotations are taken from the King James Version of the Bible.

Scripture quotations marked NKJV are taken from the New King James Version®. Copyright © 1982 by Thomas Nelson. Used by permission. All rights reserved.

Scripture quotations marked CSB are taken from the Christian Standard Bible®, Copyright © 2017 by Holman Bible Publishers. Used by permission. Christian Standard Bible, and CSB® are federally registered trademarks of Holman Bible Publishers.

Publisher's Note: This is a work of fiction. Names, characters, and incidents are a product of the author's imagination. Some actual locales and businesses are used for atmospheric purposes. Any resemblance to actual people, living or dead, is completely coincidental.

Cover design by Hannah Linder Designs

*To the children and families served by
Clinic for Special Children and the amazing staff
who care for them—body, soul, and spirit.*

*To the men and women who,
through adoption or otherwise, love and care for
children whose parents are unable to do so.
"Whatever you did for one of the least of these brothers and
sisters of mine, you did for me" (Matthew 25:40 CSB).*

*But as for you, you meant evil against me;
but God meant it for good, in order to
bring it about as it is this day.*

GENESIS 50:20 NKJV

GLOSSARY

Most Old Order Mennonite groups in Lancaster County, Pennsylvania, speak *Deitsch* (Pennsylvania Dutch) as their first language and use English only with non–*Deitsch* speakers. To give readers a taste of the language, some words and phrases are occasionally used in this book. *Deitsch*, like German, generally capitalizes all nouns, but for the sake of the reader, I've used the English rules for capitalization of nouns.

ach: oh

ay-yi-yi: an expression that shows frustration, sadness, etc.

Bisht alright?: Are you all right?

daadi: grandfather

daadi haus: grandparents' house/in-law suite

daed: dad

danki: thank you

Dee flickel fleeya, ava's hatz vaased da vaag haem: The wings do the flying, but the heart knows the way home.

dumme gedanke: foolish idea

Ebbes letz?: Something wrong?

Es dutt mir leed: I'm sorry.

Funkeleit: progressive Mennonite

gmay: Old Order Mennonite community

gmayhaus: Old Order Mennonite church house

Gott: God

guder mariye: good morning

guder nacht: good night

guder owed: good evening

gut: good

Ich wees sell: I know that.

kumm: come

macht nichts: It doesn't matter.

mamm: mother

mammi: grandmother

nee: no

nichts: nothing

Ordnung: set of rules and regulations followed by the church

outsida: Non–Old Order Mennonite

schtobbe: stop

Sell isht gut: That is good.

Sie alright?: Is she all right?

verhuddled: confused

Was hot's gewwe?: What happened?

Was iss letz?: What's wrong?

ya: yes

Wenger: Formally named Groffdale Conference, Wenger Mennonites are a horse-and-carriage-driving Old Order group that formed in Lancaster County in 1927.

Horning: Formally named Weaverland Conference, Horning Mennonites are a car-driving Old Order group that formed in Lancaster County in 1927. This group split off the group that took the name Groffdale Conference, primarily over the use of automobiles.

A New Beginning

If what didn't kill you made you stronger, Janna could have singlehandedly upended the fifty-foot pine tree that had sliced through the second floor of her new home. As it was, she struggled to get a handle on her racing mind while steering her Honda CR-V to the curb and then shoving the gearshift into park.

"Mama!" Kayla's wail from the backseat suggested tears would follow. "What happened to our house?"

What happened was obvious. Horrifyingly so. But how? Everything had been fine twelve hours ago when they returned to their old apartment for the night before bringing the last carload of belongings to Akron this morning. The white clapboard house with its green trim, quaint front porch, and small flower garden had even felt like home already.

Oh no. Mrs. Bollinger. Their sweet seventy-something landlady who lived on the other side of the twin house had been sitting in a chair on the front porch when they left last night. Where was she now? Surely not inside. Yellow caution tape had been strung from the rightmost porch post to the street sign at the left corner of the property and along the side street. But had she been hurt? The tree barely touched her side of the house, but who knew what damage was inside.

Janna pulled the keys from the ignition, then glanced in the sideview mirror before getting out of the car. Hot, humid air enveloped her as she opened the back door.

Still in her booster seat, Kayla clung to her ratty stuffed rabbit and stared past her with wide eyes. "Our house, Mama."

Janna's chest tightened at the raw anguish in her daughter's voice. She released the seat's five-point harness and tried to portray a calm she didn't feel. "I know. But it'll be all right. Come on." She helped Kayla out, then held her hand as they crossed the street. A white pickup truck and a red-striped fire department SUV sat in front of the neighboring house, but no one was in sight.

Stopping where the sidewalk met the brick walkway, Janna stared up at the pine that had fallen sideways onto the roof above three of the four second-story windows. The middle two windows had cracked, but the one to the left of them fared much worse. Pine branches had broken through the frame from the inside, thrusting shards of glass and the old air conditioner onto the porch roof.

The tightness in her chest surged into her throat. That was the window of the bedroom Kayla had chosen.

"Don't go any closer!"

She turned at the deep voice's warning, clutching Kayla to her side. Two men, one maybe forty and the other old enough to be his father, approached from around the right side of the house. The younger one wore a navy-blue T-shirt with a fire department crest on the chest, so they had to be the drivers of the pickup and SUV.

The older one smoothed his thinning white hair. "You Joanna Carpenter?"

They knew her name—sort of. A good sign. "Janna, yes. We moved in yesterday. Is Mrs. Bollinger okay?"

The other, nearly a head taller, nodded once as the two stopped a few feet away. "She's fine. Gertie's outlived cancer twice. A tree in her roof barely fazed her"—he glanced down at Kayla—"though she was sure glad you weren't here. She wanted to call you but misplaced your number."

"Where is she?"

"At her son's place. A tree service is coming today, but no one can go in the house till it's inspected and deemed structurally stable."

Ugh. Not what she wanted to hear. "We can't even get our things from the first floor?" Only their bedframes, mattresses, and a dresser had been carried upstairs by the movers. "Almost everything's still downstairs."

The older one scrunched his face. "Sorry, hon. Justin's with the fire department. He can take your number and let you know what the inspector says. Probably won't be till Monday, though. Do you have somewhere to go?"

Hardly. Their old apartment was an hour and a half away, and she'd turned in the keys that morning. As well, everything she owned, save what filled their small car, was held hostage by the house.

"How'd that tree fall down?" Kayla scowled up at it, now looking more curious than upset. That wouldn't last long.

Justin leaned down and rested his hands on his knees. "We had a bad storm here last night. The ground was soft and wet from the rain, and the strong wind blew it over." Straightening again, he met Janna's gaze with concerned eyes. "Do you have somewhere to go?"

If only she could think straight. "Well . . . no." And she

didn't want to go far in case they could get into the house sooner. Staying at a motel was an option, but finding a room in Lancaster County in late June would be nearly impossible. Except for one possibility. "Is the Flying Dutchman still the least-expensive place around?"

Both men eyed her. "It is," the older one said, "but for good reason. You don't want to stay there."

Not at all if its clientele were anything like they were years ago. But after paying the early termination penalty on their apartment, the movers' fee, and the first month's rent here, she needed to scrimp until she got paid again.

"It'll be fine . . . till we figure something out." Which she needed to do elsewhere. Swallowing down the lump in her throat, she returned her gaze to Justin. "If I give you my number, will you call me as soon as you know anything about the house?" And for nothing else.

Goodness. She had no right thinking that way about him. Not every guy was bad news. Justin had to be fifteen years older than her, and he seemed nice enough. He also spoke with a hint of the accent common to *Deitsch* speakers, so he was probably Mennonite and married even though he wasn't wearing a wedding band.

"Sure." He pulled a pad of paper and pen from the back pocket of his jeans and handed it to her. "Anything else we can do?"

Besides wave a magic wand and make this all go away? She clenched her jaw as she wrote out her name and cell phone number. "No. Thank you." She handed him the paper and pen, then grabbed Kayla's hand. "Come on, honey."

Kayla pulled away, her blue eyes alarmed below the curly wisps of damp strawberry-blond hair stuck to her forehead. "Where are we going? My toys are inside."

Janna picked her up and spoke quietly as she crossed the

street. "I know. But we can't go inside the house right now. They'll let us know when we can." Thank goodness Kayla's favorites were in the car. "We have Rabbit and your blanket. We'll get the rest as soon as we can."

"But . . . Mama, noooo! I want . . . I want . . . Noooo!"

By the time they were both in the car, Janna was soaked with perspiration and wanted to cry just as hard as her wailing five-year-old in the backseat. She pulled away from the curb, only to slam on the brakes when a car horn blared alongside her. As soon as the street was clear, she headed toward Main Street.

Somehow, in less than twenty minutes, their fairy-tale new beginning had turned into a nightmare.

Ten minutes later, Janna turned off Wanner Road and onto Division Highway. Kayla had finally stopped crying and now clutched her rabbit and blanket as she leaned sideways against the headrest of her booster seat. Another ten minutes and they'd be at the Flying Dutchman. If nothing else, renting a room would give Kayla a place to take a nap—much needed after the move yesterday and their late night—while Janna decided what to do next. They had some clothing and food in the car, but not what they'd need for even a few days at a motel.

Suddenly, the car sputtered and slowed. Janna released the gas pedal and pressed it again, but nothing happened. Although K-LOVE still played through the speakers, the air conditioner blew warmer air and their speed gradually decreased.

"Mama?" Kayla already sounded sleepy.

"Hold on, Kay. Something's not right with the car." She

glanced down at the dashboard. The only warning light lit was the low-fuel indicator, but that one hadn't gone out since the gas gauge stopped working six months ago. Since then, she'd been watching the trip meter to make sure she filled the tank every three hundred miles.

Except the full mileage was displayed instead of the trip mileage. "Please, no," she whispered as she tapped the trip meter button.

Three hundred and sixty-six miles.

No, no, no. Could this day get any worse?

"Mama? My tummy hurts."

What? *Oh, please not now.* A glimpse of Kayla's pale face in the rearview mirror confirmed her fear. Carsickness. Apparently, the day could get worse. Much worse. All because she'd taken hilly, curvy Farmersville Road so she wouldn't have to drive past the house where she and Mom had lived for six years of her childhood. "Okay, honey. We have to pull over anyway."

The car slowed even more as they climbed a hill, then Christian Aid Ministries' white wooden sign appeared on the opposite side of the road. Steering was much more difficult now, but if she could just get into the parking lot, they'd be safer than if she stopped on the shoulder.

"Please, God. Please, God," she whispered. "Just a little farther." At least no vehicles were oncoming.

The car was going too slow to make it fully into the parking lot. Cutting the turn into the driveway as soon as possible, she maneuvered the barely rolling car onto the grass between the sign and the bush alongside the exit lane.

Safe. Now to help Kayla.

She got out and opened the back door. Kayla peered at her through half-closed eyes, her usually pink cheeks almost colorless. What to do, what to do? Janna didn't want her to get sick in the car, but the late-morning sun beat down from a hazy sky, and the temperature was already in the low nineties. Hardly comfortable for anyone, let alone a child who didn't feel well.

"Hello! Are you needing help?"

An all-black carriage—Old Order Mennonite—now sat on the other side of the car in the parking lot's exit lane, and its passenger was leaning her head out the side door. Before Janna could answer, the stout sixty-something woman wearing a muted pink dress climbed out. "Are you all right? Going by the look on your face, you're not."

Not by a long shot. "My daughter's carsick. And we ran out of gas." *Oh, and we're homeless.* She helped Kayla out of her seat. "Don't get out yet. Just sit on the floor with your legs out the door. If you need to get sick, tell me and we'll get to the grass."

Kayla nodded, still clinging to her rabbit, and sat down as instructed. Janna squatted and smoothed her hair back from her face.

The woman rounded the car door with a black thermos and a folded white handkerchief in one hand, then opened the thermos and poured water on the handkerchief. "My nephew used to get carsick whenever we hired a van, it seemed. Putting a cool cloth on his forehead or the back of his neck always helped. Here."

Janna took the offered handkerchief without looking away from Kayla. "Thank you." She wiped her daughter's face, then folded the handkerchief in half and placed it on the back of her neck, beneath her long ponytail.

"Can you call your husband to bring you some gas?" The woman dragged the back of her arm across her forehead, then adjusted the white head covering she wore over her graying dark hair. With dress sleeves that came below her elbows and black stockings and shoes on, she had to be sweltering.

"I . . . no. We just moved here and don't have family nearby."

"And a big tree fell on our house last night," Kayla added.

The woman gasped. "Oh my. Is that right?"

"Well, we weren't in it at the time." Janna stood, then looked into the woman's kind face for the first time—a face she knew well. "Malinda Martin?" No wonder the voice had sounded familiar.

"*Ya*. Have we . . ." She smiled brightly. "Janna. Oh my. We had no idea you were back in these parts." Malinda pulled her into a tight embrace.

Both were sweaty, but Janna didn't care. She needed a hug, and Malinda had always had a way of making things all right. "Just as of today," she said when they released each other.

Crazy. What were the odds that someone from the family that had once practically raised her would come to her rescue—just like they had when she was only a year older than Kayla. "I planned on stopping by once we'd moved in." Her lame excuse only made her feel worse. She should've done that long before now.

Malinda's grin didn't fade a bit. "Come home with us. *Mamm* and Luke will be so happy to see you, and he's got a little boy about your daughter's age."

Mamm and Luke. What about *Daadi* Eli? Her not mentioning him could only mean—

"What's your name, dear one?" Malinda bent forward.

"Kayla. But Mama sometimes calls me Kay." She held up the rabbit. "This is Rabbit."

"Janna, we always have gas on the farm. Luke can bring you back here with some and get your car driving again." She returned her attention to Kayla. "Have you ever ridden in a carriage?"

Kayla's face brightened. "No. But I love horses. Can we, Mama?"

Janna fought to rein in the conflicting emotions that threatened to overwhelm her. Malinda's offer of help was a huge blessing, but she hadn't seen or spoken to the Martins since she and her mother moved away almost fourteen years ago—not that she hadn't tried at first. "Are you sure? I wouldn't want to impose."

"Impose?" Malinda shook her head, her brown eyes crinkling with a combination of what looked like disbelief and sadness. "Never. And *Gott* calls us to show mercy to those in need. Please. Will you come?"

Only a fool would refuse such kindness, no matter how awkward this might be. Nodding, she stroked Kayla's hair again. "Are you feeling well enough to go for a ride?"

Kayla stood. "Oh yes, Mama. My tummy doesn't hurt as much now."

Once the Honda was locked, they walked around to the carriage.

Beulah, Malinda's sister—and also sister-in-law since they'd married two Martin brothers—now stood by the passenger-side door of the carriage, glowering. Though the two dressed and even looked similar, their personalities had always been so different. "Plenty hot to be standing around," she grumbled.

At least Janna was wearing a calf-length summer dress and Kayla a knee-length skort and short-sleeved shirt. Her dress was sleeveless, but it covered more than the clothing she'd originally considered for such a hot day. Beulah certainly would have complained about their immodesty had they dressed in shorts and tank tops.

"*Ya*, 'tis. Especially when you're stranded." Malinda placed her hand on Janna's back. "Sister, you remember Janna, and this is Kayla." She winked at Janna. "Go ahead and get in. We'll be home in ten minutes."

Janna leaned into the carriage and pulled the back of the bench seat forward, then helped Kayla climb into the backseat. After following, she drew the front seat back into place. Her apprehension eased a bit at the ecstatic smile Kayla wore as she peered through the carriage's open back.

The sisters got in, then Malinda looked over her shoulder. She'd never been attractive by worldly standards, even when younger, but the warm, sincere smile that rounded her face gave it a genuine beauty. "*Ach*, Janna, *Mamm* will be so glad to see you," she said again.

Beulah grabbed the reins, huffing as she glared through the carriage's storm front. Her unpleasant demeanor was why Janna had spent six years of her childhood avoiding the woman as much as possible.

As the horse pulled the carriage out onto the shoulder of Division Highway, Janna slowly breathed in and out. If *Mammi* Salena would be so glad to see her, then why hadn't she or Luke ever responded to the letters she wrote to them fourteen years ago?

CHAPTER 2

The Reunion

Luke regretted pairing his cell phone to his truck's Bluetooth. Edie Stott, the most high-maintenance customer he'd ever built furniture for, had called four times this morning—the last two times during the fifteen-mile drive home from *Mamm*'s optician's office. Even more, he wished he hadn't given her his cell phone number. That had been his mistake of the century. At least one of them, anyway.

And now her phone number again appeared on the screen on his dashboard.

He glanced toward the passenger seat. His grandmother, though he now called her *Mamm*, had pursed her lips. She disapproved of cell phones, let alone a smartphone that could ring through the truck's speakers. While she no longer complained about the CD of acapella hymns he played whenever she rode with him, the phone ringing—multiple times, no less—was intolerable.

Sure he would regret this as well, Luke tapped the button

on the steering wheel to answer the call. "Good morning, Mrs. Stott."

"Luke, I hate to bother you." Her high-pitched voice filled the cab.

He sighed. *Then don't do it.*

"My son and his family will be here to stay with us for two weeks starting next weekend. I just wanted to make sure our dining table and chairs will be delivered by then. The table we have right now won't seat all of us, and being Amish and all, you must know how important it is for families to sit down together for meals."

Mennonite, not Amish. Not that mentioning it would matter. He'd already done it at least twice. "Yes, I do, Mrs. Stott," he said as kindly as he could. "Lord willing, I plan to deliver the set on Friday at the latest."

"You swear to me it will be ready by then?"

Ach, he'd never sworn to anything and he never would. "The Bible says our yes should be yes and our no should be no—nothing more. But I can tell you I've never missed a delivery date." Hopefully, this wouldn't be the first.

After a few-second pause, she exhaled. "Well, I'll have to trust you on that, I guess."

"Thank you, Mrs. Stott. I'll talk to you soon, then, and you have a nice day." Before she could say more, he pushed the button on the steering wheel to end the call.

The acapella lyrics of "Though Troubles Assail" again filled the cab in four-part harmony. Fitting. Troubles were assailing, that was for certain.

Mamm folded her hands in her lap as she watched out the side window. "She's making you earn every penny of this order, not?" The black bonnet over her head covering obscured her expression, but the empathy in her tone came as a relief. He didn't need chastisement right now, especially with Joah in the backseat.

"*Ya*. And I've explained why I'm a bit behind schedule and assured her I take my delivery dates seriously. I'll just have to go back out to the workshop after Joah's in bed each night."

"*Ach*, you work so much yet." Grimness now replaced the empathy.

"I know." But Mahlon was away till Wednesday at his grandfather's funeral in Ohio, which left Luke with all the work. On top of that, Joah had therapy appointments in Lancaster on Tuesdays and Fridays, and that cut close to two hours out of those afternoons.

He stopped at the red light at Martindale Road. "*Gott* always provides. He will in this too. After next week, things should slow down." Seemed like he'd been saying that for months.

"Daddy, can we go fishing today?" Joah asked.

Luke's stomach sank as he glanced in the rearview mirror. Joah peered out the back window at the tree-lined river on the other side of the intersection. They hadn't fished in close to a month, but he needed to be in the shop for the rest of the day. Cousin Miriam had been kind enough to tend any customers who came in this morning, but Saturday was their busiest day, and the customers who wanted custom furniture often expected to speak to him directly.

"I think it's a little too hot for fishing, son," he said. "But we'll go soon."

"Okay, Daddy."

Glancing in the mirror a couple more times, Luke saw Joah staring at the river as they crossed the intersection and then the bridge. His son said nothing more, but Luke knew how much he loved fishing—as much as, if not more than, Luke had when he was a child. The difference was *Daadi* had taken him often.

Luke blew out his breath, praying for wisdom. The furniture business was important to him. It was not only what he loved to do but also what supported his family. Yet sometimes he felt like it took precedence over what was best for Joah.

Something needed to change, and right quick.

Janna could see only so much through the carriage's storm front as they turned off Division Highway. The Martins' lane was now paved instead of gravel, but otherwise the property appeared mostly unchanged.

Beyond the two-and-a-half-story brick house stood the attached *daadi haus*, and the furniture and quilt shop and its parking lot sat across the lane. The *Conestoga Valley Quilts & Custom Furniture* sign still stood between the parking lot and the road, but it had been repainted. And the white picket fence that surrounded the house and *daadi haus* had been replaced.

The only other change stole her breath and brought a sting behind her eyes when she realized it. When they'd passed the row of five side-by-side black mailboxes—two for the house across the road—the one with the nameplate that read *Luke D. Martin* had once borne *Daadi* Eli's name. Her suspicion had been correct. He was gone.

"Mama, look!" Kayla whispered, her face animated as she pointed ahead.

Janna blinked her eyes dry. Behind the shop sat a large playset and a trampoline with a safety enclosure around it. Also new, they'd taken the place of the tall A-frame swing set where she and Luke had spent so many hours.

Malinda grinned back at her. "Perhaps you and Joah can play together."

"Oh yes, please." Kayla bounced on the seat, still holding Rabbit. At least her carsickness had resolved quickly this time.

After Beulah stopped the carriage, they all got out. A thin cloud veiled the sun now, and the breeze provided some relief, as did being out of the enclosed space of the carriage. Birdsong enveloped them, stirring reminiscence so strong that it brought goose bumps to Janna's arms.

Kayla pointed again. "Look at all the birds!"

Just as Janna remembered, the large martin house sat high on its pole, bright white against the dark-red carriage house beyond it across the lane. Birds perched on it and flitted all around, chirping. "They're purple martins."

A fairly new black pickup approached and slowly passed them. It continued toward the carriage house up the lane behind the *daadi haus*, then parked next to a black minivan. Strange. Customers always parked in the lot, and only one of the six parking spots was taken.

The truck's back passenger-side door opened, and a blond boy wearing black jeans, a light-colored plaid shirt, and white suspenders climbed down. Tugging his hat onto his head, he jogged toward them with an awkward gait.

Janna realized why as he neared. The poor boy wore a black cast and cast shoe on each foot.

"Here comes Joah now," Malinda said. When he stopped about twenty-five feet away, she motioned him to her. "*Kumm.* I have some friends for you to meet."

The truck's driver-side door opened, and a tall man got out. He was dressed much like Joah and wore the seagrass hat Old Order Mennonite men and boys wore in warm weather. But he drove a truck? "Is that . . ."

"Luke? *Ya.*" Malinda watched as he rounded the front of the vehicle.

"He left the *gmay* and married a Horning girl," Beulah said.

Crossing her arms, she shook her head. "And now he's going to some *Funkeleit* church."

Well, that explained the two vehicles, but Luke and Joah still dressed Old Order. And how surprising. He'd once said he would never leave the *gmay*—although he'd been only a child at the time.

When Janna returned her attention to the truck, Luke was helping a slim elderly woman out of the passenger seat. She gained her footing, then smoothed her green cape dress as she started toward them.

Mammi Salena. Janna would've recognized her anywhere. Her gray hair was now whiter, and she wasn't as light on her feet, but she walked steadily. Luke followed and grabbed Joah on his way, swinging him up onto his hip.

Suddenly choked up, Janna covered her mouth and tried to blink away the tears that flooded her eyes. She'd thought about this for years, hoping to one day reunite with the Martins but also fearing that they would be standoffish with her. Now the time had come, and she almost felt sick.

Beulah climbed back into the carriage, muttering, and the horse took off up the lane toward the large farmhouse she and Malinda shared with their husbands, two of Salena's sons. Janna hadn't used *Deitsch* in years, but the last two words of Beulah's jab —*dumme gedanke*—made her opinion clear: this is a foolish idea.

Perhaps she was right.

"Who're they?" Joah asked as Luke carried him toward the woman and little girl standing with Malinda near the carriage. "Malinda said they're friends for me to meet."

They didn't look familiar, but Malinda's kind heart earned her more friends—from inside their community and outside it—than could be counted. "I don't know, son."

Neither wore pants and both had long hair, so they might have belonged to a somewhat-conservative church. The woman didn't wear a head covering, though, instead with her hair in a thick braid that hung over one shoulder.

As they got closer, the woman dropped the hand held over her mouth.

Janna?

He second-guessed himself, but it was definitely her. Many years had passed since her mother moved them to somewhere near Philadelphia, but the light-auburn hair, fair skin, and green eyes confirmed it. Tears streamed down her face, not unlike the last time he'd seen her. But then she'd been an almost-thirteen-year-old girl sobbing as she peered through the open passenger-side window of a beat-up Ford Fairmont. Now she was taller, and her pixie face and string-bean build had been replaced by natural beauty.

A few steps ahead, *Mamm* cried out and then hastened toward the three, her arms outstretched. She and Janna hugged each other, laughing and crying at the same time, while Malinda held the little girl to her side and wiped away her own tears.

Luke couldn't blame her. Though *Mamm* rarely spoke of her, she'd missed Janna. The *Ordnung* prohibited the use of cameras, but *Mamm* still had several public-school photographs of Janna in her hope chest.

He'd missed her as well, terribly at first. That had faded over the years, but he still thought of her on occasion, remembering all the time they'd spent together and wondering what had become of her. Now she stood before him, and by the way she responded to *Mamm*, she hadn't forgotten them as he'd assumed she had.

Malinda smiled as he neared. "Look who we found out front of Christian Aid Ministries. Their car ran out of gas right as we were leaving."

Mamm and Janna still showed no sign of releasing each other, so he set Joah on the asphalt and looked down at the curly-haired girl who hugged a scruffy brown stuffed rabbit. No doubt who she belonged to. "I'm Luke and this is Joah. What's your name?"

She didn't answer, watching him solemnly through long eyelashes.

Malinda patted her shoulder. "This is Kayla, Janna's daughter."

The little girl looked up at her, her face pinched. "How come Mama's crying?"

"*Ach*, not to worry, dear one." Malinda drew her closer. "She's happy, not sad. When your mama was not much older than you, *Mammi* Salena was like a grandmother to her, but they haven't seen each other in a long time."

Nee, Mamm had been like a *mother* to her, much more than Janna's own mother ever was. During the time the Carpenters lived in the rundown house across the road, Janna had spent many more nights sleeping in a bedroom next to his than she had at home. *Mamm* had cared for Janna when she wasn't in school and throughout each summer, all while her mother slept most of the day—not always at their house—and worked overnight at a nursing home.

"Joah is six," Malinda told Kayla. "How old are you?"

The little girl grinned, showing the gap of a missing tooth. "I'll be six in August. I was born on Mama's birthday." Her mouth then opened as she stared at Joah's feet. "How did you break your legs?"

Joah smiled. "They're not broken. They're getting fixed."

Hopefully, they were. "Lord willing, he'll have the casts for two more weeks, then he'll wear braces," Luke said.

"You can run with casts on your feet?"

Joah's grin broadened. "*Ya.* And I can climb the rock wall." He pointed to the colorful plastic climbing rocks attached to a slat wall on the playset. "And I can ride my scooter and my bike. I just can't jump on the trampoline 'cause I kept falling. Carin my therapist says after I get my AFO braces and can wear regular shoes, I can jump on the trampoline again."

"Luke." Janna's voice sounded much like it always had, kind and soft-spoken.

He faced her. For a moment he thought she might hug him as well, but she must've thought better of it. That was for the best anyway.

She smiled shyly. "It's good to see you again." Even with her eyes red and a little swollen, she was lovely.

Ach, he had no place entertaining such thoughts. He nodded, brushing them aside. "*Ya*, 'tis." It would've been better if she'd intended on visiting them, though. Their car had run out of gas less than two miles away. How many times had she driven by the farm but not stopped? "Are you living in the area?"

She swallowed as she swiped any last wetness from her cheeks. "We started moving into a twin over in Akron yesterday, but a tree fell on it in the storm here last night. Then we ran out of gas."

"All will be well." *Mamm* slipped her arm around Janna's waist. "*Gott* cares for the lilies of the field and the birds of the air, and so much more for us. 'Twas no coincidence that Beulah and Malinda came upon you."

Janna nodded, pressing her lips together.

"You're able to take her and a gas can to her car and get it driving again, not?" Malinda asked him. "If you don't have gasoline, we have plenty."

"I have some." Eating a quick dinner and getting over to the workshop would have to wait. Janna and her daughter's needs were more pressing, and taking care of car problems shouldn't be a woman's concern. "Do you want to go now?"

Her lips parted but then closed again. "If it's not too much trouble."

Why would she think that? "Of course it's not."

Kayla moved away from Malinda and peered up at Janna. "Can Joah and I play till you get back?"

"That's a fine idea," Malinda said, perhaps a bit too quickly. "If the clouds pass, it'll be too hot later." She shifted her attention from the children to Luke and Janna. "I can stay with them."

He'd intended to take Joah and Kayla along, but such eagerness brightened their expressions. "Is that all right with you?" he asked Janna.

She hesitated. "I . . . well—"

"Oh, please, Mama?" Kayla begged.

Janna stroked her hair. "Yes, that's fine. But you need to be careful and obey Malinda and *Mammi* Salena. And nothing to eat till I get back. Understood?"

"I promise." Kayla turned and grabbed Joah's hand. "Come on."

They skipped off toward the playset together.

Mamm released Janna and dabbed her eyes with her handkerchief again. "Go on now. When you get back, I'll have dinner ready. You'll eat with us, not?"

"We'd love to. Thank you." Janna looked and sounded more at ease, but then the seriousness returned to her expression. She pulled a long, thin insulated bag from her purse. "Kayla's allergic to peanuts. Her EpiPens are in this, but a lot of people aren't familiar with using them. If you'd rather she go with us—"

Malinda took it with a smile. "I know how to use them. But she'll be fine."

Janna hesitated, then nodded and looked at Luke.

"You can get in the truck a while," he said. "I'll get the gas can and be right there."

At least her car wasn't far away. Much had changed in his life, and no doubt Janna had plenty of questions, many of which had such complicated answers that he couldn't possibly address them on a short ride.

Especially since he still hadn't figured out some of the answers himself.

The Invitation

Sitting in Luke's truck, Janna gripped the handkerchief Salena had placed in her hand. If only she could hold on to her emotions as tightly. What a day of lost and found. Their new home lost—and who knew for how long—yet her connection to the Martins found. And by the way Salena had held her like she might never let her go, Janna dared to hope they could regain the relationship they once shared.

As she wiped her eyes, the faint scent of lavender took her back to her childhood. She'd struggled with anxiety on and off until the age of ten, and whenever those awful feelings threatened to suffocate her, Salena would have her smell a handkerchief sprayed with lavender oil. Even after all these years, the sweet woman still kept a scented handkerchief tucked into her dress's cape.

Tears came to her eyes again. The Martins, along with the faith in God they instilled in her, had been her refuge growing up. For perhaps the thousandth time, she refused the impulse to wonder how life would've been different if Mom hadn't moved them away. Her already aching chest squeezed even more, and she lifted the handkerchief to her face. If she'd ever needed the calming the lavender brought, it was now.

Luke carried a red gas can out of the shed, and she dropped the hand holding the handkerchief into her lap. She needed to get ahold of herself.

He put the gas can in the truck's bed, then opened his door and climbed into the driver's seat. The truck started with a rumble that echoed off the side of the *daadi haus*, but he didn't put it in gear. When she glanced at him, the beautiful blue eyes she'd always loved—the color of a clear spring sky—peered into hers from below his hat brim. In addition to losing the gangly build of an energetic boy, he'd also grown into his nose, which had seemed a little too large for his face when he was a young teenager.

"You all right?" The words came out short, but his expression held sincerity.

She swallowed. "Yes."

He nodded once, then headed for the road.

Janna concentrated on the view out the passenger-side window as they waited at the end of the lane. Several cars passed, followed by a tractor trailer, all going faster than the speed limit. Some things never changed, though traffic seemed heavier than when she'd lived here. Thank goodness the area where Joah and Kayla played sat back a hundred and fifty feet from the road.

Concern for Kayla again materialized, but she rationalized it away. Janna had thrived in the care of Salena and Malinda for years, so Kayla would certainly be safe with them for ten or fifteen minutes. Still, she wasn't used to entrusting Kayla to others—not outside school, anyway.

Luke pulled out onto Division Highway, and once they were on their way, Janna faced forward, determined to relax.

She needed to get past this silliness. The house where she and Mom had lived was hardly one of the better parts of her childhood, especially the last memory she had of it, but she couldn't refuse to look at it forever. Living in Akron, she'd be traveling this section of Route 322 whenever she needed to go east. Going around it every time wouldn't be practical.

As well, something else vied for her attention. Luke sat only feet from her, and she couldn't help thinking about his wife. Beulah said he'd married, and he had a son and a second vehicle parked behind the *daadi haus*, so he obviously had a wife. But married Old Order men didn't ride alone in a vehicle with a woman who wasn't family, especially one from outside the Plain community. Yet here they were, even if only for a short ride. Hopefully, his act of kindness wouldn't stir up trouble.

She cleared her throat. "I can't thank you enough for doing this." Uneasy or not, she could at least show some gratitude.

"I'm glad to help." He kept his eyes on the road. "Are you sure your car's just out of gas?"

She hoped so. A car repair bill on top of everything else would be too much. "Pretty sure. The gas gauge stopped working a while back. I've been using the trip meter to know when to get gas, but the last few days have been . . ." Crazy? Exhausting? Overwhelming? All of those, really, but she didn't want Luke to think she was incapable of handling life. It was bad enough she'd let the car run out of gas. "Busy, and I guess I wasn't thinking about that."

They ascended the hill, and Christian Aid Ministries' sign came into view. Beyond it, her dark-blue CR-V sat on the grass.

"Is that it there?" he asked.

"Yes."

He turned into the driveway, then swung the truck around

and parked in the first of the parking spots parallel to the road, about six feet from the CR-V's front bumper.

Janna opened the door and jumped down from the truck step. Luke had already grabbed the gas can and started toward the driver's side of the CR-V. She followed, unwilling to stand there like a typical helpless woman with an out-of-gas car. "What can I do?"

He opened the fuel door and unscrewed the gas cap. Within a minute, he'd emptied the contents of the half-full gas can into the tank. "You have your keys?" He set the can on the ground.

Keys. Right. They'd need to start the car. She pulled them from her purse, unlocked the car with the key fob, and opened the driver's door.

"Let me have them."

She spun to face him. Why? Because a woman couldn't turn a key to get an engine running? "I can do it." After sliding into the seat, she put the key into the ignition and turned it.

Nothing.

She tried again. Still no hint of starting. Maybe it wasn't out of gas after all? But that had to be it. She'd seen the trip meter mileage. Heat washed over her—from the broiling car interior or her embarrassment, she didn't know—and perspiration slid down her back.

Luke opened the car door wider. "Let me do it now, please?"

With no choice but to oblige, she got out and handed over the keys. What were the chances a man who'd grown up driving a horse and carriage would be any better at starting a car anyway?

He sat down sideways on the seat, then inserted the key and turned it two clicks. After a few moments, he returned it to the original position and repeated the process. On the third time, he turned the key all the way, and the CR-V started right up.

Hearing the purr of the engine had never made her so happy, even if his success irritated her too. Now she just needed him to get out of the car.

"You won't be able to drive forward with the concrete parking stop there, even without my truck in the spot." He reached under the seat and adjusted it so he could swing his long legs inside. "I'll back it around into the driveway for you."

Seriously? Woman or not, she'd been driving a vehicle longer than he had. And backing up wasn't hard to do, even if it involved turning. "I can do it." The impatient edge in her voice brought guilt, as did the way he just stared at her blankly in response. This was how she repaid his kindness? "Sorry, I . . . It's fine. Thanks, but I can do it."

He readjusted the seat, then got out of the car and grabbed the gas can. "Better than you were able to start it, I hope." He headed for his truck but not before she caught the wry grin on his face. "I'll follow you, then."

Janna gritted her teeth as she got back into the car. Luke had always had a sense of humor—too much of one at times, according to some people in the *gmay*. For once, she agreed with them. Because now it seemed less like good-natured teasing and more like arrogance.

Luke again prayed for wisdom as he followed Janna home. Life was stressful enough right now, and it seemed like her return would only add to that. He would never turn away someone who needed help, especially someone who'd once been like family, but Janna was different now. They'd rarely bickered as children, yet she'd snapped at him twice. Because he was trying to help her, no less.

Then again, she'd spent the last fourteen years living among *outsidas*. Her picking up some of their ways seemed unavoidable.

Ach, he shouldn't be judging her. She'd never had an easy life. His own mother's lifestyle had been just as immoral and irresponsible as her mother's was. But he'd had the blessing of grandparents who'd raised him in a loving, faith-filled home. As well, the *gmay* considered him an *outsida* now too. He needed to cut Janna some slack.

But her sharp words hurt. He'd only tried to care for her needs, just as he'd always done, but she'd rejected that. It didn't make sense. And the last thing he needed was more confusion in his life.

Janna turned into their lane, and he followed her back behind the *daadi haus*. She parked, then got out and waited for him at the back of her car.

Across the lane, Kayla climbed the playset's rock wall while Joah knelt in the doorway of the playhouse at the top. Malinda sat on the bench beneath the large oak that shaded the playset and trampoline, watching them.

Kayla jumped down as they neared. "Mama, our car! You fixed it."

Janna hugged her. "Well, it is fixed, but I didn't do it." She looked at him with a slight smile. "Luke did."

Some of the tension in him eased. Not an apology, but it was something.

Kayla's grin disappeared. "We don't have to go already, do we? I wanna stay longer. This is the best playset ever. Joah's so lucky."

Janna glanced around at their surroundings. "Yes, he is." The wistfulness in her tone confirmed her words. "We're not leaving yet. But we should go in and help *Mammi* Salena with dinner."

Kayla stepped away from her. "I wanna keep playing with Joah."

"I don't mind watching them, Janna." Malinda crossed her arms over her middle, looking as comfortable on the bench as she would in an easy chair. "Really, I don't."

Not that the children needed someone to watch their every move. He and Janna had played together on their own, even wandering the farm, when they weren't much older than Joah and Kayla.

Janna took the insulated bag Malinda held out. "Are you sure? It's pretty hot, and I'm sure you must need to make dinner as well."

"Not so much in the shade, and Beulah can start our dinner. Enos and Ivan won't be in from the barn for a little while yet." Malinda shooed her with her hands. "Go on now. They're fine. Enjoy some time with *Mamm*."

"Thank you." With a genuine smile, she left for the house.

Luke sat down beside Malinda. Leaning forward and resting his elbows on his knees, he focused on the children to try to get Janna off his mind. Kayla was again scaling the rock wall, and Joah reached for her hand. She took it and hoisted herself into the playhouse, then helped him off his knees. Seconds later, they were giggling as they slid down the sliding board one right after the other.

Malinda chuckled. "Our old swing set was never as fancy as all this, but they're not the first towheaded boy and red-haired girl to frolic out here together." She watched as the children climbed the rock wall again. "Kayla looks so much like Janna did. Lighter hair, but the same sweet face."

He nodded, not trusting himself to respond. Too much had him *verhuddled*. Exhaling, he rubbed the back of his neck.

"You feeling all right?" she asked.

He lifted his head and looked at her. "*Ya.* I'm just . . ." Just what? Even he couldn't explain it.

Sympathy drew her expression as she shifted toward him and placed a hand on his shoulder. "I know. It's been a long time, and—"

"She's changed."

Malinda raised her eyebrows at him, her way of reminding people of something they should already know. "I'm sure she has. But so have you. So have I. Time changes all of us—and many things as well."

He groaned. How true that was.

She squeezed his shoulder. "Give her a chance. I'm afraid you'll regret it if you don't."

Nodding, he glanced over his shoulder at the house. If there was one thing he didn't need, it was another regret in his life.

Janna stepped back into the kitchen after opening the screen door to call Luke, Joah, and Kayla inside. Even all these years later, little had changed in the Martins' home. Spotless linoleum or wooden floors. Simple yet quality furniture, some of it antique. Curtain-less windows with just a shade for privacy. White walls decorated only with framed Bible verses and antique cross-stitch pieces. The stove and refrigerator were newer, but the rest of the kitchen had to be seventy years old. And it was still in perfect condition.

Salena placed a bowl of potato salad on the kitchen table, then pulled a glass pitcher of what looked like mint tea from the refrigerator.

"Let me get that, Salena." Janna hurried to take it from her.

She handed over the pitcher, grinning slightly. "Too old to call me *Mammi*, are you?"

Janna smiled. "I suppose." That, or she just wasn't sure what to make of their relationship now. Probably the latter. But she'd claim the former and hope for the best. "Do we need anything else?"

"*Nee. Danki*. And you can call me whichever you're comfortable with." By the way Salena kept looking her over, she could barely believe what she saw. "Perhaps I should be speaking only English. Do you remember *Deitsch*? And what about Kayla?"

"I remember some." Although their ride here made her question that. Beulah had prattled so quickly to Malinda that Janna had understood only a few words. Beulah's exasperation had been quite comprehensible, though. "Kayla knows a few words. By the time she was born, I'd forgotten a lot of it."

"She's young. The young ones learn quick. I started teaching Joah when he was three, and he spoke it well within a year."

"Really?" Children in the *gmay* always spoke *Deitsch* first and didn't learn English until they went to school. But then again, Luke had joined the Hornings. They used English in their church services, and she'd heard only their older adults use *Deitsch*. "Luke didn't want him to learn it?"

"*Ach*, he did." Salena glanced at the door. "Luke's wife couldn't speak it, and she didn't want to learn or for us to teach Joah." She opened her mouth like she might say more but then just shook her head.

Couldn't. Didn't. Past tense, so his wife wasn't around anymore. How sad.

Footsteps clattered across the porch floorboards, and then the screen door opened. The children rushed in followed by

Luke, who looked around the room with purpose. The wooden door slapped shut behind him.

"Kayla said you were on your way to the Flying Dutchman when you ran out of gas," he said when their gazes met. "Is that true?"

Oh, why had she said the name? She should've just told Kayla they were going to a motel.

He stared at her. "You know what it's like there. That's no place for any decent person, let alone a woman and child."

This day just kept going from bad to worse—or worse to worse. "I don't have a lot of options." Her words came out too brusque, but the morning's events had sapped her patience, and she wouldn't be shamed by someone who knew nothing about her situation. "It's June. Lancaster County is always crawling with tourists by now, and I need a place that can give us a room today and won't cost a fortune. Where am I—"

Salena grasped Janna's elbow. "Joah, take Kayla up to your bedroom and show her how your marble roller works. Then wash your hands before you come down."

Without a word, Joah led Kayla into the hallway to the living room.

Janna paced across the floor. She needed to chill. Losing it wouldn't help. When she turned around, Salena and Luke still stood by the table, their expressions solemn. "I know the Dutchman isn't the best place to stay."

He rested his hands on his hips. "But you still want to stay there?"

Was that what he thought—that she *wanted* to stay there? "No, I don't want to stay there. What I *want* is to stay in our new house, to unpack and make it our home. We've been looking forward to this day—to a new start—for almost three months. But now there's a tree through our roof and we can't even get any of our belongings."

Goodness. She'd said way more than planned. With a deep breath, she softened her tone. "I didn't mean to be short with you, and I promise I'm never this much of a mess. I'm just trying to do my best with circumstances I never expected."

Luke held her gaze for a few moments. "I can't let you stay at the Dutchman. It's not safe."

As if that was his decision to make. She was perfectly capable of taking care of Kayla and herself, and she had no intention of allowing someone else to do it ever again.

Salena came closer, her brow pinched with empathy. "Will you stay with us, then?"

She'd figured it would be only a matter of time before that suggestion was made. Even so, how could she impose when she hadn't seen them in so long? "I can't ask you to do—"

"You're not." Luke followed his grandmother and rested a hand on her back. "We're asking you."

"We always have the *daadi haus* ready for visitors," Salena went on, her tone hopeful. "We'd be happy to have you stay there."

"For Kayla's sake if not your own," Luke added.

Another low blow, but she was too tired to bicker with him anymore. She managed a smile. "We'll stay."

"*Gut.*" Salena took her by the shoulders. "This is best. You'll see."

Janna could only hope. She nodded, reminding herself to be thankful for the Martins' kindness, then gathered the courage to face Luke. The least she could do was recognize their generosity.

Except when she turned, he was no longer in the room.

CHAPTER 4

Catching Up

Luke had just gulped down the last of the mint tea in his thermos when the sleigh bells on the shop door jingled. Cousin Miriam's *Deitsch* greeting carried through the doorway into the workshop, so whoever had entered probably wasn't a customer. Most likely it was Beulah or Malinda coming to take over so Miriam could leave.

But *Mamm*'s voice responded.

He moved closer to the doorway into the shop. With Janna there, he'd expected *Mamm* would spend the afternoon catching up with her. Unless . . .

Hopefully, Janna hadn't taken his near silence during dinner to heart and decided to check into that motel after all. He went into the shop.

Mamm stood behind the counter to his left. "You go on now," she was telling Miriam. Her cheery tone assured him that Janna hadn't left. "I'm sure your *mamm* can use your help at home with your having company tomorrow."

Miriam refastened one of her covering pins as she came

toward the counter. "I'm just glad you could get an appointment today, and that your glasses were fixable." She pulled the dusting cloth from beneath her arm and set it on the counter, then smiled at Luke. "And I'll be praying you're able to get done all you need to this week."

The world needed more people as kind and eager to help others as his eighteen-year-old second cousin. "Thanks, Mim, and we appreciate you coming on such short notice. Be sure to take your pay. Would you like a ride?"

She started to say something but then stopped. Her grin returned, now apologetic. "*Danki*, but I have my bike."

Of course she'd decline, just like she had when he offered on other occasions. Most of the family would now ride in his truck or van if where they needed to go wasn't close by, but Miriam's father insisted that she not accept rides from him unless he used the carriage. She'd be more than halfway home by the time he hitched the rig.

When Miriam headed for the back room to gather her belongings, he asked, "Where are Janna and Kayla?"

"Out at the playset with Joah." *Mamm* pulled her stool to the counter and half sat on it. "She helped me finish redding up the house. I thought I'd relieve Miriam so she can get home. You do remember we're invited to the noon meal at their place tomorrow, not?"

He had forgotten, but she didn't need to know that. "We'll be there."

"*Gut*. I invited Janna and Kayla, but she said they'd rather stay here and rest." Her blue eyes seemed to bore right through him. "You could always come to our church in the morning, you know. We'll be going right to their place from the *gmayhaus*."

Miriam reappeared carrying her lunch bag. "Salena, a woman called this morning to ask about having a quilt made. I wrote everything down, but let me go over that with you before I leave."

With *Mamm*'s mind on something else, Luke retreated to the workshop. He needed to get back to the chair he was working on, which wouldn't happen if they got into another debate about his and Joah's church attendance. That had become a subject he preferred to avoid—as much as *Mamm* let him, anyway.

As he neared his workbench, the window overlooking the playset and trampoline caught his eye. It was open, and Kayla's squeals drew him toward it. Though she'd been shy when they sat down to dinner, by the time they'd finished eating she was chattering sparkly-eyed to *Mamm*. So much like Janna she was, in both looks and demeanor.

Outside, Kayla jumped on the trampoline while Janna and Joah rode back-to-back on the playset's tandem glider. Janna faced the other direction, but Joah was laughing and kept twisting around to say something to her.

Guilt prodded Luke. He hadn't seen Joah so animated in weeks. Since school finished for the year, he'd grown almost somber. *Mamm* did her best to keep him occupied when he wasn't helping in the shop and workshop, but being the only child living on the farm could be lonely. Even all the toys in the world wouldn't measure up to having someone else to play with. That Luke knew firsthand. His cousins who'd grown up on the farm were all older than he was, so having Janna move in across the road had been one of the best things to happen during his childhood.

Now Janna was here again, bringing out the same happiness in Joah that she'd brought out in him. That churned up such contrasting emotions that he didn't dare try to sort them out. He needed to concentrate on the chair measurements.

Just as he was about to move away from the window, Janna

dropped her feet to the ground and dragged them to stop the glider. She and Joah got off, then she followed him to the trampoline and up the metal ladder onto it. Joah grabbed her hands and jumped, cautiously at first and then higher and higher. Kayla soon joined them.

Luke had to smile as they jumped together, obviously having a wonderful time. Janna was good with children. Her interaction with Joah and Kayla during dinner only confirmed that. Of course, she always had been. When they were growing up, she'd loved taking care of younger children.

Ach, he needed to get back to work. If he didn't, he'd spend the rest of the afternoon watching them—and thinking about the Janna he remembered and the one who now made it difficult for him to think about anything else.

Finished talking with Cynthia, Janna set her phone beside her on the *daadi haus*'s porch swing and looked across the lane at the quilt and furniture shop.

The chirp of crickets and cacophony of cicadas was as thick in the darkness as the humidity. When she closed her eyes, listening and breathing in the scent of the roses in the beds along the fence and the farm smell that wafted from the milking barn beyond Beulah and Malinda's farmhouse, time seemed to stand still. Or go back to years past. Many summer nights she'd sat outside with Luke, and sometimes with Salena and *Daadi* Eli.

Daadi Eli. Just the thought of him brought the squeezing ache to Janna's chest again. Salena had told her he died of a heart attack when Luke was eighteen, so he'd been gone ten years. A tall man with a quiet nature but a keen sense of humor, he'd been the closest thing to a father she'd ever had. He'd never said the words, but his care for her had made it clear how much he loved her.

Lifting her bare feet onto the swing, she pulled her nightshirt over her legs and wrapped her arms around her knees. She ached with exhaustion, but after lying awake beside Kayla in the *daadi haus* bedroom for more than an hour, she'd realized sleep wasn't coming. The porch swing and the farm's serene surroundings had beckoned her, and that combined with hearing the voice of the woman she and Kayla had once lived with had brought much-needed peace to her heart. Her problems were far from solved, but Kayla was safe and happy. That was what mattered.

A noise across the lane drew her attention, and in the moonlight she saw movement beneath the roof sheltering the front of the shop. A tall figure wearing a hat closed the door, then strode toward the lane.

Luke.

The chain of the porch swing creaked as she shifted, and he looked right at her. At the lane, he walked directly across instead of heading toward the kitchen porch. A long-ago-familiar clink sounded when he opened the gate that separated the lane from the *daadi haus*'s slate-slab walkway and tiny front yard.

Janna lowered her legs and smoothed her nightshirt over them. At least it covered her knees while she was sitting and the light above the door wasn't bright.

He stopped at the porch step, sliding his hands into the front pockets of his pants. "It's after eleven."

"I know. Were you in the workshop?"

"*Ya.*"

So he'd spent the afternoon working, and then she'd seen

him return to the shop around seven thirty. He'd probably worked some that morning too. "Long day."

He adjusted his hat. "Every spring, Mahlon and I—you remember Mahlon Eschbach, my second cousin who apprenticed with *Daadi*? Well, he's my partner now, and every spring we donate several pieces of furniture to Clinic for Special Children's auction down in Leola. The auction was last Saturday, and about three weeks ago Mahlon's grandfather in Ohio got real sick and he had to go out there." He shrugged. "With him gone, I had to finish all the pieces, and I got behind on our custom orders. Now I'm trying to catch up."

Daadi Eli's generosity had clearly rubbed off on him. "That's kind of you. The donations, I mean."

He stared at the porch floorboards for a few moments, then looked up at her. "It's the least I can do. My wife—late wife— was a patient there."

Janna's throat nearly closed. A number of the people in the *gmay* were patients of the clinic, which diagnosed and treated genetic disorders that primarily affected the Amish and Mennonite communities. Many had maple syrup urine disease, a metabolic disorder fatal without treatment—and sometimes despite the most diligent care. "Did she have MSUD?"

"*Ya*. But because of the clinic, she was able to live a mostly normal life with only a few complications." He snorted. "Then three years ago she got the flu, and . . ."

He didn't finish, and he didn't need to. As children, she and Luke had a good friend with MSUD, and Janna had seen how even a minor illness could quickly make her very sick. "I'm so sorry," she said. At the next thought, her heart skipped. "Joah?"

"He's fine. I'm not a carrier, so we knew he wouldn't inherit it."

She should've known that. Joah had eaten foods containing

protein at both dinner and supper, which people with MSUD couldn't do.

He stepped onto the porch and leaned against one of its posts, crossing his arms. Though the light above the door illuminated him, the brim of his hat shaded his eyes, making it hard to discern his expression. "I want to apologize for today. I said some things I shouldn't have, and I could've been more friendly-like."

That was for sure, but he sounded so genuine that she couldn't hold it against him. And it wasn't like she had behaved much differently. "Accepted. And I apologize for being snippy with you at the car."

"Accepted." Canting his head, he watched her for a few moments—long enough to make her feel self-conscious. "What have you been up to all these years, Janna Carpenter? Although I guess it's not Carpenter anymore."

So much for hoping they wouldn't have that conversation so soon. But maybe it was better to get it over with. She looked down at her hands folded on her lap, then back to him. "It's still Carpenter. I made some decisions in college that weren't the best, but I've never regretted having Kayla. I can't imagine life without her."

"Children are a heritage from the Lord. No matter the circumstances. *Mamm* and *Daadi* made sure we knew that."

That they had, and Janna should've realized Luke wouldn't hold what had happened against her. Though he was part of a community where marriage almost always preceded children, he was the son of an unwed mother and had never met his father. "When did you start calling her *Mamm?*"

"When Priscilla couldn't even come home when I was hit by a car when I was fifteen. I was barely conscious for two days. She may be my mother, but she'll never be my *mamm.*"

Goodness. No wonder he felt that way. But how sad that he and his mother still had such a complicated relationship.

He crossed his arms. "How's your mother?"

If they were going to have that discussion, she'd need sustenance—chocolate, specifically. "Your *mamm* gave us a tin of the chocolate chip cookies she baked. Are you hungry?" He'd probably refuse her offer, but if nothing else, that would allow her to wait till another day to talk about Mom.

"Starving, actually."

Oh. Tonight it was, then. "Let me get them." Standing, she remembered her nightshirt. It almost reached her knees, but Luke wouldn't be comfortable with it.

Inside, she sneaked into the bedroom and changed back into that day's clothing. Kayla slept soundly, even when the dress's hanger fell on the linoleum floor, and Janna hurried into the living room and through the doorway into the small kitchen.

She paused after opening the refrigerator. What was she thinking? After vowing she wouldn't let herself get close to another guy, she'd offered cookies to one at eleven fifteen at night.

Then again, it was Luke. He might not be attending an Old Order church now, but he was still clearly quite conservative in his dress and mindset. They would never be anything but friends.

No doubt about that.

Luke took a step away from the porch post and turned his back to the door. Agreeing to her offer hadn't been a good idea. They had plenty to eat in the house kitchen, and he should've declined and gone inside. Being seen on the *daadi haus* porch with Janna late at night—her in only some sort of oversized T-shirt, no less—could cause trouble he didn't need. Good thing the chance of that—

The wooden screen door creaked open, and he turned. Janna quietly closed the door behind her, holding a plate of cookies and now wearing the dress she'd had on earlier. At least she still respected their ways.

She glanced around. "Where do you want to sit?"

The only seating was the swing, but unlike the swing on the porch outside the house kitchen, this one had barely enough room for two adults. "Here's fine." He lowered himself onto the porch step, then took off his hat and set it behind him on the floorboards.

Janna sat down beside the other porch post.

Neither said a word as they munched on the plate of cookies set between them, and he looked up at the sky. Clouds obscured the stars and kept the warmth of the day from rising into the atmosphere. Up the lane, a rooster crow ended with what sounded like a donkey's bray.

Janna looked at him. "That isn't Hank."

"*Ach, ya.*" He laughed. "You remember him?"

Her expression softened with genuine delight. "He's still around?"

"*Ya.* And still crowing at all hours. He has to be sixteen, I reckon. Ask Malinda, she knows. The orange barn cats, Millie and Tillie, they're still around too."

Janna only nodded, and her gaze shifted to the shop's parking lot and the road beyond it. He'd understand if she didn't want to talk about her mother.

She drew a slow breath. "Mom died almost four years ago. Lung cancer. Forty-four years old."

He stopped chewing and swallowed. That he hadn't expected. "*Es dutt mir leed.*"

"Not completely surprising, I guess. She smoked three packs a day for almost thirty years." Her emotionless tone gave no clue about their most recent relationship.

"But no less tragic. It's never easy to lose a loved one."

She inhaled again and released her breath, then shifted toward him. "When she had a hospice nurse call to tell me the doctors had given her less than six weeks to live, I hadn't spoken to her in more than two years . . . since she showed up for my college graduation, saw I was about to have Kayla"—she shook her head, looking away—"and told me I was just like her."

His jaw clenched. Typical Missy Carpenter cruelty—belittling others to make herself feel better about her own self-destructiveness. Janna was nothing like her, and he knew that after spending only a couple of hours with her. "That's not true."

"Anyway, I decided then that she'd never treat Kayla like she treated me. I didn't even call her when Kayla was born, and I never answered the few times she called me. Then right before Kayla turned two, Mom had the hospice she was in leave that message, and I went to see her." She smiled, although sadly. "Believe it or not, she'd become a Christian. Kayla and I visited her just about every day, and for three weeks, she was the mom I'd always wished she'd be—well, for the most part."

His heart ached for her. He fully understood the longing for a good relationship with an estranged parent. Or at least he used to. That desire had diminished in the last few years, but he could imagine the way he'd feel in such a situation. How bittersweet to gain that relationship only to then lose it. And how considerate of Janna to give Missy another chance. "That must've been difficult."

"It was. But it could've ended much worse. I'm so thankful for those three weeks."

As they sat in silence again, his conscience jabbed him. Something had been weighing on him since dinner. He now had the chance to bring it up, though part of him hesitated, not knowing how she would take it.

No matter, it had to be said.

He cleared his throat. "I need to ask what your intentions are, for *Mamm*'s sake. Having you here today brought her joy, but I don't want to see her hurt if you don't plan on staying in touch."

She grimaced. "I wouldn't do that to her."

He hoped not. But it couldn't be ruled out either, considering how many years had passed since they'd seen Janna. She'd known where they were and could've called or visited anytime. "I just need to be sure. Priscilla makes it hard enough on her."

She leaned back against the porch post. "How is she?"

That was a good question. He hadn't heard from his mother since Christmas. "Priscilla is Priscilla. She hasn't changed. She visited for two days when Joah was born, but we haven't seen her since. We get a call from her once or twice a year, and she did send a sympathy card when Rayanne—my wife—died."

Janna lowered the cookie she was about to bite. "She didn't come for the funeral?"

At least she saw the shamefulness of that. "*Nee*. And *Mamm* wonders why I don't want her in our life. She keeps hoping Priscilla will change, that she'll come home and be the daughter, mother, and grandmother she should be. I'm not holding my breath."

Janna looked into his eyes, her expression sympathetic. "That could still happen. I didn't want to give my mom another chance either, but she changed."

Her words pricked him, mainly because she was right. And as a Christian, he was called to forgive and to love even his enemies. He did that as best he could, but allowing Priscilla the opportunity to hurt him again—or worse, Joah—seemed foolish and unreasonable. "I know, and I'm glad she did. But . . ."

"I know," she said, looking into his eyes. "And I can't blame you. You have yourself and your son to protect. I understand."

Ya, she did. She always had. That was why, growing up, his closest friend hadn't been another Old Order Mennonite boy but an *outsida* girl. An *outsida* girl who'd just walked back into his life, bringing a tangle of uneasiness and anticipation that ensured he'd get little sleep tonight.

God help him.

CHAPTER 5

The Proposal

Three men stood on the sidewalk in front of the Akron twin when Janna parked at the curb across the street on Monday afternoon. She recognized the tallest one as Justin, who'd called a half hour ago to let her know the inspector was there. Neither of the other two was the man who'd been with him on Saturday, though the same municipal pickup sat parked behind her.

She checked the rearview mirror, then got out and started across the street. The roof and side of the house now had a blue tarp covering it, and the pine tree that had ruined her weekend —and who knew how many weeks to come—was now a long row of stacked logs near the side street. One of the men started toward the side yard on her half of the house.

Justin held up his hand and started to say something, but the younger guy with him—a twenty-something in jeans, a red T-shirt, a ball cap, and work boots—laughed. "Well, look at this. Janna Carpenter, right?"

She stopped, the hair on the back of her neck raising at his sly grin. He looked familiar, but not enough that she could place his name. A car approached, and she hurried to the curb. "Yes."

"You don't remember me, do you? Tony Lowery? We went to school together."

Oh, now she remembered. Though she would've been more than happy not to. They'd ridden the same school bus, and he'd teased her for years about living with "Amish people" and called her "Dutch girl." The white embroidery on his red hat—*Anthony Lowery Construction*—made her stomach uneasy. He must have been the builder Justin said was coming out to give a repair estimate for Mrs. Bollinger's homeowner's insurance. "Hello, Tony."

"Ah, no worries. I'm nothing like I used to be."

Right. Not by the way he looked her up and down. "Thank you for calling me," she said to Justin.

He nodded once. "I wish I had better news for you, but it looks like you probably won't be able to move in for four to six weeks, maybe longer, depending on how quickly the insurance company comes through."

She'd figured that. "What about what's inside?"

"The inspector says it's fine for you to get what you need from the first floor. I believe you said there wasn't much upstairs anyway?"

What a relief. "Just our beds and a dresser, and we don't need them right now." Thank goodness they'd sold most of their furniture, keeping only what they loved and planning to find what they needed at secondhand stores and yard sales once they'd settled in. "Everything else is down here, and it's not a ton of stuff."

"Maybe not, but where you going to put it?" Tony eyed her with one eyebrow raised. "That little car of yours isn't gonna hold much."

He had a legitimate point. Unfortunately.

Oh, she should've asked for Luke's help after all. He'd said he would take her to the house once she could get their belongings, but after talking to Justin, she'd decided not to tell Luke what she was doing. He was so busy with work. Now she wished for the space his truck provided as well as his strength to help carry out the boxes and bags. Some things about being single never got easier.

"No, it won't." She looked up at the sky. *Now what, Lord?*

"Where you stayin'? If you're not too far, I can load up my truck"—Tony jutted his chin at a jacked-up red pickup parked in front of the house next door—"and follow you there."

She hardly wanted him being able to find her, although keeping him from it might not be possible. He knew where she'd lived growing up. If he wanted to look for her, that would probably be the first place he'd go.

Oh, she needed wisdom. As much as she wanted to part ways with Tony as quickly as possible, the sooner her and Kayla's belongings were safe with them, the better. "I'm at the Eli Martins' place again. Over on 322."

His smirky grin returned. "With the Amish people?"

"They're Mennonite." And he said he'd changed.

He clapped his hands together. "That isn't real far. Let me move my truck closer, and we can start loadin' up."

She inhaled through her teeth as he headed for his pickup. Hopefully—

"If you're not sure about this, just say so," Justin said. His kind hazel eyes, strikingly similar to the light brown of his short hair, looked into hers when she turned. "I'd help you, but I'm on duty and have to stay around here in case we get a call. We can still find another way."

They could, but who knew how long that would take. Kayla missed her toys, and Janna would feel more at ease—and more able to figure out their next steps—once they had their belongings. "I'm sure it'll be okay. But thank you. For everything."

Again the one nod, much in the way Luke did. "I'll help bring out your things. You call me if you have any problems after you leave. Will someone be where you're staying when you get there?"

"Yes."

Tony had always been harmless. Annoying too, but harmless. If dealing with him for an hour or so meant gaining some normalcy to her and Kayla's life, she could handle that.

Luke hung up the workshop phone and let his head fall back. No matter how much Edie Stott insisted she didn't want to rush him or "micromanage," whatever that meant, he was pretty sure she was doing just that. But maybe after today's reassurance, she'd be content enough to let him be the next one to call—to schedule delivery, as he'd said he would.

Remembering the sound of the loud truck engine he'd heard while on the phone, he went into the shop. Malinda stood with an elderly couple who were examining a wedding-ring quilt, but he doubted they would've arrived in such a vehicle. He went to the front door and stepped outside.

Janna's car was parked on the lane in front of the *daadi haus*, its open back facing the lowered tailgate on the red Dodge backed up within six feet of the car's bumper. Joah stood beneath the Honda's liftgate holding a pink backpack as Kayla jumped down beside him with a blond-haired doll in her arms.

Anthony Lowery Construction. The name lettered in white on the truck's front door sounded familiar.

A man came out the *daadi haus*'s door with Janna following.

Whatever was going on, Luke didn't like it. "Janna?" He started toward the lane.

The man halted at the propped-open gate at the end of the walkway, and Janna almost lost her balance trying not to bump into him. He turned and grabbed her arm, saying something Luke couldn't hear.

"What's going on?" No matter what it was, she shouldn't have a man in the *daadi haus* with her.

She pulled away and walked between the vehicles to meet him. "Justin from the fire department called to let me know the inspector was looking at the house. When I got there, they said I could get most of our belongings. Tony was there to give Mrs. Bollinger a repair estimate and offered to help me bring them here."

The man followed with his hand held out. "Tony Lowery. Don't look so serious, brother. Me and Janna go way back. We went to school together."

Ya, and Janna had complained about him throughout elementary school and into junior high school, if Luke remembered right. She'd quickly moved away from him and now stood stiffly with her hands clenched at her waist, so she wasn't any more comfortable with him now. Yet here he was, and at her bidding. Did she have no common sense?

Brushing off the urge to shove his fists into his pockets, Luke shook the man's hand. "Luke Martin." Only one box still sat on the pickup's tailgate, and he lifted it and set it on the ground. "Thanks for your help. We can take it from here."

Tony turned to Janna, seeming to expect her to say or do something.

She swallowed. "Thank you, Tony."

He scowled, then shrugged. "Catch you later." After shutting the tailgate of the truck, he climbed into it, then started the engine and got down on the gas as he headed for the road.

When Luke faced Janna again, Joah and Kayla were carrying the backpack and doll toward the *daadi haus. Gut.* "I told you just last night that I'd take you to get your belongings. Why didn't you tell me you were going over there?"

"Because I know how busy you are," she said calmly. "I wasn't sure if I'd be able to get anything. I just knew Justin and the inspector were there, and I wanted to talk to them. Malinda told me to go and offered to watch Joah and Kayla. Then when Justin told me I could get whatever I wanted from the first floor, I realized my car would only hold so much. Tony was there and offered to help, and it was either that or call you."

"And you chose him?"

She looked away. "I chose to not interrupt you. You already said you'll be working late every night this week."

Whether she was angry or hurt, he couldn't tell. She didn't sound insincere, but she'd also balked when he tried to help her before. More than once. That bothered him, maybe more than it should've. Still, if she was going to stay with them, she ought to respect his requests. "You should've called me. Better yet, you should've told me before you left. Busy or not, I would've taken you."

She picked up the box. "Fine."

He stared after her as she headed for the *daadi haus.* Her response was hardly an apology—he didn't know what it was, really—and now she was going to just walk away? "Janna."

She stopped on the porch but didn't turn around.

"Men don't belong in the *daadi haus* with you."

She spun to face him. "Is that what this is about? Well, here's the truth: I told him to just set the boxes and bags on the porch. I never said he could go inside, but while I was putting a box in the kitchen, he came in anyway." After shifting the box to one arm, she opened the screen door. "I have no intention of pursuing that kind of relationship, not with him or anyone else for that matter."

The door closed behind her.

Luke shook his head. No matter what he did—or how he tried to help—it backfired.

Ach, he needed to get back to the workshop. Right after finding some ibuprofen for his head.

"One more story, Joah. Then it's time for bed," Salena said as she stood at his closet, hanging up shirts. "Janna needs to get Kayla to bed yet." Just as it had been years ago, Monday was laundry day.

"Okay, *Mammi*." He gave Janna the sweet top-tooth-less smile that had melted her heart pretty much from the moment she'd met him. Scooting closer to where she sat against the pillow at the bed's headboard, he laid his head against her shoulder. "Can you read *Bobcat in the Woods*? That's my favorite one."

"What's it about?" Kayla snuggled in on Janna's other side.

He giggled. "A bobcat, silly."

Kayla joined in, and Janna couldn't help grinning. She'd never seen children from such different backgrounds take to each other so quickly. Kayla's sadness about moving away from her friends had seemingly disappeared as soon as she met Joah, and his initial shyness had quickly dissolved. "Okay. Show me where it is."

Joah paged through the book of short stories until he found it.

Just as Janna was about to start reading, Luke appeared in the doorway. He frowned briefly, so much so that she questioned whether she'd seen it or imagined it. Then he walked toward the bed.

She closed her mouth and looked down at the book. Maybe he didn't like the way the three of them were nestled together against the pillow at the headboard? But Salena hadn't said anything about it, and she never had difficulty speaking her mind if she felt something was improper.

"I need to get out to the workshop." Luke stopped beside them and lifted Joah onto his hip.

Joah wrapped his arms around his neck. "*Guder nacht*, Daddy."

"*Guder nacht*, son." Luke kissed the side of his head and set him back on the bed. "What are you reading?"

Oh, he was talking to her. She closed the book, holding the page with two fingers. "*Brookside Farm Stories*." When she stole a peek at him, he looked away. Still stewing over their argument that afternoon, apparently.

He nodded, then left the room.

"Ready, Mama," Kayla said. "I wanna hear about the bobcat."

Janna forced her attention back to the book, trying to ignore the apprehension that edged at her. Salena had said she and Kayla were welcome to stay with them, but Luke's aloofness seemed to contradict that. He wouldn't even look at her.

And with *Daadi* Eli gone, Luke was the head of the household, so his decisions trumped even Salena's. If he changed his mind and decided not to have outsiders live on the property, she and Kayla would be looking for another place to stay. Again.

The thought of living here for several weeks unsettled her too. She needed independence, which she wouldn't have on the farm. Not the kind she wanted.

Looking into other housing options would probably be best.

Rain spritzed from the sky and thunder rolled in the distance as Luke left the shop at ten fifty-five that night. Janna wasn't on the *daadi haus*'s porch, but light shone through her screen door and the window on either side of it. She had to be awake.

Whether he wanted to or not, he needed to get this over with. He jogged to the gate on the other side of the lane, then opened it and hurried up the walkway to the *daadi haus* porch. With one knuckle he knocked on the wooden door.

Inside, Janna stood from the couch in the small living room. "Hey, I need to go," she told whoever she was talking to on her cell phone. "I'll call you soon." Nearing the door, she stopped and then inched toward it. "Hi."

Maybe he should've waited till tomorrow to do this—during daylight instead of here at night. But he'd spent the last three hours thinking everything over and had finally come to a decision. At least she was still fully dressed. Well, shorts and a T-shirt wasn't fully dressed, but it was daytime clothing. "I wanted to talk to you, if it's not too late."

She hesitated. "Do you want to come in?"

"Could we talk out here?" He stepped back.

Still holding her phone, she pushed the door open and crossed the threshold onto the porch. Thunder rumbled far off as she quietly closed the door behind her.

"Come sit down." He indicated the swing. As she did, he

lowered himself onto the porch railing. "I know you won't be able to live in the place you're renting for a while, and it wonders me if you'd consider not just staying here during that time but also helping us out. Keeping the house, working in the shop, and quilting, as well as taking care of Joah, has become a lot for *Mamm* in the last year or so, and how you've helped her so much over the last few days has been wonderful. Joah also has occupational therapy on Tuesdays and physical therapy on Fridays in Lancaster, and if you could drive him and *Mamm* there, that would allow me more time in the workshop. In return, you'd live here, and we'd take care of any needs you have."

Her mouth opened, and then she sank against the back of the swing.

"Is something wrong?"

"No, I . . ." She looked down at the phone on her lap.

"Janna." He waited until she looked at him. "I know we've already had some . . . difficulties, and that does concern me. But I'm willing to give it a try if you are. Difficulties or not, you were part of our family. You have nowhere to go, and we have room. I could never in good conscience turn you away, and I don't want you in a place like the Dutchman. This seems practical for all of us."

She didn't move or say anything. Not a great sign.

"Will you at least think about it and let me know?"

A few nods this time. "May I ask about Joah, about his feet? He said something about getting casts again and then AFOs, but that was all."

Luke crossed his arms. "He's always walked on his toes. Well, on the balls of his feet. Rayanne never worried about it because she walked that way when she was small too. Then when Joah was four, I made a dining set for a woman who was a physical therapist at New Beginnings Pediatric Rehab down in Lancaster. She saw the way he walked and asked me about it, then suggested we take him to a specialist. We went to a doctor at Children's Hospital in Philadelphia, and he recommended PT and OT evaluations since Joah was showing some fine motor issues too. Since then he's been getting PT and OT at New Beginnings."

"And the casts are to lengthen his Achilles tendons so he can walk with his heels down?"

Interesting. Most people knew nothing about that. "*Ya*. Therapy alone wasn't helping enough. We started serial casting three weeks ago, and Lord willing, he'll have his last recasting on Friday. Then next week he'll start wearing the AFOs he was fitted for last week. You're familiar with toe walking?"

"Some. When Kayla was born, I took a job with a medical transcription company so I could work from home. One of the clients I transcribed for regularly was a pediatric rehab."

In that case, her knowledge would come in handy with managing Joah's care. "You probably know more than I do, then."

She smiled, the same gentle smile he remembered. "I don't know about that. It sounds like you've done a great job of getting him what he needs. Being a single parent isn't easy, especially when your child has medical issues."

Indeed, and having someone truly understand and commend that lifted his spirits. *Mamm* was wonderful, and Luke didn't know how he'd rear Joah without her, but she didn't know what it was like to handle the emotional responsibilities of bringing up a child without a spouse to assist. "You have experience with medical issues too?"

"Kind of. Kayla's peanut allergy. She used to be allergic to milk too, but she outgrew that about a year ago. It's made life a little more complicated."

Mahlon's youngest son had a nut allergy, as did one of

Malinda's granddaughters, so he'd seen that firsthand. "I'm sure."

Thunder rolled a bit closer, and the sky lit up to the south. "Well, I'd better get inside before it starts to pour." And before he spent the next hour—or more—talking to her. He straightened and walked to the step, then turned around. "You'll think about what I said?"

She got to her feet. "Of course."

Heavy rain suddenly pounded the ground and porch roof. Too late.

Instead of going out to the lane and down to the walkway to the house, he walked to the end of the porch and stepped over the shared railing onto the house's kitchen porch. He glanced back before going into the house, hoping to catch her eye one last time, but Janna was watching the storm.

Inside, he closed the door. With that conversation out of the way, hopefully he'd sleep better tonight. Except he'd thought she'd give an answer right away. She obviously had some reservations, maybe more than he did.

Ach, he needed to leave this in the Lord's hands. If it was his will, she and Kayla would stay. And if not . . . well, he'd figure that out when the time came. Hire a helper for *Mamm*, maybe.

Ya, like she'd agree to that. *Ay-yi-yi.*

A Difficult Decision

Unable to go back to sleep at five thirty in the morning, Janna got up and made herself a cup of coffee, then carried it and her cell phone out to the porch swing.

The sun barely peaked above the rolling hills way beyond the shop, tinging the muted blue sky a mixture of pink and orange and casting a golden glow across the far-off pasture. Farther up the lane, voices called, cows mooed, and other noises echoed. No doubt Enos and Ivan in the barn for the four a.m. milking. Despite the hint of manure, the air smelled freshly of dew and roses after last night's rain. She'd forgotten how much she loved the peaceful beauty of early mornings on the farm.

Knowing her best friend would be on her way to her seven-to-seven shift at the hospital, Janna called her.

Arissa picked up on the third ring. "Girl, what're you doing up at this hour?"

She laughed, her stress level already easing. "I just couldn't wait another minute to talk to you."

"Aw, you're so sweet. So what's going on? I tried calling you when I got home last night, but your phone just went to voice mail."

"I know. The battery died, and I didn't realize you called until late last night." She tucked her foot under her other leg and set the swing in motion. "How was your cousin's wedding?"

"Beautiful. Happily-ever-after. But enough about that. I want to hear about your move. Are you settled in now? And how's Kay doing with it? I thought you'd call me on Saturday."

She almost had. "I didn't want to bother you while you were with your family."

Arissa sniffed. "Like you could ever bother me. How's your place? Do you love it?"

That she did. She'd love it even more when it was fixed and they were living in it. "Actually, we're not there." Between sips of coffee, she offered the abridged version of their last three days.

Arissa listened without a word, then *mm-mm-mm*'d. "That's crazy. And you're sure you're all right where you are? 'Cause you can always stay with me."

Except that her studio apartment was barely big enough for one person—and in Center City. Janna had moved them to Akron—or tried to—to find a slower, quieter life than the one Philadelphia and its suburbs offered. "We're fine. They've been very kind to us." Well, except for Luke, and even though he could be frustrating, he'd shown concern for their well-being. She had to give him that. "Actually, they've offered to let us stay in their *daadi haus* for as long as we need to."

"Their *what*?"

"*Daadi haus*. It's a little house attached to a larger house, usually for grandparents. They use theirs for visiting family and local missionaries home on furlough, but they offered it to us in exchange for helping out here."

"What about work? Don't you have projects scheduled for this week?"

"Not till Thursday. And I'll be working early in the morning and late at night. That's what I'd planned with Kayla out of school for the summer anyway." Except she still wasn't sure how she'd manage that at the Martins'. Internet usage had been forbidden when she'd lived with them before, and that probably hadn't changed. "And that's if we decide to stay here."

"*If?* So you have other options?"

"Well, not exactly." They could stay at a motel, but even the Dutchman would get expensive. And Luke was right. It was no place for her and Kayla. Finding an apartment quickly, especially one that would allow them to move out once Mrs. Bollinger's house was fixed, was unlikely and would require two moves. She'd done enough of that in the last few days. "I'm still thinking about it."

On the other end, Arissa slurped the last of a drink—her morning Starbucks, no doubt—through a straw. "Girl, do you not see God in this?" By her tone, she was shaking her head. "These people have offered you a place. Your ending up back with them like this can't possibly be just a coincidence. Sounds to me like God's told you where you belong right now."

Janna couldn't deny the coincidence part. Even so, after all these years, why would God put her back with the Martins? Growing up here had been wonderful, but then that had ended. Life had taken such a different path than what *Daadi* Eli and Salena hoped for her, and although Salena had welcomed her back with open arms, it would be only a matter of time before her conservative beliefs clashed with Janna's reality.

Not that she could go into that now. They'd be on the phone forever. Janna took another sip of coffee. "I know. I'm just not sure what's my best option. I can't help thinking that if we belonged here, I'd feel more comfortable with staying."

Arissa stayed quiet for a few moments. "Well, I can't tell you what to do, Jan. We've talked about this family, but I'm sure I don't know everything. All I can do is remind you how you always make decisions—by thinking about Kay. What's best for her, you know?" A noise sounded on the other end. "Hey, I need to hustle so I don't miss my train. I should go, but keep in touch. Let me know what you decide."

"I will."

"And don't let your ego make your decision for you." Her tone had softened. "I know you're set on being independent now—moving on, forgetting about Mitch, and taking care of everything yourself—but sometimes we need other people."

Janna's skin crawled at the sound of his name. "Thanks, Riss. Talk to you later." Sighing, she ended the call.

What was best for Kayla. That didn't take a lot of thought. All she had to do was imagine the smile that lit up her little girl's face as she played with Joah or helped Salena bake. Taking Kayla away from them—and away from the farm that had been such an amazing, stable place for Janna to grow up— and making her endure two more moves seemed unthinkable.

Still, staying just felt wrong. Not because of the *daadi haus*. Even though it was half the size of their new place and didn't give Kayla her own bedroom, it was adequate in the short term. Not even because of the lack of internet connection. A USB stick modem would fix that.

Maybe Arissa was right. After the nightmare with Mitch, she'd wanted to start over. A quieter, safer town. A nicer place to live. A better school for Kayla. A new life, really. One where she called the shots. What was wrong with that?

Nothing, except that living in the *daadi haus*, she'd be working for the Martins—and Luke would in essence be her boss. Luke who believed women needed to be reliant on a man and with whom she'd already battled about that more than once. He might not want them to leave now, but if they stayed, chances were good it wouldn't be long before their differences and the resulting disagreements changed his mind.

Closing her eyes, she rested her head against the back of the swing. Would life ever get easier?

Janna spent the day thinking over her options, and as much as she wanted to determine that staying with the Martins wouldn't work, by late afternoon she still wasn't convinced. Really, the time she spent helping Salena, reminiscing with Malinda while Joah and Kayla played, and then driving Joah, Kayla, and Salena to Joah's occupational therapy appointment at New Beginnings made the day one of the best she'd had in months.

She'd soon need to start working again, but doing that in the early morning and at night would allow her plenty of enjoyable time during the day. Was it really worth giving up that—and being close to the Martins again—just to assert her independence for a month or two? She and Kayla wouldn't be staying in the *daadi haus* forever, after all. Once Mrs. Bollinger's house was fixed, they'd move in as planned.

With Joah and Kayla doing chores in the house while Salena made supper, Janna went in search of Luke. She found him in the workshop as expected, but at entering the large room to find him on the phone, she stopped and backed up.

From his stool at the workbench, he summoned her back in. "Yes, Mrs. Stott."

Goodness. The woman he'd told her about simply wouldn't leave him alone.

The pungent smells of oak and maple, wood stain, paint, and polyurethane filled her nostrils as she slowly made her way across the room, giving Luke time by perusing the furniture. In one area the pieces were built, finished, and ready for sale. Those in another area were built but awaited stain or paint. Running her hand across the top of an unfinished table, she smiled at its almost velvety smoothness. *Daadi* Eli had taught Luke well. Every piece was a work of art.

"Yes," he said again. "I'll call you to set up a time for delivery . . . Thank you. Have a nice evening."

As she turned and headed for the workbench, he leaned over to hang the ancient black corded receiver on the wall. Even the sincerity of his smile couldn't hide its fatigue. "I know you're busy, but I was hoping to talk to you about what you said last night."

He raised his eyebrows. His expression brightened a bit, but the way he set his jaw indicated concern.

She slid onto the stool at the other end of the workbench. This view of the room immediately took her back to the countless times she'd sat in the workshop, first with Luke while they watched *Daadi* Eli work and later on her own while Luke and his grandfather worked together. When she closed her eyes and breathed in the mixture of scents, she could almost hear *Daadi* Eli's baritone voice singing a German hymn.

"*Ebbes letz?*"

She opened her eyes. "*Nee.*" Apparently, she hadn't forgotten as much *Deitsch* as she thought. "Nothing's wrong. I was just . . . remembering."

His next *Deitsch* sentence she couldn't understand, and he

glanced around the room when she didn't respond. "Not much has changed in here, I said."

"Yeah." Time seemed to stand still on the farm. Well, except for with the people—what she most wished hadn't changed.

Luke rested an arm on the workbench and looked into her eyes. He might have matured—taller and broader, more strongly built, light-blond hair now sandy—but his blue eyes were as beautiful as always. And equally as able to seemingly see everything she felt.

She looked away. "I've been thinking about what you said. It's kind of you, and I truly appreciate your concern for us."

His sigh was barely audible. "But?"

She met his gaze again. His expression gave no suggestion of what he was thinking, but disappointment tinged his tone. "It's not that I don't want to stay. My biggest concern is . . ." She shook her head. Why did this have to be so hard? It was what it was, and he knew it, so why balk? "It's just . . . us, Luke. We're different people, from very different cultures. That will trip us up and put us at odds."

"You lived with us for years and never seemed bothered by our ways."

True. But she'd been a child then. Somehow that mattered, although she wouldn't be able to give a concrete answer if he asked why. "I know, but . . . I just don't want to do something wrong and have things not work out."

"If something were to happen, we'd address it. You were part of our family. We'd like you to stay, and I don't think you'd do anything that would make me think it would be best for you to leave."

Also true—she hoped. "Could you at least give me an idea of the rules we'd need to follow? So I know what's expected."

Staring at something across the room, he inhaled. "We're not tyrants. Our rules have reasons behind them."

Here came another argument. "I know that. Please, just . . . I'm only trying to make this as painless as possible, for both of us. I'm not judging you or implying you'd judge me."

He crossed his arms. So much like *Daadi* Eli, the way he took his time thinking about what to say. "It's not our way to enforce our rules on others. That said, you'll be living here, and we'll expect you to respect our beliefs. Our ways haven't changed much. No television. You can listen to music, but only in the *daadi haus* and if you keep the volume low. No smoking or drinking, and no men in the *daadi haus*."

He really had to bring that up again? "I think I made my stance on that clear."

His lips tightened for a moment. "And if you have a smart-phone or computer, Joah's not to touch it or be around Kayla if she's using it."

Touché. Kayla did love her phone, probably too much. Maybe this would be a way to put a stop to that. "What about clothing?" When living with the Martins, she'd dressed in regular clothing for school, mainly due to Mom's insistence, but worn handmade dresses when on the farm. She still loved skirts and dresses, especially in the summer, but she couldn't wear a cape dress or head covering.

"In the *daadi haus* you can dress as you like. I don't think it's too much to ask for modesty otherwise, especially in the shop. You'll be representing the family, so skirts below the knees, tops with a proper neckline and sleeves to the elbows, and little or no face paint."

She rarely wore makeup as it was, and her dresses were no shorter than knee-length and unpretentious, at least in her opinion. Elbow-length sleeves could pose a problem since most of her summer dresses were sleeveless, but she did have a lightweight three-quarter-sleeve cardy or two. And while Kayla would need a few more skorts and short-sleeve shirts, that wasn't the end of the world. Hardly ideal, but not a deal breaker.

Although yard work would be. The Martins had quite a bit of lawn around the house and alongside the shop where the playset and trampoline were, and yard work was usually done by women. "Would I be expected to mow the lawn?"

"*Nee.* Two of Enos and Beulah's grandsons take care of that every week or so, depending on how tall the grass is."

Good. It wasn't like she had a bunch of other housing options anyway. She forced a smile. "Agreed."

"So you'll stay?"

"We'll stay."

Making some changes for a few weeks wouldn't be that big a sacrifice. Then life would move on as planned.

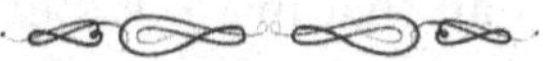

A heavy load seemed lifted off Luke's shoulders as he tidied the workshop before heading to the house for supper. Even if Janna and Kayla stayed for only a month or so, he and *Mamm* would have help, and he'd also have time to decide whether he'd need to find another helper when they left.

As well, he'd have the Stotts' dining set completed Thursday morning, Lord willing. Other custom orders waited, but Mahlon should've returned from Ohio today and would be back to work tomorrow. Things would soon settle down.

He grabbed his cell phone from the high shelf above the workbench and shoved it into his back pocket, then turned out the lights and went into the shop. Beulah stood behind the counter, adding up the money from the cash register.

He nodded to her. "*Guder owed.*"

She looked up, her expression solemn as always. As he passed the counter on the way to the door, she closed the register drawer. "Luke."

He stopped. Her face rarely reflected contentment, but today she looked like she'd been sucking lemons.

She folded her arms across her chest. "Do you think this is wise? Inviting *outsidas* to live here?"

So she *had* heard. After Janna left, he'd realized Beulah had been in the shop the whole time. Apparently, thinking she wouldn't eavesdrop had been giving his aunt too much credit. "I wouldn't do it if I thought it foolish. *Mamm* can use the help, and Janna and Kayla need a place to stay. I can't send away a woman and child who have nowhere to go. The Bible tells us to care for widows and orphans."

Beulah eyed him. "Is that what she is, then?"

"She's a woman with a child and no husband or father to care for them. That's all that matters. Besides, they're not just *outsidas*. Janna lived here."

She grunted. "Until she left and broke *Mamm*'s heart."

Surely Beulah realized Janna had nothing to do with that. "Missy took her away. Janna didn't even know about it till the day before they left. It was the last thing she wanted."

"Then why didn't she stay in contact?"

He'd asked the same question himself, more times than he could count, but that had nothing to do with what was happening now. "She wasn't even thirteen at the time. Who knows what kind of situation Missy put them in. She's returned now, and—"

"Not of her own doing. Only because Malinda insisted on bringing them here." She shook her head. "Luke, 'tis not the same. You need to think about Joah. How is bringing in an *outsida* to help care for him in his best interest? I'm not saying you're wrong in thinking *Mamm* could use some help. I agree, and Malinda and I are too busy making quilts and running the shop to do much for her, but a girl from the *gmay* would be better suited."

"I grew up with Janna. She's always been an *outsida*, but that didn't have a negative effect on me."

She huffed. "Didn't it? Janna was much more like us then, and you ended up leaving the *gmay*. She's different now, and so is her daughter, and yet you're making her a role model for Joah and thinking it won't affect him?" She tossed her hands in the air. "*Ay-yi-yi.*"

He didn't even know where to start in responding to that. She had a point. But citing Janna as a reason for his continuing shift in beliefs? She had just arrived.

"Does *Mamm* even know about this?" she asked.

"Not unless Janna's just told her, but I have no doubt she'll be delighted to have them stay."

"*Ya*, but what happens when their house is ready? What if Janna decides she doesn't need us anymore, like she did the last time she left? Then what?"

"She won't. We've already talked about that." And hopefully, Janna meant what she'd said. "I've prayed about this, Beulah. I've *been* praying for a while now, and I can't believe it's by chance that Janna showed up, needing us as much as we need her."

Scowling, she shook her head. "'Tis not our way. God calls us to be separate from the world, not to invite it into our homes and let it rear our children. Introducing Joah to their worldliness is asking for trouble. I just hope *Mamm* can see that too, and keep you from making a big mistake."

Nothing he said would change her mind. No use arguing further. "I appreciate your concern, but I've made my decision," he said as sincerely as he could. "It'll only be until their place is ready. Now, *Mamm*'ll have supper on the table soon. *Guder owed.*"

As he left the shop, he wasn't much hungry anymore. The load might have been off his shoulders, but now it sat in the pit of his stomach. Because he couldn't deny most of what Beulah had said.

Stepping Up

At hearing the door to the shop open and then close, Luke looked up from running steel wool over the seat of a dining chair. Six forty-five, early for anyone to be coming in. The shop didn't open till eight thirty, and Mahlon rarely arrived before seven fifteen. He set the pad on the seat and stood.

Whistling preceded his cousin, who walked through the doorway with his insulated cooler bag under his arm. "Hey, Luke. You're in early."

Ach, Luke was glad to see him. Over the last sixteen days, two trips to Ohio—one to visit his sick grandfather and the other for the man's sooner-than-expected funeral—had allowed Mahlon only two days in the workshop. Luke had greatly missed his help and, even more, their close friendship.

"Getting a head start on the day." He held out his hand. "You're a sight for sore eyes."

Mahlon pulled him into a brief one-armed embrace

instead. When he stepped back, he looked at him more closely. "Your eyes do look sore. Everything all right?"

"Just busy is all. Early mornings, late nights. I set up delivery for the Stotts' dining set tomorrow morning, at least." But that really didn't matter when compared to Mahlon's last couple of weeks. "How was your trip?"

He sobered. "It went well. God provided safe travels for all, and Gramma's doing better than we thought, being the doctors thought Grampa would have more time. It was a blessing to see so much of that side of my family at once. We hadn't all been together since our reunion four years ago." He set his bag on the desk by the door. "I'd planned on calling last night, but we didn't get home till almost nine. The last four days, Kendra's been sick at her stomach every morning, so we didn't get packed and on the road till after one yesterday."

Luke smiled, trying to ignore a twinge of longing. Although only five years older, Mahlon already had four children as well as a wife. Envy was a sin Luke would never entertain, at least not for more than the instant it surfaced, but he couldn't say he didn't yearn for the same. "You're going to need a nine-passenger van before you know it."

"Maybe. Don't say anything yet."

"*Nee.*" As if he would. Mahlon's more progressive family talked almost openly about such things, but his didn't. "I'm on my way in for breakfast. Join us?"

"Sure. I could use another cup of coffee. Anything new around here?"

Luke outened the lights and followed him into the shop. "I've found a helper for *Mamm*—for a little while, anyway."

"Someone I know?"

"*Ya.* You won't believe who, though."

A mischievous grin spread across his face. "Nancy Jane Hershey?"

Luke stopped, facing him.

"What?" Mahlon laughed. "It's not like she isn't in the shop a few times a month for one reason or another, and peeking into the workshop to say hello to us."

Ya. But he'd never encouraged her attention. She was a nice-enough girl, but he was no longer in good standing at their church. Pursuing a relationship with her would bring consequences, especially for her, and he wasn't ready for remarriage anyway. "Not Nancy Jane."

Mahlon shrugged. "I give up. Tell me."

The shop door flew open, and Joah rushed in with Kayla on his heels.

"Mahlon!" Joah ran toward them, and Mahlon met him halfway and scooped him up.

Kayla moved closer, watching them tentatively but with interest. She wore an unbuttoned sweater over her skirt and shirt, so Janna had taken his instructions seriously. "*Guder mariye,* Luke." Before he could stop her, she threw her arms around his waist.

Placing his hand on her head, he stepped back. Kayla hugged everyone, but he wasn't accustomed to affection like that except from Joah and from Mahlon's children. "*Guder mariye.*"

Mahlon set Joah back on the floor, then smiled at her. "What's your name, sweetheart? I don't think we've met."

She went to Joah's side. "Kayla Carpenter. I live here now."

He raised his eyebrows. "Really? Well, it's nice to meet you, Kayla. I'm Mahlon."

"Daddy, Janna said breakfast is ready," Joah said.

"*Danki,* son. We'll be right in."

Mahlon watched as Kayla grabbed Joah's hand and the two of them skipped back outside. When he faced Luke again, his eyes lit. "Wait. Janna Carpenter?"

He nodded. "Kayla's her daughter. They'll be living in the *daadi haus* and helping us out for a month or so."

Mahlon stared for a few moments, then slowly smiled. Chuckling, he started toward the door. "You've a story to tell me later, cousin. I never would've guessed that."

Ya. Even after five days, sometimes Luke couldn't believe it either.

"Mama, how come we have to wear dresses now?" Kayla looked up at Janna, her delicate eyebrows squeezed together. "I like shorts too."

Janna took another dress off the girls' clothing rack in the Ephrata Re-Uzit Shop and looked it over, then held it up to Kayla. "I know you do. But you love dresses." Thank goodness Kayla was a girlie-girl, at least when it came to clothing. "And we can wear shorts in the *daadi haus*. Just not outside it."

So far, she'd found one skirt with shorts underneath it, a short-sleeved shirt that matched, and three cotton Carter's dresses. One of the dresses was sleeveless, but the lightweight white button-down sweater Kayla already had would fix that issue. Some of the clothes were on sale too.

"You don't like me playing on the playground in a skirt. And Joah and me go on the playset every day."

"Joah and I, honey." Janna faced her. "And what I said was that when you're wearing a skirt, you should wear the bike shorts I got for you underneath it." She tapped her on the nose. "That's why we bought you those, so you could wear dresses and skirts to school and still play at recess, remember?"

Kayla gave a scrunchy smile. "Yeah." She looked toward the

front of the store. "Can I get some hair bows? I saw a basket of them near where you pay."

"We'll see how much this comes to."

She huffed. "You said we'd have more money for stuff once we moved here."

"I know. And we will. Soon." Except she'd already had to pay a bill she hadn't anticipated—a hundred and sixty dollars for a USB stick modem and the first month's internet service—just that morning. The bill had gone on her credit card since she bought it online, but that couldn't keep happening. She'd finally paid off their debt and needed to keep it that way.

"But why can't we wear shorts?"

Janna drew a deep breath. How in the world could she explain this to a not-quite-six-year-old so she would understand? "Well . . . the Martins believe women should wear dresses. They want to be modest, and to them, that means keeping a lot of their skin covered. Dresses do a good job of that. That's why Luke and Joah don't wear shorts either."

"I wish I could still wear shorts. Outside, I mean. Especially when it's really hot." She stepped away from the rack and twirled around. "I wish I had my own room too. You said when we moved, I would have my own room and we could paint it pink."

"Kayla Grace." Janna placed her hand on Kayla's shoulder to stop her. "I know you really want your own room, but do you understand how fortunate we are? Would you rather be living in a motel, in one little room with no living room, no kitchen, and no dining room? And no playset and trampoline?"

Kayla grimaced. "No."

Janna felt a little guilty. They'd both been so looking forward to living in the house in Akron, and she'd fought to accept staying with the Martins herself. She still struggled with some aspects of that arrangement, so how could she expect a little girl not to do the same? "Honey, I know this isn't what we planned, but right now it's what we have to do."

Kayla shrugged. "We could go to Florida. Cynthia said we can stay with her anytime we want to."

Kayla wasn't the only one who missed Cynthia. Amid all the craziness, Janna had also considered going to Florida—more than once. Cynthia would never turn them away. Still, she and Kayla were finally on their own, and that was how it needed to be. She was too old to be relying on others. "She said we could visit, not live with her. How about we call her tonight to talk?"

Kayla bounced up and down. "Oh yes, please!"

Janna checked her watch. Almost two thirty. "We'd better get going. *Mammi* Salena and Joah should be up by now."

"How come Joah had to take a nap today? He's older than me."

"His legs were hurting last night because of his casts. He didn't sleep very well, and *Mammi* Salena wanted him to rest."

Kayla wrinkled her nose. "The casts make his feet stinky too. We can smell it when we play on the floor. I'm glad he's getting new ones tomorrow."

Oh, goodness. "Kayla, that's not kind."

"Even he says so, Mama." She giggled. "He thinks it's funny."

Typical boy. "Maybe so, but I hope you're not saying anything to him about it."

"I'm not. I don't want to hurt his feelings."

That was more what she wanted to hear. "Good."

Maybe, just maybe, she was doing something right as a parent.

Salena had said Joah's Friday afternoon appointments at New Beginnings always took a long time, and she was right. First, Janna had helped Luke hold Joah, who needed noise-canceling headphones and repeated assurances that the saw would do nothing more than tickle, while two techs removed his casts. Then she washed his legs and feet and applied the homemade cream Salena had sent along.

Finally, after Carin, his physical therapist, guided him through exercises, she and an orthotist took measurements of Joah's feet and ankles before recasting his legs.

"No wonder *Mammi* Salena wanted to stay home," Kayla said from where she lay next to Joah on the exam table, coloring with him while his black fiberglass casts dried. "She'd be really tired by now."

"*Ya*, she would." Luke stood from his chair and moved around the room. So much sitting probably wasn't easy for him either, being he spent most days in constant motion in the workshop.

The door opened, and Carin came back in. "Okay. Joah's range of motion and the bone alignment in both feet look really good." She grinned as she sat on the stool and rolled over to him in one motion. "These should be your last casts, buddy. If everything goes as planned, you'll be ready for your AFOs next Friday. We'll remove your casts, get your AFOs fitted, and do some therapy to make sure nothing needs further adjustment." She turned to Luke. "Do you have new shoes?"

He stopped by the table, closing his eyes as he exhaled. "Not yet. We looked at Good's and Mellinger's, and I called the New Balance outlet too, but none of them had what we were looking for. Then it slipped my mind."

"The extra-wides can be tough to find," she said kindly. Carin's expensive clothing and perfect hair, makeup, and nails had intimidated Janna a little at first, but she was as personable as she was put-together. "We still have some time." She glanced at Janna, who sat on a chair beside the exam table, before looking back to him. "Online is often your best bet. Do you know someone who has a computer and internet access?"

She took the hint. "I do. If you tell me what he'll need, we can take care of it."

Luke dropped into one of the chairs along the wall, then leaned forward and rested his elbows on his knees. "*Mamm* has it written down. We'd need to order soon so we'll have them in time."

Not a problem, especially since her laptop was back online as of that morning. "We'll do it today, then."

Tension eased from his face. "*Danki.*"

Joah squirmed, his face pinched. "Janna?"

She leaned closer. "What's the matter?" Hopefully, the casts were all right.

"I need to go to the bathroom," he whispered.

Carin checked the clock on the wall, then felt his casts. "You're dry. Go ahead. Why don't you have Dad carry you, though? Then when you're finished, we'll add the lifts and inserts in your cast shoes and make sure you're walking the way you should." She patted his shoulder. "After that, you can get out of here."

Luke lifted his son off the table, then carried him out of the room.

"I'll give you the information about shoes in case you need it." Carin rolled over to the desk where her tablet computer sat, then pushed her shoulder-length dark hair behind her ears and met Janna's gaze. "And thank you. I was afraid they might have trouble finding shoes locally."

"I'm happy to help." That was her job now, after all, but it was more than that. Joah was such a sweetheart that she'd do just about anything for him. "Joah's a great kid."

"He is, and his dad's a good guy too. He's making sure Joah gets all the services he needs, and not without sacrifices."

Sacrifices? Luke had never mentioned anything like that, but it did make some sense. Old Order people didn't carry health insurance, and the prospective cost of two and a half years of specialist visits and PT and OT appointments made Janna cringe inside. Carin might have meant he was also sacrificing in ways other than financial, but Luke and Joah would certainly return before Janna could tactfully question her intent.

No matter the reason, staying with the Martins suddenly seemed a bit easier to accept. Maybe Arissa was right. Maybe God had put her there—and maybe for the Martins as much as for her and Kayla.

Luke looked in the rearview mirror as he took the Oregon Pike exit off Route 222.

Joah had been talking to Kayla about one of the books Janna read while they were at New Beginnings, but he suddenly sat forward. "Daddy, where are we going?" His tone held the eager anticipation Luke expected.

He grinned. "I thought we'd stop somewhere on the way home."

Joah's eyes widened. "Oregon Dairy?"

"The Stotts' dining set is finished and delivered, and you did well at your appointment today. We even got out of there a little early. Time for a celebration, not?"

"*Ya!*"

"What's Oregon Dairy?" Kayla asked.

"A big grocery store and restaurant," Joah said. "They sell yummy ice cream and have all sorts of animals and a playground and the Jump Pad."

"What's the Jump Pad?"

"It's like a large blown-up trampoline." Luke checked the clock on the dash. "Joah can't go on it with his casts, but you can. What's your favorite ice cream, Kayla?"

"I don't eat ice cream."

"*Nee?*" He looked over at Janna in the passenger seat.

She gave an apologetic look. "Even though she's not allergic to milk anymore, she's never wanted to try ice cream. She does eat sorbet. I'm sure I could get her a little container of that in the store."

They did just that, then went back outside and around to the Milk House next to the restaurant. Joah wanted his usual—chocolate marshmallow ice cream in a waffle cone with rainbow sprinkles—but Janna declined anything, which he expected. She'd finally allowed Luke to pay for Kayla's sorbet, but not without objections. She wasn't getting off that easily.

After paying for their ice cream, Luke found his little group at a picnic table on the playground, not far from the Jump Pad. Joah and Kayla sat opposite Janna with their backs to her, eating and watching sock-clad kids bounce. The whitetail deer enclosure across the gravel lane to their right held Janna's attention.

He sat down beside her and set his Mud Pie Sundae on the table. "Brought you something."

"But I said—" At turning to see him holding out the extra spoon he'd requested, she smiled. That still didn't disguise her hesitance.

"I know what you said. But unless something has changed,

you love ice cream. And brownies. Besides, if I finish this on my own, I'll never be able to eat my supper, and *Mamm*'ll send me to bed early as punishment."

Her grin brightened. "After your last couple of weeks, going to bed early might not be such a bad thing."

He laughed. That was the sweet sense of humor he remembered. "*Nee*. But I'd still like your help."

"All right. But only because I wouldn't want you to get in trouble." Taking the spoon, she eyed the dish. "Oh my goodness. I'd completely forgotten about Wilbur Buds. I haven't had them since . . ."

Since a month or so before Missy moved them out of Lancaster County, probably. *Daadi* had hired a van to go to Lititz, and while the women shopped for what they needed in town, he'd taken Luke and Janna to the Wilbur store so they could watch the candymakers. "Since *Daadi* took us there?" he guessed.

"Yeah."

Kayla turned sideways on the bench, her container of sorbet in one hand and spoon in the other. "What's a Wilbur Bud?"

"These here." Luke picked up one of the mini chocolate drops sitting atop a mound of whipped cream and showed it to her. "They're made not far from here. Sometime we'll have to take you there. The whole town smells like chocolate."

"Really? Yum." She faced the Jump Pad again.

Janna lifted her head from a bowed position and moved her spoon toward the dish but then stopped. Chances were she wouldn't start eating until he did, so he offered a silent prayer of thanks, then dug in.

By the time they were halfway through the sundae, the merry atmosphere and children's giggles—and the dessert, if he remembered Janna's preference right—had banished her seriousness.

She laughed at Joah's ice cream mustache and beard. "Come here, honey," she said when he finished his cone. After fishing a baby wipe from her purse, she cleaned his face and hands.

Kayla turned around, then placed her plastic spoon on the table and put the lid on her half-finished sorbet. "Can we play now?"

Janna pulled out another wipe and cleaned her hands and face too.

"For about twenty minutes," Luke said. "Then we'll need to get going."

"Wait. Hold on." Janna dipped a hand into her purse again, this time pulling out a pair of black socks. Luke's own, it appeared. "Sit down and loosen the Velcro on your shoes, Joah. I'll put these over your casts so you don't get wood chips in them."

At least she thought about such things. He never would've considered the playground a problem, but she was right. Wood chips in the casts wouldn't do. "Do you always carry a pair of my socks around?" he asked as Joah and Kayla ran off to play.

Her expression tensed. "Actually, I just put them in my purse the other day." Slowly, she sat down again. "I hope that's okay."

She thought he was chastising her? "Of course. I'm glad you did."

"The last time we were folding laundry, I realized it wouldn't hurt to carry a pair in case we ever need to cover his casts." She shrugged, her grin returning. "I just didn't think that would happen so soon."

As he looked into her eyes, the breeze rustled through the wavy, shorter strands of hair that framed her face. Years ago

Mamm had often tried to slick them down, usually with only temporary success. Now he reached up to brush some away from her eye, then caught himself. Instead, he plucked a piece of wood chip from the arm of her sweater and flicked it away.

Joah called to them from the edge of the Jump Pad, then pointed to Kayla, who bounced nearby. Just beyond it, an older black sedan slowly drove along the exit road. Both the woman in the passenger seat and the man driving sat forward to look out the open passenger-door window.

Sam and Ina from church.

Luke raised a hand and Ina did the same, but she didn't smile and they didn't stop. Strange. They were always so friendly, even in the last few months when some church members had distanced themselves. Except right now, he sat alone at a picnic table with an *outsida*—sharing an ice cream sundae with her.

Sam was one of the ministers, so no doubt the ministry would be visiting again. Soon.

CHAPTER 8

The Visitor

With Joah asleep and *Mamm* preparing for bed, Luke went downstairs to the kitchen. The door that separated the house kitchen from the *daadi haus*'s dining area stood open, and Janna sat on the recliner by the living room's front window, her computer on her lap.

He stopped, searching for something to say to her, but nothing of importance came to mind. When she looked up, he nodded, then walked to the refrigerator and opened its door.

"Still hungry after all that ice cream and supper?" Her soft voice came from behind him as he pulled out the dish of apple crisp.

The teasing in her tone—how it reminded him of years before—brought a smile to his heart. But he knew better than to show that. "Late dessert. I couldn't eat a bite of it before."

"I can imagine." She came into the house, then moved to the counter by the sink and took down a bowl before grabbing a spoon from the drawer below it.

While still wearing the same dress she'd worn earlier, she'd shed the beige sweater, and her hair was now damp and hung loose. A flowery scent surrounded him as he set the dish on the counter, and he moved away. The stack of mail on the counter beside the refrigerator caught his eye, so he sorted through it.

"I think I found shoes for Joah online." She finished filling the bowl, then returned the dish to the refrigerator. "Do you want to take a look? If you want me to order them, I should do it soon so they'll be here in time."

Joah's shoes. Already Luke had forgotten about them. Again. "*Ya*, let's." But where? *Mamm* would never abide Janna's computer in the house. That would be a test of membership for her, and he wouldn't risk that despite the slim chance that anyone would find out. Being alone in the *daadi haus* with Janna wouldn't be best either, but the only other option was taking the computer onto the porch.

He grabbed the bowl and spoon and carried it to the *daadi haus*'s dining area, where he took the seat at the head of the table.

Janna brought the laptop and sat on the side bench, then turned the computer so they both could see the screen. "These are on eBay. Carin said to order two pairs—one that's a size larger than Joah usually wears and one that's a size and a half larger, both extra-wide. These would be here in time too."

The shoes were New Balance, all black and leather. They looked sturdy and practical, and thirty dollars per pair was reasonable.

"She thinks the size-two-and-a-halves will fit. Then he'd have the threes to grow into, and if the two-and-a-halves are too small, he can wear the threes and I'll exchange the two-and-a-halves for three-and-a-halves. I'd just have to pay return shipping. He'll need knee-high socks too, but I should be able to get them at a sporting goods store. Carin wrote down the brand she suggests."

Janna hadn't changed in one regard. Even as a child, she'd been one to take charge and do what needed to be done. She might take that a little too far at times, but right now he couldn't have been gladder for it.

"Will these work, or do you want to keep looking?"

"*Sell isht gut.* Order the two pairs." After taking his wallet from the back pocket of his pants, he pulled out four twenties and placed them on the table. "There's an extra twenty for the socks. If you need more, tell me."

"Thanks."

"I should be the one thanking you." He spooned a bite of apple crisp into his mouth but stopped mid-chew. *Mamm* would've scolded him for not offering some to Janna. "You didn't want any?"

"I ate myself full." She smiled and pressed her hand against her middle. "That sundae was worth it, though."

"*Ya.*" He swallowed and scooped up another spoonful.

She didn't look up from typing on the keyboard. "It kind of seemed like you weren't so sure about that after those people in the black car drove by."

Another thing about Janna that hadn't changed. She didn't miss much. "You saw that?" He set the spoon in the bowl. "I reckon it would've been difficult not to."

She closed the computer. "The shoes should be here by Wednesday."

"Sam's a minister at the Horning church."

Her eyebrows drew together for just a moment. "Can I ask what happened? Your *mamm* mentioned that you never joined her church, but then Joah said you've been going to Mahlon's church. I'm not trying to be nosy. I'd just like to understand.

Kayla and I are spending a lot of time with Joah, and I don't want to do or say anything you wouldn't approve of."

And Beulah had insisted Janna would be a bad influence. On the contrary. "I appreciate that."

But being alone in the *daadi haus* with her for any longer, even with the door to the house open, wouldn't be wise, especially after what happened earlier. Using the computer there was one thing. Better there than out in plain sight. But now they were just talking. That could be done in a public place. "Let's go out on the porch."

Janna followed Luke onto the porch and sat down on the swing. She left room for him to sit there too, but once again he lowered himself onto the railing across from her. Not surprising. Sitting beside her that afternoon had probably caused enough trouble.

Crossing his feet at the ankles, he folded his arms. "When I was sixteen, *Daadi* hired Rayanne to work in the shop. She'd grown up in New York, but after she finished school, she came here to live with an aunt and uncle to be close to the clinic. *Daadi* knew her uncle, Wilmer, and while he was looking for help in the shop, Wilmer was looking for a Plain employer for Rayanne."

A common scenario in their community—although *Daadi* most likely ended up regretting that decision, considering the result.

"Anyway, Rayanne and I became friends." He paused, then looked up from the porch floorboards. "And then our feelings for each other became more than friendship."

"That's why you didn't join the church?"

"*Ya.*" His voice had softened. "In the Horning church, youth join at a younger age—usually around fourteen—and she was already a member. I wasn't, and she refused to consider joining our church, so when I turned eighteen I started attending her church on the alternate Sundays. We began dating about six months later when I became a member, and I pretty much stopped attending *Mamm* and *Daadi*'s church then."

Right. Since many of the Wenger congregations shared a church house with a Horning congregation, the groups alternated Sundays and visited family and friends on off weeks. "I'm sure that wasn't easy."

"*Nee.*" He shook his head. "It broke *Mamm*'s and *Daadi*'s hearts. Some of the *gmay* blamed Rayanne. Others said I'd given in to the worldliness of wanting to drive a car. In the end, *Mamm* and *Daadi* mostly accepted my belief that God intended Rayanne and me for each other." His face contorted into a grimace. "Although it's probably no wonder *Daadi* had his heart attack only two months after I joined her church."

Heartbreaking, to say the least. "I'm sorry."

He sighed. "*Ya.*"

"You still hold to a lot of the Wenger ways, though."

"It's in my blood, I reckon." With a shrug, he smiled slightly. "That's what I used to tell Rayanne when she complained that I was too Wenger. And aside from the beliefs about some things—driving a car, speaking *Deitsch*, using more-modern machinery, things like that—the two churches have a fair amount in common. With each decision, I've prayed mightily to discern what God would have me do."

That made perfect sense—and yet he now attended a more progressive Mennonite church. "How does Mahlon's church fit into all this, then?" Hopefully, she wasn't being too intrusive.

He drew a slow breath and let it out. "That wasn't so much

my doing. Well, it was, I reckon, but . . ." He bowed his head for a moment, then looked up again. "When Joah started his PT and OT, Carin recommended applying for state medical assistance for him, to help pay for his services. I refused, obviously, but then the bills started adding up. The church had already contributed a lot toward Rayanne's care, and I didn't feel comfortable asking for more help, especially since Joah's problems aren't life-threatening. After talking to Mahlon and praying about it, I finally agreed, and a caseworker at New Beginnings helped me apply for the assistance."

Janna's heart sank. "And having insurance is grounds for losing membership."

"Buying insurance goes against the Discipline. We're not technically buying it since it doesn't cost us anything, but government assistance isn't acceptable either. Last fall, Wilmer questioned how I was affording all Joah's therapy and doctor appointments, and I couldn't be dishonest. He had to inform the ministry, and they admonished me. But on top of what we paid for Rayanne's care, we couldn't manage Joah's services without it."

She didn't doubt that a bit.

"For years, Mahlon and I have talked about the differences in our churches' beliefs. Then when I was counseled about Joah's insurance, he and I got into discussions about manmade rules some churches follow. He encouraged me to visit his church on our in-between Sundays, and back in March, Joah and I did. That got back to the ministry, and I was counseled again."

He shrugged. "For the past month or so, since Joah finished the school year, we've been attending just Mahlon's church. We're more conservative in some ways, but a lot of people there come from Old Order or very conservative backgrounds, and they've readily accepted us."

Maybe so, but the shine in his eyes and the way he clenched his jaw confirmed how much it also tore him apart. "Yet it's not what you've wanted."

His arms still crossed, he lifted one hand to prop his chin on it. "A lot isn't what I've wanted."

Janna's heart ached at the dejection in his tone.

He pushed off the railing, still averting his gaze. "It's getting late. I'd best say good night." Without another word, he headed for the opposite end of the porch.

Perhaps she'd gone too far with her questioning. "Luke." Rising from the swing, she followed him.

He turned around but wouldn't look at her.

Oh, how she wished she knew what to say. Leaving a church was never simple or easy—she knew that all too well. And leaving a close-knit Old Order congregation was often a devastating decision that severed a person from not only their church but also the entire community. The despair in Luke's eyes confirmed that.

She stopped by the door, giving him space. "You're only doing what's best for Joah."

After a few moments, he nodded, then stepped over the railing onto the kitchen porch and entered the house. The door closed behind him.

Janna sighed. Carin said Luke was making sacrifices, but she probably had no idea how much they really cost him.

Luke said goodbye to the older couple who'd just placed an order for an entertainment armoire, then carried the order form into the workshop. Mrs. Stott might have been one of his most challenging customers yet, but she'd sent him two new customers within two days of delivering her dining set—a woman who'd bought a coffee table and two end tables off the shop floor yesterday and today's couple.

As he tacked the order to the bulletin board by his workbench, an excited squeal carried in through the open side door, quickly followed by a shriek.

"Kayla!" Joah sounded frightened.

Luke hurried outside. Joah was climbing out of the playset's house while Kayla lay sprawled on her belly at the bottom of the rock wall, crying. Luke jogged over and dropped to his knees beside her. "*Was hot's gewwe?*" he asked Joah as he gently lifted Kayla so she sat on the grass.

"She was waving to a woman and fell." Joah pointed toward the front of the shop.

"From where? In the playhouse?"

Kayla clutched her right wrist but otherwise looked uninjured. Hopefully, her tears were more from the fright of falling.

Joah jumped down and squatted beside them. "*Ya. Sie alright?*"

"I think she's fine." Luke lifted her chin. "What hurts?"

"My wrist."

"Did you fall on it?" He took it in his hands and turned it over. No swelling or bruising.

She nodded, then reached upward with both arms, waving her hands. Janna must have come running from the house. He helped Kayla to her feet, then stood and turned around.

A tall young woman with tanned skin and chin-length black hair rushed toward them. Certainly not Janna, especially the way she was dressed.

"Aunt Rissa!" Kayla squealed.

The woman lifted her onto her hip, hugging her. "Are you okay, sweetie?"

Kayla pulled back, smiling brightly. "Mama didn't tell me you were coming to see us." Her sore wrist now seemed forgotten.

"That's because she didn't know I was coming." She kissed Kayla's forehead, leaving a red lipstick mark. "Oh, I've missed you so much. Where is your mama?"

"In the house making dinner with *Mammi* Salena." She squirmed. "I wanna go tell her you're here."

The woman smiled, resting her forehead against Kayla's. "Let's go together. We'll make it a surprise." She set Kayla back on the ground, placed her hands on her hips, and looked Luke up and down. "Do you have any idea how many Luke Martins live around here?"

Odd way to greet someone. Joah stepped closer to him, watching her warily, and Luke rested a hand on his shoulder. "Several, I expect."

"Fourteen. Good thing I knew what road Janna used to live on. I'm Arissa Otero, her best friend, by the way."

Having already glimpsed her formfitting blouse and black shorts, he kept his eyes on her face. "Welcome." Other words escaped him. This woman, with her bright lipstick, high-heeled black sandals, and bold jewelry, had little in common with Janna. "Well, feel free to go into the house. Kayla can show you the way."

"Thanks." The two of them headed off with Kayla skipping as she held Arissa's hand, and Luke turned to take Joah back into the workshop with him.

Beulah stood in the doorway he'd come out, her arms folded across her chest and a frown on her face as she shook her head.

Ya. He had a bad feeling about this visit as well.

"Well. This is . . . quaint," Arissa said as Janna followed her into the *daadi haus*. "It's farmhouse, I guess, but definitely not the Joanna-Gaines-farmhouse you've become so enamored with." She meandered across the dining area, then peeked through the doorway into the kitchen before walking back around to the small living room. Her nose wrinkled. "What's 'Gott seg-ney dye-sus haws'?"

Janna glanced up at the antique framed cross-stitch piece hanging above the couch. "*Gott segne dieses Haus*," she corrected with the proper pronunciation. "It means 'God bless this house.' Salena's grandmother made that when she married in 1885."

"Mmm." Arissa turned in a circle, taking in the white walls, mustard-colored linoleum floor, and simple furnishings and decorations. The addition of Kayla's toys and various stacks of still-packed boxes made the living area look smaller than it was, and Janna could almost feel minimalist Arissa's clutter anxiety rising. "Are curtains against the rules?"

She shrugged. "Shades work fine."

Arissa walked to the doorway into the bedroom and attached bathroom. "No TV?"

"I left it at the Akron house."

She turned around. "What's Kay doing without *Daniel Tiger's Neighborhood*?"

"She can watch it on the computer or my phone." But Kayla now spent so much of her time playing with Joah, following Malinda around the barnyard, and helping Janna and Salena that she only occasionally asked for a TV show. No harm in that, really.

"At least you've got an air conditioner in the bedroom

window." Arissa came toward her and sighed. "Girl, I'd be lying if I said I wasn't concerned about you."

Concerned—about what? Sure, the *daadi haus* looked like it had been decorated in the 1970s, but living there was temporary. "Riss, we're fine. I know it's small, but it's only for a few weeks. And weren't you the one who said our ending up here had to be a God thing?"

"I'm not talking about *this*." She held her arms out to the sides. "I'm talking about *you*. Have you looked in the mirror? I get here, and I find Kayla playing outside in almost ninety-degree weather with a dress and a *sweater* on. Then you're wearing a long skirt and a sweater too, and you're barefoot in the kitchen with your hair up in this braided-bun thing. All I could think was, *Who are you and what have you done with my bestie?* Because the last time I saw her, she wanted nothing to do with being some man dependent 1920s housewife."

Now that wasn't fair. "These are clothes I've had for years. And I put up my hair when I'm in the kitchen because it gets in the way. I'm not a housewife, and I'm certainly not man-dependent. We're living here, but not for nothing."

"No, you're working for room and board—doing laundry, cleaning, preparing meals, running a cash register, and doing whatever Luke says, according to Kay."

"I doubt that's how she described it."

"Maybe not with those exact words, but aren't you?"

True, but . . . "I'm doing what I have to do. We don't have the money—or the time or the desire—to move again. I started working again yesterday, and we're here to stay until our rental in Akron is fixed. Yes, we're helping out around the house and in the shop, but not all the time. I have plenty of downtime too. And so what? Salena took care of me for years when I was a kid, and for nothing in return except my love. How can I complain about helping her for a few weeks?"

Arissa sighed, then walked around the coffee table to the orange-and-brown-floral sofa. "I'm not trying to be mean, you know? I just . . ." She plopped down. "When I walked into the kitchen and then sat at the table during lunch, all I could think of was my dad's fundamentalist cousins. The modesty culture, the submissive women, the controlling men." She arched her eyebrows. "The abuse in the name of patriarchy."

"None of the Martins are abusive." Well, Beulah maybe, but that was different. She was mostly just a grumbler, and everyone tried to ignore her grousing. "Salena is the gentlest person I know, and Luke can be set in his ways, but he's certainly not the abusive type."

A wry grin twisted Arissa's lips. "Seems like he prefers the silent treatment."

That she couldn't deny. "He is quiet, especially around women he doesn't know—"

"And who dress like this?" She swept a hand from her head toward her feet. "He would barely look at me, and when he did, he'd only look at my face."

Goodness. What was wrong with Arissa today? "That's how he was raised. You're the one who's always talking about how men treat women. He's being respectful. You can't have it both ways. Would you rather he stared? Or catcalled like the construction guys in the city?"

Arissa exhaled loudly. "No, but . . ." She shook her head. "I'm just concerned, that's all. You're an hour and a half away, and you and Kay are out here by yourselves. I get that you've been on your own for a while now, but I just worry, you know? The last six months have been hard enough. You deserve better."

Which was why Arissa would always be her BFF despite her occasional craziness. Dropping onto the couch, Janna put her arm around her. "This isn't what we planned, but it is what it is. I'm a big girl. I can handle it. We're in a better place than we were—on multiple levels."

Arissa drew back to meet her gaze. "Just . . . be careful, okay? I know you grew up here, but you've been away for twice as long. You're not like them anymore. Don't forget who you are."

That definitely wouldn't be happening. "Never."

CHAPTER 9

Falling Out

The sky was just beginning to lighten in the east and the purple martins were chortling their dawnsong over the chirp of crickets as Luke stepped outside. He pulled on his barn boots and quickly tied them, then stepped off the porch and started for the milking barn. Sleep had come slow last night, not for the first time in the last week, and he wanted coffee. His uncles needed help with the milking, though, so caffeine would have to wait.

He slowed as he reached the lane. The front door of the *daadi haus* was open, and light shone through the screen door and the window on either side of it. Awful early for Janna and Kayla to be up, especially on a Sunday. *Mamm* pushed breakfast off till seven fifteen on the Lord's Day.

After hustling up the *daadi haus*'s walkway and onto its porch, he rapped on the screen's wooden frame.

Janna appeared in the doorway between the dining area and kitchen. "Luke." Wearing denim shorts and a black tank top, she came toward him with a furrowed brow and a travel mug in her hand. "Is something wrong?"

"I was going to ask you the same thing. It's barely after five. Ivan just called and asked if I'd help with milking since Enos's sciatica's bothering him. I saw the light on and wanted to make sure you and Kayla are all right."

The worry eased from her face, but she didn't respond right away. Nor did she seem appreciative of his concern. If anything, she looked uncomfortable. "We're fine. I . . . I'm back to work now."

Work? "You mean like a job?"

Still holding the mug, she crossed her arms. "I'm a free-lance editor for a Christian publishing house and my own personal clients. During the summer, I work before Kayla gets up and after she goes to bed."

He didn't know what to say. "I had no idea."

She shrugged. "We haven't talked about it. But you must've realized I support us somehow."

Ya. While the *gmay* assisted its widowed mothers so they didn't need to work outside the home, Janna had no help that he knew of. Her mother was gone, her father hadn't been a part of her life for decades, and neither she nor Kayla had ever mentioned Kayla's father. "Reckon I never thought about that." But she shouldn't have to bear that burden while staying with them. "You're here now, working for us. I've told you I'll take care of anything you and Kayla need."

She raised her shoulders slightly, a strange reaction to what should've provided some relief. "I know. But . . ." With a shake of her head, she looked away and then back to him again. "Luke, I run a business. My clients rely on me. And we need my income like your family needs yours. I can't stop working any more than you can. It won't affect my working for you, I assure you that."

That wasn't his concern. Her well-being was, as well as her demeanor. Yesterday she'd been so kind—although he hadn't talked to her since Arissa had taken her and Kayla out for supper last night. Now she watched him with the cautiousness due an enemy. "So you'll work early in the morning and late at night and then help *Mamm* during the day? You'll be exhausted in no time. And today's the Sabbath. It's a day of rest."

"I try not to work on Sundays, but sometimes it can't be helped. I have a deadline for the publisher, and with the Akron house issue, I couldn't get started on this project as quickly as I'd planned." Her eyes narrowed. "I don't see how my working right now is any different from what you're doing. Milking's much more labor intensive."

Not true. Not at all. "Milking is necessary for the health of the cows. Jesus pointed out that if a sheep fell into a pit on the Sabbath, what man wouldn't lift it out? Certain work is necessary, such as caring for the needs of livestock. But we must take care to limit our labors, not only out of deference to God's instruction but also for our own physical and spiritual health."

She didn't respond, and the quick rising and falling of her chest warned him that an argument was imminent. "I need to get back to work," she said, clearly striving to keep her tone polite, "so I'll let you get up to the barn now."

He opened his mouth but couldn't speak. If that wasn't a command, he didn't know what was. What place had she to . . .

Nee. Quarreling with her would reap no benefit. Besides, Enos and Ivan waited on him. Heeding the nudging to hold his tongue, he nodded, then turned and hurried back to the lane.

Suddenly, the caffeine was no longer necessary. The adrenaline pumping through him had woken him more than sufficiently.

One thing was certain—they'd be discussing this further at another time.

As Luke headed up the lane in the direction of the milking barn, Janna pressed a hand to her chest. This wasn't how she'd planned on starting her day. All she'd wanted was to get a good number of hours in on her current project, a devotional to—ironically—help couples embrace biblical partnership in marriage. And what was she doing? Disputing with a man who believed his gender gave him authority over her simply because she was female and lived under his roof.

Not that they were a couple or ever would be. She appreciated what he was doing for her and Kayla, but she had every intention of working in exchange for it. Being under Luke's thumb had never been—and never would be—part of their agreement.

After moving to the recliner, she set her mug beside her laptop on the end table and then slid the computer onto her lap. Time to put the conversation out of her mind and get working. At least Luke hadn't insisted on pushing his agenda.

And at least she'd managed to change the subject when, the evening before, Joah had asked her if she and Kayla would come to church with him and Luke that morning. As much as the children would love that, sitting in a pew with Luke would now be beyond awkward.

It was bad enough they'd be at the same table for breakfast in a couple of hours.

By noontime, Janna's mood was finally improving.

Breakfast had been uncomfortable, with she and Luke barely looking at each other, but she'd been able to get out of going to church. Appeasing Joah did require her assurance that she and Kayla would go with him and Luke to Mahlon's house for Ephrata's Fourth of July fireworks on Tuesday night, but she could handle that. Even better, Salena had been so preoccupied with preparations to help Beulah and Malinda host family today that she hadn't questioned Janna's plans.

With the Martins out of the house, Janna had been able to finish the first pass of her edit. If she continued at this pace, she'd get the manuscript back to the publisher before the deadline, and finishing sooner meant getting paid sooner. Things were starting to look up.

Suddenly, the door to the house's kitchen opened and closed.

Salena walked by the doorway that led from the kitchen into the *daadi haus*'s dining area, but then stopped. "*Ach*, I didn't know you were here." She came into the *daadi haus*, and as she passed the dining table and could see Kayla on the couch, a frown replaced her smile.

Janna's stomach sank. Kayla still lay on her belly, watching a video of her favorite TV show on Janna's phone—even though she'd been told to turn it off five minutes ago. Of all the times for her to disobey, it had to be now?

"I thought you girls were going to church."

"Mama said maybe next week." Kayla sat up, pulling off her pink Hello Kitty headphones and setting the phone on her lap.

Salena eyed Janna, her expression solemn. "'Tis the

Sabbath, and a beautiful day at that. Why would you want to be inside?" The dissatisfaction in her tone made it clear she didn't agree with their modes of entertainment either.

Janna closed her laptop and set it on the end table beside her. Explaining that she'd needed to work certainly wouldn't help the situation. "I know. We were about to have some lunch and go outside."

"Why don't you come eat dinner with us? I just have to get the macaroni salad I forgot to take with me." She moved toward Kayla. "Some of Malinda's and Beulah's grandchildren are there. I'm sure they'd love to have you play with them."

Kayla smiled. "Can we, Mama? Joah said he won't be home till later 'cause they're eating at someone's house after church."

Spending a few hours under Beulah's disapproving stare was hardly what Janna had intended for the day, but declining would land her in even more trouble, especially after Kayla's reaction. "That would be nice." She stood, glancing at her traitorous daughter. "Go use the bathroom."

Kayla jumped up, tossing the phone—face up and video still playing—onto the couch cushion, then skipped to the bedroom.

Janna got up and grabbed the phone, then shut it off and pulled out the headphones' plug.

Salena stood with her hands clasped at her waist and her lips drawn into a thin line. "'Tis a Sunday—the Lord's Day. A day set aside for rest and worship. When you told Joah you couldn't go to church with them, I assumed you were planning on attending another church, not staying here doing"—with a hand she indicated the phone Janna held—"that." She shook her head. "Kayla's a little girl, and so very impressionable. You must guard what you allow into her heart and mind, and what you allow into your own."

Swallowing, she nodded. Everything in her wanted to

defend her actions, but the close companionship that she and Salena had been rebuilding all week threatened to disintegrate before her eyes. "I know."

"*Ya*, which is why this has me so *verhuddled*. You do know. Why would—"

"Ready, Mama!" Kayla skipped back into the living room and went to Salena. "Do you know what we're having to eat?"

Salena stroked her hair back from her face. "Baked ham-and-cheese sandwiches, macaroni salad and potato salad, green beans, and chow chow. For dessert, peach pie and apple crumb cake. Oh, and Malinda made her mint whoopie pies."

Kayla bounced on her heels. "Those are my favorite. Joah will be sorry he missed them. Do you think I could bring one back for him?"

Salena took her face in her hand. "You have such a kind heart. I'm sure he'd appreciate that."

With a lump in her throat, Janna headed for the bedroom. "I'll be ready in a minute."

This morning's spat with Luke had been one thing. She'd stood her ground and ended their discussion. But while that conversation had incensed her, this one felt like a punch in the stomach. All she wanted was for Salena to be proud of her—of the woman she'd become and the mother she strove to be. Instead, she felt like an inept parent and a complete disappointment.

In the bathroom, Janna stared at her reflection. She needed to get herself together and keep it that way. That meant she'd need to avoid Beulah, if that were possible. So much for her day getting better.

Really, should she have been surprised by this? The Martins might have raised her, but so much had changed since then. It had been only a matter of time until something like this happened.

Luke sat on the kitchen porch's swing, teaching Joah how to play his harmonica, when a black minivan pulled into the lane. It turned into the shop's parking lot and parked in the spot nearest to the house.

"Who's that?" Joah lowered the harmonica as he stood. "We're shut on Sunday."

Hard to tell. Plenty of people they knew owned Dodge Caravans—including Rayanne's uncle, whose stout frame soon rounded the back of the van. Dressed in his Plain suit and hat, he started toward the house.

"It's Wilmer." And he wasn't there for the shop.

Joah went to the porch railing and waved.

Maybe this was best. Luke had known Wilmer all his life, and after he started dating Rayanne they'd become even closer. The man was as considerate and fair as folks came. He was a deacon at church, but since he'd come alone, this wouldn't be formal counsel.

Luke stood and headed down the walkway. "Evening, Wilmer."

"Luke." Wilmer smiled at Joah, who'd followed. "How are you, young man? I think you're taller every time I see you."

Joah grinned back.

His smile faded when he returned his attention to Luke. "Do you have a few minutes?"

"Of course." He placed his hand on Joah's shoulder. "Go on inside now. It's time to get ready for bed anyway."

Once Joah was in the house, again blowing notes on the harmonica, Luke glanced around. They could sit at the kitchen table or on the porch, but too many people might be in earshot.

No one else needed to hear what was said. "You up to taking a walk?"

Wilmer responded by starting for the lane with his hands clasped behind his back. "We missed you at church again today," he said as Luke stepped into pace beside him.

"*Ya.*" What else could he say?

The older man walked slowly, his gaze fixed ahead. "Sam and Ina invited us for the noon meal, and while we were talking, he mentioned they'd seen you at Oregon Dairy with a woman from outside the community . . . and that it appeared you were on a date."

Luke clenched his teeth. This was how rumors spread. Folks jumping to conclusions. "We weren't on a date."

Wilmer's gray eyebrows disappeared beneath his hat as he looked at him. "You were there with a woman, then?"

Luke kept his voice low as they passed the *daadi haus.* "Janna Carpenter, the girl across the road *Mamm* and *Daadi* reared when I was a child, is staying with us for a few weeks. She'll be driving *Mamm* and Joah to his therapy appointments for me, so she and her daughter went with us on Friday. We stopped at Oregon Dairy on the way home. When Sam and Ina saw us, we were sitting at a picnic table while the children played."

He nodded a few times. "I see. And how is Joah doing?"

"Quite well." This might be easier than he'd thought. "Lord willing, he's in his last casts now. If all goes as planned, he'll get his braces this Friday."

More nods. "And the government insurance?"

So much for easy. "He still has that."

"Am I correct in assuming that you're still attending the liberal church?"

"It's not liberal. They're a Bible-believing congregation.

They just put an emphasis on spreading the gospel instead of on rules about dress, hairstyles, and the like."

"Mmm." Wilmer inhaled, then let out the breath slowly. "Luke, I understand the last few years have been difficult for you. Losing a spouse, especially so young, is very hard, and then you've had Joah's . . . issues as well." He met his gaze. "But I can't understand this path you're taking. If Rayanne were—"

"I know." But a lot would be different if Rayanne were still alive. Or maybe it wouldn't. Joah would still need care, and they'd still be hard-pressed to afford his eight to ten therapy sessions each month—and that didn't include the casting and AFOs. "I know how the church feels about the insurance. But I don't believe it's unreasonable in some situations. Joah's therapist says that without the services he's receiving, he'd almost certainly have worse problems in the future."

"Having this type of insurance takes our dependence off God and the community and places it on an institution we wish to separate ourselves from as much as possible."

He realized that, and he'd struggled with it himself at first. But he also felt at peace with his decision. After much petitioning the Lord, he'd not been convicted that accepting the insurance was wrong. Actually, it felt like an answer to prayer.

"Folks have been asking about you," Wilmer said. "They're concerned."

"The ones who are still talking to us, you mean?"

"Luke."

"It's not like I'm stretching the truth." He shoved his hands into his pants pockets. "More than a few have been keeping their distance."

"I understand. But are you really thinking about what you're doing? Are you counting the cost of your decisions? Attending a liberal church. Having a young woman and child from outside the community live here." Wilmer halted and faced him. "There will be consequences, not only for you but also for Joah. You must know that."

"We started attending Mahlon's church because I no longer felt welcome at ours, and because I no longer agree with some of our church's beliefs. And having Janna stay with us was *Mamm*'s idea. I agreed because she and her daughter have nowhere else to go. If anything, it's been a blessing." Well, for the most part. "Having Janna here has lightened *Mamm*'s load considerably."

Wilmer glanced toward the playset, then nodded at the bench beneath the oak tree. They ambled over, and after they sat, he folded his arms and stared up the lane toward Enos and Ivan's farmhouse. "It's been more than three years since Rayanne died. You're young, Luke, and you have a child. God intended for children to be reared by both a father and a mother. Perhaps it's time you consider remarriage."

Luke sat forward, leaning his elbows on his knees. As if things weren't complicated enough, now he needed to think about marriage too? Like that would fix everything? It wasn't that he didn't know any suitable women. He just didn't know the single sisters in the Horning congregations well. Having come to the church as an adult, he'd spent time primarily with men and couples.

Then there was the issue of his attending another church. Between that and the insurance mess, no woman's parents would agree to her entering a courtship with him. Although maybe that was Wilmer's intent, to point that out so Luke would rethink his actions. Of course, he didn't believe all that church's tenets were indispensable anymore, so did he even still belong there? Too many questions and not enough answers.

He gave the only reply he could. "I'll pray about it."

"You need to be praying about what else is going on in your life too. You're struggling, Luke, and we both know it. If I can help in any way, I will. You know you can talk to me, or to any of the ministry." Wilmer placed a hand on his shoulder. "Evelyn and I care very much for you and Joah, and I'd be remiss if I kept silent. You're walking a grievous path. If you don't make haste in getting your life in order and following the Discipline, you'll be expelled. You need to contemplate the consequences of that, for yourself and for Joah."

He nodded. "*Ya.*"

Wilmer squeezed his shoulder, then stood. Neither said a word as they returned to the lane.

When they neared the *daadi haus*, the screen door opened. Kayla came outside in what looked like a pink bathing suit with a short mesh skirt. "Luke!" she called, waving, then twirled around. "Aunt Rissa got me a ballerina outfit!"

Just when he'd thought things couldn't get worse. He held up a hand but looked straight ahead. Hopefully, she'd stay on the porch and not say another word.

The door opened again. "Kayla, I told you to get your pajam—" Janna froze at seeing them, then swiftly ushered her daughter back inside.

Wilmer kept silent, but his grave expression said enough.

Ya. Grievous didn't even come close to describing the path Luke was walking.

CHAPTER 10

Unexpected Friends

"Mama, your phone was ringing when I was using the bathroom." Kayla held out Janna's cell phone as her dirt-smudged bare feet propelled her through the doorway between the *daadi haus* and the house's kitchen.

Janna turned from the table just as the phone emitted its voice mail notification. Of all the times for the phone to ring, it had to be when Kayla would hear it. "I'll take it."

Kayla stopped and pressed the home button, lighting up the screen. "It was Cynthia. Can we call her back?"

Janna took the phone and slid it into her cardigan pocket. After Salena's tongue-lashing the day before, she'd been trying so hard to tread carefully. Leaving her phone in the *daadi haus* all day hadn't worked after all.

Kayla's eyebrows drew together, although not in their usual full scowl. "Can we, Mama?"

She grasped her shoulder and went back to the table, where Luke was helping Joah read aloud an article from the *Plain Communities Business Exchange* magazine that had come in the mail that day. "Later, honey." She resumed collecting their supper dishes.

"'Tis fine if you need to call her." Salena spoke quietly as she turned on the faucet to fill the double sink.

Janna swallowed. Did she or didn't she? Part of her wanted to wait until after the dishes were washed and the kitchen cleaned up, but it wasn't like Cynthia to call this early in the evening. "I'm sorry. Maybe I'd better listen to the message real quick." She steered Kayla to the table. "Take the dishes to the counter. I'll be right back."

A short replay of the message in the *daadi haus*'s dining area assured Janna there was no need to call back right away, and she returned to the kitchen.

"What did she say?" Kayla met her as soon as she came through the doorway.

"That we can call her later on. Which we will."

She opened her mouth but then closed it. "Yes, Mama."

Amazing. Just a week before, Kayla would've begged to call now. Spending time with more-reserved Joah, as well as experiencing Salena and Luke's expectation of immediate obedience, had knocked her exuberance down a few notches. Although Janna wasn't sure how she felt about that.

"May Kayla and I be excused to go play a game?" Joah asked.

Luke took the magazine from him. "*Ya.*"

The children eagerly headed for the living room.

"Kayla says Cynthia is like a grandmother to her." Salena's words, spoken as footsteps sounded on the stairs, were phrased as a statement but felt more like a question.

Janna started to gather the remainder of their dishes. Salena had made other such mentions, both of which Janna had skirted, but perhaps the time had come for her to be completely honest. Though she'd chosen to not go into much detail about the last fourteen years, the truth would eventually come out.

"When Mom moved us from here, our new apartment was right up the street from the town library. She started working days, but I didn't like being home alone"—she gave a light grin in Salena's direction—"and you'd made me a book lover, so I spent hours at the library. Cynthia was a retired school psychologist working there part-time, and we became friends."

Salena met her gaze when Janna set the last plates on the counter beside the sink. "I always prayed the Lord would provide the care you needed, whether that came from your mother or from someone else."

That he had—and Cynthia, unlike the Martins, had stayed in close contact after they were apart.

Janna looked away. Such thoughts would do no good. The past was the past, and the Martins had been more than kind to her since she'd arrived. Mostly.

"We were perfect for each other. Her husband had passed away and she had no children, and Mom was too wrapped up in her own issues to worry about me. Cynthia lived in a big Victorian house around the corner from us, so I was there or at the library more than I was home. She was my foundation throughout school, and with her help, I applied to colleges and got a full scholarship."

"You always wanted to be a teacher." Luke's quiet baritone came from behind her. "Is that what you went to college for?"

She glanced over her shoulder. He wore an unreadable expression—one he exhibited far too often. "Yes. I double-majored so I could teach English at the middle-school or high-school level." And she'd graduated in three years, no less, which had been a blessing she hadn't anticipated. If she hadn't taken the AP classes in high school and extra classes during her freshman and sophomore years, finishing college would've been much more challenging.

Salena brightened. "You were a teacher, then?"

And now came the difficult part. Nothing like the truth to change the mood—just like it had completely changed her career plans. "Well . . . I never got to teach, aside from student teaching to earn my degree. Kayla was born about two months after I graduated, so I found a job where I could work from home and take care of her instead."

Salena's expression sobered as her wet hands hovered above the soapy water. "And you've done that all on your own."

"Well, with Cynthia's help." Janna moved to the other side of her and grabbed a dish towel for something to do. "Mom moved again my last year at college, so I lived with Cynthia after graduation. Kayla and I were with her until two years ago, when she moved to Florida to be close to her sisters. Then Kayla and I got our own apartment."

"And Kayla's father." Salena lowered her voice. "He is . . ."

"Somewhere. Probably Colorado, where he was from." Janna weighed her words before saying more, knowing how the discussion was moving into territory the Martins avoided. "I found out I was expecting Kayla a month before winter break. He went home for Christmas and didn't come back."

Salena sighed and nodded a few times. "Sometimes one decision can change everything."

"*Ya.*" Luke set the magazine on the table. "The Bible tells us all have sinned and fallen short of God's glory. None is righteous; no, not one. But we're justified by his grace through the redemption that's in Christ Jesus."

Salena turned to look at him. "*Ach, Ich wees sell.*"

"I know you know." He stood, then pushed in his chair. After walking to the back door, he grabbed his hat from the pegboard on the wall. "You and *Daadi* always understood that."

His solemn gaze moved to Janna. "If we ask for his forgiveness, God is merciful and no longer remembers our sins. If that's the case, neither should we remember them. Not?" He set the hat on his head and went outside before she could respond.

Janna almost laughed. If anyone could lecture about redemption while looking as serious as an accuser, it was Luke. She faced the sink, still trying to make sense of him. "Point taken."

Salena sniffed as she started the washing, then muttered something in *Deitsch*.

Janna looked at her. "I'm sorry?"

She shook her head. "*Nichts*."

Meaning she had no intention of saying more. Even so, Janna had understood her gist. Luke needed to practice what he preached.

Whatever that meant.

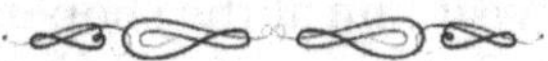

When Janna agreed to go with Joah and Luke to watch Ephrata's Fourth of July fireworks at Mahlon and Kendra's house, no one had mentioned that the Eschbachs' entire church would be there as well. She wouldn't have agreed so readily had she known that. Spending the evening with Mahlon and Kendra and their four children was one thing. Sharing a backyard, albeit a large one, with a swarm of people she didn't know was another.

But it was too late to back out now. She had just followed Joah and Kayla behind the house, and Luke was parking his truck up the street.

With the children running off toward the playset and trampoline at the back of the yard, Janna stopped and looked around. Maybe it would be better to wait for Luke so she'd know where to go or what to do. Slow cookers and dishes of picnic foods covered several tables on and around the concrete patio, while men of all ages and middle-aged and older women sat in lawn chairs, stood in groups of various sizes, or congregated near where the children played. Younger women, most dressed in skirts or dresses and wearing some form of head covering, stood by the food tables or carried more food out the back door.

"Janna!"

She turned to find a slim woman, maybe thirty-five, coming toward her. Wearing a loose-fitting floral cape dress, a white head covering, and green flip-flops, she smiled warmly and held out her hands to take the bowl of coleslaw Janna carried. "I'm Kendra, Mahlon's wife. We're so glad you and Kayla came along." She tucked the bowl into one arm. "You may not remember, but we met years ago. Mahlon and I had just started dating, and I used to visit him at the shop on occasion."

Now that she thought about it, she did recall a dark-haired girl visiting Mahlon in the months before Mom moved them away. "Actually, I do remember that. I think you brought us a bushel of peaches once."

"Yes, from my parents' orchard. You have a wonderful memory."

Sometimes too wonderful. But at least Kendra put her more at ease. She couldn't have been more welcoming. A good thing since Luke had been even quieter than usual since their tiff on Sunday morning.

"Mahlon told me your daughter has a peanut allergy," she went on. "Our youngest does too, and a few of the other children here are allergic to peanuts or tree nuts. I know it's concerning when food has been provided by many people, so I just wanted to let you know our church building and any events that include food are nut-free. Not that we parents don't still need to be vigilant, but as a church family, we want to keep our little ones safe."

Good to know. "Thank you. That makes me feel better."

"Come and I'll introduce you to some of the women from the young moms' Bible study that meets in our home on Thursday mornings." Kendra set the bowl on the table. "Our families watch the fireworks here each year, and this time we decided to host anyone from church who wanted to come. If you're interested in joining a study, we'd love to have you."

Within moments, about ten women between the ages of twenty-five and forty-five had gathered around and started introducing themselves. Quite a difference from how the women at Janna's last church had treated her, at least right before she stopped attending. These women's genuine smiles and sweet greetings almost made her rethink her initial decision to decline the Bible study invitation. Almost.

Kendra excused herself to find Mahlon so he could bless the food before they ate, and Janna scanned the back of the yard for the children. Joah, pumping his legs on a swing, was easy to find since he was the only boy wearing suspenders and a hat. Kayla jumped on the trampoline with two other girls, then went to the edge where Luke stood, grinning as she held her arms out to him.

He lifted her off the trampoline and pretended to drop her in what had become a game of sorts he played with her and Joah. She wrapped her arms around his neck, laughing, and he carried her to the playset, where he started pushing Joah on the swing. When Luke set her on the ground, she stayed right at his side, and he rested a hand on the back of her head.

Interesting. Kayla was affectionate—more so than Janna had ever been—and while Luke had seemed a bit uncomfortable with that at first, in the last few days he hadn't been as resistant. Any stranger looking at them now would probably think they were father and daughter.

Maybe it was time to talk to Kayla about that. Not that Luke was doing anything wrong, but she didn't want her daughter becoming too attached to him. That had happened with Mitch, and when Janna's relationship with him went south, it resulted in two broken hearts. She and Kayla would be moving out of the *daadi haus* as soon as the Akron house was ready, and she didn't want anything making that transition more arduous than it needed to be.

Kayla stepped around in front of Luke, and he leaned down to listen to what she was saying. Janna couldn't see her full expression but both laughed. Despite herself, Janna warmed inside. After all the struggles of the last few months, she loved seeing Kayla happy, and the occasional glimpses of the Luke she remembered—the one who wasn't so grim—heartened her.

Kayla turned and, at seeing Janna watching, waved wildly. Beside her, Luke nodded his acknowledgment.

Janna waved back and started toward the playset. Whether she liked it or not, they needed to get into the Akron house as soon as possible. For Kayla's sake if not her own.

As it neared dark, Joah and Kayla returned to the picnic blanket where Luke sat talking with Mahlon's older brother Adam.

Kayla dropped down beside him and took over gently stroking the sweat-dampened hair of Adam's eighteen-month-old son, who slept in the cradle made by Luke's crossed legs.

Joah looked around. "Excuse me, Daddy. Do you know

where Janna is? Naomi said the fireworks should be starting soon."

"Last I saw her, she was over by the tables, talking to some of the women." And she probably still was, because the last time he'd stolen a glance—well, more than a glance—had been less than a minute ago. "There she is." He pointed to the patio. "With Kendra and Sharilyn."

Joah jogged off in her direction, and Luke shifted his gaze back to Janna. In the glow of the light above the patio door, she smiled as she spoke, much more animated than earlier. She'd visibly tensed when they arrived at the house, but the women had welcomed her just as he knew they would. In the last fifteen minutes, as she talked and laughed with Kendra and a few others, she looked comfortable. A change for the better since she'd seemed hesitant to attend any kind of church-related event.

Joah stopped at her side, then rested his chin against her middle when she slipped an arm around him. Moments later, she hugged Kendra and Sharilyn, then walked across the yard holding his hand.

Her grin returned as they neared the blanket. "He looks quite comfortable."

"Weston just loves Luke," Adam said, then stood. "Here, you can have my seat. I should take him inside before the fireworks start." After crouching, he carefully lifted his son into his arms and straightened. "It's good to see you again, Janna. We'd love to have you join us for church some Sunday."

She nodded, her expression sincere. "Thank you." As he walked away, she sat down beside Luke, then tucked her legs to the side and smoothed her black-and-gray striped skirt. She motioned Joah closer by patting the blanket in front of her. "Come sit. How are your feet?"

He slowly seated himself, straightened his casted legs, and wiggled his toes. "They don't hurt. They're just hot."

"Good." She rubbed his back as Kayla crawled over next to him. "Two more days, then the casts will be off."

"And the AFOs will be cooler?"

"I would think so. The nighttime ones will definitely be cooler, and the daytime ones should be too."

"I can't wait." He looked at Luke. "Daddy, we might come to Bible study here on Thursday morning."

"If that's all right with you and your *mamm*," Janna added quickly. "Kendra invited us, but I told her we'd have to see if it would suit."

"That's fine." He'd expected the invitation, and Janna sounded interested in going, which he hadn't anticipated. Since she wanted to attend, he'd do everything he could to make it possible. "They're a wonderful group of women, and I think you'll enjoy the study and the fellowship. So will Joah and Kayla. The women all bring their children, and the older girls watch them. They read a Bible story and make a craft. One week they made cards for residents of a nursing home."

"Ooh, I love crafts! Maybe *Mammi* Salena could come with us too," Kayla said, twisting toward him. "Do you think so?"

Ach, how he wished she would. "*Nee*, she doesn't go to Bible studies or Sunday school. But I think she'll be fine with you going." He looked at Janna. "If she isn't, just tell me and I'll talk to her."

"Well . . . I don't want to cause any trouble." Clearly, she'd overheard some of his and *Mamm*'s discussions about what was and wasn't acceptable.

"*Macht nichts*. If you want to go, I want you to go."

And if it made her look at him the way she was right now—eyes smiling with appreciation—he'd deal with *Mamm* as much as necessary.

CHAPTER 11

The Reprimand

I'm so glad you and the children could come today," Kendra said from where she stood at the kitchen sink, washing the mugs and glasses used during Bible study that morning. She smiled sweetly at Janna, but it didn't mask her tired-looking eyes. "And thank you for staying to help with redding up."

"I'm happy to. Thank you for inviting us." Janna glanced out the window as she dried a mug. At the back of the yard, Joah and Kayla climbed on the playset with Amanda and Caleb while Naomi pushed Drew on a toddler swing.

Kendra dunked a washed glass in the rinse water, then set it on the drying rack on the counter. "Fellowship with other believers is so important. Did you attend a church before you moved?"

"Well . . ." Just how much should she say? Only Arissa and Cynthia knew everything that happened at their last church, and she kind of wanted to keep it that way. The past was in the past now, where it belonged. "We did—until March. We haven't attended anywhere since then."

Kendra met her gaze, her brown eyes sympathetic. "Several people in our church were hurt by their previous church family. It's very hard."

Apparently she hadn't been as vague as she'd thought. "Yes."

"Was it doctrine related?"

"Yes and no, I guess." That is, if condemning a woman for a man's poor choices and the consequences of those choices would be considered doctrinal. At her last church, it seemed to be. But did she really want to go there?

The gentleness of Kendra's gaze eased her hesitation. Kendra had such a kind heart, and Janna couldn't imagine her being judgmental. "Long story short, I started dating the lead pastor's son, and after nine months, I found out he wasn't at all who I thought he was. I ended our relationship, and when his boss—who went to one of our satellite churches—somehow found out why, he decided it was in the company's best interest to let him go. Most of our church basically blamed me."

Kendra rested a hand on her arm. "I'm so sorry."

"That's why we're here now. It was time to start over."

She smiled lightly. "And now you're back with the Martins. God is so good."

Janna couldn't deny that. Things could've been much worse. "Yes. I haven't told them what happened yet, so could you not mention it to Mahlon?"

"Of course." After a few moments, she glanced at her. "I certainly don't want to seem pushy, but we'd be very happy to have you worship with us on a Sunday morning." She rinsed a mug and placed it on the drying rack. "You wouldn't need to dress any particular way. On our website, we state that modesty is appreciated, but we don't require attendees to wear head coverings or follow clothing guidelines."

That would certainly make Joah and Kayla happy. But

attending church with Luke could be a bit uncomfortable, especially if—or more likely, *when*—they had more disagreements. Or perhaps it would help with that. She wouldn't mind spending more time with this woman who made her feel so loved and accepted. "Maybe we will."

"Oh." Kendra swayed, grasping the counter, and ran the back of her other hand across her forehead. "I'm sorry. I need to sit a moment." Her face had paled.

Janna helped her to the kitchen table, then pulled out the chair at the end of it. "Are you all right?"

Kendra sat down. "Would you mind getting me some Coke from the refrigerator? My blood sugar's just a bit low, I think."

Janna quickly retrieved the two-liter bottle and poured some into a clean glass from the counter, then brought it to her. Low blood sugar seemed likely, considering. While the women had helped themselves to fruit salad and coffee cake before and after their study, she'd never seen Kendra do anything more than sip one cup of tea. "Here." She placed the glass in her hand. "What else can I do?"

Kendra took two swallows. A bit of color had returned to her cheeks, but not enough. "Thank you, but I'll be fine. It happens on occasion. A little rest works wonders." After another sip, she managed a smile, though it seemed forced. "It's after eleven thirty. You'll need to get home for dinner. If you wouldn't mind calling the children inside, Naomi and Amanda will finish the dishes."

Janna didn't want to leave yet, but she didn't want to be in the way either. And putting the girls, who were perhaps eleven and eight, in charge? "You're sure?"

"We'll be fine." Her gentle tone also held a firmness. "Really. And thank you."

Janna opened the back door and called the children.

Naomi—tall, slim, and with her dark hair in a single

braided ponytail down her back—turned around, then lifted Drew out of the swing and started toward the house. The other four children followed.

Janna would have to trust Kendra's judgment. Her girls were quite responsible, and apparently this had happened before. As well, how many times, when she'd been barely older than Kayla, had Janna taken care of her mother, who'd been drunk and in much worse shape than Kendra?

When Luke looked up from moving an end table to the section where they kept pieces to be finished, he found Janna standing inside the doorway between the shop and workshop.

"I just wanted to let you know we're back." She gave him a light smile, but something about her demeanor didn't seem right. "And to talk to you about something."

That didn't sound good. Hopefully, nothing disturbing happened at Bible study. He brushed his hands on his pants as he walked over. "*Ebbes letz?*"

She glanced at Mahlon. "Is Kendra diabetic?"

"*Nee.* Why?"

"She got pale and had to sit down after Bible study. She said it was just low blood sugar and insisted she was fine and we should go, but I really didn't want to leave her with only the children there. I thought maybe Mahlon should know."

Now her question made sense. Mahlon had mentioned Kendra having a similar episode last week, and it had happened when she was carrying their other children as well. "*Ya,* wouldn't hurt to tell him." He touched her back to lead her toward where his cousin was sanding a chair on the far side of the room. "Mahlon."

Mahlon looked up and then stood, arching his eyebrows, as they neared.

"When we left Bible study, Kendra wasn't feeling well. I wanted to stay to make sure she was all right, but she insisted she'd be fine with Naomi and Amanda there."

"Sounds like what you told me about before," Luke added.

Mahlon gave a few slow nods as he rested his hands on his hips. "She hasn't been feeling so good the last week or so. That's made it hard for her to eat as much as she should, and if she does too much, her blood sugar drops." Mahlon didn't sound overly concerned, but he had to be. Luke would be if she were his wife. "What was she doing when you left?"

"Lying on the couch while the girls finished the dishes."

He nodded one last time. "Thanks for letting me know. She should be fine, but I'll give them a call."

Luke faced her as Mahlon strode to the workbench where he kept his cell phone. "You enjoyed the study, then?" Throughout the morning, he'd been praying she would. Of course, he still wasn't sure how he felt about the possibility of Janna and Kayla attending church with him and Joah. That could get complicated.

Her eyes brightened. "I did. Joah and Kayla had a great time too."

Happy voices carried into the workshop as the children played on the playset, and she looked to the open door. Her green eyes then met his again, and after several seconds, she swallowed. "Well . . . I'd better get inside. Your *mamm*'s probably started dinner already."

And he needed to get back to work.

After she left, he headed to where another end table awaited its last sanding before being stained and then polyurethaned. The window drew him.

Joah and Kayla knelt in the playhouse while Janna stood

beside it talking to them. Joah pointed overhead, and they watched two purple martins flying in. After circling several times, the birds tucked their wings and dove toward their towering house. Janna and the children smiled even though they watched the birds' in-air acrobatics all the time.

"Everything all right?"

Mahlon's voice from behind made him step back. He'd watched longer than planned. "*Ya.* Just checking on the children. How's Kendra?"

"Better. I've asked her if one of the other women could host Bible study for a while, but she didn't want to do that. At least not yet. We'll see. I'm going home for dinner." Mahlon gazed out the window. "The children, you say?"

"*Ya.*" Resisting one last glance outside, he headed to the end table.

"But no one else?"

Luke couldn't see Mahlon's face with his back to him, but he didn't need to. His tone conveyed his smile. Luke shook his head. "That chair isn't going to sand itself."

Mahlon laughed. "Neither's that table—especially if you're at the window."

Ach, his cousin knew him too well.

Janna couldn't determine what Luke was feeling as Joah stood before them all in the exam room at New Beginnings. The legs of his black jeans were rolled to the knee, and Carin had just secured his new black AFOs over black knee socks. Luke was a pro at wearing a taciturn expression, but she suspected he was a little overwhelmed.

Watching Joah try to walk right after his casts were

removed had been almost painful. His feet seemed to have forgotten what to do, and despite Carin's assurances that his loss of muscle tone would be temporary and that the AFOs would give him more stability, Luke had looked apprehensive.

As well, Carin had provided so many instructions. The hinged AFOs were for daytime wear. The unhinged ones were for nighttime wear, never to be walked in. Joah would need an hour of physical therapy at New Beginnings each week, then home exercises for about an hour on the other days. They were to check for skin irritation from the AFOs every morning and night or if Joah complained. Such a long list of what to do and what not to do. Thank goodness Carin always gave written instructions at the end of each appointment.

Joah looked at his feet and smiled. "Look, Daddy. My heels are down."

Luke, seated next to Salena on a chair against the wall, gave a tight-lipped smile. "*Ya*, they are, son."

"All right, buddy. Let's see about some shoes now." Carin stood and glanced at Janna. "You have them?"

Janna retrieved both pairs of black sneakers from her tote bag and handed over the smaller pair. "These are the two-and-a-halves. We have threes if they're too small."

"Great." Carin loosened the laces, then removed the insoles and squatted in front of Joah again. "These look like they'll be a good fit." After putting one shoe on, she squeezed its sides together and used her thumb to check the position of his toes. Then she did the same with the other shoe. "What do you think, Joah?"

Grinning again, he nodded.

She took his hand and walked him back and forth across the room. "Do they feel a little funny?"

More nods.

"That's normal. As your feet and ankles get stronger, that'll change." She clapped her hands together. "Okay. Let's go over to the therapy room and do some walking and PT to make sure the AFOs aren't rubbing anywhere."

Ten minutes later, Janna stood beside Luke, watching through the plate-glass walls of the therapy room as Carin and a PT aide worked with Joah. Salena and Kayla now sat on a couch against the far wall as they read one of the books Kayla had collected from a table in the corner.

Luke let out an almost shaky sigh that drew Janna's attention. He had his arms crossed and tears in his eyes.

She stepped closer, touched by his unusual show of emotion. "You okay?"

He kept his gaze on Joah. "His whole life, I've never seen him walk with his heels on the floor," he said softly. "That probably wouldn't seem like a big deal to most people, but it is to me. These weeks he's been in the casts, I've prayed it would work, but I knew there was a chance it might not. And then what would I tell all the people who've questioned the necessity of his treatment? Wilmer, the people at church, Rayanne's father . . . *Mamm*."

Mamm? "She questioned it?" she whispered.

"*Ya*. Eventually she granted that it was my choice since Joah's my son, but we've had it out over the medical assistance and his PT and OT more than a few times. I've really hoped everything we've been doing wouldn't be all for nothing."

Perhaps that was why Salena was so reticent at the New Beginnings appointments. She always listened when the therapists gave instructions but otherwise remained more subdued than usual.

Janna went back to watching Joah. Carin and the PT aide each held one of his hands as he walked one foot in front of the other across a low, wide balance beam. His steps looked much steadier with the AFOs on, and with them being the same color as his socks and shoes, most people probably wouldn't notice them. Her previous sadness that Joah hadn't been allowed the printed design he'd wanted on the AFOs slipped away. Perhaps not drawing attention would be best after all, considering the situation.

"It's not been all for nothing," she murmured. "Just look at him. He managed the casts like a champ—better than I would've, no doubt. Now he'll learn how to walk the way he should, and you won't have to worry about the long-term problems Carin said he would have if he kept toe walking. You did what you knew in your heart he needed, and God answered your prayers." She met his gaze and smiled. "*You* are an awesome dad."

He grinned back, chuckling, and rested a hand on her back. "I appreciate that, and what you've done to help. *Mamm* says I'm not so good at expressing my gratitude, so I hope you know."

"Luke."

At Salena's reprimand from across the large room, he lifted his hand and dropped it to his side. "*Es dutt mir leed.*"

Janna gave a shake of her head at his apology. "No need."

But had she said that because she saw his touch as nothing more than a friendly gesture? Or because she was in denial about missing it as soon as it was gone?

Luke closed the door after *Mamm* got out of the passenger seat, then followed her around to the front of the truck. She took Joah's and Kayla's hands and started across Oregon Dairy's exit road, while Luke waited for Janna to join him on the strip of grass between the road and the parking lot.

"Want to split a Mud Pie Sundae again?" he asked her.

"Sure." Her expression then took on seriousness as she looked at him. "Are you sure that's a good idea? I'm thinking it wasn't a coincidence that a man from your old church showed up only two days after the last time we were here."

He couldn't deny that. Still, they weren't doing anything wrong. They'd shared ice cream countless times as children. The only difference now was their age. Besides, what were the chances of someone he knew seeing them again?

The playground was busier this time, and a Plain-dressed young woman and her three children stood at the nearby goat pen. She smiled and waved at *Mamm*, but she didn't look familiar to him.

As they crossed the road, Joah stood on the other side, not far from where *Mamm* and Kayla sat at a picnic table while Kayla pulled off her shoes. "Can I jump now that my casts are off?"

He sounded so hopeful, and Luke didn't know the right answer.

"Not yet, honey." Janna's voice was gentle as she took his hand. "You have to jump in just socks, and your feet and ankles aren't strong enough yet without the AFOs on. Maybe in a few weeks. We'll ask Carin about it next week, okay?"

He sighed.

She tipped his hat back on his head so she could see his face. "Would you like to go into the store with me to get Kayla's sorbet?"

His smile returned. "*Ya.*"

"What kind of ice cream do you want?" Luke asked him.

"Chocolate marshmallow with sprinkles."

He pulled his wallet from his pocket and opened it. Five dollars had more than covered Kayla's sorbet last time.

"You don't have to do that," Janna said before he'd even pulled out a bill. "Really."

Just as he figured. He handed a five to Joah. "Will you buy Kayla's sorbet for her?"

His grin returned, even bigger. "I'll get her peach. She likes that the best."

Luke patted his shoulder, then met Janna's gaze and raised his eyebrows. "Mud Pie Sundae? It's a lot for one person to eat this close to supper, you know."

She pressed her lips together. "I just . . . I don't want to cause you trouble."

"I'm not worried about it." Well, that wasn't fully true, but he needed to stop letting others' opinions dictate what was or wasn't acceptable. "If Jesus were here with us, which he is, he'd find no problem with it. Isn't that what truly matters?"

Janna hesitated, then exhaled and managed a smile. "All right. You're just going to get an extra spoon for me anyway, so it's not like I have a choice. We'll be back in a few minutes." She led Joah toward the store, walking slowly with him as they held hands. Never before had a person stirred such conflicting feelings in him.

He headed for the picnic table to ask *Mamm* what she wanted.

As he neared, she watched him, her eyes barely visible through the sun-darkened lenses of her wire-rim glasses. Suddenly the reality of the situation hit him. Other people weren't who Janna was worried about. She was worried about the woman who'd already given him one warning today—and would probably be giving him a second one after she saw the Mud Pie Sundae with two spoons.

Ach, so be it.

Priscilla

Janna looked up from the book she was reading to Joah and Kayla when tires squealed on asphalt out at the road. A red sedan with darkened windows had turned into the lane and now made its way back toward the house.

Kayla sat forward on the kitchen porch's swing, placing her bare feet on the gray floorboards. "Who's that?"

On the other side of Janna, Joah shrugged. "Maybe a customer. Sometimes they come by after supper because they work during the day."

The battered old Ford Focus stopped at the gap in the picket fence where the slate-slab walkway met the lane. The driver's door opened moments later, and a too-thin sixtyish woman with short and spikey bleached hair got out. Dressed in black flip-flops and a knee-length blue tube dress, she started up the walk toward the porch.

Janna set the book on her lap. "Can I help you?" Something about the woman seemed familiar.

The woman stopped at the porch, twirling her keys around

a finger as her stare moved from Janna to each of the children, then back to her. "Who're you?"

Janna stood. "My name's Janna. Can I help you?"

A smirk spread across her face. "Well, what d'ya know? Never thought you'd come back." She gave a short, cynical laugh. "Although they'd probably say the exact same thing about me."

The clear-blue eyes, high cheek bones, and pointed chin suddenly reminded Janna of someone—Salena, especially when she was younger. And considering what the woman had just said, that could mean only one thing. "How are you, Priscilla?"

Cocking her head, she held Janna's gaze. "That's something, you remembering me. Last time I saw you, you couldn't have been more than ten." Priscilla looked beyond her to Kayla and Joah, still on the swing, and her hard gaze softened a little. "Well, my grandson's a cute little guy, isn't he?" She returned her attention to Janna. "Obviously the girl's your kid, with that hair and all. You get married to Luke?"

Janna almost choked. "No, we're just staying here—in the *daadi haus*—for a few weeks." And she needed to get Luke out here, like now. If he knew she was talking to Priscilla with Joah right there, he'd probably lose it.

"Mama, who is she?" Kayla's soft voice came from beside her.

She placed her hand on Kayla's head but turned to look at Joah. Still on the swing, he watched with a confused expression. He probably didn't realize who she was—or maybe didn't even know she existed? "Honey, go tell your dad Priscilla's here."

He slid off the swing, but then looked down at his feet. Janna had allowed him to take off his shoes while they were reading, and now he stood there in just his socks and AFOs, which he knew to wear only with shoes. She crouched down and put on his shoes and tied them, grateful Priscilla didn't ask more questions. "Go ahead."

"Something wrong with his legs?" Priscilla asked after he was inside. She sounded more irritated than concerned.

"They're braces to help him walk correctly. He just got them four days ago." Luke was protective of Joah when it came to Priscilla, and Janna would let him do whatever explaining he saw fit.

Priscilla hacked from deep in her chest—the same cough Mom always had—then crossed her scrawny arms. The wrinkled, sallow skin of her face made her look at least fifteen years older than she was. Such a shame.

The screen door creaked open behind Janna, and Salena rushed out. She crossed the porch and stepped down onto the walk, then hugged her daughter. Moments later, Luke came out onto the porch. He said nothing, but his solemn expression spoke volumes. "I sent Joah upstairs," he told Janna when he stopped beside her. "Would you help him get ready for bed?"

She almost protested, realizing he had no intention of allowing Joah to see his grandmother that night, but that wasn't her place. And the pleading in his eyes expressed how troubled this had him. "Of course."

"I'll be up to say good night to him in a few minutes."

She guided Kayla toward the door.

About twenty minutes later, Janna led Kayla back downstairs. Luke had already said goodnight to Joah, and he now sat at the kitchen table with Salena and Priscilla. The two women talked amicably, but he only stared at his folded hands resting on the table.

Janna gave an apologetic smile. *"Guder nacht."*

Kayla went to Salena and hugged her.

"*Guder nacht.*" Salena's eyes sparkled just as they had on the day Janna and Kayla had arrived.

Luke only glanced up for a second and gave a nod of acknowledgment.

Her heart went out to him, but there was nothing she could do. "Come, Kayla."

As they reached the doorway into the *daadi haus*, chair legs squawked across the floor. "You two can catch up." Luke strode to the back door. After grabbing his hat from the pegboard, he stepped outside, letting the screen door slap closed behind him.

Kayla looked up at Janna, her forehead wrinkled with concern. "Is Luke mad at us?" she asked when they closed the *daadi haus* door behind them.

"Oh no, honey. Not at all."

That wasn't a lie. He wasn't mad—at least not at her and Kayla.

The tension pulling at Luke's shoulders eased some as he stepped off the porch of Enos and Ivan's farmhouse in the humid darkness. Far across the property, light shone inside the *daadi haus*. At least Janna was still up. He hadn't visited her at night since learning she worked after Kayla was in bed, but tonight he needed to talk to her. His uncles and aunts had shared his concerns about Priscilla's arrival, but no one could truly understand like Janna would.

The sky brightened behind the cloud cover in the west, and several seconds later thunder rumbled. He picked up his pace on the lane, then took a shortcut over the lawn between the trampoline and playset and crossed the lane to the *daadi haus*'s walkway. The gate clinked closed behind him, and as he stepped onto the porch, Janna appeared on the other side of the screen door.

Waiting for him, maybe? That thought lifted his spirits more than it should have. "I know it's late—"

She pushed the door open. "Come in. Or do you want me to come out?"

With a shake of his head, he stepped inside. "Storm's coming." Besides, the humidity was oppressive. The *daadi haus* had an air conditioner in the bedroom, and between that and the oscillating pedestal fan that cooled the living room and dining area, the temperature was comfortable.

The laptop on the end table beside the recliner caught his eye. "If you're working—"

"I'm not." Her eyes searched his, no doubt trying to sense his frame of mind. She knew how he felt about Priscilla, and he'd seen the concern on her face when he'd left the house. "Do you want some lemonade?"

"*Ya.*" Once she was in the kitchen, he hung his hat on the peg by the door and sat down at the end of the table.

Soon she carried in two full glasses, then set one before him on the beige tablecloth before lowering herself onto the side bench.

He drained half the lemonade in the glass, then wiped the cool surface across his forehead. "I stopped and talked to Enos and Ivan, just to let them know."

"What does Joah know about Priscilla?" she asked.

For the first time, the truth almost embarrassed him. "Nothing. She hasn't been here since he was a newborn. *Mamm* and I have spoken of her, so he's heard her name from time to time, but I've never told him she's his grandmother." He looked her in the eye. "Did she say anything to him before I came out?"

"Not directly. She said he was cute. And she did refer to

him as her grandson. I sent him in to get you as soon as I real-ized who she was."

He ran his thumb over the condensation forming on the glass, then slowly inhaled. "And now I'll need to tell him some-thing, but how do you tell a six-year-old his grandmother wants little to do with her family—her own son and grandson, even—except when they happen to have something she wants?"

Empathy drew her expression. "Well . . . you tell the truth —what you think is necessary for him to know—and make it clear that she's had a difficult time in life because of some choices she's made. You tell him she doesn't have a relationship with Jesus and we need to pray for her because of that, and that he and the rest of the family are in no way part of the reason she does what she does."

He considered that. Wise words, and he suspected she had experience with this. "Is that what you told Kayla?"

She looked away, her eyes following her finger as it traced the cross-stitched flowers on the tablecloth. "Not about her grandmother. She only knows that she died when she was two." Janna cleared her throat quietly. "But that's basically what I told her when she asked about her father last year."

He nodded, unsure how to respond to that. What little she'd shared about Kayla's father *verhuddled* him. Why she'd ever gotten involved with such a man, especially in the way she had, made no sense.

"Did Priscilla say why she's here?" she asked.

"She just wanted to see us." He snorted. "Not that I believe her. Whenever she's visited, she's wanted money. The last time she was here, it was after *Mamm* called to tell her about Joah being born, but she only used that as a reason to visit—and then asked for five hundred dollars."

Janna frowned slightly, but it seemed sympathetic. He'd expected disgust.

"What?"

She seemed to be considering her words. "Luke, you saw her. She and my mom were right around the same age, so she's not even fifty. She looks so much older."

For good reason. "Living on alcohol and cigarettes for so many years will do that."

"I know. Honestly, I do." She hesitated again as if deciding what to say. "But what if she's sick and that's why she's here? It's not unlikely. I just . . . I understand how much she's hurt you and how much you don't want her to do the same to Joah, but I also can't help wondering about her reason for coming. When the hospice called about my mom and left me a message, I deleted it. But I couldn't stop thinking about her, and after a few days I looked up the facility's number and called. I've thanked God for that opportunity so many times since, and I'd hate to see you live with regrets if you don't have to."

His jaw clenched. Really, he'd expected her to offer different advice—like validation. "Kayla was only two at the time. Your mom had changed, and you also knew that whatever happened, Kayla wouldn't understand. Joah will be seven at the end of next month. If Priscilla mistreats him, he'll understand."

Janna fingered the cross-stitched flowers again, then finally looked up at him. "I still think it's something you should think about—and pray about."

He couldn't deny that, as much as he wanted to. "*Ya.*"

Lightning lit up the night beyond the windows, and thunder followed. Moments later, rain poured from the sky, pounding the roof. But it still didn't hold a candle to the storm raging inside him. He got up and walked to the screen door. The weather app on his phone had warned that damaging hail might fall in some places. So far they had just rain.

"You're Joah's father," Janna said as she came beside him.

"You know him best, and whatever you decide, I'll respect your wishes. Joah's with me a lot of the day, so you tell me what you want me to do and I'll do it."

He looked at her. Hard to believe this was the same woman who'd struggled to keep her cool as she dismissed him to the milking barn a little over a week ago. She could be fully and unreasonably exasperating, but then at other times her encouragement and support heartened him in ways he hadn't experienced since . . . well, since Rayanne was alive. "*Danki.*"

Now he just needed to figure out what to do.

Janna's prayers for Luke's situation seemed to have had some effect. Everyone had talked mostly pleasantly during breakfast, dinner, and supper, and Salena and Priscilla had spent most of the day together. At Luke's request, Janna had ensured Joah was never alone with his grandmother, and while she'd thought Luke might be miffed about her advice the night before, before breakfast he'd asked for her help in explaining to Joah what he needed to know about Priscilla. As well, going by Salena's cheerful demeanor, Priscilla hadn't mentioned ill health.

After they finished dessert, Luke excused Joah and Kayla, then grabbed the *Die Botschaft,* a weekly newspaper that detailed local news from individual scribes in Old Order Amish and Mennonite communities all over North America. Apparently, his mother's presence gave him no reason to postpone the household tradition of his reading aloud from it while the women washed the supper dishes. Or perhaps he did it as a reminder of how her father had done the same thing when she was growing up.

Priscilla watched the screen door close behind the children, then looked at Luke. "You've raised a fine boy."

He set the newspaper on the table and nodded at Salena. "I've had the best help I could ask for."

Ever humble, Salena waved off the compliment.

"You could've told him about me." A hint of irritation had crept into Priscilla's tone.

Luke's expression sobered. "And what should I have told him? That he has a grandmother who's only come to see him once, calls no more than twice a year, and couldn't even show up for his mother's funeral?"

And now it began. Janna had figured it would happen eventually. She stood from her chair and began collecting their dessert dishes. Staying at the table seemed improper since she wasn't part of the family.

Priscilla rested her crossed arms on the table in front of her, pinning him with narrowed eyes. "I knew you wouldn't want me around him. Isn't that what you did today?"

"You had limited contact with him today because *you've* limited your contact with him for years—by choice. Actions have consequences."

She huffed. "Not always, apparently. Janna moved away, what . . . ten years ago? Fifteen?"

Janna set the dessert plates on the counter by the sink and turned around. Surely Priscilla wasn't bringing her into this.

"I've at least called." Priscilla kept her gaze on Luke. "I came to see Joah when he was born. But she decides to suddenly reappear after all these years, and what do you do? Invite her to live here. She never contacted you at all after they left."

Never contacted them? That wasn't—

"*Nee.*" Luke spoke firmly. "There's no comparison at all, and I won't allow you to try to make one."

"That's not true anyway," Janna said. "I wrote letters almost every day for weeks. So many that Mom told me I couldn't write more than one a week, and I did that for probably two months."

Salena looked at her, eyes wide behind her glasses. "We never received letters from you. Luke and I wrote several but never received any back."

Then what had happened to . . .

Janna tried to swallow but couldn't. "But I wrote you. I did, and I gave them to . . ." *Mom.* She'd given them to Mom. So what had Mom done with them—and the ones written to her? Thrown them away?

Probably. Just like she'd disregarded everything else that mattered to Janna.

She almost felt sick. Inhaling, she pressed her fingers over her mouth. "We didn't have stamps. The post office was right near where she worked, so she said she'd mail them for me. And we had a post office box, so she always picked up our mail."

Salena stood. "*Ach,*" she whispered as she neared. "*Es dutt mir leed.*"

Janna couldn't have this discussion. Not now, and not with Priscilla there. Luke and Salena had their own issues to handle. "I'll give you privacy so you can talk," she said, then headed for the doorway into the *daadi haus.* "Just leave the dishes. I'll take care of them later."

Because if she touched them right now, they'd all end up smashed.

Luke pushed his chair back and stood.

Priscilla scowled as he rounded the table. "Where you going?"

"Don't worry, I'll be back. We're definitely not done talking."

"Luke." *Mamm* met his gaze, her eyebrows arched, as she still stood beside her chair. "I'll go."

Nee, he needed to do this. "Give me a minute." Janna had pushed the door behind her when she hurried into the *daadi haus*, but it closed only partway. If she was in the bedroom, he'd leave her alone, but he hoped otherwise.

She wasn't in the dining area or the part of the living room he could see, so he checked the kitchen as he passed the doorway. At finding her, a combination of empathy and anger filled him. She sat on the floor against the refrigerator with her knees pulled up beneath her skirt and both hands over her face. He grabbed two tissues from the box on the kitchen counter, then lowered himself onto the floor beside her.

She wiped her eyes.

"Here." He placed the tissues in her hand. When they were children, he'd just sit with her when she was upset like this, and that seemed best now. What could he say that would help?

After wiping her eyes again, she leaned her head back. "I owe you an apology."

She owed him? "*Nee*."

"Yes, I do. Because last night I said you should give your mom a chance—because I was so glad I did. But right now . . ." She shook her head. "Right now I'm trying not to hate my mom, and it's not working. She knew how much I missed you, how many times I wrote to you, and how I waited every day for a letter from you. And she didn't care." Her voice broke and she covered her face again. "How could a mother do that? *How?*"

His throat stung. Knowing the torment she was feeling all too well, he would've done just about anything to take it away.

Of course, that would mean not having learned the truth. It would be a lie to say he wasn't relieved to know why they'd never heard from her. He'd always hoped there'd been a reason other than her simply not writing. "*Es dutt mir leed.*"

Ya. Never had the literal translation—*it does me harm*—been more accurate.

"You did what you could. I should've realized it was her and not you. If anyone needs to apologize, it's me. I should've known you would never ignore my letters."

He reached for her, but again he caught himself and instead smoothed some loose hair back from her face. "We always suspected something had happened. We never blamed you."

She wiped her eyes again, grimacing. "I wish I could say the same."

That made sense. She'd been reluctant to trust them for the first few days she'd been back and even seemed to consider herself an inconvenience. Now he understood why. "*Macht nichts.* We know the truth. And you're here. She may have wronged you, but God had a plan. He redeems the evil done against us."

She sighed. "Too bad that doesn't make it hurt less."

How true that was. He placed his hand on her shoulder and squeezed it. Leaving when she was so upset bothered him, but he had to. "I need to go back in the house. You'll be all right?"

"Yeah." She shook her head. "It's just par for the course in my life."

"I know the feeling." After standing, he offered his hand and helped her up.

Words of comfort didn't come, and before he could stop himself, he'd pulled her to his side. She stiffened for a moment, bracing her hand on his middle, but then rested her forehead against his shoulder.

His breath caught when her arm slipped around him. No matter the situation, what they were doing wasn't . . . well, it just shouldn't be done. Even if it didn't feel wrong.

He gently put her away from him, but when she looked up, neither his hands nor his eyes could let her go. She managed a faint smile despite the tears in her green eyes, and a streak of dampness glinted on her cheek. He brushed it away with the side of his thumb.

"Luke?"

He inhaled and stepped back. *Mamm*'s call from in the house told him he'd been alone with Janna for too long.

But by the way his heart skipped, he already knew that.

CHAPTER 13

If Not for Grace

Nothing. It meant nothing.

Janna swiped her palms across her cheeks and breathed deeply after Luke returned to the house. Somehow she could still feel his blue-and-white-plaid shirt and elastic suspender against her face and smell their scent—laundry detergent with hints of sawed wood and furniture stain.

Luke was simply being kind, trying to offer some consolation. Just like any friend, especially one who understood the situation so well, would have.

Except he wasn't one of her other friends. He was a man who'd grown up in the *gmay*, and the *gmay* had rules about interaction between men and women. As did the church he'd joined. Neither condoned any show of physical affection outside marriage, and certainly not with someone from outside the community.

Still, this was different. She and Luke had grown up together. They'd been like siblings. And Luke wasn't attending the Old Order churches anymore. He'd been at River View

Mennonite Fellowship, whose members were prudent in their contact with those of the opposite gender but not as strict as the Old Order groups. Luke had hugged Kendra on the night of the picnic—or perhaps it was the other way around. But either way, he hadn't seemed uncomfortable with it.

If that was the case, his embrace tonight—could it even be called that?—should fall into the same category. Same with his wiping her cheek. Innocuous gestures between friends. An indication that he understood.

As well, he'd let go of her almost as soon as she responded in kind. Not that she'd intended for that to happen. Touching his side had been an immediate defense that allowed her to keep some control of what was happening. But what about after that? She'd willingly hugged him. It made no . . .

Oh, forget it. She couldn't think about this now. Trying to wrap her head around what her mother had done was difficult enough. She pressed her hand to her chest, still vying for the air she needed.

How in the world could a revelation bring such relief and bitterness at the same time? She could practically taste the latter. After almost four years of feeling at peace with Mom, resentment had reared its ugly head again.

Just par for the course. As much as she hated it, that was true. She really shouldn't be surprised. Even so, why hadn't Mom come clean about the letters before her death? She'd admitted to and apologized for plenty of other things. In some ways, this even trumped all the years of neglect and indifference. She'd severed any relationship Janna had with the people she loved most. On purpose.

Who knew how differently her life might've turned out, and how much hurt and despair she'd have avoided, had she been allowed to keep her connection with the Martins. Salena had promised she would always have a home with them, and

Janna had kept every intention of returning as soon as she finished high school. Until she never heard from them and the doubts crept in, bolstered by Mom's ridicule when Janna went through the mail each evening. How could any person be so cruel?

"Hurt people hurt people." Those words had been Cynthia's reminder to her on so many occasions—that Mom's treatment of people reflected her own pain and self-loathing and not the inadequacies of those on whom she inflicted her animosity. Still, knowing that didn't make it any less horrid. For goodness' sake, the woman was dead now and still twisting a knife in her back. A knife Janna had thought was gone for—

Luke's voice, raised but muffled by the wall and closed door between the house and *daadi haus*, startled her out of her thoughts. She couldn't make out what he said after his outburst, but he'd never been one to yell.

Her heart went out to him. She certainly didn't agree with everything he said or did, but he strove to do what was right. He didn't deserve how Priscilla treated him. Knowing how it hurt him, Janna wished she could comfort him as he had her.

What sounded like a distant scream beckoned her to the screen door, and she stepped out onto the porch. Up the lane, beyond where it curved to the left around the playset on its way toward Enos and Ivan's farmhouse, Kayla stood from squatting on the asphalt. "Maaamaaa!"

Joah. He lay on the lane maybe six feet from his scooter and bike, not moving.

Moments later she was rushing through the gate and jogging toward them.

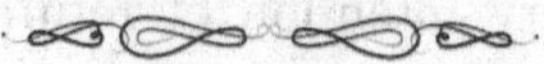

Malinda, who'd come bustling out the front door of the farmhouse, reached Joah first. She had him on his feet by the time Janna reached them. "*Was hot's gewwe?*" she asked as they both looked him over.

Blood smeared his chin, the tip of his nose, and his palms, but Malinda's gentle blotting with a handkerchief showed road rash only on his chin and hands. He must've wiped some onto his nose.

Janna's racing heart slowed as she held his wrists, inspecting his palms and then the rest of him. He didn't seem hurt otherwise. "Did you fall?"

He nodded, still crying. "She rode in front of me."

"I didn't mean to!" Kayla's chin quivered. "I was riding his bike and turned in front of him by accident. He tried to go around me and jumped off the scooter but fell. I didn't mean to do it. I thought he was way behind me."

No one was at fault, then. And the AFOs did make him clumsy at times. "Joah, are you hurt anywhere else?"

This time he shook his head.

"Okay. We just need to clean you up." She looked at Malinda, who held Kayla to her side. Both children were now crying, although Kayla's tears fell in silence. "Honey, it's okay. It was an accident and he'll be fine." She met Malinda's gaze again and lowered her voice. "Can we go to your place? They're talking to Priscilla, and things were getting tense."

She made a sympathetic face. "*Ach, ya.* That's probably best, then."

Ten minutes later, Joah's hands and chin were cleaned and bandaged, and he and Kayla were headed back outside to the playset. Malinda closed the first aid kit on the counter by the kitchen sink, then faced Janna and looked into her eyes. "The children aren't the only ones who've been crying tonight, not?"

Janna exhaled. Her red eyes had probably given that away, so there was no use denying it. "We just figured out my mom never sent all the letters I wrote after we moved away, and she never gave me the letters written to me."

"*Ay-yi-yi*." Malinda shook her head, tsking. "How that must hurt."

Her throat had tightened so she couldn't have verbally agreed if she wanted to.

"Enos and Ivan are out in the barn, and Beulah's talking to her son's family on the phone." Malinda canted her head. "How about we sit on the bench and visit while the children play?"

She could handle that—as long as they talked about something else. For years, she'd tried not to let herself dwell on the what-ifs. Now more of them bombarded her like darts to the soul. Things could have been so different, even if they'd left Lancaster County but she'd been able to stay in touch with the Martins. But how did she not think about that? Or about why she—

"We don't have to if—"

"No, it's not that. I just . . ." Janna cleared her throat, trying to rid its aching. "Have you ever had someone do something to you, and even though it wasn't your fault, you felt guilty about it? Like they did it because you deserved it?"

"*Ach,* dear one." Malinda rested a hand on her arm. "You did nothing to deserve your mother's actions. When we have thoughts like that, it's the evil one doing what he does best. Satan is the father of lies, but we don't have to believe him because we belong to Jesus—the Way, the *Truth,* and the Life."

Janna nodded. Getting her heart to remember that wasn't always easy. "But have you ever felt that way?"

She led her toward the living room. "Without a doubt."

Of course she would have. Malinda had lived with Beulah's cynicism all her life, and while the two women loved each other, that didn't shield her from her sister's criticism. Janna had witnessed that many times over the years she was with the Martins, as well as been moved by Malinda's gracious responses. "You're always so kind, no matter how people treat you."

She chuckled. "I try, anyway."

At reaching the front screen door, Janna opened it, and they stepped onto the covered porch. "That can't be easy."

Malinda stopped, considering that. "*Nee*. But grace is for those who don't deserve it, not? As sinners, we don't deserve God's grace, but he gives it. And if we don't forgive others, he won't forgive us. That's not a chance I want to take."

The truth of her words inspired and convicted Janna at the same time.

"My *daed* always told us we can't control what others do," Malinda said as they headed for the playset, "but we can control how *we* respond. Ever since I was a little girl, I've asked Jesus to help me respond the way he would."

Maybe Janna needed to do the same. Regularly. But still . . . "I just wish I could stop thinking about how things might have been different. I know I can't change anything and it's not doing me any good, but my mind keeps going there. What if we hadn't moved? Or what if we had but Mom had let me keep in touch?"

As they crossed the lane, Malinda rested a hand on her back. "Are you sure you'd want to change the past if you could?" Though her tone was light, the words were anything but.

She stopped. "Why wouldn't I?" How could she not wish for something different? Like the love she'd felt living with

Daadi Eli, *Mammi* Salena, and Luke. The stability. The Martins had been her family, and she'd never fully gotten over losing them, not even now. So much could have been—

"Oh, dear one," Malinda murmured, her voice thick with emotion. "I understand. I do. But truly think about what would be different." She turned Janna toward the trampoline, where Joah and Kayla jumped within the mesh enclosure. "Think about where that sweet little girl would be."

Reality stole Janna's breath. If things had been different, Kayla . . . *wouldn't* be. The person she loved most—the one she'd give her life for without a second thought—never would have been born. Just the thought made her eyes sting.

"My *daed* also used to say we need to take the bad with the good, because sometimes the worst kind of bad can result in the best kind of good." Malinda smiled, watching as Kayla held Joah's wrist to give him stability on the trampoline while not hurting his scraped hands. "That precious child is the best kind of good."

Yes, she was. And Janna wouldn't give her up for anything.

Luke rubbed his hand over his face. Aside from a miracle happening, seemingly nothing would get Priscilla to see the wrongfulness of her behavior. Something else was always to blame—the *gmay*'s strictness, church leadership who didn't like her, her lack of having a sister growing up, or *Mamm* and *Daadi*'s refusal to condone her teenage rebellion. She simply would not take responsibility for the things she'd done and how she'd treated her family, and trying to explain what should've been obvious had Luke exhausted.

And now she'd blamed her sporadic communication with

them on his detachment from their relationship and mistrust of her. Did she truly expect that in spite of her minimal—not to mention self-seeking—contact, he would welcome her back into his life whenever she felt like showing up?

Sure, *Mamm* welcomed her, and in some ways he understood that. If Joah were to do the same thing when he was older, Luke would certainly react differently. But right now he was more concerned about protecting his son.

When he lowered his hand, *Mamm* and Priscilla watched him. And apparently expected a response. "The detachment and mistrust are only because you've given me reason after reason for them. We have no relationship because that's been your choice. When I was three months old, you went to Pittsburgh—supposedly to visit a friend for a weekend—met a man, and decided he was more important than your child. He's long gone now, but plenty of other things and people have since taken his place. Your choices over the last twenty-eight years have proven what's important to you and what's not."

"But you *are* important to me." Priscilla's protest almost sounded genuine. "I think about you a lot."

He sighed. That still didn't make up for her absence. "There's more to a relationship than thinking about someone."

She dropped her head and dug the fingers of both hands into her messy hair. "You just don't understand."

And there it was again—the excuse she gave every time they had this discussion. *He* didn't understand. How could anybody understand?

"*Nee*, I don't, and I doubt I ever will. Because I'm a parent too, and I can't imagine not seeing Joah for one day, let alone years. I can't imagine not hearing his voice, not seeing his smile, not feeling his arms around my neck."

She looked up, grimacing. "You think I've never thought about that? I stayed in Pittsburgh because I just couldn't be here. I never belonged in the *gmay*, no matter how hard I tried. And don't tell me you don't understand that, because you left it too."

That wasn't the same. "I've stayed in the Old Order community." But had he, really? He might still be a member, but who knew for how long. The ministry would allow his disobedience for only so long. Of course, Priscilla didn't know that, unless *Mamm* had told her. He doubted it.

She shook her head. "Luke, I've always wanted what was best for you. That's why I never tried to bring you to Pittsburgh. Believe me, I thought about it. I wanted to be a good mother. Really. But I couldn't give you what *Mamm* and *Daed* could. You were better off here, and every time I visited just proved that to me even more." She glanced at *Mamm*, then back to him. "I did what I could, and that was leave you with the people who would provide the best life for you."

That he couldn't deny, and perhaps she was telling the truth. He'd always thought she'd simply not wanted the responsibility of parenthood, but maybe her intentions had been less self-centered than they seemed.

Mamm excused herself to the bathroom and slowly stood. She looked tired, but he suspected it was more emotional than physical. How could Priscilla keep doing this to her?

Priscilla coughed harshly as she watched *Mamm* leave the room, then returned her attention to him. She took a deep breath and released it. "She and I haven't always seen eye to eye, but she did what I couldn't. I wish I was half the woman she is."

The sadness in her voice softened his defensiveness a bit. "It's not too late. People change all the time."

She snorted. "Easier said than done." The hardness had edged into her tone again.

"*Ya*. But things worth doing often aren't easy, not?"

Priscilla's mouth twitched as she considered that. "I suppose." After staring at the table for several moments, she looked up at him. Her eyebrows crinkled together. "I'm not getting any younger, and I do want to do better. But there's no use in me trying if you're not willing to give me another chance. So will you do that . . . please?"

As much as he wished he could give an immediate, honest affirmation—for her sake if not for his own—he couldn't. Missy Carpenter's changed life came to mind, but so did the stolen letters. Of course, that had happened long before Missy became a Christian, so he couldn't hold that against her.

As well, Luke served a God who offered forgiveness—and expected it from his followers. Knowing that, and the way it would wound *Mamm* if he refused, how could he deny Priscilla's request, especially when she finally seemed earnest? Despite the wall he'd put up between them, part of him still longed for reconciliation. And hadn't he just pointed out that things worth doing weren't always easy?

He nodded. "*Ya*."

She reached across the table and took his hand in her much-cooler one. "Son, I can do this. You'll see. I *want* to do this—for you, Joah, and *Mamm*. I promise."

Son. Never had she called him that. Luke squeezed her hand gently, and the joy and contentment of doing what was right in the eyes of the Lord welled in him.

Praise be to God.

Luke watched as Priscilla stood several feet from their picnic table at Oregon Dairy, eating an ice cream cone and grinning at Joah, who climbed on the rope spiderweb near the back of the playground. Her demeanor had indeed changed since their discussion two nights ago. She smiled readily, looked happy for perhaps the first time he remembered, and gave more of her attention to her family than to her cell phone. Even her visit with Enos, Ivan, Beulah, and Malinda had gone better than expected.

Yesterday she'd accompanied *Mamm* to visit *Mamm*'s sister, this morning she'd driven her to the fabric store, and this afternoon she'd come with them to New Beginnings while *Mamm* rested. Her attention had never left Joah as Carin took him through his therapy and Luke explained the treatment he'd been receiving, and now she beamed at Joah like a proud grandmother. Perhaps a bit too proud, but she'd lived outside the *gmay* for decades, so that shouldn't be unexpected.

Beside him on the picnic table's bench, Janna was finishing Kayla's pint of peach sorbet. She'd declined sharing a sundae with him, claiming she was in the mood for something fruity this time, but who knew if that was the case or if she was putting some distance between them. The time he'd spent with Priscilla had limited his interaction with Janna the last two days, and after what had happened in the *daadi haus*'s kitchen, he hadn't visited her at night. She had work deadlines to meet anyway. And maybe some distance was wise.

But he wanted to know what she was feeling, especially regarding the letters. She didn't appear upset—quieter than usual perhaps, but not troubled—though that didn't mean anything. Living long term with difficult circumstances could make a person a good actor.

Priscilla startled, interrupting his search for something to say to Janna, and then she reached into her purse. She pulled out her cell phone, shoved the last bit of cone into her mouth, and answered the phone all while heading for the shaded area where the ice cream shop's covered deck jutted out toward the playground below. No more than two minutes later, she returned to the table.

The ice cream in Luke's stomach turned heavy as she sat down across from them. With her smile gone, she again wore the hard expression that made her appear years older. "Everything all right?"

Priscilla looked away, staring somewhere across the parking lot behind him. "I gotta go."

"Go?" As in back to the house?

"Back to Pittsburgh. Tonight."

Pittsburgh? But it was already past four o'clock, and the city was a four-hour drive away—if traffic wasn't bad. Besides, her Saturday was already planned. "You told *Mamm* you'd take her to visit Jake and Ellie tomorrow morning. He's your brother, and you haven't seen him in seven years."

She shook her head. "Can't. I need to leave tonight."

"Why?" He couldn't let her off that easy. "What's so important that it can't wait?"

"I just do," she said. "You wouldn't understand."

Unbelievable. After she'd raised *Mamm*'s hope of finally having a relationship with her—and claimed she wanted another chance and made a *promise* to him—now she was leaving suddenly, just like she had every other time. He swallowed, struggling to keep the anger from his voice. "But you'll stay in touch? Visit again soon?"

She met his gaze for a moment, then averted hers to the picnic table's top. "Luke, I'm no good for you. You, *Mamm*, and Joah deserve better."

Except it wasn't unbelievable. It was what she did. And he'd given her the benefit of the doubt and believed her lies. Now *Mamm* would be heartbroken—again—and he'd have to explain the inexplicable to Joah. "Is that a yes or a no?"

She sighed. "It's . . . it's an *I'll try*."

An *I'll try*. He never should've—

A muted rock song played from within her purse.

She got up, then pulled out her phone and answered it as she hurried away from the table.

Hands surrounded his clenched fist as it lay on his leg.

Janna. He'd forgotten about her. At some point she'd slid closer to him, and now she looked at him with such compassion as she slipped her fingers into his palm and entwined them with his.

Somehow the feel of her hands around his eased his anger, and he shook his head and repeated her words from two nights before. "Just par for the course in my life."

"I know the feeling." She squeezed his hand. "Shall I let the children know we'll be leaving soon?"

"*Ya.*"

Best to get this over with as quickly as possible.

CHAPTER 14

The Purple Martins

Janna had just carried her coffee onto the porch when she caught sight of movement up the lane toward Enos and Ivan's. The dark jeans, plaid shirt, white suspenders, and hat could've belonged to any of the Martin men, but only one was that tall.

Instead of going to the swing, she leaned against the porch post to wait. Thank goodness it was Sunday and she'd already dressed for church. Had Luke come by at this time yesterday, he would've found her on the swing in leggings and a T-shirt as she worked. Not that there was anything wrong with that. Well, except that it would've made him uncomfortable. But according to Arissa, that was his problem, not hers.

"Morning." As he neared the gate, his eyes took in the alternating pink and red rose bushes in the beds along the picket fence. "The roses haven't looked this beautiful in years. You never lost your green thumb."

"Cynthia had an English garden on her property when she lived up here. Roses have always been my favorite, though."

"Yours and *Mamm*'s both."

She glanced at her watch. A few minutes after six. They wouldn't sit down to breakfast till quarter after seven, and considering the direction he'd come from, he'd probably just finished helping with the milking again. "I just made coffee if you'd like some."

"Best thing I've heard today." He opened the gate and strode up the walkway.

"Take this one." She held out the travel mug in her hand. "I'll go pour another." When their gazes met, she smiled. "You look like you could use some caffeine."

Stepping onto the porch, he took it. "Early mornings." One eyebrow arched beneath his hat brim. "Sound familiar?"

Her grin widened, but only for a moment. Was he teasing her or making a point of how they'd argued about her working on Sunday two weeks ago? "*Ya*. But I'm not working this morning."

"*Gut*."

Right. Instead of responding, she turned and went inside. Hopefully, he wouldn't say any more about it. She wasn't in the mood for an argument, and after having it out with Priscilla on Friday night, maybe he wasn't either.

When she returned to the porch, he was on the swing. She stopped after shutting the screen door quietly. They'd never shared this swing since it barely accommodated two adults.

He slid toward the armrest. "You can sit. Except I might smell like the barn."

Well, if the close quarters didn't bother him . . . And drinking her coffee on the porch railing wouldn't be nearly as relaxing. "I always kind of liked that smell." She sat down, leaving a couple of inches between them, and crossed her feet at the ankles. "The hay, the top-dress, the animal scent."

He chuckled. "The manure?"

"Well, not so much that." She smiled. At least he'd forgotten what they'd talked about before she went in for more coffee. "Though I don't mind the hint of it I catch on the breeze from here."

He swallowed another sip. "I need to apologize for two Sundays ago, for the way I acted. I'm not saying I want you working on the Lord's Day, but I shouldn't have been so short."

Or he hadn't forgotten. But she'd take an apology. "I really do try not to work on Sundays. That was just a weird week with not being able to start as soon as I'd planned. I never want to miss a deadline."

He pushed off with his black work boot, setting the swing in motion.

Janna closed her eyes, and as she breathed in, déjà vu flooded through her with such strength that her breath audibly caught.

"*Bisht alright?*" Luke was looking right at her when she opened her eyes.

"Yeah, I just . . ." Amazing how something could bring such solace and sadness at the same time. "When I closed my eyes, it seemed almost like going back in time. The movement of the swing. The coolness of the air. The scent of the roses. The sound of the purple martins. It took me right back to years ago."

He opened his mouth but didn't say anything. After a few moments, he lifted the mug to his lips again. The set of his jaw deterred her from asking his thoughts.

A pair of purple martins flew in, and she smiled as they glided over the playset and dove toward the martin house. Despite how morning had broken almost an hour before, one bird continued chirping out his dawnsong at the top of his lungs. "It always amazed me that they came back every year— that they knew which nesting site to return to. *Daadi* Eli said they would go all the way to Brazil for the winter, and yet their scouts showed up again in April."

"*Dee flickel fleeya, ava's hatz vaased da vaag haem.*" Luke's quote of his grandfather's words brought goose bumps to Janna's arms as their meaning came to her: *The wings do the flying, but the heart knows the way home.* His voice and inflection even made him sound like *Daadi* Eli. "Kind of like you."

Like her? She met his gaze. "What do you mean?"

"You found your way home too."

Well, she'd tried, anyway. And in a few weeks, the Akron house would be repaired and they'd move in. Until then—

"It took more time, but here you are." A brief smile tugged at onc side of his mouth.

He meant here. On the farm, with them.

She swallowed. "Yeah."

But how did she feel about that? They'd been with the Martins for three weeks now, and she and Kayla were comfortable —mostly. The *daadi haus* was tiny, she'd be glad when she could shower instead of taking a bath, and sharing a bed with squirmy Kayla was hardly ideal, yet they were happier, even despite the rules they had to follow. Still, they couldn't stay forever.

She sipped her coffee, watching the purple martins again. The birds went where they needed to go, and she would do the same. She'd promised herself she and Kayla would start over and thrive on their own when they moved, and that was a promise she intended to keep.

Luke had just passed from the shop to the workshop when the phone behind the shop's counter rang. With Malinda outside carrying an elderly customer's quilt purchase to her car, he turned around and answered it.

"I'm trying to reach Janna Carpenter," a woman said, sounding a bit anxious. Or maybe determined.

Odd that someone would ask for Janna specifically. "She's not here at the moment. May I take a message?"

"This is Arissa Otero, her best friend. I've been trying to call her, but she's not answering her cell. I need to talk to her, like ASAP."

Arissa—the bold, flashy young woman who'd visited a couple of weekends ago. The hesitance he felt at hearing her name tempted him to just take a message, but perhaps that wouldn't be in Janna's best interest. "Let me see if she's still here. She was about to go out. If you'll hold on, I'll check."

"Yes. Please."

He walked to the front door, then stepped outside and glanced around. Janna and the children were nowhere to be seen, but her car was still parked beside his truck. The *daadi haus*'s front door squeaked open, and she followed Joah and Kayla onto the porch. "Janna!" He motioned her to him.

She hurried the children down the walkway to the lane and across it.

"Your friend Arissa's on the phone," he called as she approached. "She said it's important she talk to you."

Her expression sobered. "Wait right here," she told the children, indicating the bench under the roof overhang. "I'll be right out, and then we'll go."

He followed her into the shop but continued to the workshop. Then yesterday's stack of mail on the desk inside the doorway caught his eye, and he stopped to flip through it. As much as he knew better than to eavesdrop—that was sin—he couldn't move. Arissa's call concerned him, and not just because he had misgivings about her. It was more the urgency in her tone.

He wasn't truly eavesdropping anyway. The shop's counter was on the other side of the wall from the desk, but he could only hear that Janna was speaking, not what she said.

"He *called* you?"

That he heard clearly, and the emotions in Janna's voice—disbelief and possibly even fear—confirmed his suspicion. Something had to be wrong.

The rest of what she said was indistinguishable, but less than two minutes later, the phone receiver clicked as it was hung back on the wall. He set the mail on the desk, waited several seconds, and then went back into the shop.

Janna leaned against the wall with the fingers of one hand over her mouth and her eyes closed. He'd been right.

"*Ebbes letz?*"

Opening her eyes, she dropped her hand to her side and shook her head. "It's not a big deal." She came out from behind the counter. "It's almost one. I don't want Joah to be late for his appointment."

Nee, that wouldn't do. He'd have to wait till they returned before trying to get more out of her. "Let me know when you're back?"

She nodded, then rounded him and headed for the front door.

Malinda came back inside only moments after Janna went out. She held his gaze, her brow creased. "Is she upset about something?"

Malinda was too kind to accuse, but she probably suspected he was the reason for it. That had been true more than once lately, and it wasn't unlikely that Janna had mentioned it. She and Malinda had always been close. "Her friend who visited just called, looking for her. Janna said it wasn't a big deal, but I don't know."

She sighed, then moved behind the counter.

Nothing more he could do now. He returned to the workshop and the coffee table he'd been working on before stopping for dinner. Running his hand over the surface assured him that the steel wool he'd used on it had fully smoothed the first coat of polyurethane, so he just needed to wipe it down with a damp cloth before applying the second coat.

He was carrying the can of polyurethane to the table when Janna rushed through the open back door and almost crashed into the workbench beside it. Even her maneuvering didn't keep her from catching her hip on the corner of it.

"My car won't start," she blurted. Then seeming to suddenly realize her hip hurt, she stopped and pressed her hand against it. "It won't even turn over."

This definitely wasn't her day. "It's probably more than out of gas, then." He set the can on the workbench.

She grimaced. "But it was fine when we went out yesterday."

The battery, maybe. Not that they needed to worry about that right now. She already had enough on her mind. "Do you think you could drive the van?" The Caravan was bigger than her little Honda, but he doubted she'd have trouble with that. It wouldn't hurt for the van to get some use, either. He drove it only on Sundays, mainly to keep it running well.

"I . . . Sure." Even so, tears flooded her eyes. She exhaled and turned away.

Catching her by the arm, he stepped around in front of her, then placed both hands on her shoulders. Maybe she *could* drive the van, but *should* she? "You're upset. More than just I-don't-want-to-be-late and I-just-whacked-my-hip upset. If you need me to take you, I will." Not that he wanted to give up an hour and forty-five minutes of work time, and Mahlon wasn't even back from going home for dinner, but she shouldn't be driving if she wasn't in the right state of mind. And maybe while Joah did therapy, she'd tell him what was going on. "Do you need me to take you?"

Somehow, she collected herself and shook her head. "I'm fine. Really." She even sounded convincing, though her eyes blinked a few times to dry the tears. "I can drive the van."

He rubbed his thumbs over both her shoulders. She relaxed, but when the almost vulnerable look in her eyes turned to typical Janna determination, he released her. "Come on. I'll get the keys for you."

"You have work to do. I know where they are. I can get them." She managed a smile. "But thanks."

"Janna," he said as she crossed the floor.

She glanced back at reaching the doorway into the shop. "Luke, we really need to go."

Right. Now wasn't the time. "Just let me know when you're back."

"I will."

He sighed after she left. Whatever that phone call had been about, it wasn't good.

"You've been awfully quiet tonight, and you barely ate any supper," Salena said when they were nearly finished washing the dishes. She set a handful of silverware in the rinse water and met Janna's gaze with concern in her blue eyes. "This afternoon, Malinda asked if all was well. She mentioned you'd received a phone call at the shop that *verhuddled* you. Would that be why?"

Janna hesitated. While she'd managed to get through the day without more questions about that, she knew they would eventually come from someone. She just hadn't expected it to be Salena. And Malinda hadn't even been in the shop when she was on the phone. How would she know, unless—

"She asked me what happened," Luke said, confirming her suspicion from behind them. When she turned around, he looked up from the magazine he was perusing. "She could tell something was wrong when you left."

And now all three of them knew something was up. As much as she didn't want to go into it—from day one back with the Martins, she'd hoped she wouldn't need to explain that part of her life to them—now she didn't have much choice. Especially since it could affect them. A lot.

Janna dried the silverware within the dish towel she held, then set it on the counter by the silverware drawer. Where did she even start?

"Arissa called because my ex-boyfriend called her and then texted her when she didn't answer. Back in April, about a month after we broke up and he lost his job, his parents sent him to a Christian rehab facility in Massachusetts. By that time I'd already changed my cell phone number and begun making plans to come back here once Kayla finished school in June."

Realizing she now wrung the towel in her hands, she set it on the counter. "He was released from the rehab program last week. Arissa didn't respond to his text either, but she wanted me to know he's trying to find me—to apologize, he claims."

Luke got up from his chair, then came around to the nearer side of the table and leaned against it. "Do you think he'd try to find you here?" His expression and tone were solemn but otherwise impossible to decipher.

She forced herself to keep looking at him. "I don't know." After spending a good part of the afternoon trying to figure out the best way to explain this if she had to, all the answers seemed to have flown out of her head. "He knows I grew up in Lancaster County, and I mentioned I'd considered moving back here once or twice."

She might've said it wasn't too far from New Holland too, since they'd talked about Shady Maple Smorgasbord. And he definitely knew the Martins' last name. So many people here had that surname, but had she also talked about the quilt and furniture shop? She just didn't know.

Salena pressed her lips together—from disappointment or compassion, Janna couldn't tell. "Would he try to hurt you?" The gentleness of her words confirmed compassion.

That brought some relief, but Janna still needed to answer the question. He had once, but . . . "No. I don't know. I don't think so." She shook her head. How did she even explain? "I've forgiven him for things he did, but I don't want him in my life again. We came here to start over. And I don't want this to cause any trouble for you." The realization of that possibility made her eyes burn and her throat close to the point that she couldn't say more.

"*Ach.*" Salena clasped her shoulders. "God is always with us. One who's trusting isn't worrying, and one who's worrying isn't trusting."

Janna nodded. How many times had she repeated those words—Salena's motto for as long as she could remember—in her head over the years?

Luke pushed away from the table and headed for the door. "I'll be back."

Salena faced him. "Where are you going?"

"To see if Don's home."

She started toward him. "Luke, it's not our way."

"I'm just going to talk to him." After grabbing his hat, he left.

Janna looked between the closing door and frowning Salena. "Who's Don?"

Salena clicked her tongue in disapproval. "The police officer who lives across the road. He owns the house your *mamm* rented."

Oh. She'd planned to go after Luke if he was doing something he shouldn't, but not anymore. He might want her to go with him, and she wasn't going there.

Once *Mamm* and Joah were in bed, Luke went down to the kitchen. The door into the *daadi haus* stood open as he'd hoped, but he stopped in the doorway. "I know you're working . . ."

Janna looked up from her laptop, then set it on the end table and stood from the recliner by the front window. "Not tonight." Her attempted grin was mostly unsuccessful as she came toward him. "My mind's not in it."

Understandable.

"You talked to a police officer?" She sounded uneasy, probably because she knew the Old Order groups avoided contact with law enforcement, preferring to handle issues their own way.

"*Ya.*" When she sat down on the bench at the table, he took the chair at the head. "Don's a good man. A few years back, he was investigating vandalism on some local Amish properties. We'd only talked a couple of times before, but he asked for my help in understanding the Plain mindset and being respectful of that while doing his job. We went fishing a couple of times that fall, and then Rayanne died that winter and he visited several times. He'd lost his wife too, so we had more in common than people might think."

Her eyes searched his face. "What did you talk to him about? Tonight, I mean."

"I explained what you'd told us." Which hadn't been as helpful as he'd thought, and hopefully, she wouldn't be angry that he had. "He asked some questions I didn't know the answers to, and told me nothing can be done right now. If your —" He couldn't get himself to say *ex-boyfriend*. "What is this man's name?"

"Mitch Anderson."

"Well, if he were to come here and cause a problem, we could call the police and they'd respond." Although the family wouldn't be happy about that. "Even if we simply didn't want him here, it would still be trespassing. I wanted to talk to Don because we allow strangers on the property all the time because of the shop, and I didn't know if that would affect our being able to do anything about this. But he said if this man were to show up and make anyone uncomfortable, we could ask him to leave and involve the police if he didn't."

Shaking her head, she looked up from staring at the tablecloth. "I didn't want to bring your family into this. He was supposed to be at the rehab till mid-August. When I agreed to stay here, I figured we'd be in Akron by the time—"

"Janna." She couldn't be serious. "The last thing I'd want is you dealing with him by yourself."

"I know, but . . ."

Remembering Don's suggested questions, he drew a breath. "What did he go to rehab for?"

She stared at the tablecloth again. "Alcohol, mostly. I didn't even know about his drinking until last fall when it got out of hand."

Still not looking at him, she conveyed a disturbing story that had begun fifteen months earlier. Her starting to date her pastor's son. Red flags she overlooked, although he'd been a different person in the beginning. Her concerns about his behavior, and his increasing mistreatment of her. And then someone calling to tell her he was at a bar with a woman, her confronting him in the parking lot as he escorted that woman to his car, and her ending their relationship then and there. By the time Janna finished with how people at the church blamed her for his losing his job, Luke was disgusted.

She met his gaze for only a moment. "And now I'm starting over. Again. Just like when Mom moved us away from here, and just like when Kayla's father went back home. Having seen Mom's life, I tried so hard to be careful about who I dated. But both times I trusted the wrong people. My decisions haven't been any more—"

"Janna." He took her hand. She startled, but he didn't let go. "With Kayla's father, you were young and made a decision. It wasn't a right decision, but you repented and God forgave you. But with this Mitch, you did nothing wrong. You do understand that?"

"Yeah." She sighed. "I'm just ready to be done with having to start over again."

Ach, he could relate. In some ways, he'd been trying to do the same for more than three years now. "Maybe that's why God brought you here, then—to start over where you were forced to leave off."

She considered that. "Maybe."

Realizing he still held her hand, he released it.

Honestly, having her and Kayla here was starting to feel like a new beginning for him. *Mamm*'s quality of life, physically and emotionally, was better. Joah loved having an ever-present playmate. And despite his occasional spats with Janna, Luke appreciated having her back—perhaps more than he should and for reasons he shouldn't at times.

But all things considered, what should he do with that?

CHAPTER 15

Unwelcome Visitor

Joah and Kayla sat on stools at the workbench by the back door when Janna went to check on them. A cool drizzle had been falling steadily all morning, keeping the children in the shop and workshop. They had an unfinished wall shelf to sand, with each one working on an end while giggling about something—probably Luke and Mahlon's two-part singing of an Old Order hymn as they assembled a dining table.

Janna joined the children at the workbench, grateful for the quiet Wednesday morning. Only one customer had come in, and there was just something about the workshop on rainy days. The usual woodworking smells, combined with the rain-scented breeze, the dim light from the open windows, and the familiar song from her childhood, brought a peace she savored.

Joah grinned, showing his missing top front teeth. "Daddy said you and him used to sand pieces together."

"We did. We used to sing that song as well."

Kayla looked up, her face scrunched. "It sounds funny."

"Kayla." But it wasn't like she could scold her. Janna had

also thought the singing was odd when she first started attending church with the Martins. "It's German, and the words are sung slow and drawn out. If I remember right, that song is taken from one of the psalms."

"Psalm 130." Luke's pleased confirmation from behind her brought butterflies to her stomach. She'd noticed that he'd stopped singing but hadn't heard him approach. He held her gaze for a few moments, smiling just enough to make the butterflies intensify, then slid his hand across the shelf. "You're doing a wonderful-good job."

As he looked back to Janna, the bell that announced a car had turned off the lane into the parking lot sounded. Good thing. For some reason, she was particularly enjoying his attention. Maybe because she was feeling so nostalgic. "Keep it up. And no arguing."

"We know," they said in monotonous unison.

She headed for the bathroom since she had time before the customer could park and come inside, then made her way to the shop.

In the doorway, she stopped as her stomach clenched tight. The customer had his back to her as he examined a quilt hanging near the front door, but she'd recognize the gelled dark hair, athletic build, and tight gray T-shirt and dark jeans anywhere. Her hope that Mitch would leave her alone, since he hadn't shown up in the week since Arissa's call, had been just wishful thinking.

She backed up into the workshop. Someone grasped her shoulders, and she clapped a hand over her mouth as she spun around. Luke stood only inches away. She pulled him away from the doorway. "He's here. In the shop."

After a moment, recognition lit his eyes. "You're sure?"

She nodded. What should she do? Seeing Mitch might frighten Kayla, but Janna had no idea how to get her out of there quickly. Maybe send her and Joah out the back door with instructions to hurry to the house? But Salena had women from church visiting. And how would Janna explain to the children why they suddenly needed to leave?

Or perhaps it would be best to have them stay in the workshop with Luke and Mahlon while she handled Mitch in the shop. "Keep the children back here while I talk to him."

Shaking his head, he opened his mouth.

She gripped his arm tighter. "He told Arissa he wanted to apologize. I can give him the chance."

"All right," he agreed, but with reluctance. "But if he causes any trouble, I'm coming in."

Good—maybe. Luke had enough contention in his life right now without having to defend his actions because of her too.

As she went into the shop, she silently repeated Salena's motto. "Good morning. Can I help you?"

Mitch turned around. His initial scowl at seeing her shifted to a grim smile as he crossed his arms. "If you wanted to hide, you should've parked your car in the barn. As soon as I reached the parking lot, I could see it in back of the house."

She stepped behind the counter, glad for something to put between them, and strove to portray a calm demeanor. "I'm not hiding." Maybe she should've tried to conceal the car better, though. Except he probably would've eventually found her anyway.

He stepped toward the counter. "You pulled a pretty good disappearing act. Took me a whole week to put together enough of what you'd told me about where you grew up."

"We were ready for something different."

He glanced around. "Farms. Cows. Horses and buggies. No electricity. Different, all right."

Had he missed the lights in the ceiling? "We have electricity. It's the Old Order Amish who don't."

Stopping five feet from the counter, he stared at her. Then his expression softened. "You look good, Jan. You're almost tanned."

Typical Mitch. She ignored that comment. "So do you. You look . . . happier."

"Well, I was. Until I went to your apartment and you were gone. No goodbye, no nothing."

So much for just apologizing.

"Mitch, I ended our relationship five months ago, and really, it was over before then. I was just trying to salvage it for Kayla's and your parents' sake. But after what you kept from me . . . what you were doing behind my back, I didn't owe you anything. You weren't the only one who suffered because of your choices. Kayla and I did as well."

He shifted his gaze to the floor, then returned it to her. His eyebrows knit in what looked like remorse as he moved closer. "I've missed her. Is she here?"

What he really meant was he wanted to see Kayla, but that wasn't going to happen. "She is."

"Can I—"

"That's not in her best interest."

He slammed his palm on the counter. "How can you say that? She's known me almost half her life."

She took a step back but kept her composure. Her heart now raced and her insides quivered, but he didn't need to know that. "The last time she saw you, you slapped me. That's not what I want my daughter—"

"Janna?" Luke came into the shop, thank goodness. "Everything all right? It sounded like something fell." He stopped beside her but stared at Mitch.

Mitch's jaw clenched. "Who's he?" He never took his eyes off Luke. "The guy you grew up with?"

This conversation needed to end. It was bad enough Luke

had probably heard what she'd just said, but Mitch's eyes narrowed like that only when he was furious. "Mitch, please," she said softly. "You told Arissa you wanted to find me so you could apologize. If that's the case, your apology is accepted. If not, I need to get back to work."

"Either way, it's time for you to leave," Luke added.

Mitch shook his head. "Unreal. I go and drive all this way and—"

The bells on the shop's front door clanged against the glass, and a tall, fiftyish police officer walked in. "Good morning, folks."

Relief and an incredible thankfulness washed through Janna. Luke must've called him, but how had he gotten here so soon?

Mitch had spun around, but now he glared at her. "You called the *police* on me?"

"I live across the road." The officer watched him with arched eyebrows as he neared where Mitch stood. "Just making a neighborly visit on my break. There a reason they'd need to call the police on you, son?"

"Ah," he growled. "I'm done here." Heading for the door, he tossed a hand out to his side without looking back. "Take care of yourself and Kayla."

Janna's chest ached as the door closed behind him, and she released her breath.

"I'll make sure he finds his way out of the area and let the other units know to keep an eye on you all." The officer nodded at Luke. "Don't be afraid to call again if you need to."

"We will. Thanks, Don."

As the man left, she remembered the children. "Where are Joah and Kayla?"

"They're fine." Luke stepped closer, grinning slightly.

"Mahlon has them in the storage room with him, looking for something that may or may not be there."

She laughed, but tears then filled her eyes. Whether they were from apprehension, embarrassment, or relief, she didn't know. Maybe all three. "Sorry."

"It's all right." He drew her to his side and rubbed her back.

This time she welcomed his consolation.

When Janna relaxed against him, Luke resisted the urge to wrap his arm around her. She still breathed heavily. Either that or she was trembling—or both. After what she'd said, he couldn't blame her. Not that he would've let Mitch lay a hand on her. Nonresistance didn't mean not protecting another person, especially a woman or a child. But thanks be to God, it hadn't come to that.

As much as he didn't want to move away, he should. Being so close to comfort her for a moment or two was one thing. Doing it for longer because it comforted him was another. He stepped away.

She swiped her hand across one cheek, then took a deep breath and released it.

Mahlon appeared in the doorway. "Everything all right?"

"*Ya*." Luke returned his attention to Janna. "Go on to the house. Mahlon and I can take care of any customers who come in."

She nodded, still not looking at him. Rounding the two men, she called, "Time to go in to make dinner."

Mahlon went back into the workshop, and moments later Joah and Kayla came jogging into the shop. On their way to the front door, they happily discussed what dessert they'd be having with the meal.

A hand on his side brought Luke's attention back to Janna, who now stood right next to him. "*Danki*," she whispered, then followed the children.

Her touch rendered him speechless for a moment, but he found his voice as she reached the door. "Janna."

She turned.

"We'll talk more later?"

She nodded, and the door closed behind her.

He definitely needed to know more about this Mitch Anderson—as soon as possible.

As Luke stood on the porch watching darkness begin to descend on the rolling fields beyond the shop, Don Smith's white pickup slowly made its way back the lane to the house. Luke wiped his arm across his forehead, then headed for where he parked near the end of the walkway.

Don got out still dressed in his uniform. "Sorry for the late visit—busy day today—but I wanted to check in with you folks."

"No problem. Janna was putting her daughter to bed, but let me see if she can come out." He turned toward the *daadi haus*, but she was already on the porch. With a hand he motioned her over. "We appreciated your help today."

Don nodded at Janna as she neared. "I'm Don Smith, since we didn't get to introduce ourselves earlier."

"Janna Carpenter. And thank you."

He gave a tight-lipped smile. "Well, I have some news. Probably good news for you, but definitely not for this Mitch fellow. He got himself stopped for speeding in Blue Ball. Turns out his license is suspended for a DUI back in March, and that means he's looking at a fine and sixty to ninety days of jail time."

Janna's eyes widened. "He's going to jail?"

"If he's convicted."

"For goodness' sake." Her expression and tone reflected sadness Luke hadn't expected. "He keeps getting himself into more and more trouble."

Guilt pricked Luke. His first reaction had been relief.

"Anyway, I just wanted to let you know," Don said. "If you want to file a complaint against him, I can take that."

She shook her head. "That won't be necessary."

Gut. Just having Don here in his uniform could bring discord, and perhaps Mitch's self-inflicted consequences would discourage him from causing more trouble.

"All right. Have a good night, then. And don't hesitate to call if you have more problems." After getting into the truck, Don lowered the window and smiled at Janna. "Luke said you lived in my place years back. If you want to come see it sometime—you know, for old time's sake—have him bring you over."

Janna stiffened but grinned. "Thank you."

Don backed up, then turned around in the shop's parking lot and headed for the road.

"He's done a real nice job renovating the whole house." Luke spoke as casually as he could. "I've only seen the half he lives in—he rents out the other half to a young couple—but his is the same side where you lived. The inside's even nicer than the outside."

She exhaled, staring past the parking lot to the far-off pasture and the road beyond it. "I don't know if I could go inside."

Just as he'd expected. "Because of what happened right before you moved?"

She grimaced. "The night that ruined my life."

His breath lodged in his chest. Had more happened than he realized? He hadn't been there for the whole incident. He'd been standing on the front porch waiting for her to get what she needed from inside when she screamed. That sent him running into the house, but he'd thought her mother's boyfriend had only frightened her. When Luke got through the front door, the man moved away from where he'd cornered Janna, and Luke rushed her out of there and back home with him. "What do you mean?"

"Less than two weeks after your *mamm* told Mom what happened, she moved us away. I think she did it to get away from the guy. Even she said he was crazy, and that day was the last straw." She met his gaze. "In a way, she deserves credit for protecting us, but she took me away."

With a hand on her back, he led her toward the *daadi haus*. "I always thought that had to do with you telling her you wanted to wear a head covering to church on Sundays like the other girls."

She stopped at the gate. "I never thought about that. But I did tell her right around then too." Scowling in thought, she opened the gate and walked toward the porch with him, then they sat on the step. "Maybe it was both. She wasn't happy about either."

And that gave him the opportunity to ask something else that had been on his mind. "How do you feel about that now? Wearing a covering, I mean."

"I certainly don't have a problem with women wearing one. Just about everyone I'm around now does. If you're talking about me specifically, though, I don't know that women *have* to wear one. A lot of Bible scholars claim it was cultural and not an instruction to all women. But if women want to do it, I'm fine with that."

Not the answer he'd hoped for, but not an unexpected one either.

Shaking her head, she sighed slowly. "Our beliefs may be similar, but I'll never be a sweet, serene Mennonite girl—not like the women from church. What happened today is proof of that. Our lives have been so different."

No way would he accept that, especially since many of her hardships hadn't been her fault. "The Bible says in Christ we're a new creation. Old things have passed away and all things have become new. You came here to start over, and you have. And you *are* sweet and serene"—he nudged her arm with his— "most of the time, anyway."

"Funny." She wrinkled her nose at him.

He chuckled. "At least someone thinks I am. And that's the same face you made at me when we were young."

She stared into his eyes, and the amusement turned to something else. Esteem—or even fondness? "You're so much like *Daadi* Eli."

Her tender smile, the sincerity in her voice, and the significance of those words seemed to paralyze his tongue. Finally, he grinned. "*Danki.*"

"He was such a good man. So are you." She stood. "I'd better start editing. Have a good night."

By the time he got up, she was in the *daadi haus*. And he was trying to figure out what just happened.

In the kitchen, Janna stopped and tried to catch her breath. What was wrong with her? After promising herself she wouldn't get too close to Luke—and doing a fairly good job of that—today had completely derailed her. This morning she'd welcomed his touch, even reciprocated, and now tonight her feelings were way out of control. Part of her and Kayla's new beginning included her not getting involved with a guy until they were settled and she was ready. And Luke, of all guys?

She jumped at the sound of her cell phone, then turned and grabbed it off the counter. Arissa. "Hey."

"You have got to be kidding me. I can't believe he found you."

Janna walked into the living room, where she'd be farthest from the doorway into the house, and plopped onto the chair outside the mostly closed bedroom door. "Well, we had talked about where I'd grown up, and he knew I'd thought about moving back."

"Still, it's crazy. And why aren't you more upset?"

Arissa didn't know everything yet. After lunch Janna had texted her what happened that morning, but she hadn't had the chance to send an update. She caught her up on the latest news.

"No way." Arissa drew out her response after listening without a word in. "Although I guess I shouldn't be that surprised. He's been in major self-destruct mode since, like, Thanksgiving. Did you know about the DUI?"

"No, that happened in March. After we broke up." Janna pulled her feet up and crossed her legs.

Arissa huffed. "Well, I'm just glad you're all right and that Luke stepped up for you. I didn't think he would."

Now that wasn't fair. "I did. I know you don't believe it, but he really is a great guy."

Silence.

Then Arissa said, "I don't like the way that sounded."

"What?"

"That you suddenly think he's a great guy. That's how you ended up with Mitch. His confronting that other guy at church who was pestering you—how he got him to leave you alone—is what attracted you to him. But then that protectiveness turned domineering after you two got together." She paused. "Honestly, it was probably the same way with Chad, if you think about it."

Janna squirmed at the mention of Kayla's father—and at the realization that Arissa might be right. She'd been drawn to how both men were protective and wanted to be in charge, but that had ended badly both times, just in different ways.

"And chances are, that's because of your growing up with the Martins," Arissa went on, now in full psych-nurse mode. "In their culture, the man is the head of the family, and you loved *Daadi* Eli and how he took care of you, so you probably went looking for that." She paused. "Now you're back with them, and Luke's the head of the family and being the care-taker. I just don't want you doing it with him too. Especially with him."

Arissa had a point. Multiple points, really, and good ones. Janna couldn't refute what she'd said, not that she'd admit it. "I'm just saying he's a good guy. That's all."

But was that all? Some of her feelings for Luke had changed today—deepened in ways she hadn't expected—and now they seemed so blurred. That scared her. Too much was at stake. She didn't want anything to damage her renewed rela-tionship with the Martins, and then she had Kayla to think about too. Kayla adored Luke even more than she had Mitch, and Janna couldn't risk her being hurt again.

Bottom line, no matter what she felt, her friendship with Luke needed to stay just that—a friendship.

CHAPTER 16

A Hard Decision

"Evening, folks."

At the familiar voice, Luke stopped talking and turned to look behind them. Wilmer and their church's elderly bishop, Harold—both dressed in black pants, a white shirt, and a black hat—slowly approached where he and Janna sat on the bench by the playset.

Ach, this had been such a pleasant day. He'd been able to get away from the shop early to take Joah fishing, and sitting out here had him completely relaxed. Until now.

Luke stood and rounded the bench.

"Your mother said I'd find you here." Wilmer glanced at Janna, who'd also risen. "I hope we're not interrupting."

"Not at all. Maybe you remember Janna Carpenter? She stayed with us a lot when I was growing up."

Wilmer nodded at her. "Eli spoke about you."

"This is Rayanne's uncle Wilmer who she lived with when she moved here," he told Janna. "And Harold is our bishop."

Well, *our* probably wasn't the right word. This visit most likely meant Luke would soon be put off the church.

"It's nice to meet you." After an uneasy silence, Janna shifted her gaze to Joah and Kayla on the swings. "I'm going to go push the children for a bit."

The men would speak their minds no matter who was listening, but he appreciated her discretion. "Would you like to sit?"

The two lowered themselves onto the bench, and Luke did the same.

"I was speaking to one of the brethren today," Harold began, "and he mentioned that a police vehicle was seen leaving here yesterday."

Luke stifled a sigh. Sometimes it seemed like eyes were everywhere. "Our neighbor across the road is an officer. He stopped to talk to me while he was on duty." That wasn't a lie, and he saw no reason to go into more detail unless questioned.

Wilmer's posture relaxed a bit. "Ah."

Luke stared at the grass a few feet in front of them so his attention wouldn't drift to Janna and the children. The men most likely hadn't come just to ask about the police, so he'd let them steer the conversation.

Wilmer cleared his throat. "Luke, it's been two months now since you and Joah have been at church, either on a Sunday or a Wednesday night. We've spoken a number of times, and I know the ministry and some of the other brethren have talked to you as well." Resting his hands on his knees, he looked directly at Luke. "If you're not at church tomorrow, that will prove your intention to no longer be a member of the congregation, and it will be announced that you're expelled from membership."

Every ounce of energy seemed to drain from Luke's body. He'd known this point would eventually come, but it still left him barely able to breathe.

Wilmer stared at him with his face drawn with what looked like physical pain. "I cannot understand why you would do this."

Luke bent forward, leaning on his elbows. "It has in no way been a simple decision for me. It's just that some of my beliefs are no longer in line with the congregation's anymore—and it's not that I want to live less plainly." He turned his head to the side to look at him and then Harold. "My beliefs have changed because I've read the Bible. For example, it clearly states that, as Christians, we're called to spread the gospel intentionally. But how can I teach my son that unless we're part of a church that encourages it?"

"Are you confirming that you have no intention to return to our church, then?" Harold asked.

What did he say to that? Cutting his ties to the congregation—to the people who'd been his family in faith for ten years —was *not* what he wanted, but he had only two options. Stay or leave. Granted, even as an expelled member he could attend church services and remain in fellowship with the other members, but some brothers and sisters had already distanced themselves, considering him disorderly.

"*Nee.* What I'm saying is that I need to do what I believe God would have me do, as determined by what the Bible says. My differing beliefs will eventually become a problem, not just for me but also for Joah."

Wilmer now stared straight ahead with his brow furrowed. "I see. And have you spoken to Ray and Titus?"

He hadn't, but that was nothing new. Rayanne and her mother had always initiated the phone calls and visits, and after her mother died, Rayanne had contact with her father only if she called him. Luke had tried to keep in touch with Ray after Rayanne's passing, but he'd spoken to him only once since Christmastime. His interaction with her only living sibling,

Titus, a brother twenty-one years older who had a large family, had been equally sporadic. "Not lately."

Wilmer rested a hand on Luke's shoulder. "Evelyn and I care very much for you and Joah. Rayanne became like another daughter in the time she lived with us, and I've always appreciated your honesty and integrity." His eyes watered as he shook his head. "This decision is so difficult for us to comprehend, but we'll continue to pray that you'll count the cost and realize the effects it will have."

Luke didn't respond. He'd never be able to explain in a way that Wilmer and Harold would truly understand, especially now since he doubted his ability to speak more than a few words without breaking down. "*Danki*," he said.

For the second time in ten years, he was considering something he'd once said he'd never do—leave his current church for one less conservative. It wasn't that he wanted a more worldly life, as many who left did, but that wouldn't change the end result.

He would be more than leaving a church. In some ways, he would be formally ending life as he and Joah knew it.

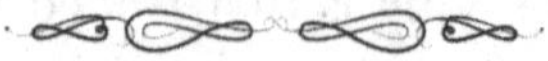

It was after nine o'clock when Janna could finally go into the house's kitchen for one of the brownies Salena and the children had baked that day. She'd headed there as soon as Kayla was in bed, but the sound of Luke and Salena's *Deitsch* conversation stopped her before she even reached the doorway into the house. Though their voices were hushed, the words she understood and their tense tones said enough.

Now with the house silent, Janna again heeded the call of the brownies. She wanted to finish her edit tonight, and some chocolate would give the cognitive wherewithal to get it done.

Not even two steps into the darkened kitchen, she collided with something that made her cry out as she went careening toward the back door.

A hand clamped onto her wrist, and a moment later Luke held her by both arms. *"Bisht alright?"*

Janna's heart raced as she took a step back. "I'm fine." When she looked up at him, thoughts of herself dissolved. The lamp in the *daadi haus*'s living room provided barely enough light to see in the kitchen, but when her eyes adjusted, the distress lining Luke's forehead and setting his jaw was obvious, and she doubted it had to do with their unexpected meeting. "Are *you* okay?"

Sighing, he released her and then shook his head. "I should be. I knew this was coming."

"This?" Part of her hesitated to encourage his confiding in her. That had brought them closer over the last several weeks, maybe closer than was sensible. But even so, she cared about him and wanted to know.

"Aren't you working?"

"I was, but now I'm getting a brownie. I'm thinking you were about to go for a walk, but if you'd like to talk, I can offer chocolate and a sympathetic ear."

He relaxed a little, and after a moment he nodded.

Minutes later, they sat at the table in the *daadi haus*, he on the end and she on the side bench. He took his first bite of brownie and washed it down with a swallow of milk. "If Joah and I aren't at church tomorrow morning, I'm going to be put off the church."

"Put off?"

"Expelled from membership."

Exactly what she'd suspected. It made her sad, knowing

how conflicted he must feel, then worry pricked her. What if he returned to his old church? He and Joah seemed so happy now, and she and Kayla enjoyed attending River View Mennonite Fellowship with them. Not that she should be making it about herself. "What are you going to do?"

He stared at the plate in front of him. "Follow my conscience. I believe God has led us to River View."

That was the answer she'd hoped for, but it didn't negate the reality of it. "That won't be easy for you."

"*Nee*. I've already talked to Joah. He'll miss his friends at church and school, but he's getting to know the children at River View and loves the service and Sunday school." He gave a sheepish grin. "So do I."

"He won't be able to go to his school anymore?" She hadn't considered that.

"They'd probably allow it with the hope I'd mend my ways and rejoin the church, but I don't want to stir up trouble. I've already talked to the principal at the school most of the children from River View attend. It's only ten minutes from here, and Mahlon's love it." He looked at her. "Hard to believe, but school starts in four weeks."

"I know." And she needed to get Kayla registered in Akron.

"You could enroll Kayla there too. She'd already know some of the children, and I'm sure you'd like her to get the same teaching at school that she gets at home and in church."

True, but . . . "That probably won't be in the budget."

He focused on his brownie while breaking off a piece. "River View encourages Christian education so much that it has a scholarship fund that pays a portion of tuition. And if it's still too expensive, we could help."

No. No way. She stopped chewing, but she couldn't respond with her mouth full and swallowed hard. "I couldn't let you do that."

"*Ya*, you could. The money we have is not ours but the Lord's. I think he'd consider it a worthwhile use, not?"

Undeniably. Still, she wouldn't allow it.

"At least think about it? Look at their website?"

No harm in that, except that it might weaken her resolve. But she did need to consider something else. "How far is it from Akron?" Their rental was only a five-minute walk from the public school Kayla would attend—one of the reasons Janna had chosen it.

He blinked, and she thought she saw disappointment in his brief scowl. "Maybe fifteen minutes. Or she could ride their bus." He lowered his gaze to the plate again and broke off another piece of brownie. "Has anyone given you an idea when the Akron house will be ready?"

"I talked to Mrs. Bollinger last week. The work was delayed because of the insurance company, but she thinks late August, just before school starts."

"So about four weeks for your move too."

Now she was sorry she'd brought it up. His night had already been difficult, and she'd just made it worse by reminding him he was losing her help.

And truth be told, the thought of moving no longer brought her just happy anticipation. She and Kayla would miss the Martins and the farm, more than she wanted to admit.

Luke was sitting at the desk in the workshop, talking to Mahlon who'd just returned after going home for dinner, when Janna came in from the shop.

"I just wanted to let you know we're leaving for Joah's PT," she said when they looked at her. "*Mamm*'s taking her rest, and

Malinda should be here shortly to take care of the shop. Do you need anything while we're out?"

Ah. The perfect time to ask what he needed to. "*Nee.* Are you busy with anything tomorrow?"

She scowled in thought. "No. Why?"

"A customer who works for Strasburg Rail Road sent me four tickets as a thank-you." He picked up the envelope he'd set aside. "Mahlon and I are going back to not working Wednesdays now that we're caught up on custom orders, so what do you think about you and I taking Joah and Kayla tomorrow? Strasburg sells discount tickets for Cherry Crest Adventure Farm, so we could get off the train at Groff's Grove and walk over there, spend some time, then ride the train back in the afternoon."

Her face brightened as he'd hoped it would. "They'd love that. One of the boys from church told them about Cherry Crest, and Kayla's asked about going there."

"Then it can be a kind of three-days-early birthday present for her"—he arched his eyebrows at her as he stood from the desk chair—"and you."

She crossed her arms. "I told you, no birthday present, at least not for me. If you want to do something little for Kayla, that's fine, but not for me."

Mahlon laughed and headed for the workbench. "Good luck with that, Janna. Salena tells him the same thing every year."

Luke held up both hands. "I promised I wouldn't buy anything, and I won't." Of course, buying a gift wasn't his only option.

She eyed him skeptically, but that faded as she unfolded her arms. "Are you going to tell them or make it a surprise?"

He grinned. "Surprise. I thought about not telling you either, but I didn't know if you had anything planned."

Her smile returned, and she just looked at him for a few moments. Then she inhaled. "I'd better get going."

"Let me know when you're back. And be careful."

She wrinkled her nose at him. "Always." Moments later she was gone.

Luke crossed the floor to their work area but stopped short. Mahlon sat on a stool at his workbench, watching him. "What?"

Mahlon shrugged. "Just observing."

That meant he'd soon be questioning. Might as well get it over with. "And what do you observe, wise cousin?"

"A friendship that both delights and concerns me."

Definitely not the response Luke had expected, but he knew Mahlon well enough—and Mahlon knew him well enough—that he respected his counsel. Instead of replying, he sat on the other stool at the workbench and waited.

"It delights me because you're starting to live life again. Smiling. Laughing. Enjoying yourself. Having Janna and Kayla here has been good for you."

Luke couldn't deny that.

"And lately I've seen the way you and Janna interact. How you look at each other every now and then, how you're comfortable with each other. Now tomorrow you're taking the children to Strasburg. So I have to wonder—"

"We're friends." Best to make that clear. "As far as I'm concerned, she's family." That wasn't a lie, but was it true? Never had hugging a family member elicited the contentment and happiness he felt when he'd held Janna. Only one other person had done that, and he'd been married to her. Which made this a slippery slope.

Mahlon nodded. "But . . ."

Ach, what did he say? Even he had difficulty sorting it all out. "I care about her. And not just because she's been the help we need. Because she's . . . *her*. She's part of my childhood . . . part of me, even. We have our differences, but we also have things in common that outweigh that." He sighed, determining to be honest. "And yet I hesitate too, because Rayanne—"

"Rayanne has been with the Lord for more than three years now." Mahlon spoke the words matter-of-factly as he looked Luke in the eye. "It's not at all wrong for you to move on with your life."

He couldn't deny that either. "I know. But I can't help feeling that . . . that I should've been there when she got sick, that I should've made sure she went to the hospital right away and the doctors there contacted the clinic for care instructions." There. After all this time, he'd finally said aloud what had been tormenting him. "And that's made moving on seem so . . ." How could he explain it?

Mahlon stared at him. "Luke. It wasn't your fault, and I truly hope you don't believe it was. Rayanne chose to go to New York even though you couldn't go along. You wanted her to wait until you finished the custom orders that were already scheduled."

Ya, and he should've insisted on it. But he didn't that time. Instead, he gave in to her independence and let her have her way despite how it put him ill at ease. Less than a week later he was driving the five hours to her hometown, where he found her in the hospital, almost comatose from cerebral edema. "Worst decision I ever made."

"We've all made decisions we wish we could change," Mahlon said, "and by far, some are harder to accept than others. But we also need to remember that the Lord determines our days. He has a plan for each person's life, whether or not we understand that plan while we're here on earth."

"I know, and I wouldn't say I blame myself. The circumstances just make it . . . difficult, I guess. I haven't wanted to even consider a relationship with a woman." Until Janna. But he couldn't say that. "But having Janna back—her help and friendship—has reminded me how men and women complement each other."

Mahlon nodded. "Indeed we do. And I can't imagine that Rayanne would want you to stay a widower. If the tables were turned, wouldn't you want her to remarry—and for Joah to have a father in your absence?"

Yet another thing he couldn't refute. In light of Rayanne's MSUD, they'd discussed remarriage, so he knew Mahlon was right. "Of course."

Mahlon sat up straighter. "Now, back to Janna. As much as it brings me joy to see you happy, I have concerns too. You've lived your life in the Old Order communities. She's lived in the world. Even though you're both at River View now, you must realize your differences would make a relationship complicated . . . even imprudent."

He realized it, all right. Especially in the middle of the night when he was supposed to be sleeping, not trying to come up with a solution.

"I'm not saying there's no hope," Mahlon added. "With God all things are possible. But compromises would be necessary. You'd need to address that before entering a courtship."

"*Ya*." Complicated was right. And that wasn't even taking into consideration that Janna and Kayla would soon be moving off the farm to Akron—back into the world.

Ach, he had a lot of praying to do.

The shop's front door opened and closed, followed by Malinda's cheerful greeting.

With a nod, Luke stood. Time to get back to work and get his mind on something else. If he could.

CHAPTER 17

Photographs

The day couldn't have gone much better. Joah and Kayla had loved the steam train ride from Strasburg Rail Road to Groff's Grove, their early picnic dinner—cold fried chicken, coleslaw, fruit salad, and cookies—had been delicious, and the four and a half hours spent at Cherry Crest had been even more fun than Luke had imagined. Even the cloud cover, which kept the weather unusually comfortable for the second of August, now gave way to clear-blue sky. The day had been just as much a gift for him as for Kayla.

"Thirsty?" He stopped beside Janna, who still stood by the hay bales that fenced in the pedal carts Joah and Kayla were driving around the track for smaller kids.

She turned and smiled at the cup of lemonade he held out to her. "I was wondering where you went. *Danki.*"

Gut. He was hoping she wouldn't give him a hard time about spending money on her and Kayla. That had to mean she was as glad for a drink as he was. Apparently, the children were thirsty as well, because they parked their pedal carts and came running.

"Here." He handed his cup to Joah while Janna gave hers to Kayla, then chuckled as Joah drank. "Make sure you leave me some."

Joah gulped down another swallow and handed the half-full cup back to him. "Daddy, my legs are sore."

Janna smoothed the curls of Kayla's hair that had come loose from her two braids. "It's almost four o'clock anyway. We need to get back to Groff's Grove to catch the train."

Ya. The last train of the day left at four, so if they didn't get it on its way to the turnaround or on its way back, they'd be walking the two miles back to Strasburg.

Kayla returned her cup to Janna. "Can we come back another time?"

"Like for my birthday?" Joah's question cut off what Janna was about to say. "And maybe Mahlon's could come along. Naomi, Amanda, and Caleb would love it. Drew too, even though he's little."

"I'm sure they would." With a hand on Joah's shoulder, Luke guided him toward the exit to the railroad tracks.

Joah's steps soon slowed, and he stopped before they were halfway to the tracks. "Will you carry me, Daddy?" He'd never been a complainer, and his drawn expression confirmed his words. After nearly a month in the AFOs and with continued PT and home exercises with Janna each day, his feet and ankles were considerably stronger than when the casts came off. Still, they'd done a lot today.

He downed the last of the lemonade, then tossed the cup in a nearby trash can and lifted him onto his hip. Really, he should be thankful. Before he knew it, Joah would be too old to be carried. And unlike Mahlon, Luke didn't have more little ones to come.

"I'm tired too," Kayla said. "Mama, will you carry me?"

"My daddy can carry you." Joah wrapped his arm around Luke's neck as he looked over his shoulder. "He picks up furniture all the time. He can carry both of us."

That was true. And Janna already had their backpack of belongings on her back and still held the remainder of her and Kayla's lemonade. He held out his free arm. "Come on, sweetheart."

"Luke, are you sure?" Janna said.

He scooped Kayla up onto his other hip and grinned at Janna. "That they're lighter than furniture? *Ya*."

Smiling back, she stepped into pace beside him. "Funny."

The children obviously thought so. Looking across his shoulders at each other, they giggled away.

When they reached Groff's Grove, all the picnic tables beneath the canopy of trees were empty except for one. A white-haired couple who looked to be in their seventies sat side by side on the bench of a table directly behind the train-stop shelter, holding hands.

Luke smiled and nodded to them, and they responded in kind.

"Can we play on the seesaws?" Kayla asked, pointing to the play area, as he set her and Joah on the ground.

"*Nee*, stay here." Janna slipped off the backpack and set it on the bench of the nearest picnic table, then sat down. "The train should be here soon, and we'll need to get on quickly so it doesn't have to wait for us. Why don't you come sit with me and rest awhile."

They obeyed, Kayla on her lap and Joah beside her, and Luke lowered himself onto the bench on Joah's other side.

Kayla twisted around. "Where's your phone, Mama? We should take a picture of us all together."

Janna balked, glancing at Luke.

He shrugged. Seemed harmless enough. "Why not?"

She hesitated again, then pulled her phone from the backpack's front pocket. While she readied the phone, Luke lifted Joah and slid next to her, placing Joah on his leg.

"May I help?" The older woman had stood and now walked around their table. "If you can show me how to take a picture with that, I'll do it for you."

"Oh. Yes, thank you." Janna quickly demonstrated, then handed the phone over.

The woman took a few pictures, grinning. "Now that wasn't so hard." As she handed the phone back, the train whistle sounded in the distance. She glanced at her husband, who slowly rose. "Merrill proposed to me right here in this grove fifty-three years ago today. I wasn't even eighteen and he was nineteen, and our families said we would never last because our backgrounds were so different. We married two months later and had seven children over the next twenty years." When her husband joined her, she took his hand and smiled. "Every year since, we've come back to celebrate."

"That's so sweet." Janna smiled. "Happy anniversary to you."

The whistle sounded again, this time closer, and the children jumped up and headed for the wooden steps that led down into the shelter.

She grabbed the backpack and followed. "Keep back from the tracks. Stay by the bench to wait."

Luke nodded again as he stood. "Thank you. And may God bless you with many more years together."

The woman glanced down to where Janna held each of the children in front of her as they looked down the track toward the coming train. "You have a beautiful family. Enjoy them. Time passes quickly."

"Oh." He almost let it go rather than correct her, but that

wouldn't be right. It wasn't truthful, and what if they ended up on the same train car and talking more? "They're not my family. Well, the boy's my son. She's a family friend, and the little girl's her daughter."

A family friend who just happened to live in his house, care for his child, and help and care for his grandmother—and him, really. *Ya*, that was the truth. Janna was just a friend. And after the day they'd had together, the truth hurt.

"Kayla brought me your cell phone this morning." Salena cast a sideways glance at Janna as the two of them stood at the sink washing the dinner dishes. "She showed me a picture of the four of you and said a woman you met at the picnic grove took it."

Janna groaned inwardly. Maybe it was time to start hiding her phone when she left it in the *daadi haus* while she was in the shop. Either that or she needed to change her PIN so Kayla couldn't use the phone on her own. "Oh?" She had no idea what else to say. Salena didn't seem upset, but there had to be a reason she'd brought it up.

"She also said yesterday was the best day of her life." A slight smile came to her lips as she slid the plate she'd washed into the rinse water. "Joah said the same thing."

Janna removed the plate and dried it with her hand towel. "They had a really good time. We all did."

"I could see that." Salena's reserved tone made it hard to determine how she felt about the photo, though she'd never hidden the fact that she disapproved of cell phone and camera use. "'Tis been a long time—years, for sure and certain—since Luke's looked as happy as he did in that picture."

Janna removed the next plate and dried it. When she and Salena discussed things they didn't agree on, it was better to just listen. Too often, Janna's attempts to explain came off sounding like she was trying to rationalize something she'd done wrong. Maybe because that was how she usually felt—that she needed to defend a poor choice.

"I've seen a change in him, and in Joah." She picked up another plate but just held it instead of placing it in the sudsy water. "It does my heart *gut* to see them happy. But it *verhuddles* me too."

"Why is that?" Not that she needed to ask.

She set the plate on the counter and faced her. "Luke has made some troubling decisions, especially in the last six months, and they've not come without cost. Now, I'm not saying you had anything to do with those decisions—many were made before you were here—but people are watching him. He could still have his church membership reinstated, or even join our church, but not if he doesn't take care with his actions."

Janna might as well just save time and say it. "You mean his friendship with me."

Salena pressed her lips together, her eyes searching Janna's face. "Is that what it is, then?"

Surely she couldn't think there was more to it. They lived under the same roof, and any other setup would hardly be appropriate. And that was only one part of what would be a problematic relationship on so many levels. "Yes."

But going by Salena's response, or lack of one, she wasn't convinced.

"It's the truth. Dating is the last thing on my mind anyway. Luke's a good man—the kind of man a woman should desire for a husband—but I'm not what he'd want for a wife." Well, that had been more than she'd planned on saying, but she might as well finish. "Being here has been a blessing for Kayla and me, but in a few weeks our house will be ready. I need to concentrate on getting us settled and on our feet."

Salena nodded and placed her hand on the back of Janna's arm.

Janna swallowed. That was the truth, and she did have more important things to attend to. So why did hearing it aloud make her heart feel so heavy?

When Luke stopped in the doorway into the kitchen, the two women stood at the sink with their backs to him. *Mamm* held onto Janna's arm. "*Ach*, you'll be sorely missed."

"*Ya*, you will."

They both spun around at the sound of his voice, and he stepped into the room.

Mamm stared at him. "I thought you'd gone back to the workshop."

Just as he'd expected—though she never shied away from making her thoughts known, and what she'd told Janna were all things she'd said to him too. "I was upstairs. Then in the living room paying a couple of bills."

Janna's lips parted as her brow creased with what could be sympathy or remorse. Probably sympathy. Nothing she'd said should bring guilt. She'd told the truth.

Not that all of it was what he wanted to hear. What she'd said about him being a good man had sent his spirits soaring, probably too much. But the part about her not being what he'd want in a wife, and then her desire to settle in Akron—just her and Kayla—had felt like a blow to his chest.

He started toward the back door. "Janna and I are friends, and her and Kayla being here has been good for us. We had a great time yesterday, and I saw no reason why we shouldn't have a reminder of that memory." At the back door, he grabbed his hat off the pegboard and put it on. "Don't be giving her a hard time about the picture. I'm pretty sure you still have your photos of her from when she was a child, not?"

Mamm pursed her lips.

Janna faced her, her expression brightening. "You have pictures? Will you show me?"

She sighed but then smiled. "Of course. As soon as we're finished here."

"*Now* I'm going to the workshop." Luke went out the screen door and let it slap behind him.

While the picture of the four of them was a reminder of a day he didn't want to forget, somehow that memory now seemed bittersweet.

Janna still couldn't believe it as she followed Salena up the stairs. Photos—from when she was a child. Why hadn't Salena mentioned them before? She'd had plenty of time to do so.

Actually, Janna did know why. Photographs, especially ones solely of people, were considered prideful by the *gmay*. But Salena had photos of her, and surely she knew Janna would want to see them. Unlike how she didn't allow Janna into the bedroom she'd used as a child, even to clean—it was Luke's now, after all—not showing her the photos made less sense.

In her sparsely furnished bedroom, Salena lifted the lid of the hope chest sitting against the footboard of the antique oak bed. "That there." She pointed to the square cardboard box nestled among neatly folded bed linens. "Would you get it for me?"

Janna lifted it out and set it on the end of the bed. Not wanting to seem too eager, she stepped back.

Salena closed the chest lid, then sat down on it and indicated the bed on the other side of the box. "Sit." With slightly shaking hands, she unfolded the box flaps.

On top sat pink double-knit fabric Janna would've recognized anywhere. "My dress," she whispered, then grasped it by the shoulder seams, letting it unfold onto her lap. The small-floral-print dress had been her favorite for years, thanks to how Salena had sewed it to fit loose and have a deep hem that could be let out as Janna grew. "I always loved this one."

Salena smiled, albeit sadly, as she touched the long sleeve. "That's why I kept it instead of passing it on to someone else." When their eyes met, she asked, "Would it fit Kayla, do you think?"

"Not yet. I was probably ten or eleven the last time I wore it." And would she really want Kayla wearing it, even if it did fit her? Something about Kayla wearing a Plain dress seemed off—although Janna never had a problem with it when she was a child. "But I'm glad you kept it."

Next Salena pulled out a white eight-by-ten envelope. She opened the end and tipped it till a small stack of five-by-seven school pictures slid into her hand. "I remember the first time you brought pictures home. You were so happy you had one to give us, and neither *Daadi* nor I could refuse it."

Janna's throat tightened as she took them. Finally, she'd know what she looked like as a child. Salena and Malinda had both remarked how much Kayla resembled her, but Janna had no photographs from her childhood. Mom never had a camera, and who knew what had happened to the school pictures. They hadn't been in the three storage bins the hospice gave her when Mom died.

The photos were in chronological order, from second grade

to sixth grade. Her hair was long and wavy like Kayla's though a little darker, her eyes were green instead of blue, and she had more freckles. But the resemblance was undeniable. "Wait till Kayla sees these," she murmured, again looking at herself as a seven-year-old. "Would it be all right if I took them to Walmart and had copies made?"

Salena shifted on the chest but didn't answer.

Janna looked up to find her expression sober. Then she realized why. Chances were good that no one—well, except Luke—knew she had the pictures. And she needed to keep it that way.

"You could have the copies made and then show them to the children, I reckon." Though her tone sounded unsure, she nodded.

"Of course. I wouldn't mention your having them."

Salena nodded again, concern no longer lining her forehead. "And then I have this." She pulled out a four-inch-by-six-inch brown photo album. "A few years ago, we were at a family reunion, and Mahlon's mother had brought some books of pictures from past reunions. Some of the pictures had you and Luke in them, and she must have seen how I enjoyed looking at them, because later that week Mahlon brought me this book she'd put together."

Janna took the album, then moved the box so she could slide next to her. When she opened it, sure enough, the album's clear plastic sleeves displayed back-to-back pictures of her and Luke. In most of them they were with other children—playing games, eating ice cream cones, sitting at a picnic table eating pie —but a few of the photos were of just the two of them. In one, they were smiling at the camera while each holding a black-and-white kitten. She was probably eight, so Luke would've been nine and a half.

"Goodness. I remember this. Those kittens were so soft. I see a little bit of Joah in him—in the eyes, I think."

Salena grinned, canting her head to look at that picture more closely. "He's always looked more like Rayanne, but he has Luke's eyes and hair. And the freckles Luke had. That's one of my favorites. There's another one too." She turned the page and pointed. "This one."

Tears filled Janna's eyes. Before them was a photo of *Daadi* Eli, with his black hat and suspenders, sitting on a porch swing between Luke and Janna. He had an arm around each of them, and all three were smiling for the camera. Maybe ten years old, Janna wore the pink dress that now lay on the bed, and her hair hung in two long braids. "I love that." The one on the facing page was similar, except only *Daadi* Eli was looking at the camera. She and Luke both leaned forward, looking at each other and laughing about something. "And this. That's how I remember us."

"*Ya*, that's how I remember you too. Two peas in a pod, and usually up to something." Salena's smile faded, and she tapped the picture with her finger. "This is why you and Luke must be careful. Growing up, you were the best of friends, and that still connects you in a special way even after all your years apart, I think. But you're not children anymore."

No, they weren't. And Salena was likely right. While Janna had felt that type of connection with Luke only a few brief times during the first month she and Kayla had been living there, in the last weeks that had changed—especially since Wednesday. Clearly, Salena had seen it too.

"You *must* take care, for your sake and his."

A flood of emotion suddenly brought tears to her eyes, and Janna wiped away the one that slid down her face.

Salena placed a hand on her shoulder and squeezed it.

"Things happened that hurt all of us. But now here you are. And I hope you know how much *Daadi* loved you."

Unable to answer, she nodded as more tears fell. Salena thought they were shed for the past—for *Daadi* Eli—and that was best. But they were also for the years with the Martins she'd loved and then lost.

And for the connection with Luke she'd missed and again longed for, but didn't dare pursue.

Unexpected Gifts

Kayla gasped as she pushed aside the white tissue paper that covered her birthday present. "An American Girl?" she squealed, snatching the auburn-haired, blue-eyed doll from the cardboard box on her lap. "A Truly Me doll!" Her eyes sparkled as she looked up at Janna. "You really got me one!"

Janna's heart twinged at the combination of joy and disbelief on her daughter's face, thrilled that she'd been able to get her something she desperately wanted yet sad that it had taken her two years to do it. Even now such a gift had been possible only because she found the doll at the Re-Uzit Shop. Thank goodness Salena had been with them and could occupy the children at the back of the store so Janna could purchase the doll and hide it in the back of the van.

Kayla jumped up from the *daadi haus* couch, knocking the box to the floor, and held the doll out so she could look over its silver-star-emblazoned bright-pink sweatshirt dress and gray leggings. "Mama, she looks just like me!"

The happy tears in her eyes tightened Janna's throat. "Yes, she does." That had been a birthday present to her from God. Finding an American Girl doll for just fifteen dollars was incredible, but finding one exactly like Kayla wanted—just two weeks before her birthday? That had to be a God thing.

"I love her so much!" Kayla hugged Janna as tightly as she did the doll. "Thank you!"

"We have something for you too," Joah said from the recliner where he sat on Luke's lap. "The bigger box is from Daddy and me, and the other one is from *Mammi* Salena. Open them."

With the doll tucked under one arm, Kayla untied the pink yarn that held the larger cardboard box closed with a tied bow on the top. Lifting the flaps brought another gasp from her. "A bed for her!" She set the doll on Janna's lap so she could lift it out of the box.

"We made it for you." Joah smiled shyly. "I helped Daddy sand and paint it. And *Mammi* Salena sewed the pillow and quilt."

The white sleigh bed with its patchwork quilt of pastel calico squares was gorgeous. The fine craftmanship and expert sewing made it look like a piece that would be found in an expensive furniture store, just in miniature.

Kayla set the bed on the floor, then dropped to her knees next to it and tucked the doll under the bedding. "She fits perfectly." Beaming at them, she got up and hurried to the side of the chair and embraced both of them at once. "*Danki.*"

Luke squeezed her shoulder. "We're glad you like it."

"I *love* it."

"Open the one from *Mammi* Salena too." Joah pointed to the last box.

Kayla obliged, and within moments she was holding up clothing for her doll. A white nightgown came out first, then two double-knit dresses, one purple floral and one light-blue floral. She looked at Salena. "These are like your dresses!"

Salena grinned from her place at the end of the couch. "I made them from my leftover material. There's something else in there too."

Kayla removed more tissue paper, then more of the light-blue floral fabric. "A dress for me! Just like my doll's—and just like yours!" Standing, she held it to her torso and looked down at herself. "And it's just like—" She clapped a hand over her mouth.

"Just like what?" Janna asked.

Kayla didn't respond. Apparently, she'd said too much. After hugging Salena, she knelt and slid a shirt box decorated with crayoned flowers from under the couch, then got up and set it on Janna's lap. "This is from *Mammi* Salena, Joah, and me."

So this was what the three of them had been scheming about for the last week. "Thank you."

After slitting the tape on the sides, she lifted the lid and read the equally colorful handmade birthday card inside. Underneath the tissue paper sat a folded square of the same blue floral fabric.

A dress for her too? Oh dear.

Kayla unfolded it. "We didn't have enough fabric to make a dress for you, so we made a skirt. Now we'll all match."

Relief washed through Janna. As much as she loved the idea of matching Kayla, wearing a double-knit dress—even one without a cape—wouldn't feel right. She'd agreed to Salena making Kayla a simple dress, but Janna wearing one made of the fabric Old Order Mennonites used was a different story. A skirt she could handle, though, and the fabric was lovely.

Kayla picked up her doll again. "I helped hem it. And Joah and me wrapped it."

She smiled around at each of them. "It's beautiful. I love it . . . and the card."

Joah turned to look at Luke. "Can we have cake now?"

"Sounds like a good idea to me." He set Joah on the floor.

As they all headed for the house's kitchen, Joah slipped his arms around Janna's waist. "Did you have a happy birthday?"

She squeezed him to one side and Kayla and her doll to the other. "The happiest."

Kayla grinned up at her. "'Cause you got to spend it with us?"

Out of the mouths of babes. "That's exactly why."

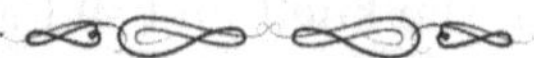

Luke had just walked into his bedroom after coming inside from taking out the trash when his cell phone vibrated in his pocket.

Ah. Janna must've found her birthday gift—finally. He'd expected her to realize its presence as soon as she and Kayla returned to the *daadi haus*, but that had been a half hour ago. At least she hadn't gone to bed without seeing it.

Mamm was still awake and getting ready for bed, so he shut the door behind him and pulled out the phone. Sure enough, Janna had texted him.

OMGoodness. Can you come down?

She didn't sound upset, thankfully, although gauging tone in a text was difficult. One of the reasons he didn't like texting. Well, unless it was with Janna.

Be right there.

Shoving the phone back into his pocket, he quietly went downstairs.

The door between the kitchen and the *daadi haus* was now open—it had been closed just minutes before—and Janna stood in the front corner of the living room. Her back was to him, but one hand sat atop the black corner desk decorated with the pink gift bow he'd picked up at Dollar Tree.

"Everything all right?" he asked as he neared.

She turned around, moving her hand to the matching ladder-back chair, and smiled despite how she also worked to keep her chin from quivering. "I'm thinking you know something about this?"

He stopped a few feet from her. Keeping a straight face was hard. "What? Because I happen to make furniture?"

"*Ya*, and because this is so much nicer than anything online. Only you could build something this beautiful."

Not exactly true. "Well . . . Mahlon could too."

She exhaled in amused exasperation, though still close to tears. "But he didn't make it. You did."

Ach, he'd had his fun. Now it was time to fess up. "Happy birthday."

The look of admiration she cast at the desk confirmed her delight—just the reaction he'd hoped for. "How did you know? And how did you get it in here without me knowing it? We were together all evening."

"I asked Kayla if she knew what one piece of furniture you'd want if you could have it. She said you really liked a black corner desk you'd seen online, and I had her show me on my phone."

Of course, he'd added the narrow shelves underneath between the side legs and the back leg, as well as the low hutch with drawers on the top. "I just added a chair and gave it a few more features. There's a keyboard shelf under the big drawer, so if you want to work on your computer here, you can, and the top is the right height for writing letters or Bible study."

He shrugged. "And when I asked you to get Joah ready for bed so I could help Ivan with something . . . well, I was helping him bring it over from the shop. What did Kayla say?"

"She didn't see it. It was dark when we came in, and we went through the kitchen to the bedroom. She was so excited about putting the nightgown on her doll and getting her into her bed, and then we called and talked to Cynthia. She was asleep when I got off the phone and came out here. Did she and Joah know about it?"

"*Nee.* I was afraid they'd slip up and say something."

She shook her head. "I can't believe you managed to make it without my knowing. I'm out in the shop at some point almost every day." After glancing back at it again, she smiled. "I'd scold you for getting me something after I told you not to, but I love it too much. You have no idea how much it means to me." Tears filled her eyes, and she covered her mouth with one hand.

Ach, something had to be wrong. "Hey now." He moved closer. "Those are more than just tears of joy. *Was iss letz?*"

She wiped her eyes, recomposing herself. "Sorry. I don't know. I guess . . . It's just been so long since I got a tangible gift for my birthday. Arissa's always taken Kayla and me to Ocean City for the weekend around our birthday—which was wonderful—and Mitch took me to an expensive restaurant, but that was his choice, not mine."

"What about Cynthia?"

"She's Quaker. Quakers traditionally didn't celebrate birthdays, and her family kept that practice even after most everyone else left it behind."

Hmm. Even Old Order Mennonites weren't quite that stringent—well, most of them. His family had never been extravagant by any means, but they gave practical gifts on birthdays and at Christmas.

Scowling, she sighed. "I'm being ungrateful. I should be thankful for everything, and I am, but when I turned on the light and saw this, and it was a complete surprise and so amazing . . ." She exhaled again. "I'm talking too much. It's perfect and I love it." Stepping closer, she slipped her arms around him. "Thank you."

Her sincere response touched him. Wrapping his arms around her, he cradled her head against his shoulder and rested his cheek against her hair. "And I was afraid you'd be upset with me."

"*Nee*." She drew back slightly. "Between Wednesday and now today, this has been such a perfect birthday." Her hand cupped his cheek, and as he lifted his head, her lips gently pressed against his.

Adrenaline coursed through him, and it took every ounce of his self-discipline to not respond.

Abruptly, she pulled away. "I'm so sorry. I wasn't trying to . . . I was just going to kiss you on the cheek, not . . ."

Ach, this was exactly why any show of affection outside marriage was asking for trouble. He released her but kept hold of her arms. It seemed she might run if he didn't—although who knew where—and that would complicate the situation even more. "*Macht nichts*. It wasn't your fault. No harm done."

"*Ya*." She swallowed. Even in the dim light of the one lamp in the room, the redness of her cheeks obviously deepened. "It's getting late."

But would just walking away without saying more be best? Talking it out seemed prudent, although they'd already clarified it was unintentional. What more was there to say? With a light squeeze, he released her arms and stepped back. "*Guder nacht*."

She only nodded.

The walk to the doorway into the house seemed never-ending, and after closing the door, he leaned against the kitchen counter to collect his wits.

No harm done? His mouth may have said that, but everything else in him said otherwise.

As soon as the door closed, Janna lowered herself onto the couch. Her heart pounded so hard she felt light-headed.

What had she done? What in the *world* had she done? Kissing him had been a bad idea, even the peck on the cheek she'd planned. At the time it hadn't seemed inappropriate—just a way of showing her thanks for everything he'd done to make her and Kayla's birthday special. Just like she'd kissed Salena earlier that evening.

Apparently he'd moved, because she'd had no intention of kissing him on the lips. That had been coincidental, no doubt, but what about afterward? Neither of them had withdrawn right away. And had he held her there, even? His hand had already been on the back of her head, and he didn't release her until she pulled away.

It happened so fast, she couldn't remember—and yet it hadn't happened as quickly as it could have. Or should have.

Now what? In less than eight hours, they'd be sitting at the same table for breakfast. How would she pretend nothing was amiss when she couldn't look him in the eye? He'd acted like what happened was no big deal, but surely he didn't feel that way. Old Order men didn't show any type of affection to a woman who wasn't their wife or a close family member, not even in a platonic way. How would he not be disturbed by a woman—one from outside the community, no less—kissing him?

Granted, they were friends. Good friends again, lately. And granted, Luke was probably less strict than most Old Order men. Maybe he simply considered it nothing more than an accident and saw no reason for concern. He was so good at curtailing his feelings sometimes. For all she knew, he was angry. Well, probably not. Whenever he got upset with her, he made that clear.

After drawing a breath, she released it and stood. It was getting late, and her current editing project awaited her. She could even sit at her new desk tonight—if she could get herself in the right frame of mind to work.

Goodness, the desk was beautiful, even in its simplicity. Hours of work had to have gone into it, and her stomach fluttered as she ran her hand over its smooth top again.

Just last week, Luke had said that as he worked on a piece, he took time to pray for whoever would become its owner. So he'd prayed for her as he built and finished it. That warmed her heart as much as the thought of him holding her. This time it hadn't been the obligatory side hug, either. He'd embraced her with tenderness. And she'd relished every moment of it.

Oh, she needed to do some praying. For him. For her. For wisdom to know how to handle the ever-building feelings for him she'd promised herself she wouldn't allow for any man— certainly not anytime soon.

Luke stopped at the top of the staircase. Down the hall, light came through the partially closed door to *Mamm's*

bedroom. She was almost always asleep long before now, so she probably knew he was still up. Just what he needed.

Ach, he wasn't a child, and he hadn't done anything wrong. He should at least make sure she was all right.

"Luke." *Mamm*'s soft voice broke the silence just as he was about to knock.

He opened the door enough to go in, then closed it behind him.

Wearing a cotton nightgown and robe, and with her wavy gray-and-white hair unbound but her head covered by the white kerchief she wore at night, she sat against two bed pillows with a homemaking magazine open on her lap. "Were you downstairs?"

"Janna found the desk. She asked if I could come down."

"She asked? How?"

He slid his hands into the front pockets of his pants. "She texted me. On my phone." Remarkable that even after having a smartphone for months, which *Mamm* knew full well, he still hesitated to mention it.

After closing the magazine, she set it on the table beside the bed and returned her gaze to him. "Surely you understand that propriety is needed in your relationship with Janna."

"I do. We've done nothing improper." That was true. What just happened was unintentional and therefore merited no reproach. And thanks be to God that Janna didn't wear lip paint. "She only wanted to thank me for the desk. I was there for no more than ten minutes."

Mamm stared down at her hands folded in her lap, then looked up with an expression drawn with concern. "You need to keep in mind that eyes are watching. The eyes of those who give you business, I mean. Many of your customers are Christians, and if your uprightness comes into question, that will affect whether people come to you for furniture or refer others to you."

Here they went again. "Do you honestly—" At hearing the edge to his tone, he clamped his mouth shut. She spoke the truth, and her intentions were good. "I would never compromise my honor—or Janna's—and not simply because of the business. My first priority is to live a life that glorifies God. Never has my relationship with Janna been in any way improper."

"I'm not saying it has. I'm saying eyes are watching."

Ach, eyes were always watching. And sometimes seeing things that weren't there. They both knew that. "*Ya*."

She scowled again, though it seemed more from sadness. "And with you being put off the church, people are talking."

"That's idle talk. Christians should know better."

"They should. But I want you to be mindful of it. Propriety matters."

"*Nee*, the appearance of propriety matters," he corrected. "Because if propriety mattered, then tongues wouldn't be wagging when they shouldn't."

Unbelievable. He pulled over the Windsor chair that sat against the wall, then sat down. A tirade about people minding their thoughts and deeds seemed warranted, but what good would it do? Instead, he rested his elbows on his knees and rubbed his hands over his face. No matter that he should just live rightly and not worry about people's opinions, part of him still struggled with the desire to feel vindicated by others in the Plain community.

Mamm's hand on his shoulder made him straighten.

"Luke, you need to look at your life and take it to the Lord in prayer. That's how you can determine what he would have you do. We've reared you to shun worldliness, and yet it's made its way into your life. First it was leaving the *gmay* and buying and driving a vehicle. Then it was agreeing with Rayanne to not teach Joah *Deitsch*. Then it was a computer system for the shop, then government insurance, and then a cell phone. Now it's going to a *Funkeleit* church and enrolling Joah in a school with twelve grades." Her eyes glinted as she shook her head. "You mustn't allow yourself—and your son—to be led astray. God calls us to be separate from the world."

He knew that, and though he no longer believed it in the way she did, he'd grappled with each of the decisions he'd made. He still wrestled with some of them. But then he considered Mahlon's life and everything became so hazy. Mahlon was one of the godliest men he knew—no doubt the man Luke respected most since *Daadi*'s death—and yet he didn't follow all the Old Order ways. Sometimes determining God's will was so difficult.

"'Tis late now," *Mamm* said. "But I hope you'll think about all this."

With a nod, he stood.

Chances were good he'd have plenty of time tonight to think. Because as tired as he was, sleep would likely be slow in coming. Again.

CHAPTER 19

Confrontations

J anna turned over, trying to find a comfortable position for probably the tenth time. On the bedside table, the alarm clock's glowing red 3:36 mocked her. For as tired as she was—or should've been—her mind was wide awake. It started with rehashing everything that happened after Luke came down to the *daadi haus*, then spiraled into thoughts about her and Kayla leaving the farm, whether she should register Kayla for public school or put her in Christian school, and even Mitch and whether he would show up again.

Sighing, she rubbed her eyes. Lying here trying to make herself sleep wasn't doing any good. Then there was the chance her restlessness would wake Kayla. As carefully as possible, she slid out of bed and crept to the door.

In the living room, she pulled the bedroom door closed and turned on the lamp on the end table. Of course, the first thing her eyes found was the desk in the corner. Something tugged in her belly, and more emotions flooded through her. The *daadi haus*'s vintage furniture and minimal simple décor surely wasn't the farmhouse style she'd been dreaming of since the day she'd started looking for a place to live in Lancaster County, but after six weeks this had become home. And the Martins had again become family.

But for how much longer? Another three weeks, maybe. She didn't want to think about that.

Janna sat on the couch and picked up her Bible from the middle cushion.

"When I can't get to sleep, I don't count sheep; I talk to the Shepherd."

She almost laughed. The words echoing in her mind sounded just as silly now as they had when spoken by one of the women during Sunday school, but they were also true. And even though worries swirled in Janna's head, taunting her with uncertainty, God already knew what her future held. He had a plan for her and Kayla—a *good* plan. Again and again he'd proven himself worthy of her trust, so why couldn't she trust him now?

She let the Bible fall open, and a tract appeared. *The Christian Woman's Veiling.* After Bible study that week, a newer attendee had asked about head coverings. A discussion ensued, and several women kindly explained the relative Bible passage in 1 Corinthians 11 and shared their own experiences. Kendra had offered a tract to anyone who wanted one and posed a question Janna hadn't considered before: "Many people claim that Paul's instructions on covering the head were cultural—just to the Corinthians—but where else in the Bible are Christians instructed to follow what the culture tells them to do instead of what God wants them to do?"

Since then, that had been on Janna's mind as well. Should she be wearing a head covering? With all her heart she wanted to be obedient to God—even though the idea of women submitting to men flew in the face of her desire for independence. But it wasn't like she had a father or husband to submit to anyway.

She'd read through the tract a few times in the last few days, but the women's discussion of what they called *godly order* was what had resonated with her. The way they'd talked about the love and respect they shared with their husbands, and how she'd seen that lived out in Mahlon and Kendra's marriage, brought an unexpected longing for the same.

It didn't help that her friendship with Luke was built on a similar foundation. They weren't married or even dating, but she'd heard the woman at Groff's Grove tell Luke what a beautiful family he had. And they fulfilled complementary roles. She handled all the domestic tasks, even mending clothes and helping Salena can produce from Beulah and Malinda's garden, and assisted in the shop. Luke treated her and Kayla as he did his own family, providing them with food and a place to live, and faithfully ensured they had everything they needed—well, as much as she allowed him to.

Whether or not she wanted to admit it, that had her wishing for . . . more. With him. But how did she handle that? It sure wasn't what she'd signed up for when she accepted the Martins' invitation to stay here. And even if Luke felt the same way, he'd never pursue a relationship with a woman who didn't wear a head covering, no matter how he felt about her. He wouldn't capitulate, but she didn't want her feelings for him to influence her decision about covering her head. That needed to be between her and the Lord.

Besides, she didn't know if Luke felt the same way about her.

Except she did. Tonight had made that clear. Who knew how many hours he'd spent making her desk and chair, and then there was the way he'd held her. That said enough.

Goodness. What had she gotten herself into?

She leaned her head against the back of the couch, and the clock on the wall caught her eye. Time to go back to bed. If Luke was helping Enos and Ivan that morning, which he'd been doing a lot lately, he'd be heading for the milking barn in about ten minutes. He would knock on the door if he saw a light on, and no way was she in a frame of mind to face him yet.

Janna stopped short, her heart quickening, as soon as she rounded the last stall in the ladies' room after church. In front of the row of three sinks stood a tall young woman with a Bible clutched to her middle, staring her down. Janna had seen her before, usually sitting with an older couple near the front of the church, but she didn't know her name. That was unfortunate since greeting her by name might provide a way to diffuse whatever had her so indignant.

Janna smiled as she sidestepped to the nearest sink. "Good morning. And excuse me."

The woman turned. Her expression hadn't changed, and her pale skin, dark dress, and the way her almost-black hair was tightly pulled back under her head covering didn't soften it any. "You live with Luke Martin." Her quiet words sounded like an accusation.

What in the world was this about? Everyone at River View knew she and Kayla were staying with the Martins temporarily, and that had never been a problem. She rinsed her hands and grabbed a paper towel from the dispenser. "Yes, we're staying in their *daadi haus*." She nearly added *only for a few more weeks* but stopped herself. Saying that might seem like she thought they were doing something wrong.

"You're an unwed mother. By living there, you're putting his integrity at risk. Surely you don't want that."

Janna realized she still held the crumpled paper towel in her hand and tossed it into the trash can beside her. "No." But what else could she say to that? "Excuse me. I need to go." That wasn't a lie. She'd run into Sharilyn on her way to the bathroom, and they'd ended up talking for close to fifteen minutes. Luke might come looking for her, and he didn't need to get involved in this. "Thank you for your concern."

But it wasn't concern. The woman's dark-eyed glare confirmed that. She was angry, and her whole demeanor made the hairs on Janna's arms stand up. "Satan is always prowling around, seeking whom he may devour," the woman said. "As long as you're living there, you're risking temptation."

That was the furthest thing from the truth. Living with the Martins had strengthened her faith and desire to please the Lord.

Janna grabbed her Bible from where she'd set it by the potted African violet on the wall shelf. "Luke and I are friends, nothing more."

"The Bible warns us to abstain from all appearance of evil."

A retort about the evil being directed at her came to Janna's mind, but such a response would only make the situation worse. She pulled the door open and walked out, heading for the sanctuary.

Strangely, being away from the woman did nothing to calm her, and after turning a corner she stopped and leaned against the wall.

With everything else going crazy in her life right now, this was the last thing she needed.

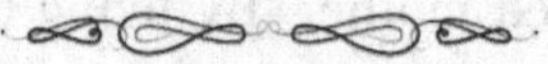

A hand on the back of Janna's arm startled her out of her thoughts as she stood at the counter in the Eschbachs' kitchen.

"Are you all right?" Kendra's brown eyes held concern instead of their usual serenity. "You seem out of sorts today. Even after church you did."

Janna's gaze dropped to the coleslaw she'd been mixing. Who knew how long she'd stood there with the spoon motionless in the bowl. She exhaled. The incident in the ladies' room had happened almost an hour ago, but it was still on replay in her mind. She'd hoped their time at the Eschbachs' for dinner would banish it, but no such luck. "Sorry. I'm lousy company today."

"Not at all." Without moving, Kendra checked the stockpot of corn boiling on the stovetop. "Is something wrong?"

As much as she wanted to brush off what happened, that might be a bad idea. If the young woman was brazen enough to confront Janna in the restroom, what else might she do? She would never forgive herself if Luke's character was marred because of her. And right now she and Kendra had privacy since the children were playing outside while Mahlon and Luke tended chicken on the grill. "Something happened at church."

Kendra listened as she recounted the incident, then asked a few questions. When Janna answered the last one, giving a description of the woman, Kendra sighed. "I'm so sorry. I know who that was, although I suspected it was her from the start."

That made her feel a little better. "Has this happened before?"

"No." She grimaced, hesitating as if she wasn't sure if she should say more. "But Rhonda's shown interest in Luke. Not openly to him that I know of, but by asking me and even Naomi about him. She's twenty but in no way mature enough to be in a dating relationship."

Now what happened made some sense. "So because I'm living on the farm, she thinks I'm . . . competition?"

Kendra gave a tight-lipped grin. "I'd say she thinks you're competition because you are."

Because she was? What was that supposed to . . .

Kendra laughed softly. "It's just that there's chemistry between you and Luke, and I'm not the only one who's noticed it."

Oh, she didn't need this right now. After such a long night, she was more emotionally spent than she'd been in months. Unable to stave off the tears that came to her eyes, she turned around and leaned against the counter.

Kendra's smile faded. "I'm sorry. I didn't mean to—"

"It's not you." She shook her head. "I was already a mess today, and Rhonda was the last straw."

Kendra stepped closer. "What can I do?"

"I don't know, aside from pray for me. Not that prayer isn't important. I know it is."

"It's more powerful than we often realize. Can I pray for anything specifically?"

"Well . . . Kayla and I will be moving to Akron in a few weeks." She paused, trying to put her thoughts in order. "And then Luke's and my relationship—our friendship, I mean. And he's going to have to find someone to help Salena. And now what to do about Rhonda."

"That's a lot to have weighing on your heart. And the issue with Rhonda will need more than prayer. We need to tell Mahlon and Luke what happened. If nothing else, I think church leadership needs to know. Then they can decide how to address it."

Janna had been afraid of that. Telling Kendra was one thing. Talking to Mahlon and Luke—especially Luke, and especially after last night—was another. But in the end, that had to be better than saying nothing and having the situation escalate, and then having to admit that she hadn't said something when she should have. "*Ya.*"

"I'm sorry if what I said upset you. That wasn't my intention. Is everything all right between you and Luke?"

"Sure." Janna's response came out too knee-jerk, and she sighed. Kendra was so easy to talk to, yet Janna had no idea how to explain what she was feeling. Even she didn't completely understand it.

Kendra looked into her eyes. "You and Luke care for each other very much."

She nodded, her eyes watering again. "I think so," she whispered, "and it's so complicated. I just don't know what to do."

"Oh, Janna." Kendra took her hands. "Let's pray right now. I know the four of us will pray together after we talk to Mahlon and Luke, but I want to pray with you now."

Thankfully, Janna could respond with another nod. Because that was the only reply she could manage.

Luke held out a glass of lemonade as he sat down beside Janna on the bench beneath the oak tree.

She grinned and took it from him, but the smile seemed forced.

He'd still take it, and at least she'd looked at him. She'd barely made eye contact since telling him and Mahlon about what happened at church. He'd spent the first part of the day thinking she was still embarrassed about last night, but now he didn't know which incident had her so stoic—or if it was some-thing else entirely.

She took a sip as she watched the children on the playset.

Leaning back, he downed a few swallows from his own glass. "Do you trust me?"

Her shoulders tensed slightly. "I . . . Yes." She didn't sound annoyed. Just puzzled. "Why?"

"On the way from church to Mahlon's, I knew you were upset. But when I asked if something was wrong, you said no. Why didn't you want to tell me?"

Again she watched the children. "Joah and Kayla were in the backseat. How could I?"

She had a point. But somehow he didn't think that was the full reason. "So you would've told me if they hadn't been with us?"

Janna now stared at the glass, which she rested on her leg. "Right at that moment? I don't know. But it wasn't that I didn't want to tell *you*. I didn't want to tell anyone. But by the time Kendra asked why I was so distracted, I'd realized the situation could get worse if I ignored it. And then you'd be bothered that I didn't tell you"—she glanced at him—"like you are now."

"I'm not bothered." He even managed to attest to that by keeping his tone gentle. "I just want you to know you can trust me."

When she met his gaze, her eyes held less seriousness. "I do trust you—as much as I trust any person, anyway. As far as men go, I trust you more than anyone."

Gut. That was what he wanted to hear.

"And please don't think it's you. It's not. It's just the way I am. Aside from you and *Daadi* Eli, the few men I've let into my life have turned out to be very different from what I thought." She scowled beyond the playset toward Enos and Ivan's farm-house. "And whenever something like this morning happens, I always think it's my fault—like I did something wrong or I deserved it. That makes it hard to talk about."

"Janna." He didn't know what pained him more, that she felt that way or that she spoke about it with such resignation. "Why would you think that? Rhonda was the only one at fault."

Her soft snort and smile came out nothing short of cynical. "I know. Cynthia and I talked about this tendency a lot when I was in high school, but I never got fully past it, I guess. She thinks it's because of Mom—the way she used to blame everyone else, especially me, for whatever was going wrong in her life." She grinned more genuinely. "I've never told anyone else that, not even Arissa, so there's proof I trust you."

Ach, he wanted to hug her. Now wasn't the time or place, though. He settled on smiling back. "Please don't ever feel like you can't talk to me."

Her expression brightened, and her posture relaxed even more. She took another sip of lemonade, then said, "I talked to Arissa this afternoon. She told me Mitch's parents took his car away and basically have him on house arrest until he goes to court. They're hoping to get the judge to send him back to the rehab instead of jail. So at least the chance of him coming here again is pretty slim."

He hoped so. "Arissa talked to him?"

"No, but they're related by marriage. Arissa's mom's aunt is married to Mitch's mom's uncle. Her mom talks to his mom."

Luke tried to think that through, but without success. "Impressive. That's some real relational recall."

She laughed softly, possibly the sweetest sound he'd heard in a while. "How quickly you forget. I was raised by Mennonites. They're experts at decoding vague, distant relationships."

True, although he apparently hadn't inherited that gene. "I haven't forgotten at all, and I'm glad you haven't either." That brought to mind what he'd seen that afternoon, and he now felt more comfortable mentioning it. "When I went into the *daadi haus* looking for Joah today, there was a tract on the table with your Bible. It was about head coverings. Did someone give it to you, or did you ask for it?"

Either she tensed again or he imagined it. Hopefully the latter. "Kendra gave it to me after a bunch of us were talking about it on Thursday." Her quieter tone told him she had no intention of saying more.

He probably shouldn't have brought it up, especially today. He just so wished she would take that to heart. Still, hounding her about it would do no good. If she had questions or wanted to discuss it, she'd ask someone—if not him, then Kendra or *Mamm* or Malinda.

But he wanted her to talk to him. About this and about anything and everything.

That clearly wasn't going to happen tonight.

CHAPTER 20

Mistakes Made

"J oah's doing so well with his braces now," Barbie Stoltzfus remarked. "If I didn't already know, I'd never guess he was wearing them."

Janna watched as Joah, Kayla, and Barbie's twins ran from the ground below the treehouse to the swing set on the other side of the Stoltzfuses' backyard. Zach and Tirzah were a year older than Joah and faster, but even with the way the AFOs altered his running gait, Joah kept up with Kayla. Of course, she probably slowed herself so he wouldn't lag behind. She was so good with him.

"He really is. Between PT and the exercises we do at home, he's come a long way." She leaned back and crossed her ankles, enjoying the padded lounge chair in the shade of the covered patio.

Thankfully, she hadn't declined the Wednesday-afternoon invite Barbie had offered at church on Sunday. The Stoltzfuses were as welcoming as could be, and they had a lovely home decorated in the simple farmhouse style Janna loved. She and

Barbie had already spent an hour talking décor, and Barbie had even given her a box of decorations she'd been planning to donate. Those and the items Janna had picked up at second-hand stores and yard sales provided some much-needed excitement about moving to the Akron house.

She smiled at how effortlessly Joah swung across the monkey bars. His slim build reminded her of Luke when he was young. "This summer has been tough for him at times—the weeks of casts, getting used to the AFOs, and all the therapy and exercises—but he rarely complains. He's an amazing kid."

Barbie tucked some stray pieces of dark hair under the white headscarf she wore. "He's got a godly father who's taught him well."

"*Ya*, he does." Janna kept her tone neutral. After the incident at church, she didn't want to give anyone ideas.

Barbie grinned. "It's interesting to hear you speaking *Deitsch*. But I guess you hear it a lot."

"Some. The Martins mostly speak English when we're around since I've forgotten a lot of it. I'm picking it up again, though, and so is Kayla."

Barbie again watched the children as Zach and Tirzah pushed Joah and Kayla on the swings. "Ironic, isn't it? So many of us no longer use *Deitsch*—my family never did when I was growing up, and Phil's hasn't in the last twenty years or so, yet you're from outside the community and learning it."

Ironic indeed. But a whole lot in Janna's life was ironic lately.

"Mom!" Zach came running toward them, followed by the other three. Stopping a few feet away, he brushed shaggy dark-blond hair from his blue eyes. "It's so hot. Can we go to the pool?"

"Yeah, can we?" Tirzah chimed in. Her long ponytail was a few shades lighter than her brother's hair, but otherwise their resemblance was obvious. "We just bagged up the swimsuits that don't fit us anymore. They'd fit Joah and Kayla, wouldn't they?"

Kayla looked around. "You have a pool?"

Barbie laughed. "No, sweetie. We belong to the community pool. It's a five-minute walk from here." She shifted her gaze from Kayla to Janna, and her expression sobered. "But maybe that wouldn't be all right?"

Janna had no idea what to say. Old Order Mennonites didn't swim, except maybe boys in a creek or pond. Luke wasn't Old Order anymore, though, and for months he'd been attending the same church Phil and Barbie did. They obviously saw nothing wrong with belonging to a public pool. "Well . . ."

"Please, Mama." Kayla bounced on her heels. "Joah gets to swim at therapy sometimes, but I never do."

"Is the water deep?" Joah asked. "I don't know how to swim."

"We wouldn't have to go in the big pool," Barbie told him. "Zach and Tirzah actually prefer the zero-depth-entry pool. They can walk in and go only as deep as they want, and it's like a small water park."

"The slides and the mushroom waterfall are my favorites," Tirzah said, "but I love the fountains too."

Janna weighed her options as quickly as she could. Excitement animated the faces of all the children, even Joah, and she didn't want Barbie to think she was ungrateful. She just didn't know how Luke would—

"It's up to you." Barbie kept her tone light. "But we have plenty of sunscreen and suits for the children, and they're modest. Swim skirts and shirts for the girls and board shorts and rash guards for the boys. I only have one suit for myself, but if the kids are going to stay in the shallow areas, I usually just wear regular clothes. Your skirt's longer than mine, but you could knot the hem higher so you can wade to your knees."

That didn't sound nearly as problematic as swimming in a pool. And Luke had agreed to Joah doing swim therapy at New Beginnings, where he wore the same type of swimwear Barbie was offering. This wouldn't be any different, really, and the children would love a few hours of playing in the water. She wouldn't mind it either, especially since Joah's time in the pool without his AFOs would be exercise enough that they wouldn't need to do his home PT later.

With a smile, she said, "Let's do it."

Luke stopped in the doorway into Joah's bedroom to find *Mamm* searching through the neatly folded pants in the bottom dresser drawer.

She glanced over her shoulder at Janna. "Are you thinking he'll need more pants for school, then?"

"*Ya*, definitely." Janna's attention never left Joah's bare feet as the two of them sat on the bed going through his bedtime ankle stretches. Facing him, she held his shins below the rolled-up pantlegs of his pajama pants. "Last time. Heels out. Toes toward you, as far back as you can pull them. Good. Now hold it just like that." Together, they counted to fifteen. "And you're done." She picked up one of the nighttime AFOs lying on the quilt beside him. "All but one pair of his jeans are short, and only two pairs of pants have a hem that can be let out."

"Can we get me more jeans?" Joah asked. "Instead of broadfalls?"

Mamm huffed and shut the drawer, then opened the one

above it. "Nothing wrong with broadfalls. Your *daed* wears them."

Ya, Luke did. He was even wearing a pair now. But not because he felt obligated to dress Old Order. He just didn't have a reason not to wear them. They were comfortable, in decent shape, and fit fine. Why spend money on new clothes unnecessarily?

Joah sighed. "But it takes so long to do the buttons. The teacher will say I'm taking too long in the bathroom again."

At least his reaction didn't have to do with dressing more worldly. He'd hear about it from *Mamm* if Joah, mainly around children from River View now, got the notion that broadfalls were too Plain.

Janna attached the Velcro to secure the second AFO, then laid her hand on the side of Joah's head. "We can always work on buttons here if we need to, just like you do at OT."

Her sweet reassurance touched Luke, but apparently not his son. Joah sulked. "Or we could just get me jeans."

"Joah Martin." Good reason or not for disliking broadfalls, Luke wouldn't allow disrespect. Some of the children at church were more outspoken like that, but he wouldn't tolerate it in his home.

Joah looked over, his eyes widening. *"Es dutt mir leed."*

Mamm and Janna now realized his presence, as did Kayla, who'd been looking at a book as she lay across the bottom of the bed.

He moved toward them. "We need to be thankful for what we have, even if it isn't perfect. Through God's grace and mercy, we can always make do. Not?"

"*Ya*," Joah said.

Janna kissed the top of his head. "All right. You sleep well now."

Joah hugged her as if he wished to never let go, not that

Luke could blame him. Janna cared for him like he was her own child, and Joah—with no recollection of his mother—thrived on that. Not that he didn't get love and attention from *Mamm*. He did, but when it came to child-rearing, an eighty-four-year-old woman had limits that a twenty-seven-year-old woman didn't. Just watching Janna take Joah through his exercises now proved how difficult it would be to replace her.

Impossible, really.

She did so much more than just fulfill the role she'd agreed to. Life proved that every day. Beyond her expected duties, she was a doting mother to Joah and a patient, loving granddaughter to *Mamm*. And to him—how did he even articulate all she was to him? A good friend. A fun companion. A confidante who understood him even when others didn't. The reason he got up smiling, even at four a.m. How would they—

"*Guder nacht*, Luke." Kayla's sweet voice and arms around his waist interrupted.

He smoothed her hair. "*Guder nacht*."

Janna smiled and bid them all good night, then left with Kayla.

Determined to redirect his attention to Joah, Luke helped him under the sheet, then sat on the edge of the bed. The slightly pink tinge across his son's nose and cheeks reminded him of their plans that afternoon. Luke had been gone most of the day helping Mahlon build a shed, most of suppertime had been spent discussing the carriage accident on Martindale Road, and then they'd had church tonight. He'd completely forgotten about their plans. "You went to the Stoltzfuses' this afternoon. Did you have a nice time?"

A smile lit up Joah's face as he lay back against the pillow. "It was so fun. We went in their pool."

A strangling noise came from *Mamm*'s throat as she came toward them. "Pool?"

Luke had been to the Stoltzfuses' house in the spring, and they hadn't had a swimming pool then. They could've put one in their backyard since—but swimming? Surely Janna wouldn't have allowed that. "They have a pool?"

"*Nee*, it's near their house. We walked there." Joah's eyes reflected pure joy. "You should see it, Daddy. It has fountains, and slides, and waterfalls to stand under, and big umbrellas. And it wasn't deep at all, so I wasn't scared. I wish the pool at New Beginnings was like that."

Mamm's eyes, on the other hand, reflected horror as she stood with her mouth ajar and one hand on her chest. Probably covering a heart that galloped with disbelief like his own did.

A pool . . . with fountains, slides, and waterfalls?

And then it all made sense. Phil and Barbie had a community pool not far from their house—and it had indeed looked as Joah described when Luke passed it while making a furniture delivery a few weeks ago. Fortunately, it was in a part of town he had no reason to return to, because after seeing the barely clad teenage girls walking on the sidewalk along the grounds' black metal fence, he'd determined to never take that route again.

And yet his young son had ended up there today. "You went to the community pool?" The question came out louder than he'd planned.

Joah's expression sobered and he swallowed. "*Ya*."

Mamm shook her head, her face twisting.

"What were you wearing?" Part of him didn't want to know, especially when it came to Janna and Kayla, but he needed details before he confronted Janna.

"Bathing suits that Zach and Tirzah grew out of." He looked at *Mamm*, then back to Luke. "Barbie said they're modest. And Janna put sunburn cream on us."

"*Ach*, nothing of the sort is modest," *Mamm* whispered.

Joah looked close to tears. His chin quivered as he pinched his lips together. "Are you going to punish me?"

Luke's chest tightened with remorse, and he rested a hand on Joah's shoulder. He'd been swimming at New Beginnings, so why would he see any problem with swimming elsewhere? "*Nee*, son. You did nothing wrong, and I don't want you to think you did." Janna, on the other hand . . . That was another story. "It's getting late now. Time for you to get to sleep."

After their exchange of good-nights, Luke followed *Mamm* into the hallway and closed the door. He shook his head, completely speechless. How could Janna have—

"We need to talk to her." *Mamm* had tears in her eyes as she spoke softly, obviously more distraught than angry.

If only he felt the same way. Distress he could deal with. He *was* dealing with it. But that wasn't the only emotion tormenting him.

He was also furious.

For the first time in weeks, Janna had Kayla tucked into bed by quarter of nine. It wasn't yet dark outside, but the children needed to get back to a set bedtime with school soon to start. Both had been tired tonight anyway thanks to three hours at the pool. Now she could sit down and finish her current editing project. Maybe she'd even get to bed at a decent hour.

As she opened her laptop on the desk, rapping from behind made her turn around.

Luke stood in the doorway into the house's kitchen. "Come in here, please."

Something had to be wrong. He hadn't looked so grave since Priscilla's visit.

She quickly crossed the floor but then stopped only two steps into the kitchen. At the far end of the table, Salena wore an equally grim expression as she leaned back in the chair. Perhaps one of the people involved in the carriage accident had died? "What's wrong?"

"You took the children to a swimming pool?" Luke's question wasn't one to be answered with a yes or no. The disbelief in his tone conveyed he already knew the answer.

Janna looked from Salena to him, her heart sinking. "Yes, with the Stoltzfuses."

"You didn't think I'd mind you being at a public swimming pool?" He clamped his mouth closed as if realizing he'd spoken too loudly for after bedtime, then exhaled and leaned against the counter. "How could you think a pool would be a place I'd want you taking the children—or yourself?"

Oh, deep down she'd known she should have at least asked him first. But that really hadn't seemed necessary. "We didn't do anything wrong." But by the way her voice wavered, neither would believe her. "The Stoltzfuses have a membership. The visitor passes weren't expensive, and Barbie had modest swimwear for the children. Joah swims at New Beginnings, so I didn't think—"

"Swimming at New Beginnings is part of his therapy, and it's in a private pool for medical use, not a public pool used solely for recreation. Did anyone see you?"

Regret gave way to annoyance. "Do you mean did anyone we know see us? I don't know. Barbie talked to a few moms there, but I didn't recognize them. I was paying attention to the children, not to who else was there."

He blew out his breath again and stared at the counter. "What were you and Barbie wearing?"

"Luke." *Mamm*'s warning proved she'd heard him despite how quietly he'd asked.

Janna glanced at her. For a moment she hoped Salena might take her side—realize that she hadn't done anything improper—but no such luck. The stern expression hadn't left her face.

She returned her attention to Luke, ready to snap back that it wasn't his business. Because it wasn't. She and Kayla might live here, but he didn't get the last word on what she did unless it involved the shop or Joah—and this wasn't about either. Well, it did involve Joah, but she'd done nothing to harm him in any way.

"Our clothes. The water was only knee-deep where we were, so I knotted my skirt a little higher so I could be with them." Then her conscience pricked her. "I didn't think you'd have a problem with it. Phil and Barbie go to the same church we do, and they obviously don't think there's anything wrong with swimming there. And none of us were dressed immodestly."

"*Nee*, but how many others were? You took my son—and yourself and your daughter—to a place where people are clad in next to nothing."

As if this was the first time. "He's exposed to that already. When we were at Strasburg Rail Road, a woman was wearing a dress that was hardly more than a long tank top. And the last time we were at Mellinger's, which you've taken Joah into countless times, a teenage girl was wearing short shorts and a shirt that showed her middle." Not that the store staff condoned that either, but it proved her point. Even in a store run by Mennonites they could be exposed to immodesty.

"I drove by that pool last month. I saw what was worn there. It's not the same." He shook his head, scowling heavier than she'd ever seen before. Even when Priscilla left, he hadn't been so mad. "I just can't believe you did this—that you took them there without asking first. Why? All you had to do was call me."

She should have. Calling him would've taken only a minute or two. But she'd let their deepening friendship allow her to believe she knew what his answer would be—that she knew *him*. How wrong she'd been.

Tears pricked her eyes, and she dropped into the chair at the end of the table.

She didn't know him at all.

"You're both at fault in this."

Luke's head snapped up at *Mamm*'s accusation. She was blaming *him*? "I knew nothing about this until a half hour ago."

She folded her arms. "*Ya*, but you've let yourself be led astray. You say that by no longer following the rules you once honored, you've simply left legalism—man's rules—behind. But in doing that, you've also invited confusion into your life and into the lives of those you lead as the head of this household." With one hand on the table, she stood. "*Ya*, the Old Order ways may seem strict. But they give clarity by drawing lines we know not to cross. What's acceptable and what's not are clear." Her gaze moved to Janna, then back to him. "And mistakes like this don't happen."

Heat crept up his neck to his face. *Mamm*'s words had truth to them, probably more than he wanted to admit. But she could've waited until they were alone to dish out her wisdom instead of embarrassing him in front of Janna.

Then guilt born of pride stabbed him. A man needed to recognize when he was wrong, or at least could've done something differently, and be able to acknowledge it. That only made him even angrier. This whole situation was too much.

Mamm headed for the living room. "Think about what I said, and talk it out," she said over her shoulder, "before this problem gets worse. *Guder nacht.*"

He clenched his jaw, unable to look at Janna. He'd already made too many foolish decisions, and trying to talk to her at this moment would be another one. "Not now." Turning around, he walked to the screen door and pushed it open. It slammed behind him as he stepped off the porch, and he headed for the lane.

What had he been thinking, allowing Janna back into his life like he had? He should've known he was asking for trouble. Even though they'd grown up together, they were far too different now to be as close as he'd let them get. He should've permitted her and Kayla to stay here but kept a sensible distance—for everyone's sake.

But no. He'd been a fool and made irresponsible excuses for his increasing feelings for her. Excuses that he and Janna had grown up together, so having a close friendship was acceptable. Excuses that even though she was of the world, she respected his beliefs and was therefore a suitable caregiver for Joah. And excuses that her time with them at the farm and with the people at River View would make her into a woman he could properly court, fall in love with, and marry.

And now? She'd disregarded his values, overestimated their relationship, let her independence make a decision that wasn't hers, and put them all in a situation that could have damaging consequences. If certain people happened to see her, Joah, and Kayla at the pool—or even just walking there with the children in swimwear—news would spread quickly, portray their family in a negative light, and possibly take a toll on his business.

And that wasn't the worst of it.

His chest squeezed so tightly that his lungs ached, and he crossed the grass to sit on the bench beneath the tall oak. The same bench he and Janna had shared just nights before—where she'd told him that of all the men in the world, she trusted him most. His heart had soared then, but now . . .

Now it seethed. Not so much toward Janna. What she'd done was forgivable. And even though there'd been no apology, she'd seemed sincere in her claim that she hadn't thought he would mind them going to the pool. But that just confirmed what he'd spent weeks trying to deny.

He and Janna were incompatible. Some people would even call them unequally yoked, and maybe that was true. They were too different in their beliefs, and nothing more than casual friendship should have ever grown between them. Yet what had he done? Brought her into his family's life—even let her into *his* life. And worse, he'd let her fill the empty places grief had carved deep inside him.

Now the empty places cracked deep again, and he could blame only himself.

Who knew how long Janna sat in the empty kitchen, staring at the wall as tears fell from her eyes faster than she could wipe them away. Not that it mattered anyway. Neither Salena nor Luke was coming back anytime soon, so no one was there to see her crying—or for her to apologize to.

All because of one seemingly trivial decision.

She got up and went back into the *daadi haus*. Her phone lay on the table, and when she picked it up, it vibrated. At least someone cared enough to call or text, even if she wasn't in the mood to talk.

Unable to sit, she paced while punching in her voice mail PIN.

"Hi, Janna, it's Gertie Bollinger." The elderly woman's sweet voice stole her breath. "I hope you and Kayla are doing well. I just wanted to let you know I talked to Tony Lowery today, and he expects your half of the house to be ready by the twenty-third. So you should be moved in before Kayla starts school, just as you hoped. Give me a call when you get a chance."

So they'd be saying goodbye to the farm in two weeks. Fourteen days, maybe less. She'd known the time was coming but had been able to push that to the back of her mind—until now. Their time with the Martins would soon be ending.

That was probably for the best. What just happened proved it. And how ironic that the call came tonight. Perhaps this was God's confirmation that she and Kayla should move on—get back on the path he'd started them on by providing the rental in Akron.

Right. Her head might believe that, but her heart never would. And wasn't this the way it always ended—with her on her own again? Some things never changed.

Moving On

Luke had never been so glad to smell coffee brewing. Before he'd made it halfway down the staircase, the scent was strong enough that he definitely wasn't only imagining it. Janna had come into the house to make coffee for him before beginning her editing work.

Part of him had feared she wouldn't—after all, she did that each morning out of kindness, not because he'd asked her to— and that same part couldn't have blamed her if she didn't. His walking out during their argument last night had hardly been the best way to deal with the situation.

The kitchen's brightness cast some light into the living room, so she had to be still in the house. Usually all was dark when he came down, with the light above the stove providing a muted glow only in the kitchen.

When he reached the kitchen, she was heading for the *daadi haus*. Going by her quick pace, she'd probably heard him coming. "Janna, wait."

She stopped inside the doorway but didn't turn around.

Now what? Coming down earlier than usual to catch her had worked, but he hadn't thought about what he'd say. "I was hoping—"

"I need to start working."

"I know. Just a few minutes. Please."

With a sigh, she turned around. She'd dressed—well, except for putting on a sweater—and her hair was neatly braided, but her eyes looked tired. Really tired. Like his had in the mirror ten minutes ago.

Ach, pride indeed went before a fall. If they'd talked last night, both would probably be in better shape now. "I need to apologize."

Her shoulders relaxed a bit, though she only looked him in the eye for a moment.

"I shouldn't have left." He moved toward her slowly. "We needed to discuss what happened, and I made that impossible. I also didn't heed the Bible's instruction to not let the sun go down on my wrath. That's sin, and I need to ask your forgiveness."

She swallowed. "I'm sorry too. I never intended to go behind your back. Honestly, I didn't think it would be a problem. We were with Barbie, and Joah swims at PT sometimes, and . . ." She shook her head. "But I should've asked you first, and I didn't."

That bothered him. Had he not made it clear by his lifestyle that he eschewed the ways of the world? "You really thought I'd agree to it? To my son—and you and your daughter—being exposed to people dressed that way?"

"We're exposed to it in other places."

That excuse again. "This is different. Seeing people like that when we're somewhere we need to go is one thing. Paying money to spend time where people purposely dress without modesty is another."

She opened her mouth but didn't say anything. Was she really going to object? Maybe this wasn't going as well as he'd thought.

"It's just . . . Luke, it's not always clear where you stand." She crossed her arms. "You dress Old Order and are strict with some beliefs, but then you have a smartphone and go to a church that varies in how conservative people are."

And now they were back to what *Mamm* had accused, not that he could deny it. "All you had to do was call me. That's what you should have done."

"Right." The word came out too short for his liking. Her gaze shifted to the travel mug of coffee that sat on the counter next to the stove, in the same place she always left it for him. "I need to get to work. From now on, I'll ask."

"*Gut. Danki.*"

She disappeared into the *daadi haus*, closing the door partially behind her.

He picked up his coffee, then stepped out onto the porch after outening the kitchen light. Sitting on the swing, he shoved his feet into his barn boots and exhaled. How in the world had they gone from being so close only days before to now contending about something that should be indisputable?

Janna and her independence, that was how. It wasn't that he didn't understand it. She was independent because her life had required it. But all he wanted was her trust and respect. That shouldn't be too much to ask.

The weight that settled on him made it a challenge to stand. The physical tiredness would be tolerable, but the emotional exhaustion compounded it. As much as he enjoyed the early mornings in the milking barn with his uncles, this wasn't going to be an easy start to his day.

"Did you and Luke talk things out last night?" Salena asked quietly from where she sat on the stool behind the cash register.

On the other side of the counter, Janna looked up from the price tag she was writing out, then glanced over her shoulder. Joah was dusting furniture while Kayla swept the floor, and both were out of earshot. "Not last night, but we talked some this morning."

She'd wondered how long it would take for Salena to say something. Salena had eyed them at breakfast, and this time it wasn't because she fretted that they were becoming too friendly. That had been her concern last Thursday morning as they looked at the photos, but today she'd watched as they barely spoke to each other.

Salena's brows drew together. "Why not last night? The Bible is quite clear that we're not to go to bed angry."

"Luke went for a walk." Her honesty might get him chastised, but the truth was the truth. "I waited up for a little while, then went to bed." And she hadn't gotten her nightly work in. That was the rotten cherry on top of all this madness.

"*Ai-yi-yi.*" Salena clicked her tongue, shaking her head. "And this morning?"

"We apologized, and I told him I'll ask about anything like that in the future."

"*Ach, gut.* I hope you've both learned from this so it doesn't happen again. I'm just praying nobody saw you. Word gets around, and something like this would reflect badly on our family—and possibly the business."

Janna gritted her teeth and returned her attention to the price tag. Now she couldn't remember the price. "Well, you won't have to worry about that for much longer. Mrs. Bollinger called last night. Our house should be ready the week of the twentieth."

She looked up to find Salena's seriousness replaced by the same deep sadness she'd displayed when Priscilla abruptly ended her visit. Ah, what had she been thinking? Sure, a flippant answer had seemed like a rightful response to being scolded, but now she felt horrible. They had their disagreements, but Salena loved her—and Kayla.

"You'll be leaving us, then," Salena said. "Moving to Akron."

"We're moving?"

When Janna turned, Kayla stood about six feet away, staring at her in horror as she held the broom and half-full metal dustpan.

Well, word was out. All she could do was be honest. She looked from Kayla to Joah, who approached holding his dust cloth. "In about two weeks."

Kayla's face crumpled. "But I don't wanna move. I wanna stay here. I wanna go to school with Joah."

Janna moved toward her. "Honey, I know you like being here, but we knew it would be only until our house was fixed. Now it's almost ready. You'll finally have your own room."

"I don't care about that." Tears filled Kayla's eyes. "If we stay here, I'll never ever complain about not having my own bedroom again. Never. And I'll never ever fight with Joah again either. Please, Mama."

This day just kept getting worse. First Luke, then Salena, and now this. Thank goodness no customers were in the shop. "Our time here was temporary, Kay. We knew that. And I signed a lease with Mrs. Bollinger. That's a contract, and I can't back out of it. I already paid her for our first month's rent."

"I don't care! I don't want to go!" Now crying, Kayla dropped the dustpan. It hit the floor with a clang, sending its contents onto and all around her bare feet, and she cried harder.

"It's okay." Janna helped her step out of the mess.

"Everything all right in here?" Luke asked from the doorway into the workshop. His gaze moved from the children to Janna to Salena, who'd come over and taken the broom.

And Janna had thought it couldn't get worse.

"Mama said we're moving to Akron," Kayla blurted before Janna could figure out how best to answer him.

He looked at her, his expression blank.

Janna slipped her arm around Kayla, who buried her face in her side. "Our house is almost ready."

The bell rang, announcing that a vehicle had turned into the shop's parking lot, and he glanced at the front door. "Come back in the workshop."

Janna turned to Salena.

She stopped sweeping and shooed them toward the door. "Ya, go. I'm fine."

Janna led Kayla away, and Joah wiped his cheek as he followed. Now he was crying too. Goodness. She'd known this conversation would be a difficult one, and this wasn't how she wanted it to happen.

At this point, she might as well make that the tagline of her life: *This wasn't how I wanted it to happen.*

Luke glanced around the workshop as he followed Janna, Kayla, and Joah. Near one of the workbenches, Mahlon was showing Andy, the teen from church they'd hired as a helper, how to apply polyurethane to a stained wall shelf. Mahlon hearing what they said wouldn't bother him—probably—but Andy didn't need to. "Let's go outside."

He led them through the side door into the morning warmth and humidity, then to the bench by the playset. Janna sat down and pulled Kayla onto her lap, and he did the same with Joah. A tear slid down Joah's cheek, and he brushed it away.

Luke rubbed his back. "What's wrong, son?" He knew but wanted to hear it from him.

"I don't want them to leave," he said, staring at the ground. "I won't have anyone to play with, and who will take care of me? How will I get to therapy, and who will do my exercises with me? Who will help *Mammi* Salena?"

All questions Luke couldn't answer. Each day they'd moved closer to the Akron house being finished, but every time he'd tried to make a plan for when that happened, all he could do was admit he'd need to hire someone to take Janna's place. "The Lord will provide someone."

"I don't want *someone*. I want Janna. And Kayla."

"Oh, honey." Janna's eyes became watery as she took his face in her hand and lifted his chin.

Luke could relate. He felt the same way, whether or not he should. Even after yesterday's debacle. "I know you do. But we've—"

"I wish we'd never gone to Zach and Tirzah's." Joah shook his head, frowning.

The Stoltzfus's house? "Why do you say that?"

"Then we wouldn't have gone to that pool, and you wouldn't have gotten mad."

"This has nothing to do with that." Janna dropped her hand to his shoulder and squeezed it. "Our moving to Akron was planned months ago. We just ended up here because your *daed* and *Mammi* Salena very kindly invited us to stay when the tree fell on our house."

"I'd never ask them to leave," Luke said. "*Ya*, we had a disagreement last night, but that happens in families. As far as we're concerned, that's what Janna and Kayla are. And families work things out."

Joah looked at Janna. "Will we still see you?"

She blinked quickly. "Of course. We'll be ten minutes away. You'll see us at church, and we'll visit you and you can visit us, and if your *daed* needs me to drive you to PT or OT or help in other ways, I'll be happy to do that."

Kayla wiped her face with the sleeve of her sweater. "Will Joah and me go to the same school?"

"We haven't . . . I don't know yet." She drew Kayla closer. "Honey, this isn't happening tomorrow. We're here for a while yet. We'll have time to talk about everything, maybe tonight. Okay?"

Well, she hadn't said no. Hopefully, Janna was still considering sending Kayla to the Christian school Joah would be attending. Nothing more had been said about that, but she had to know the benefits outweighed the cost. And it sounded like she planned to still attend River View.

She sighed. "Why don't you go play for a while before it gets too hot?"

Kayla and Joah exchanged glances. "I didn't finish the dusting," he said.

Janna smiled weakly. "You were almost done, and thank you for your honesty. Go ahead." As the two headed for the playset, she sat back and closed her eyes. "That wasn't how I wanted them to find out."

He rested his elbows on his legs and stared at the grass between his feet. "When were you going to tell me?"

"Today." The word held none of the defensiveness he'd expected.

When he finally lifted his head, Joah and Kayla sat in the playhouse with their legs dangling out. Not happily swinging back-to-back on the glider or climbing the rock wall, just quietly talking. The irony brought a bad taste to his mouth. "Reminds me of when another boy and girl who were best friends ended up separated."

She opened her eyes and looked at him. "This isn't the same. There's nothing sudden about this, and I'm not running from anything or trying to take Kayla away."

Ach, he hadn't meant it that way. "*Nee*, I know that. I'm not comparing you to your *mamm*. I'm talking about them—what they're feeling. Fourteen years ago, that was us." He gazed toward the barn and the pasture beyond it, debating whether he should say exactly what was going through his mind. "And it's us again now, except this time you have a choice."

Janna stared at him. He couldn't be serious. Making it sound like she was leaving because she wanted to? "Luke, I signed a six-month lease and already paid the first month's rent. I can't just back out on Mrs. Bollinger now. That would be unfair, and she's had enough unfairness in her life lately."

Nodding slowly, he continued to look at something far off. "I just wish there was another way. A way to not separate them. They're so happy together." He swallowed audibly. "The day your mom moved you away from here is still so clear in my mind. I remember how much that hurt—and how much it devastated you—and the thought of them experiencing that makes me feel sick inside."

Wow. Luke was generally so reserved. He still was—speaking softly, giving no facial evidence of his feelings, and not making eye contact—but she hadn't expected such candidness, especially today. It almost weakened her resolve. "This won't be the same. Mom took us an hour and a half away, and she had no intention of allowing me to stay in touch. Kayla and I will be ten minutes away, and separating her and Joah is not my intention at all. We're just resuming our original plan."

Which she needed to stick to. Moving into the Akron house. Getting Kayla settled in a good school. Taking her editing schedule to as close to full-time as possible so she could start saving money for the future. She was infinitely grateful to the Martins, but now it was time for her and Kayla to stand fully on their own feet.

As much as she'd miss the farm, they couldn't stay here forever. Kayla should have her own room, and Janna wanted the same. They'd shared the same bed for over two years, since moving into their previous apartment, and that definitely wasn't the best scenario.

The Akron house would be their home—all two bedrooms, one-and-a-half bathrooms, kitchen, dining room, living room, porch, and yard of it. It was more than twice the size of the *daadi haus*, and she couldn't wait to decorate and make it into a haven they adored. It would be their new start—their desperately needed new start. And they could still have a relationship with the Martins.

He inhaled and let it out slowly. "It worries me, you and her living there on your own."

She looked him in the eye. Had he forgotten what her life had been like? "I've been managing on my own for a long time. Sure, I had Cynthia when I was in high school, Arissa when I was in college, and Cynthia after college, but I've always been responsible for myself. Kayla and I lived on our own for two years before coming out here, and Akron has much less crime than where we used to live. We'll be fine." More than fine.

"What if Mitch comes looking for you again?"

Really? She'd been trying not to think about that possibility. "I can't let that rule my life. Right now he has no car, and he'll eventually go to jail or back to the rehab in Massachusetts, or maybe both. After what's happened, he probably won't try anyway."

His attention returned to the fields. "You haven't decided which school Kayla will be going to?"

Would the questions never end? "Not yet." She'd certainly thought about it, and with all her heart she wished to send Kayla to the Christian school. Whether that was feasible she had yet to determine—and now wasn't the time to do it.

She stood. "I need to make sure your *mamm* is all right before we leave for Bible study."

Before he could say more, she started for the shop. No doubt they'd be talking about this again, but she couldn't handle it right now. Not when her mind kept replaying the image of fourteen-year-old Luke standing in the lane with his grandparents, his hand held up in a wave and a hollow stare on his face, as her mother drove her away from the Martin farm.

CHAPTER 22

The Scare

"Mama, I'm hungry," Kayla said as she and Joah reached the rack of candy bars and other snacks by the cash registers in Mellinger's Store. "Can Joah and me get something to eat?"

Janna stopped behind them. Usually they were home from Joah's PT by now, but an accident on Route 222 kept them stuck in traffic for twenty minutes. Now they waited as Salena picked out the notions she needed in the sewing section near the back of the store. "*Ya.* Not candy. They have plenty of healthy snacks here."

Smiling, the children turned back to the rack. Both chose a strawberry-flavored fruit and oat bar, and Janna checked the ingredients for peanuts before paying the cashier for them. Moments later, Salena joined them and purchased her sewing notions and two pairs of black compression knee-highs.

"What do you think of pizza casserole for supper tonight?" Salena asked her as they left the store.

"Sure." That was one of Luke's favorite meals, so he would

be happy—she hoped. And it didn't require a lot of prep, which would be nice. With the heat, the less time they spent cooking over the stove, the better.

At the van, Janna opened the back door for the children. Joah climbed in, but Kayla didn't follow. "Come on, Kay." Janna turned to find her standing about fifteen feet away.

Her face was scrunched up, her mouth ajar, and one hand grasped her throat while the other held the partially eaten fruit bar.

"Kayla?" She rushed toward her. "Is it stuck?"

As Janna reached her, she realized mucus poured from Kayla's nostrils, her eyes were watering, and red welts were forming around her mouth.

No, no, no. Please, Lord, no. "It's all right." *Oh Lord, let it be all right.* Janna grabbed the fruit bar and shoved it into the pocket of her sweater, then picked Kayla up and jogged back to the van.

Salena and Joah already sat in their seats, but Salena had turned around. "*Ebbes letz?*"

She sat Kayla on the floor of the van beside the captain's chair that held her booster seat.

Kayla wheezed with every breath now. "Mama," she rasped, her teary eyes terrified.

Janna's heart about broke. "She's having an allergic reaction." But to what? She'd read the bar's ingredients, and there definitely weren't peanuts in it.

She dropped her purse on the ground, grabbed the bag that held Kayla's EpiPens, and unzipped it. After quickly removing them, she pulled one from its tube, took off the end piece, lifted one side of Kayla's skort, and pressed the injector to her thigh until it clicked. *One, two, three, four, five.* She shoved the injector back into the tube and dropped it into her purse. "We need to get her to the hospital."

"An ambulance?"

Janna's mind spun. The rule was to call 911 as soon as epinephrine was given, but they were less than two miles from the hospital. The community ambulance station was farther away. "We can probably get her there before the ambulance could even get here. Come on, honey." She lifted Kayla, who leaned sideways against the back of the driver's seat. "Let's get you into your seat."

Kayla was pale except for the pink patches of hives all over her face and neck, and her eyes were swollen partly shut as she leaned against the booster seat's headrest. The wheezing continued, but she was moving some air, and hopefully the epinephrine would work quickly. *Please, Lord, let it work quickly.*

"Dizzy, Mama," Kayla whispered hoarsely.

"I know, baby." Janna stroked her hair back from her face. "That's the medicine working."

"Is Kayla okay?" Joah asked, his eyes wide.

"She will be." Janna closed the door, then grabbed her purse, got in the driver's seat, and headed for the parking lot's exit.

Fortunately, Main Street wasn't busy with afternoon traffic yet. Salena remained turned in her seat, watching Kayla. Janna tried to keep her eyes on the road, though she couldn't help checking the rearview mirror again and again as she drove and prayed.

In the ER lobby, a middle-aged woman in navy-blue scrubs who'd been talking to the receptionist immediately ushered them back to a treatment room. She called for assistance, then had Janna lay Kayla on the stretcher as she readied an oxygen mask. By the time two more women—a young one in scrubs and an older one in scrubs and a white coat—rushed into the room, she'd clipped a pulse ox onto

Kayla's finger and was wrapping a blood pressure cuff around her arm.

Janna stood by Kayla's head, holding her hand and stroking her hair. She answered the doctor's questions as best she could, but her own questions competed: Had she done everything she should have—in the order she should have? Would they chastise her for not calling an ambulance? Should she have laid Kayla down in the van instead of putting her in her booster?

Kayla still looked terrified, though her wheezing had eased, and she cried out when the nurse inserted an IV needle.

Janna kissed her temple, fighting tears and wishing with all her heart that she could switch places with her poor little girl. "It's okay. What they're doing will help you feel better. You're doing real good."

"Yes, you are, sweetheart," the doctor said kindly as she placed her stethoscope on Kayla's chest. She listened, moving the stethoscope several times, then glanced up at the monitor screen attached to the wall. "Pulse ox is ninety-three. Let's give her twenty of diphenhydramine and point-two of epi."

"You got it." The middle-aged nurse turned to the medical cart behind her, then unlocked it and opened a drawer.

The doctor leaned down and smiled at Kayla. "You're doing a *great* job. Is your breathing easier now?"

Kayla nodded. "Itchy," she whispered.

"I know. The medicine Nurse Lynn's about to give you will help that, and it works pretty quick. It's probably going to make you sleepy too."

Janna inhaled slowly, trying to calm her racing heart. The wheezing had stopped now, and even though Kayla still breathed heavier than usual, the hives were no longer spreading. Her eyes were still swollen, but she seemed more comfortable. Janna finally felt like she could breathe too.

The doctor shifted her gaze to Janna. "You did a great job too, Mom."

She managed a nod. Maybe so, but she still felt completely to blame.

Luke prayed continuously as he drove under Route 222 and neared town. As soon as his phone had rung ten minutes ago, he'd feared something was wrong. Janna had texted him earlier to let him know they'd been slowed in traffic because of an accident but they still planned to make a stop at Mellinger's for *Mamm*. When he'd seen the hospital name on his caller ID, his stomach turned cold.

That had only intensified when *Mamm*'s unusually emotional voice told him that Kayla had an allergic reaction in the parking lot of Mellinger's and they'd rushed her to the hospital. As much as he loathed hospitals, he couldn't get there quickly enough.

The speed limit was thirty-five, and he wished that was possible. With two lanes narrowing to one, the vehicles ahead slowed as they merged. He was less than three miles away now, but it might take ten minutes to get there.

Exactly eight minutes later, he quickly approached the emergency room entrance. The automatic doors opened, and as he passed the wheelchairs in the glass enclosure that led to the waiting room, *Mamm* came into view, sitting in a chair along the wall beyond the reception desk.

Joah jumped up from the chair beside her and rushed to him. "Daddy!"

Luke picked him up and joined *Mamm*. "Have you heard anything?"

She shook her head, clutching the black purse that sat on her lap. "A nurse took them away as soon as we came in. I didn't think they'd want us back there too."

That was probably best, at least for Joah's sake. He already looked frightened, and seeing Kayla treated would only intensify that fear. But Luke needed to be with her—and Janna.

When he went to the desk, one of the receptionists looked up. "May I help you?"

"Can you tell me anything about Kayla Carpenter, the little girl who came in with an allergic reaction?"

"Why don't you have a seat and I'll check." She picked up the phone and pressed a few buttons, then spoke with someone as Luke sat beside *Mamm*.

"Will Kayla be okay?" Joah asked. "She could hardly breathe, and her face got all swelled up, and she wouldn't talk to me."

"Jesus is with her," he said, "and they should be able to tell us something soon."

About a minute later, the woman at the desk stood. "Sir? You all can go back if you like. Just give her name at the nurses' station, and they'll direct you."

That had to be a good sign. If Kayla was in bad shape, they wouldn't want more people crowding around her. He thought about having Joah stay here with *Mamm*, but she'd want to see Kayla and Janna as well. After helping *Mamm* stand, he led her and Joah to the doors that opened automatically when the receptionist pushed a button.

As soon as they reached the nurses' station, he caught sight of Kayla slightly propped up on the bed in the room across from it. Janna sat in a chair beside her, talking with a nurse who stood on the other side of Kayla.

Joah let go of Luke's hand and headed for them.

"Joah." Though coarser than usual, the little voice that

called out had to be one of the sweetest sounds Luke had ever heard.

Joah stopped short beside Janna, staring at Kayla, who wore a hospital gown and had an oxygen mask over her nose and mouth. Maybe leaving him in the waiting room with *Mamm* would've been better.

Janna put her arm around his waist. "It's okay, honey. She's feeling much better now. Her face is still swollen, but that'll go away as the medicine works. And the mask on her face is just to make it easier for her to breathe."

Mamm stopped beside the nurse and smoothed Kayla's hair back from her face. She then looked at the nurse. "Thank you for everything."

"You're quite welcome." She patted Kayla's hand, then addressed Janna. "I'll check back in ten minutes or so. If you need anything, just use the call button."

As the nurse left, Luke glanced at Janna. She'd met his gaze for only a few moments when they came into the room, but she appeared calm and composed. She'd even comforted Joah. Of course, that didn't mean she wasn't a mess inside. Even seeing Kayla now—covered with red splotches, with her face still swollen and her looking so tiny on the bed—tightened his throat. He couldn't imagine how distraught Janna must've felt.

Except he could. He'd lived it for the twenty-six hours he spent at Rayanne's bedside before she died.

His breath caught, and he redirected his thoughts to Kayla. Now wasn't the time to relive horrors from the past. He needed to be here in the present for Janna and Kayla, and he should've been thanking God for a good outcome. This could have ended so much worse.

He joined Janna and Joah, and she looked up at him. She'd remained reserved in her interaction with him today, although that guardedness now seemed gone. She tried to smile, albeit not very successfully.

Stepping closer, he placed his hand on her shoulder. He shouldn't with *Mamm* standing right there—it would most likely earn him a reprimand later—but he'd been in Janna's place once, and he'd been so thankful for those who'd offered him support.

She grasped his hand tightly for a few moments, then let go and returned her attention to the children.

He squeezed her shoulder gently. If it meant giving Janna some comfort, he'd put up with all the scolding necessary.

An hour and a half later, Salena and Luke finally agreed to go home. It was nearly seven o'clock, Salena was clearly tiring, and they all had to be hungry. As it was, by the time they got home and finished supper, it would be bedtime for Joah.

Janna got up from where she sat on the foot of the stretcher and walked to the doorway with them so anything they said wouldn't disturb Kayla, who now slept.

Salena hugged her. "You call if you need us."

"I will." She tried to smile when they released each other.

"Let me know when they discharge her and you're on your way home," Luke added. "If you need *anything*—doesn't matter what it is or what time—call or text me."

Joah looked up at her, much too solemn for a not-quite-seven-year-old. "When will you be home?"

She hugged him to her side. "Probably not until after you're asleep. We need to stay here a few more hours."

"But you'll be there when I wake up tomorrow?"

She smiled and leaned down to kiss the top of his head. "Lord willing."

He wrapped his arms around her waist. "What about my bedtime exercises?" He sounded close to tears, and she expected that had nothing to do with his exercises.

She managed a more genuine smile, hoping that would lighten his mood. "This is a good time for you to show your daddy just how well you've learned them."

He nodded, and Luke rested a hand on his back. "We'll be sure to say an extra prayer for Kayla tonight, okay?"

As Luke led them out of the room, Janna went to the chair beside the bed and dropped into it. At least this one was padded and comfortable. The last time Kayla had ended up at the hospital, when she'd had a reaction to peanut butter at the age of two, the ER had been rundown and the chairs hard plastic. This hospital couldn't have been cleaner or more up-to-date, and all the staff were wonderful in every way.

With a sigh, she made herself as comfortable as possible. Kayla slept soundly, a result of the reaction's toll and the Benadryl they'd given her, and the nurse had said they'd probably be there another four hours for observation.

A TV hung from a swiveling bracket on the wall above the three glass doors that could be fanned out across the wide doorway, but Janna had no desire to turn it on. She hadn't watched TV since arriving in Lancaster County, and honestly, she didn't feel like she'd missed anything. Besides, she needed to update Kendra, who'd texted earlier that they were praying for Kayla and her.

Janna couldn't make a call—the phone wouldn't do it for some reason—but when she texted her, Kendra was able to call. For thirty minutes they chatted, then Kendra prayed with her before hanging up so she could put her children to bed.

Janna then texted Arissa, who had messaged her right as

Joah's appointment at New Beginnings was ending. She asked Arissa to call her, and talking to her passed another twenty-five minutes and ended with Arissa promising to visit on Sunday.

Just as Janna started typing out a text to Cynthia, a soft, high-pitched noise made her look up. Kayla stirred, turning her head back and forth and rubbing her neck while still asleep. The wheezing continued as her breaths quickened, though she never opened her eyes.

Janna jumped up, dropping her phone onto the chair. "Kay?"

The monitor on the wall started pinging, and she glanced up. Two numbers—the heart rate and pulse ox—blinked. "Kayla?"

She didn't respond, just continued squirming in discomfort. Hives were forming on her neck and face.

Oh, not again. Please, Lord. I'll do anything. Janna reached across Kayla and grabbed the call button. Before she could push it, Aileen, the nurse who'd taken over for Lynn at seven o'clock, rushed into the room.

Luke had just sat down in the living room with the latest issue of *Fine Woodworking* when his phone's text alert sounded in his pocket.

By the way *Mamm* looked at him from her usual evening spot in the recliner, her eyebrows raised in hope, she expected it was Janna. But it was only eight forty-five, too soon for Kayla to be released. More likely it was Mahlon asking for an update. For once, he didn't feel guilty pulling out the phone in front of *Mamm.*

But it was from Janna.

Kayla had another allergic reaction. She's okay now, but they're admitting her for observation. Could you bring me a change of clothes? They gave her an oral steroid this time and she vomited on me.

Poor Kayla. And poor Janna. She'd seemed calm at the hospital, but she was also good at putting up a front. The way she'd clasped his hand when he put it on her shoulder had told him she wasn't letting on how upset she was, probably because of *Mamm* and Joah. "Kayla had another reaction."

"Another?"

"They're keeping her overnight now, and she threw up on Janna. She asked if I could bring clothes for her. Would you get them for me?" Might as well ask. She wouldn't let him go into Janna and Kayla's bedroom anyway.

Mamm set aside the sweater she was knitting, then slowly stood before heading for the *daadi haus*.

Luke texted her back that he would leave soon, then jogged upstairs and changed into clothes that weren't smeared with wood stain. Back in the kitchen, he grabbed his hat from the peg on the wall by the door.

Mamm joined him, setting a tote bag on the counter. Within minutes, she'd filled a thermos with mint tea, made a ham-and-cheese sandwich, and packed the sandwich into a cooler bag along with several of the granola bars she'd baked with the children that morning.

He placed the thermos and cooler bag into the tote and picked it up. "Did you see Kayla's blanket and rabbit in the bedroom?"

"*Ach, ya.* She'll want those." She went back into the *daadi haus* and returned with both, as well as with tears in her eyes. "Tell Janna I'm praying for them."

He put an arm around her and kissed her forehead. *Mamm*

absolutely adored Kayla and had been worried enough before she learned about the second reaction. "If Janna's upset, I'll stay as long as she needs me to—or lets me." With how things had gone the last few days, he wouldn't be surprised if she didn't want him to stay. But he hoped not. "If I won't be back tonight, do you want me to call Malinda to ask her to come stay here?"

"*Nee.* We'll be fine. Just let me know how they're doing."

With that decided, he stepped out onto the porch and then sprinted to his truck. At least traffic would be much lighter now, so it shouldn't take long to get there.

Twelve minutes later, Luke again walked up to the desk in the ER, and the same receptionist pushed a button to open the automatic doors.

When he approached Kayla's doorway, he found Janna, dressed in a blue top and pants just like the nurses wore, sitting propped up on the bed with her arm around Kayla. He'd expected Kayla to still be wearing an oxygen mask, but that had been replaced with a nasal cannula—a good sign, he hoped.

Janna smiled, seeming quite composed, and nudged Kayla's arm. "Look who's here."

Kayla slowly opened her eyes, then grinned with such happiness—tired as it was—that his concern for her eased. "Luke."

"Hey there." He walked to the side of the bed and pulled her rabbit out of the tote. "This guy said if you were going to be here, he wanted to be here too."

"Rabbit! And my blanket!" She grabbed that too when he lifted it out of the bag.

"I thought you might want them." He set the bag on the bed and retrieved Janna's neatly folded clothes. "And these are for you."

She took them and stood, looking into his eyes with the same fondness he'd seen in them on the night of her birthday.

"Thank you so much. I'm sorry for making you come back. Right after you texted me that you were on your way, the nurse brought me these scrubs, but I'm glad to have my own clothes."

"*Nee*. I'm glad you texted me."

"'Cause if we're going to be here, you want to be here too—like Rabbit?" Kayla said, looking up at him.

He chuckled even though she was completely serious. "That's right."

Janna squeezed his arm, and as she headed for the attached bathroom, more weight lifted off his shoulders. Perhaps all wasn't lost between the two of them after all.

No Better Friend

Janna quickly dressed, then picked up the folded scrubs from where she'd set them on the bathroom sink. Glancing in the mirror, she stopped. Her hair was always a bit unruly by the end of the day, but its current state was worse than usual. At least being in a braid had kept it clean. Changing clothes was much easier than trying to wash long hair in a small sink. Things could be worse. She needed to keep that in mind.

"*Ach*, it wasn't your fault, sweetheart," Luke was telling Kayla as Janna stepped back into the room. He sat on the edge of the stretcher, smoothing the curls off her face as he gazed down at her with a gentle smile. "And don't feel so bad. I got sick on your mama once too."

Kayla looked over, her expression a combination of glee and horror. "Did he, Mama?"

Janna had to smile. She'd forgotten about that. "*Ya.* I was about eight, I think. He used to get carsick sometimes when we'd hire a van."

"And one Saturday, we went to visit some of *Daadi* Eli's

family, and as soon as we got out of the van . . ." He splayed his hands in front of him. "Your mama jumped, but not quick enough to get her shoes out of the way."

Kayla grimaced, looking sleepy. "Gross."

"But you know what? Your mama was more upset that I was sick than she was about her shoes." After a glance at Janna, he arched his eyebrows at Kayla. "Right then I knew I'd never find a better friend than her—not anywhere."

Janna grinned too, despite the sadness brought by that memory. The incident hadn't fazed her. By that time, she'd already spent a few years taking care of Mom when she was sick from drinking too much.

And if she didn't know better, she'd consider Luke's nostalgic words a peace offering. Maybe they were. He'd been unusually quiet the last two days, but not tonight. Perhaps he realized he'd overreacted to her taking the children to the pool.

Whatever the reason, she'd take it. The day had been stressful enough without worrying about her relationship with him.

Just then, Aileen wheeled a large club-type chair into the room. "Oh, good. You got your clothes." She pushed the chair toward the wall. "We're still working on getting you a bed upstairs. Sometimes that takes a little while, so I had one of the guys from patient transport find us a sleeper chair. It pulls out into a bed, and I can draw the curtain and close the doors partway so you can get some rest."

"Thank you. I appreciate it."

Aileen checked Kayla's IV, then looked at the monitor and patted her arm. "Get some sleep now, miss. I'm pretty sure it's past your bedtime."

"*Ya.*"

After taking the scrubs from Janna, Aileen left, sliding the curtain across the ceiling track and pulling the doors.

Here or upstairs, Kayla would be in good hands. Of course, Janna's ability to sleep—exhausted or not—was another thing. Every few minutes she was scrutinizing Kayla, looking for signs of another reaction.

Luke had lowered the head of the stretcher and was helping Kayla turn on her side. He pulled the blanket up to her waist. "How's that?"

"Good. Night-night." She hugged Rabbit and her blanket tighter and closed her eyes.

Janna kissed her forehead, breathing in the sweaty scent of her hair. Never had she thought she'd savor that smell. She'd never take the essence of her little girl for granted again. "Night-night."

Luke watched her intently when she straightened, so much so that she looked away for fear that he'd see how close to tears she was.

The weight of her dispute with the Martins two nights ago, her move to Akron and Luke's insinuation she was doing so by choice, the burden of wondering how the Martins would manage without her and Kayla, and her uncertainty about which school to enroll Kayla in . . .

All that had been more than enough difficulties for the week. Now this too? She'd kept it together for Kayla's sake, but only by the grace of God.

Luke stood and guided her away from the bed. "Do they know what happened?" he whispered. "Why she had another reaction, I mean."

"It's called a biphasic reaction. The doctor said they see it in kids sometimes, especially when they're right around her age." She took a deep breath, trying to keep her calm, then released it. "I just don't know why this happened in the first place. I read the ingredients on the fruit bar's label. It didn't contain peanuts, and the wrapper said nothing about it being made in a facility where peanuts are used."

"Does she see an allergist?"

"*Ya.* I need to make a post-ER appointment for her next week, but the office we go to is more than an hour away now."

"If she needs to go, we'll take her. Or if you want to find a closer allergist, we'll talk to Kendra. I know the one Drew goes to is close by."

They'd been seeing Kayla's allergist for almost four years, but switching might be best. Lancaster County was home now, and they weren't moving again.

Except they were.

Janna nodded, blinking at the sting behind her eyes. "Okay."

Luke rested a hand on her shoulder. "Don't worry about that right now."

Right. She didn't need to deal with that till Monday.

The sting intensified, and she looked away again, striving to control her breathing. Her gaze landed on Kayla, and the sight of her little girl—still blotchy where the hives had been, breathing the oxygen, and with an IV board on the arm holding Rabbit—completely undid her.

It was too much. All that had happened this week. What could've happened today. And what would be happening within the next two weeks.

Tears blurred her vision and slid down her cheeks.

"*Ach,* come here." Luke drew her close and wrapped his arms around her.

Covering her face with her hands, she leaned into his chest and sobbed.

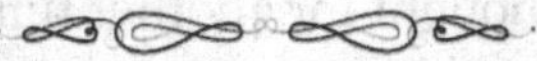

Once Janna stopped crying, Luke opened out the sleeping chair so she could sit down. He grabbed some tissues from the box on the counter by the sink, then sat beside her and placed them in her hand.

She wiped her eyes and sighed.

"I hope you know what a wonderful-good job you did today." He wasn't sure where the words came from, but as soon as they were out, something told him she needed to hear them. "*Mamm* told me how you knew exactly what to do and did it, how you kept calm and even reassured Joah when he was upset."

She stared down at the tissue in her fist. "You know what the doctor told me? She came back into the room to check on Kayla, and right before she left, she said, 'Congratulations, Mom. Most of us get to give our child life only once. You just did it a second time.'" With a shake of her head, she looked at him. "I was so relieved when Kayla outgrew her milk allergy and we only had the peanut one to deal with. But now she's probably allergic to something else too."

He slid his hand across her back. "Being a parent isn't for the faint of heart, is it?"

She smiled, albeit cynically. "Especially when you're doing it on your own."

"Two are better than one, for if they fall, the one will lift up the other." He couldn't recall the exact words from Ecclesiastes, but their wisdom wasn't lost in his version.

That reminded him of Wilmer's advice a few weeks back—how God intended for children to be reared by both a father and a mother. He'd scoffed at the notion of remarriage then, but now . . .

Ach, that was a thought for another time.

"You've been such a help to *Mamm* and me that way, and I hope we've been able to do the same for you."

"Absolutely. This summer has been amazing, for Kayla and for me, even if it started off feeling like a disaster."

"I agree."

She eyed him, her grin returning. "That it started off feeling like a disaster?"

That wasn't what he'd meant, but she was right. "Seemed that way. Mahlon was in Ohio, the Stotts' dining set deadline was looming, *Mamm* had more responsibilities than she could handle, Joah was lonely, and I felt like it was all my fault. Then you and Kayla showed up, and it's been the best summer we've had in years."

And now summer would soon be coming to an end. Joah—and maybe Kayla with him—would be starting school, and Janna and Kayla would be moving out of the *daadi haus*. Janna had assured him she would still help out, but only a fool would think their lives wouldn't revert back to how they'd been, at least in some ways.

But what other options did they have? Even if Janna hadn't signed a lease agreement on the Akron house, it wasn't like he could expect her to live in the *daadi haus*, help out in the shop, and care for his family forever. Really, he needed a wife—just as Wilmer had said. And hopefully, Janna would come to realize that all men weren't trouble and find someone she wanted to marry.

He cringed at that thought. Not because she didn't deserve to marry, but because she was the only woman who'd made him even entertain the thought of remarriage. And yet how could he marry her? There were disparities in some of their beliefs, and his were too important to him. He wouldn't renounce them. He couldn't.

Janna sighed, bringing him back to reality.

He pushed those thoughts away. Right now he needed to be here for her in any way he could, not thinking about himself. He started to ask if she wanted the sandwich Salena sent or a granola bar, but the squeaking of Aileen's sneakers interrupted as she pushed past the curtain.

"Good news," she whispered. "They have a bed for you up in the peds unit. You'll be more comfortable there."

Luke nodded his thanks. Well, Janna and Kayla would be more comfortable up there. As long as he could stay with them, he didn't care if he was comfortable or not.

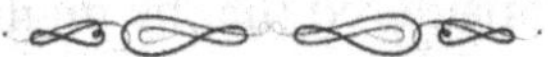

It was quarter past midnight by the time Kayla's nurse in the pediatric unit had finished everything she needed to do. Janna turned off the last of the room lights, then settled into the recliner by Kayla's bed.

Luke, who'd given no indication he was leaving, now lay on the couch against the wall. He hadn't pulled it out to make a bed despite how his legs were too long to straighten them, but that hadn't stopped him from quickly falling asleep after she assured him she and Kayla had everything they needed.

That was completely understandable. For weeks now he'd been rising early to help Enos and Ivan. He said he didn't mind —and she suspected it helped him preserve a good relationship with his family despite their feelings about his attending a *Funkeleit* church—but it tired him enough that after a day in the workshop, he was often in bed by nine thirty.

She was up early as well, although that wasn't as hard to do since he always stopped in the *daadi haus* on his way to the milking barn. They never talked long, but she looked forward to it. Still, she should be a lot more tired by now. She'd been up for twenty hours.

Reclining the chair a bit more, she turned partly onto her side and pulled up the blanket. Kayla's vital signs were being monitored, so Janna should rest while she could.

Except she couldn't slow down her mind. It replayed everything. Kayla's first reaction in Mellinger's parking lot. The terrifying rush to the hospital. Trying to care for Kayla and not let on to Joah and Salena just how critical Kayla's condition was. The treatment in the ER. The second reaction.

Then the words she'd prayed sprang from her mind: *I'll do anything.* So strange. Never before had she tried to bargain with God—or even considered that he might work that way. He didn't, and she knew it. But she'd prayed those words, and immediately the oddest thing came to mind—wearing a head covering.

She sighed. *I'll do anything.* Did that mean, deep down, she knew she could do more? Well, obviously she could. People could always do more—more relying on God alone, more acting in obedience, more developing a desire for his plan to be fulfilled. But did he want more from her? Something she was holding back? Something more she *should* do?

Wearing a head covering had crossed her mind a lot lately. Kendra and the other women's reasons for wearing one were compelling enough, at least until she thought about how people would react. Well, how Arissa and Cynthia would react. They were the only two possible opposing voices whose opinions mattered to her.

But wasn't that what God called Christians to do—to follow where he led despite what other people thought or said? Like Luke had done.

Especially over the last two months, she'd been pursuing the Lord in every aspect of her life. Living with the Martins had made that easier in some ways, since their life revolved around being faithful in everything they did, but she was putting in work too—inwardly. Trusting God more. Allowing herself to trust others. Moving on from the past and forgiving those who'd hurt her. And believing that she hadn't deserved being mistreated.

And now it seemed he might be calling her to something else. Something she needed to think through.

Just not right now, because her mind was losing track of her thoughts. Time to get some sleep. Once things settled down, she'd talk to Kendra.

Luke awoke to a faint scent that reminded him of something he couldn't quite remember. Cleaning solution, maybe. He opened his eyes. The room was dark, lit only by the glowing numbers and graphs of a hospital monitor screen. A bed came into view. An IV pole.

He sat up, slamming his feet on the tile floor, and reality took hold. Kayla, not Rayanne, lay in the bed, sound asleep on her side as she hugged her stuffed rabbit. He sat on a couch by the wall, where he'd lain after the nurse got them settled in the room in the pediatric unit. Rubbing his hand across his forehead, he inhaled, then released the breath.

In the reclining chair beside the bed, Janna lifted her head and then pushed herself up. "Are you all right?"

By the time he dropped his hand, she was out of the chair and coming toward him.

"*Es dutt mir leed.* I didn't mean to wake you."

"Bad dream?" She stopped a few feet from him.

Well, not really. "*Nee.* I just thought I was somewhere else for a few moments." The reality of his surroundings had sent a wave of incredible relief through him, but his throat still felt tight.

She watched him, scowling a little as she closed her sweater against the room's chill. "Where?" The word came out in a gentle whisper, as if she sensed his distress.

"Rayanne passed away in the hospital. I slept there, or tried to, the night before."

Her expression pinched, and she sat down beside him. "This hospital?"

"*Nee.* In New York." He'd told her that, but with every-thing going on, it probably slipped her mind. "She and Joah were with Wilmer, Evelyn, and their one son's family, visiting her parents and relatives." He swallowed. "The trip was planned pretty last-minute. Mahlon and I were too busy with orders for me to take time off, but she insisted on going, and I gave in. Four days later . . ." He glanced around the room. "*Ach,* it isn't the time for this."

"*Nee,* go on."

He hesitated, but her sincere request encouraged him to finish. "The fourth day they were there, she wasn't feeling well. She'd woken up with a fever and was achy, and I told her to call the clinic to get care instructions, which we always did when she was sick." He shook his head. "Apparently, there was some miscommunication about whether she or her mother would call, and neither did. Rayanne was much sicker the next morn-ing, and they called the clinic and were told by the on-call doctor to take her to the hospital. By the time I got there, she was barely responsive—and she died the next afternoon."

Janna lifted his hand off his leg and held it between both of hers. "I'm so sorry."

Warmed by her compassion, he tried to grin. "It's not our place to question what God allows. One day we'll understand why his plan was best. But since then, I don't like hospitals much."

"Why didn't you say something? I certainly wouldn't have expected you to stay."

The emotion in her tone put a genuine smile on his face. "I knew you were upset. Plenty more than you were letting on. I also remember what it was like, feeling alone at the hospital. Rayanne's mother was there and the rest of the family were in and out, but Wilmer and Evelyn were the only ones I knew well." He placed his other hand on hers. "God is always with us, but I still didn't want you here by yourself."

She leaned her head against his shoulder. "And that's why I'll never find a better friend than you anywhere either." Her voice sounded strained again.

Ach, how he longed for more than just friendship between them. He withdrew his hand and slipped that arm around her.

She pretended to scratch her cheek, but he was pretty sure she was wiping her eye. "Thank you so much for staying."

"'Fear thou not; for I am with thee: be not dismayed; for I am thy God: I will strengthen thee.'"

"Always," she whispered.

So many times he'd repeated those words during difficult times, but they'd fallen flat in the weeks after Rayanne's death as he strove to come to grips with his new life. Now, sitting here with Janna and feeling like the future would again be so very different from what he wanted, all he could do was cling to the words of the One who'd never failed him.

CHAPTER 24

Decisions to Make

It was nearly two o'clock when Janna turned the van onto the lane the next day. Luke had left the hospital around eight that morning since Saturday was their busiest day at the shop, and while Janna had hoped she and Kayla would soon follow, discharge took longer than expected.

Beyond the shop, children climbed on the playset and jumped on the trampoline. As the van approached, Joah and the Eschbach children ran to the edge of the grass and waved.

"Looks like you've got a welcoming committee." Janna smiled as she glanced in the rearview mirror.

Kayla placed her hand on the window, grinning brightly.

Janna parked next to Kendra's van, then got out and opened the back door. Within moments Kayla was out of the van to meet the children, who all jogged toward her. Kendra waved from the bench near the playset, where she sat with Drew's head on her lap as he slept.

"Can Kayla play with us?" Joah asked.

"Of course." Janna hugged him and kissed the top of his

head as he wrapped his arms around her. "She might get tired more quickly because of the medicine they gave her, but she can play if she wants to."

As the five of them rushed off, Janna headed for the bench beneath the oak. "How long have you been here?" she asked as she sat down.

Kendra smiled and gave her as much of a hug as she could without disturbing Drew. "Mahlon brought Caleb with him this morning. The rest of us came around eleven, figuring you'd be home soon. I made dinner since the quilt shop was extra busy and Salena was helping Malinda and Beulah."

Janna had originally hoped to be home by one thirty so they could see Salena before she took her one-hour rest, but this worked better since it gave her the opportunity to talk to Kendra alone.

"Were you able to determine what Kayla reacted to?"

"The pediatrician who discharged her looked at the fruit bar wrapper, and he thinks most likely mango. The rest of the ingredients she's had before, but I don't know about mango. When we take her to the allergist for her follow-up this week, we'll have her tested for that."

Kendra stroked Drew's hair, sweaty despite the low-eighties temperature, as she gazed down at him. "Well, I know how much of a burden another allergy will be, but I'm glad it's probably figured out."

"And it could be worse," Janna added. "We managed a milk allergy for almost five years. At least mango isn't as common."

Kendra smiled. "Even in our difficulties, we always have something to be thankful for."

True. All things considered, Janna had many things to be thankful for.

Squeals came from the children, and she looked over at them. Naomi and Amanda swung on the swings while the other three bounced around the trampoline. Joah and Kayla held hands and wore smiles so carefree that they seemed to have forgotten the events of the last twenty-four hours. In some ways, perhaps that was best.

Yet their carefree days together were numbered.

Janna put that out of her mind. "There's something I wanted to talk to you about."

"Sure." Kendra carefully uncrossed her legs and shifted toward her. "What's on your mind?"

Janna hesitated. It seemed like fully explaining the prayer and her middle-of-the-night thought process about it was her only option, so she unloaded everything. "Does that make any sense at all?" she said, finishing. "Or do I sound crazy?"

Kendra grabbed her hand and squeezed it. "You don't sound crazy at all."

Well, that was good. "Then what do you make of it?"

"I believe the Holy Spirit is speaking to you. Have you been thinking about covering your head?"

This could be hard to explain. "I have—some—for the last few weeks. Then more often since we talked about it at Bible study and you gave me the tract on the topic."

"And what are you thinking?"

"I just don't know. A lot of Bible scholars say it was cultural, that it was an instruction given only to the Corinthians, but then I started questioning that after we talked about it. And now, after last night, I feel like . . . I know I should, but . . ."

"Something's holding you back?"

Agreeing aloud felt too difficult, but Janna could nod.

"You're not the only one who feels that way. It isn't a simple decision for a lot of women, even those who've grown up in homes where it's commonplace. I questioned it when I was a teenager."

Janna looked at her. "Really?"

"My mother's one sister no longer wears a covering, and neither do her daughters, and yet they're faithful Christians—active in their church, in serving their community, and in missions. As a teenager, I struggled with that. My aunt and cousins obviously loved Jesus, and it was hard for me to reconcile that they followed him and yet didn't feel the need to cover their heads."

Yes! "That's part of why I'm conflicted. How do you do that? Reconcile the two, I mean."

"Well, I can speak only for myself, but I relied on the Holy Spirit's leading. My parents and I studied covering the head and talked through the many explanations people give for women not doing so, and between that and a lot of prayer, I determined it was something I needed to do. Same with dressing modestly. I would never condemn anyone who doesn't —and I would never insist that only certain head coverings or ways of dress are acceptable—but the Holy Spirit has convinced me of what's right for me to do."

Janna nodded. "That makes sense." It also made wearing a head covering seem less . . . judgy. Not that many people in the Plain community had ever made her feel judged, mainly just Beulah, but Janna had worried that Arissa or Cynthia might feel that way.

"Janna, you said *part* of why you're conflicted. There's another reason, then?"

Ya, there was. But that one was even more difficult to explain, even to Kendra. "I just don't want it to seem like I'm doing it only to . . . I don't know, make people happy, I guess."

Kendra kept her smile mild. "I see. And yes, some people would certainly be very happy about it."

Janna nodded, looking away. Kendra obviously knew exactly what—and whom—she meant, although she was too kind to say it outright.

"So you want to do this and for others to understand that you're doing it out of obedience to the Lord and not because of someone else's expectations or wishes."

"Exactly. But I'm not sure how to accomplish that."

Kendra held her gaze, her expression compassionate. "We can't control what others think, and God doesn't call us to. He calls us to be faithful to him. We're not responsible for others' actions or thoughts, only our own. What matters is that we obey what he asks of us."

Wise words, as always. One of the reasons she loved Kendra so much. "Thank you."

"If I can do anything else, just let me know."

Janna's mood suddenly brightened. This wasn't a life-or-death decision she was making, but it was important. "Actually, where could I get a covering? *Mamm* used to buy hers from someone, but I don't remember whom."

"Probably Ada Weaver. I get mine from her too. She runs a fabric store on their farm and makes all different shapes and sizes. I'd give you one of mine, but your hair is much thicker, and I'm pretty sure you'll need a larger crown. Does Salena have a headscarf you could wear until we can visit Ada?"

"The ones she wears to bed. I'll ask her. I just need to talk to Kayla about it first." And Arissa too, since she'd be visiting tomorrow.

Well, one decision made. Now to deal with the school situation. Kayla would be attending school with Joah, that she knew. Paying for it? She had yet to figure that out.

"Is every Sunday like this here?" Arissa asked as Janna followed her off the kitchen porch.

"Well, not every Sunday." They stepped into pace on the slate slabs that led to the lane. "But most Sundays we either have company for dinner or are invited somewhere. It's a nice way to unwind before the workweek starts, and Kayla loves getting to play with so many kids."

Today would be even more relaxing than usual. With Salena, Malinda and two of her daughters, and Beulah and one of her daughters-in-law redding up the kitchen, Janna and Arissa had been shooed out to visit together.

They walked along the rose bushes in front of the *daadi haus*'s fence, then Janna opened the gate and followed Arissa up to the porch. There, they sat on the swing.

"She certainly seems happy," Arissa said as she peered across the lane to where the thirteen children now played. Luke and two of the fathers sat on the bench talking, while Enos, Ivan, and the other father ambled toward the carriage house. "No issues since she was discharged?"

"*Nee*, she's been fine." That was another reason Janna was glad to be out of the kitchen. The pediatrician at the hospital had warned of a small chance of another allergic reaction within seventy-two hours, and even though she'd made sure Luke knew what to do if Kayla showed any sign of that, being able to see her gave Janna more peace of mind.

"Kay looks like she fits right in here." Arissa's tone now held an edge Janna couldn't quite read. She didn't sound annoyed. A mix of concerned and confused, maybe. "And she's not the only one."

Here it came. Janna had wondered how long it would take. "What do you mean?"

"Just look at her." Arissa frowned slightly. "With that dress she's wearing and her hair in the braids, she looks just like the other girls. I even heard her speaking some of their language." She met her gaze. "And I'm afraid you're not far behind."

Janna suppressed a sigh. "Why, because my skirt's the same material? It was a birthday gift from Salena, made to match the dress Kayla's wearing. And it's not like I look any different now." Well, except that she hadn't worn pants or shorts in weeks. But did that really matter? She grinned, hoping to lighten the mood. "Physically, except for size, the two of us have been polar opposites from day one. I've always been low maintenance."

Arissa grinned but only briefly. "It's not just that. It's your demeanor too. Granted, you've always been the quiet, introspective one, but now you seem . . . I don't know, submissive?"

She really had to use that word? "Try content. I'm happy, like Kayla. Until we moved, I didn't realize just how much I missed living out here. It's slower paced, it's peaceful, and I love it. I don't think being content is something to apologize for."

"I'm not saying that. You've had enough crazy in your life that you deserve some happy." She shook her head. "But when I got here and saw the girls on the porch and then realized Kayla was one of them, I was afraid I'd go inside to find you wearing one of those bonnets."

"Head covering," she said. But she couldn't deny the rest, and she needed to talk to Arissa about it. "Actually, I have decided to wear one—as of yesterday, anyway—but I wanted to tell you first."

Arissa stared at her. "But isn't that about submission? You've sworn that off."

"This is submission to God, obedience to him. That I've never sworn off, and after talking with the women at Bible study, I've realized that godly order is a blessing when men and women treat each other as the Bible instructs. I've been thinking and praying about it for a while now, and I know it's what God's calling me to do."

Arissa gave a few slow nods, then pulled her phone from the back pocket of her denim skirt. She input her PIN, and after a few swipes and clicks, held out the phone. "Does it have anything to do with this?"

The screen displayed the photo of her, Luke, and the children at Groff's Grove.

"Kayla texted it to me last week after we talked about what she did for her birthday. And today she told me Luke stayed overnight at the hospital with you, and I can see what's going on just watching you both."

Oh, this was exactly what she'd been afraid of. "We're friends. I didn't decide to cover my head because of him."

"Maybe formally you're friends, but I know you, Jan. You care about him—a lot—and I think the feeling is mutual."

She couldn't refute any of that either, even the last part. But whether or not that care went further than friendship, she still didn't know—at least in Luke's case. As well, she questioned the prudence of entering that kind of relationship before she and Kayla were on their feet. "Maybe so, but that's not why I'm doing this. I promise you that."

Arissa put her phone back into her pocket. "Jan, I can't tell you how to live your life, but you are my BFF. I love you and Kay, and I want what's best for you. You're happy here, and I get that and I'm glad. But just keep in mind what will change if you choose this life."

Janna didn't respond, allowing Arissa to speak her mind.

"Say you start wearing a head covering, join their church, and eventually get married—to whomever. Even if the differences in dress don't bother you, think beyond that. You love kids, but do you want to have six or seven more of them? At your age, you could. And what about your editing? You've worked hard to grow your business into something that supports you. Are you ready to give that up? Because you'll have to if you have a home and large family to care for." Arissa raised her eyebrows at her. "Those're just some major changes. There'd be plenty of minor ones as well, I'm sure."

Janna sighed as she gazed across the lane. Luke now sat cross-legged on the trampoline while Joah, Kayla, and two of the other children jumped to bounce him. Amid a roar of giggles, they finally unseated him, sending him onto his back, and Joah and Kayla pounced on him. He sat up, hugging them both.

She smiled, her heart warming, but then that faded. Arissa was right. She had a lot to think about. But she'd have plenty of time for that. "Right now, I need to be faithful to what God's calling me to do," she said. "The rest he'll show me in time."

Honestly, how could what she wanted in life be so opposite sometimes?

Mamm and Janna were already in the kitchen when Luke came downstairs after putting Joah to bed.

Janna glanced over her shoulder at him and smiled, then handed him a plate with a slice of Dutch apple pie and a fork.

He sat down at the table but didn't start eating until they joined him and each said a silent blessing. "What's on the schedule for this week? The usual?"

Janna looked up from her plate. "OT Tuesday and PT Friday, church Wednesday night, and Bible study Thursday morning." She gazed across the table at *Mamm*. "Malinda's watching the shop till around ten tomorrow morning so the children and I can go to Ada Weaver's with Kendra. You're welcome to come along."

Mamm set down her fork, her full attention on Janna. "Ada's. You planning on doing some sewing?"

A tinge of color came to Janna's cheeks. "*Nee*. I've decided to wear a head covering. Kendra says Ada sells all different kinds and can customize a pattern and make one if she doesn't have the right size."

Luke stopped chewing and stared at her. For a moment he wasn't sure if he'd heard right. Then *Mamm* reached across the table and took Janna's hand. Going by the way she grinned, he'd heard right.

"We'd have to follow her since one van won't hold us all," Janna said, "but I'd like you to come—if you want to."

Mamm squeezed her hand and then released it. "*Ach*, of course I do."

Luke managed to down the bite of pie in his mouth. So many thoughts came to mind. Wondering when she'd made the decision and why she hadn't said anything before now. How he wished he could go with them to Ada's, as odd as that seemed. And above all, how this decision could change everything. Maybe.

When *Mamm* stood, he realized he'd been lost in his thoughts for long enough that she'd finished her pie—and that he hadn't said anything about Janna's announcement.

Janna followed, carrying her plate to the sink as well. "It's been a long day for you. I'll take care of the dishes."

Mamm didn't object. Their having company today hadn't allowed her time to rest that afternoon, and she looked tired. She hugged Janna, then said her good-nights and went upstairs.

Luke shoved the last forkful of pie into his mouth and rose, then carried his plate to the sink. He needed to say something, but what? Jumping for joy, his heart's initial response, obviously wouldn't suit. But staying silent sure wouldn't either.

Janna didn't look up when he stopped beside her. She

finished filling one side of the sink with soapy water, then swiveled the faucet to fill the other side. Her cheeks colored again as she moved the small pile of used dishes into the wash water. While at the hospital, she'd been so open with him, so why was she now almost shy?

He added his plate to the others, then considered what to say. "When did you decide?"

She glanced at him, the barely visible smile on her face again. "Final decision? Yesterday afternoon. But I needed to talk to Arissa and Kayla first. I told Arissa today and Kayla tonight."

He could understand that. After moving around to the other side of her, he pulled a dish towel from the drawer there. "How'd that go?"

She drew a slow breath as she ran her dish cloth over a plate. "Better than I thought. Arissa wasn't thrilled, but she knows it's not her decision. And she's always stood by me no matter what. Kayla just smiled and said, 'Okay, Mama.'"

"You've been thinking about this for a while?"

"And praying about it." She slipped the plate into the rinse water. "Part of me wanted to talk to you about it—before now, I mean—but the decision needed to be between the Lord and me. I didn't want it to seem like I was doing it to improve my relationship with Salena . . . or for any other reason than I believe it's what God wants."

That made sense, and honestly, he wouldn't want it another way. But she and *Mamm* seemed to get along fine. "What's wrong with your relationship with *Mamm*?"

"Well, nothing's *wrong*. It's more that I've felt like . . . I don't know, like she doesn't approve of me. I didn't want it to seem like I was trying to . . . win her favor, I guess?"

He chuckled, mainly because he understood what she was saying all too well. "*Ach*, Janna, *Mamm* loves you so much. She always has and always will." He turned and leaned against the counter, looking at her. "Would she be overjoyed if you embraced all her beliefs and joined her church? No doubt. But don't think for a moment that she loves you any less because some of your beliefs differ from hers. I've felt the same way you have, but she's loved me no matter what."

After a few moments, she smiled. But then tears filled her eyes. "Goodness. I don't know what's wrong with me. I rarely cry, and this weekend . . ." She shook her head.

"Nothing's wrong with you. There's just a lot going on in your life."

Ach, a lot was going on in all of their lives. Even he'd wanted to cry a time or two—like right now, because even though Janna had made a decision he'd been praying for, it didn't change the fact that she and Kayla would be moving to Akron.

It wasn't the end of the world, though it sometimes felt like it, and now he had to admit that all his hoping for a different outcome had done nothing but leave him with only days to find help for *Mamm*. It shouldn't be that hard, really. Joah would be starting school a week from tomorrow, and Janna would be taking him to PT and OT after school. Just a helper for household chores and in the shop would do. So why did it feel—

"What is it?" Janna's words interrupted his thoughts.

The dishes now sat stacked on the counter in front of him, clean. He hadn't realized he'd been drying them—or that his expression must've given away his mood.

The stairs in the living room creaked, and moments later *Mamm* came into the kitchen. Nearing them, she held out what looked like a white handkerchief. "I thought you'd want these for now."

Janna smiled as she took them. "*Danki*."

When she set them on the counter, he recognized one of

the headscarves *Mamm* wore to bed as well as several long hair pins. She helped Janna coil her braid and pin it, then watched as she placed the scarf and tied it at the back of her neck. After smiling at Janna, she met his gaze. "Morning comes early."

"I'll be right up." Once he heard the creaking again, he turned back to Janna.

She had her head down as she adjusted the placement of the scarf. "How does it look?"

"Beautiful."

She looked up, laughing softly. "I meant is it straight. I'm pretty sure *beautiful* contradicts the humility it should convey."

"But humility is beautiful, not?" he said, weighing whether to be as honest as he wished. "As is the one who displays it."

She grinned. "True."

Apparently he hadn't been specific enough. "Especially in your case. In my opinion."

Her smile disappeared as she realized his meaning, then returned as she averted her eyes. With a squeeze of his arm, she murmured, "You better get upstairs before she comes back down and drags you up by your ear."

He laughed at the memory. "She hasn't done that since I was ten. Not that she wouldn't do it again." As much as he wanted to stay here all night, she was right. "*Guder nacht.*"

"*Guder nacht.*"

He headed for the stairs, his heart beating a little faster. Morning did come early, and tonight he was even gladder for that than usual.

CHAPTER 25

The Heart Knows

A prayer answered, that's what it was. When Janna, Luke, and the children had walked into the Mennonite school Joah would start attending next week, she'd been unsure how the meeting would go. Even with the nearly full-time editing schedule she'd lined up for September and October, affording private school on top of rent and everything else seemed unlikely.

And then the principal informed them that, in accordance with Janna's income, River View Mennonite Fellowship would pay sixty percent of Kayla's tuition. Despite her initial hesitance, Janna had to accept this news for what it was—the answer she'd been praying for.

Now, as the four of them got into Luke's truck, her ringtone sang inside her purse.

"Who is it?" Kayla asked.

Janna's heart sank as soon as she pulled out her phone. "Mrs. Bollinger."

"But it's only Wednesday." Not a trace of cheeriness remained in Kayla's voice. "She said not till next week."

Janna considered sending the call to voice mail, but that wouldn't change the inevitable. So she answered it. Within five minutes, and at Luke's urging, she'd agreed to Mrs. Bollinger's invitation to stop by to see the house, which would be ready to move into this Saturday.

A collective quiet gloom settled over the truck's cab. Janna drew a breath and vowed to quash her own dejection. Kayla surely wouldn't find reasons to be happy about moving if Janna didn't.

By the time they pulled up to the curb in Akron, she'd reminded herself how much she and Kayla loved the house. And, as she suspected, it was even more charming now. The peeling white clapboard had been replaced by bright-white siding, periwinkle-blue shutters had been added to the windows, and the stained roof had new dark-gray shingles. The flowers in the front beds were as lovely as they'd always been.

"It looks different," Kayla murmured.

Janna hoped she hadn't imagined the admiration in her tone. "*Ya*, it does." She got out, then led the children around to the front of the truck.

An Old Order Mennonite carriage clip-clopped toward them in the other lane, and they waited there with Luke and Joah. The driver, an elderly man wearing wire-rim glasses, held up a hand and smiled as he passed.

Janna froze as a memory sucked the air from her lungs. How many times had *Daadi* Eli done the same thing as he drove down the lane while she stood on the kitchen porch and waved back?

She stared after the carriage, overwhelmed by a longing for just a few minutes with him. To tell him how much she loved him and how grateful she was for the way he and Salena had cared for her. And to introduce him to Kayla—and Joah. He'd love them. And they'd—

"Mama, are you coming?"

Janna looked away just as Kayla grabbed her hand. Luke and Joah were halfway to the curb, and fortunately, they hadn't noticed her lagging behind. She hurried Kayla across and caught up with them as they stepped onto the sidewalk.

The new screen door on the right side of the house opened, and stout Mrs. Bollinger stepped onto the porch, smoothing her blouse and skirt. "Looks a bit different, no?" she said, greeting them with a smile.

That was for sure. Even the gray porch floorboards had been repainted, and the old chair had been replaced by two new oak rockers. "It's just beautiful."

Mrs. Bollinger blinked, then her eyes lit with delight. "Well, look at you."

Hers wasn't the first such reaction this week, and Janna grinned as she climbed the two steps to the porch.

Mrs. Bollinger placed her hand on Janna's arm. "You look beautiful too," she whispered, then glanced around at all of them. "Are you ready to see the inside? You just missed Tony, but his workers are up tiling the bathroom."

That was a relief. The last thing Janna needed today was Tony's comments.

A middle-aged man appeared on the other side of the screen door. "So what do you think?" he asked as he joined them on the porch. "While we had Tony taking care of the insurance repairs, we decided to have him make some updates too." He walked around them to the other front door. "I'm her son Rudy, by the way."

Janna almost couldn't believe her eyes when she stepped inside. The living room's white walls were now light-gray with crisp white trim. The beige carpet, dingy and a little worn but certainly not in terrible shape, was gone. Gray-washed oak flooring had taken its place.

Rudy walked toward the doorway into the dining room, holding up his arms. "Nice, isn't it?"

More than nice.

"Mama, can we go upstairs?" Kayla sounded almost excited now.

Janna reminded herself that was a good thing. "*Ya*. But people are working up there, so be sure to stay out of their way." She wandered into the dining room and then the kitchen. The same flooring continued in there, and the cabinets had been painted dark gray and topped with a marbled gray-and-white countertop. Everything was simply gorgeous—and perfect for how she planned to decorate.

The clip-clopping of another horse sounded outside the open window, drawing her to the sink as a carriage passed on the road alongside the house. And suddenly the design of the house seemed trivial.

"So what do you think?"

Rudy's voice turned her around, and Janna forced a smile. "It's lovely."

He moved toward her. "What's the matter?"

She shook her head. "The house is amazing." A little unnerved by something about his expression, she rounded him and returned to the living room. The others must've gone upstairs.

He followed. "You seem upset about something."

"It's just going to be hard to leave the people we're staying with, that's all." Hopefully, that would end the discussion.

He nodded a few times. "Well, as you must realize, this rental is worth more than seven hundred a month now. We do have to abide by the lease agreement, but I've told Mom she needs to up the rent in February—to help pay for the renovations."

He named a price well out of her planned budget, and Janna cringed. A six-month lease had seemed like a prudent option when she signed it, to make sure they were happy here. Not so much now.

Rudy slid his hands into his jeans pockets. "That said, if you're happier where you are, we'd have no problem dissolving the lease and returning your rent payment."

The children came down the stairs, followed by Mrs. Bollinger and Luke.

"I'll keep that in mind," she said just loudly enough for Rudy to hear. As if she didn't have enough to worry about, now they'd probably need to move again in six months.

She walked toward the front door, ready to go. All she could do was leave this new challenge in the Lord's hands.

The next evening Janna was sitting on the kitchen porch's step, watching the children catch lightning bugs, when Luke closed up the shop. As he started toward the house, the tension of the last two hours eased. August's sales and expenditures so far were now transferred from the shop ledger to his software program, and the picture before him—a perfect summer evening, in his opinion—brought a renewal of energy.

"Daddy, look!" Joah jogged toward him, holding a canning jar of blinking bugs. "I caught six so far."

"And I caught five!" No sooner had Kayla stopped beside Joah, she pointed. "Look, there's more over there!"

The two took off, and Luke crossed the lane and started up the walkway to the porch.

Janna smiled, sending a flutter through his middle. "All caught up?"

"*Ya.*" As much as he would've rather spent the time with her, it felt good to have the work done. He sat down beside her, probably closer than he should have. "Where's *Mamm*?"

She made no move to put space between them. "Inside. Jake called about ten minutes ago."

Gut. Mamm's weekly phone call with her oldest son's family rarely took less than an hour.

Down at the road, flashing carriage lights turned onto the lane and came toward them. The children ran to the edge of the pavement as the carriage neared, then waved to Ivan and Malinda as they drove by. When Joah and Kayla crossed the lane to the wide strip of grass alongside the shop's parking lot, their happy chatter faded.

A calf's bawl carried from up in the barn, barely audible over the constant din of crickets and katydids. Hank's telltale cock-a-doodle-bray soon joined in, making Luke chuckle. After all these years, that never got old.

Neither did sitting next to Janna.

A glance at her made his heart skip. She sat silent, seemingly staring at the far-off sky but with her eyes closed as the breeze played with the wavy strands of hair that had slid from beneath her covering. Then the slightest scowl replaced the serenity of her expression.

Reminded of a game they'd played as children, he said, "A penny for your thoughts."

She lowered her chin but didn't open her eyes. After a few moments, she whispered, "I love it here."

That definitely wasn't what he'd expected. And how did he respond to that? Well, he knew what he wanted to say, but should he? *Lord, give me the right words.*

"And not just in Lancaster County," she went on. "I love it

here. On the farm." She opened her eyes and met his gaze. "With you." Her last two words came out so softly that he barely heard them.

"With all of us, you mean? Or . . ." Now he was being too bold.

"With all of you." She smiled. "But especially with you."

Ach, how he wanted to kiss her. That was no way for an honorable man to act, though, so he took her hand instead. "Then stay."

"I just don't know how we'd . . ." She looked away as if she didn't know how to continue.

But he did. It was what he'd wanted to say for weeks. "We want you here. *I* want you here. I've drug my feet in finding someone else to help us only because I couldn't stand the thought of it. You and Kayla are so much more than helpers for *Mamm,* and so much more than a babysitter and a friend for Joah."

He paused, hoping his honesty wouldn't make her uneasy. "And you're so much more than a childhood friend doing a favor for me. You're the reason I feel like I'm living life again, not just surviving it." After waiting for her to look into his eyes, he said what he needed to. "I know you've said you're not interested in a relationship with any man, but—"

"I've decided to reconsider," she said, averting her eyes but smiling. "But only for you."

Emotion swelled in Luke's chest. For weeks now he'd prayed about his feelings for Janna, trying to discern what God wanted their relationship to be. This was the answer he'd hoped for with all his heart. "You said you'd never be a sweet, serene Mennonite girl either," he teased, "but you got the shy-girl response down pat. So I guess you were wrong about that too."

"*Schtobbe.*" She nudged his ribs with her elbow, then

became more serious. "But how will Kayla and I stay here if we're—"

"That's why I called Don Smith tonight."

"Don?" Janna stared at him, confused. "Please tell me you didn't call him about what Rudy Bollinger told me."

Luke laughed. *"Nee."* Sure, he'd been bothered when she told him about Rudy's plan to raise the rent so high, but the man hadn't done anything illegal. Of course, all Janna knew was that he'd called a police officer. "Last spring, Don mentioned that his tenants would be moving out this fall. At supper I remembered that. Turns out the couple is leaving September thirtieth, and he doesn't have a new renter yet"—he grinned—"unless you're interested."

Janna's mind spun as she tried to wrap her head around what Luke was saying. "So we could live across the road?"

"Ya. You'd have your own place but still be close enough to be here as much as suits. And we'd pay you for any help around the house or with Joah. I know you have editing work scheduled, but if you'd like to do that here, you're welcome to use the *daadi haus."*

Wow. Really, it was an incredible option. She and Kayla could come over early in the morning to help make breakfast and eat with the Martins, then once the children were on the school bus, she could help Salena with any household chores. The rest of the time, which she would have plenty of with Joah and Kayla at school, could be spent in the *daadi haus* editing. After school she would oversee homework, help make supper, and enjoy time with the Martins before taking Kayla home at bedtime. It would be wonderful, except—

"Would that work for you?" Luke's reserved tone suggested he was thinking the same thing.

"You mean because Mom and I lived there?"

"*Ya.*"

Two months ago it would've been a hard no. She hadn't even wanted to look at the house then, despite the major differences in its appearance. Now she didn't think of the old house when she looked at it, and Don's side—the one Mom had rented—looked nothing like it had. Janna had seen that herself when they happened to be at their mailboxes at the same time and Don invited her and the children inside. The rental side was just as nice, according to Luke. "God hasn't given us a spirit of fear," she said.

He squeezed her hand gently. "*Nee.*"

"What about the rent?"

"Six fifty a month. Plus electric and water, but they'd be low if you're here most of the time. And if you're helping out as much as you have been, that'll cover part of the rent."

Even less than the Akron house? "That can't be right."

"It's smaller than the Bollingers' rental, and 322's a busy road," he said. "A lot of people don't want to live right on Division Highway."

True enough.

A mix of emotions rushed through her, and she pressed her lips together.

"*Was iss letz?*"

"As we were crossing the street in Akron, that carriage went by and the driver reminded me so much of *Daadi* Eli." Her throat ached, but she determined to finish. "I know I'll never be able to make up for everything he and Salena did for me. Now he's gone, but she's still here . . . and I just . . . I want to do whatever I can for her. Just be here with her—and you and Joah."

Luke let go of her hand and slipped his arm around her,

resting his hand on her shoulder. "She'll cherish that more than anything." He jutted his chin toward the lane. "So will they. And so will I."

Janna grinned. Right now the only thing she loved more than his closeness and affection was the joy that filled her heart. Across the lane, the children stood together against the shadowy backdrop of rolling fields, bathed in the full moon's dim bluish glow. They held up their jars, probably deciding who had more lightning bugs.

What joy it brought to her heart, knowing best friends wouldn't be separated this time. Not the ones catching lightning bugs beneath the starry sky, and not the ones sitting side by side on the porch just as they had so many years ago.

Two evenings later, Luke could barely contain his grin as Janna carried Joah's birthday cake—chocolate with cream-cheese frosting, his favorite—to the kitchen table. Seven light-blue candles burned amid matching icing spelling out *Happy Birthday*, flickering light on Joah's face when Kayla outened the light.

Mamm had never been one for birthday fanfare, but he detected the slightest smile on her face as the rest of them sang "Happy Birthday." With how the children had been almost glum at supper, still thinking Janna and Kayla would be moving away, she probably couldn't bring herself to protest.

Joah blew out his candles, then proceeded to open his gifts while Janna cut the cake. He politely thanked *Mamm* for the three new shirts and two books she gave him, then took the crayon-decorated envelope Kayla handed to him.

"That's from all of us," she told him, smiling like she knew a secret.

He removed the *Jesus Loves Me* sticker that held the flap closed and pulled out the contents—eleven pseudo-tickets Janna and Kayla had drawn and colored. As he read the one on top, his face lit up. "Cherry Crest Adventure Farm! We're going there again?"

"Tomorrow!" Kayla burst out as if she couldn't hold back a moment longer. "Those aren't the real tickets, but Mama and me made one for each person going."

Mamm had been adding a scoop of ice cream and a spoon to the cake slices Janna placed on plates, and now she started passing them around.

Joah spread the tickets out on the table. "How come there's so many? I just counted eleven."

"Do you remember what you said when we were there?" Luke asked. "How maybe we could come back for your birthday and bring some other people with us?"

"Mahlon's!" he exclaimed after a moment. "They're going with us?"

"*Ya.*"

Joah looked at the tickets—all of them the same except for their colors. "This will be the *best* birthday ever."

Janna stepped to the counter, then returned with another envelope, this one undecorated. "What if I said your birthday can get even better?" She handed it to him. "Although, this isn't really a birthday gift, and it's for you *and* for Kayla and *Mammi* Salena."

Now in her chair, *Mamm* waved a hand. "*Ach*, what's this about?"

Joah looked around at all of them, then pulled out the folded sheet of white paper inside. After unfolding it, he stared at the photograph of a house printed in the center of the sheet.

Kayla got up and rounded the table to look at it. "That looks like the house across the road."

"*Ya.* That's Don's house." Joah looked up at Janna, bewildered.

"That's where Kayla and I will be living." She pointed to the front door on the left side of the house. "Right there, on the other side of Don."

"You're not moving to Akron?" *Mamm* asked.

"*Nee.* Mrs. Bollinger's son offered to dissolve the lease, and I agreed. Don's tenants are moving out the end of next month, and Kayla and I will move in then. Although I'm thinking we'll be spending most of our time here."

As Kayla squealed, jumping up and down, Joah burst into tears. He bounded out of his chair and buried his face in Janna's side. Janna hugged him back, leaning down to whisper in his ear.

Mamm now grinned genuinely.

After they'd finished their cake and ice cream, Joah and Kayla went to find a board game for them all to play.

"Why don't you just stay here, save your money?" *Mamm* said as she and Janna met by the sink, both with plates in their hands. "'Tisn't like we need the *daadi haus* for anyone else."

Janna glanced at Luke.

He nodded, and she set the plates on the counter and faced *Mamm.* "Because we can't."

Mamm looked from her to him. "*Ach,* why not?"

Luke stopped behind Janna, putting his hands on her shoulders.

She glanced up at him and grasped his one hand where it sat. "Because we can't."

Mamm inhaled quickly as realization came. "I see." She seemed circumspect, as he'd anticipated.

"We talked a long time last night," Luke said, "and we're

both fully committed to this relationship and to being patient with each other as we work through any differences. Neither of us have doubts."

Salena smiled again. "*Ach*, you make me happy. And it's not even my birthday."

Nee, that wouldn't be till the beginning of next June, but if all went as hoped, he would have an even better gift for her then—making this young woman *Mamm* loved dearly her granddaughter-in-law.

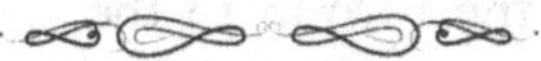

At the end of the lane, Janna kissed Joah and Kayla, then watched as they climbed the steps of the school bus. The two slid into the second seat on the side closest to her and Luke before their faces appeared in the window.

Having never ridden a bus before, Joah had seemed nervous while they waited for this one's arrival, but now he smiled and waved along with Kayla. Probably because the driver was also the children's Sunday school teacher and Luke had just reminded them that the bus would be picking up Naomi, Amanda, and Caleb too.

The driver waved, and moments later the bus pulled away.

Janna watched it until Luke rested a hand on her back, then looked up at him.

"Ready?"

Actually, she was. Although the end of summer always saddened her a bit, she looked forward to this next part of their life. Kayla loved school—as did Joah, according to Luke—and what better school environment than the one God provided for them? As well, she was ready to get back to editing regularly, and not at crazy hours.

She turned, and he took her hand as they walked toward the house. Smiling, she interlaced their fingers and stepped closer to him. Neither spoke, not that she minded. It was such a beautiful day, clear and sunny and slightly cool for the end of August, and birds sang from the tall maple alongside the lane, no longer rivaled by cicadas.

Amazing. This last year—the last couple of years—had been so incredibly difficult at times. Yet God truly had used everything for good. And his plan was turning out so much more marvelous than anything she'd envisioned.

As they passed the turn-in to the shop's parking lot, she slowed, wishing for more time with Luke. He matched her pace, but too soon they came to where the *daadi haus* was to the right side of the lane and the shop to the left.

Three purple martins flew in and landed on the martin house, their loud chirps mixing with those of the birds already perched there.

"I guess they'll be heading south in the next month or so," she said, hoping to prolong their time before he went into the workshop and she went into the house to help Salena start the laundry.

Luke didn't look away from the birds. "They'll be back come April, though, like always." He released her hand and drew her to his side with an arm around her middle. "*Dee flickel fleeya, ava's hatz vaased da vaag haem.*"

The wings do the flying, but the heart knows the way home.

Ya, theirs did, and so did hers.

DISCUSSION QUESTIONS

1. Janna and Kayla Carpenter move to Akron—or attempt to—in search of a new beginning in their life. In your own life, have you ever felt like you needed to make major changes so you could move forward? Why do you think Janna chose Lancaster County after being away for so long?

2. Luke Martin also wants change in his life. Struggling to balance running a business and caring for his aging mother and young son, he grapples with the feeling that his business, although necessary to support his family, is taking precedence. What are some ways people can deal with this common feeling?

3. Janna and Luke's relationship starts out complicated. Her desire for independence and his traditional Old Order principles set them at odds and cause tiffs between them. What events lead to their putting their differences aside and rekindling their friendship?

4. Both Luke and Janna have people who speak wisdom into their lives. Who are they for each character, and which ones are your favorites?

5. Janna is devastated when she learns that her mother intercepted the letters she and the Martins wrote to each other almost fourteen years before. How do you think she came to terms with that betrayal?

6. Luke also feels betrayed by his mother, who has been mostly absent from his life. Were you surprised when she left so abruptly even after promising Luke that she wanted to change their relationship for the better? Why or why not?

7. Toward the end of the story, Luke makes the difficult decision to change churches, stating that he believes that is God's leading. Describe a time in your life when you knew with certainty that God was guiding you to make a significant change.

8. Luke and Janna's biggest confrontation happens after a friend from church invites Janna and the children to go to the community pool with them and Janna accepts. Who did you relate to more in this situation, Luke or Janna?

9. Despite their differences, Luke and Janna also share a lot of similarities. What are they, and which ones do you think were most important in impelling their relationship beyond friendship?

10. Who is (are) your favorite character(s) in the story? Why? Which character do you relate to the most? Why?

11. What was your favorite scene in the book? Which was your least favorite?

12. What is your greatest takeaway from reading this story?

Author's Note

The Heart Knows the Way Home is a story I once told myself I'd never pen. Contemporary Plain fiction ranked pretty high on my "Things I'll Never Write" list. As someone who attended an ultra-conservative Mennonite church in my late teens and early twenties, I worried that writing about Plain people would seem like an exploitation of my former church family and those like them. My beliefs are no longer completely in line with theirs, but I would never want to disrespect them in any way.

And then God put a story on my heart—this story—and revealed a way that it could benefit the Amish and Mennonite communities. My mind began to change.

Several years ago, I learned about Clinic for Special Children (CSC), a nonprofit medical facility in Strasburg, Pennsylvania, that serves children and adults with genetic and other complex medical disorders. Many of CSC's patients are Amish or Mennonite, and this can compound their medical care since the Old Order groups and some of the conservative groups don't carry health insurance. Genetic testing is expensive, let alone lifelong medical care, but the clinic is dedicated to serving their families by providing cutting-edge yet affordable services.

As a nonprofit, CSC's ability to operate relies primarily on collaborative funding, benefit auctions and fundraisers, and contributions. In 2019, clinical and lab fees made up only 11 percent of its yearly revenue (2019 Annual & Innovation Report). I've contributed by donating and participating in CSC's annual 5K, but my desire to do more brought a question to my author mind: What if I, through my writing, could bring awareness and even some financial support to CSC? Many readers of Amish and Mennonite fiction have a deep fondness for Plain people and their lifestyle. Knowing that, I suspected that some, if they knew about CSC, would be impelled to support it, knowing their donations would greatly benefit Amish and Mennonite families.

With that in mind, I let this story unfold. My prayer is that it blessed you as a reader and will bless CSC by bringing awareness to its mission and through proceeds from this book's sales. If you've bought this book, thank you! A portion of its earnings will be donated to CSC. And if you're inspired to learn more about CSC or to contribute (God bless you!), you can do so by visiting www.clinicforspecialchildren.org.

Carry one another's burdens;
in this way you will fulfill the law of Christ.
GALATIANS 6:2 CSB

ACKNOWLEDGMENTS

My first and foremost thanks, as always, go to Jesus Christ—my blessed Savior, sovereign Lord, and closest friend; the author and finisher of my faith; and the giver of any talent I have. *Soli Deo gloria.*

Many thanks to my family for their constant support.

Anyone can write a book, but it takes a village to bring it to life. Unending thanks to all those who have helped take this story from idea to completed book:

Marlene Bagnull, for your friendship and invaluable knowledge of all things writing and publishing related.

Jean Bloom, for your exceptional editing skills, and Hannah Linder, for your graphic art prowess.

My amazing critique partners (Verna, Vicki, Lori, Lisa, Carolyn, and the rest of the Thursday-night group; Lee Carver, Tanya Eavenson, Ginger Solomon, and Cele LeBlanc), for your faithful friendship, wise input, much-needed laughs, and continuous encouragement.

Elva Hurst, Joe and Esther Keim, and Rachel Galloway, for answering my questions and assisting with the *Deitsch* used in the book.

Finally, a sincere thank-you to all my prayer warriors. You know who you are, and I'm forever grateful to do life with you.

About the Author

For as long as she can remember, Christy Distler has dreamed her most vivid dreams with her eyes wide open. Names became people—people who didn't exist in this time and place but couldn't have been more real in her heart and mind. So she did the only rational thing: gave them a voice by writing fiction.

Christy's novels, whether historical or contemporary, delve into betrayal and reconciliation, faith and grace, and always involve the intertwining of cultures. When not writing, she works as an editor for publishing houses and independent authors.

Obsession with words aside, she lives with her husband, children, and dogs in Pennsylvania.

To connect with Christy, please visit www.christydistler.com
or scan this QR code:

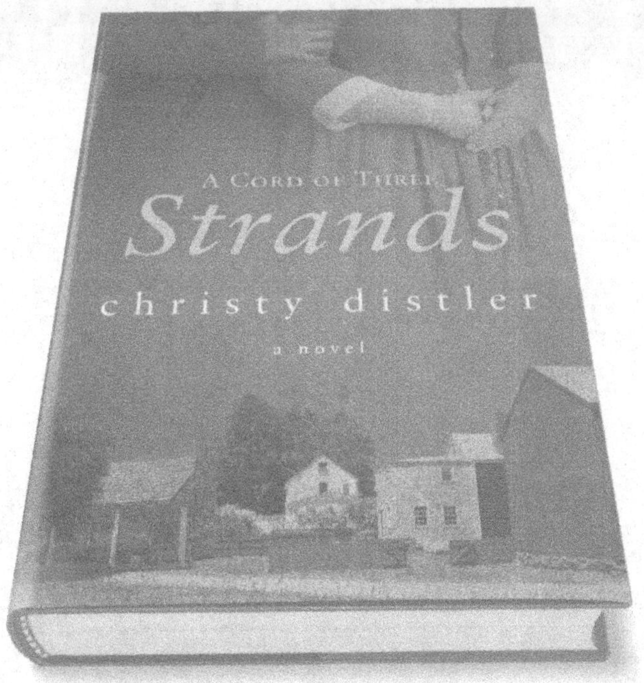

Take a step back in time to 1756 Pennsylvania as Isaac
Lukens, the son of a French trader and a Lenape woman,
returns to the Quaker community where he was reared.
There he finds his dearest childhood friend, Elisabeth
Aldan, striving to keep custody of her young siblings.

As their devotion to one another deepens, both must make
decisions that could bind them together or tear them apart.

CHAPTER 1

Isaac

Late Second Month (February) 1756
Northampton County, Pennsylvania

Even before we saw the smoke, I smelled it. Not the sweet, welcoming scent that curled from a frontier cabin's chimney but a faint yet acrid odor that foretold a scorching destruction.

I scanned the barren treetops on both sides of the road, listening. No other sound accompanied the soft crunching of snow beneath our moccasins. Still, the skin on my shoulders tightened and prickled.

"Isaac." Beside me, Sam Milham backhanded my arm and stopped. His pale-blue eyes narrowed beneath the beaver fur of his woolen cap as he scanned the clear sky and surrounding forest. Finally, he jutted his chin toward the summit fifty paces ahead. "That way."

Gripping the arms of our travois tighter, I set out for the

crest. My longer strides and the weight of his ration sack put me several steps ahead of him, but he caught up when I slowed.

Thick gray smoke rose from a clearing in the trees, about one hundred and fifty yards into the vale below and thirty yards east of the road. Dense haze blanketed the area, its concentration diminishing as the wind drove it southeastward.

Sam swore. "It's a settler plantation. You think it's Wolf Clan?"

God forbid it. But with the increasing war parties that ravaged the frontier, that seemed more likely than an inadvertent cabin or barn fire. "Let's go." I plunged through the ankle-deep snow as quickly as the road's slope allowed.

We had almost reached the wagon path to the plantation when gunshots rang out. A woman's cry resonated through the trees, and whoops followed. Moments later a shriek pierced the air. Then silence.

I stopped, lowering the travois to the ground, then crept into the wood. My heart pounded, stealing my breath. Far off, a hawk screed. Distant sounds of laughter echoed.

"They're intent on revenge." Sam's coarse whisper came from behind. "We can do nothing."

We didn't know that. Not for certain.

Navigating the trees, I headed for the upwind end of the clearing. Sam cursed again but followed.

None of what I'd seen and heard in our village last month—the warriors' reprehensible stories, the scalps they displayed atop spears, or the bound, exhausted captives they dragged behind them—prepared me for what awaited in the glade.

The cabin smoldered, one end still burning. Flames had already blackened the barn beyond. Amidst the smoke and floating ash, bodies lay strewn—a man and a boy of possibly fourteen near the barn, a younger boy by the cabin, and a woman at the edge of the wood. Crystalized blood stained the snow around their heads, confirming their fate.

Bitterness rose to my throat, and I swallowed it before it choked me. Surely this family had committed no offense, yet they had been butchered like animals.

As I neared the prostrate woman, four buckskin-clad warriors trotted from between the cabin and barn, their scalp locks swinging. Only the leader, who held a hunting gun against his shoulder, didn't use an arm to shield his nose and mouth from the pungent smoke.

They emerged from the haze, and the leader's lips contorted into a sneer. The contrast of white teeth against his black-painted face added to its malice. "Walks In Two Worlds," he called in Lenape. "Has the half-breed and his yellow-haired friend finally decided to join us?"

The others snickered and lowered their arms, baring their faces.

Wolf Clan indeed. Walks In Two Worlds was what that clan's warriors from the west, those who had forsaken our tribe's peace with the province, called me with contempt. Their thin frames and smooth skin purported they were younger than I. Even their leader had likely seen no more than twenty winters. Already they were murderers.

"These people did nothing to you!" I started toward them, shaking with anger. For the first time in many months, speaking our native language felt foreign. "Have you no conscience?"

The leader stopped five paces from where I stood, his expression sobering. Then his smirk returned. "What would our great sachems say now, seeing the one who once spewed pleadings for peace now consumed by fury?" He swept out his hand. "They took what was not theirs—our land. We are taking it back."

Sam grabbed my arm, halting my advance.

A child's shrieks carried from within the forest, then another warrior emerged with a young boy who flailed and cried out for his mama. As they approached, the warrior, no older than fifteen winters, exuded the pride of a young hunter who'd shot his first deer.

"I told you I would find him." He dropped the boy at his feet, then grabbed the child's tousled brown hair and unsheathed the knife at his waist.

Charging forward, I knocked the knife from his hand and shoved him to the ground. "Coward! He is a child."

The young warrior jumped to his feet, glaring. "So were William Penn's sons, once. If we had destroyed them in their youth, this land would still be ours. Our families would be thriving here, not starving and dying of white man's sickness."

I stood over the trembling boy. "Taking his life will neither right the wrongs nor bring back what we have lost. You will not lay a hand on him again."

Sam drew his pistol. Despite his short stature and how his veins contained not a drop of Indian blood, his thirteen years in the wilderness, apt aim, and hand-fighting skill had earned him the reputation of a man not to be crossed. But gratitude for Sam's unapologetic defense succumbed to recognition of my hypocrisy.

The young warrior spat at me. "Walks In Two Worlds speaks our language with a forked tongue. Though he is Lenape, he clings to the white man's Quaker religion. Many applaud the peace he promotes, but he is a traitor to his suffering people."

The leader swung his hunting gun toward me, but Sam trained his pistol on him and cocked the hammer before the leader could shoulder his weapon.

Scowling, the leader grabbed his gun by the barrel and dropped its butt to the ground. "The boy is ours." Spread out behind him, the others made no move. Their glares confirmed their refusal to yield.

Our rations.

"Let's trade, then." I nodded at where the wagon path entered the clearing. "Two and a half bushels of shelled corn sit on a travois near the road. Take them."

The young warrior scoffed. "Shelled corn?"

"Are you not only a coward but also a fool?" The furious words left my mouth before I could temper them. "Parched, the corn will feed your families. The boy will not."

The leader jerked his head, and one of the others ran off to the path. After peering through the wood toward the road, he turned back and nodded.

"We go," the leader said.

Sam didn't stand down. "Leave the travois."

The young warrior glowered at me as he trailed the others. "Walks In Two Worlds' days are numbered," he hissed as he passed us. "Soon he will walk only in one—the spirit world."

Sam pursed his lips as they disappeared into the forest. "That was to feed *our* village, my friend."

As if I didn't know that. The two of us had spent weeks trapping beavers for pelts we needed to barter for corn and other rations, not to mention our week traveling to and from the trading post. The rations still filled his sack, but without the corn, the gnawing hunger in our bellies would not soon relent. "They would have taken his life."

He snorted. "Now they will try to take yours."

The warriors gone, I knelt beside the boy, who wore only breeches, a shirt, and stockings. He cowered when I placed my hand on his shoulder, drawing up his knees and covering his head with his arms.

"'Tis all right. I won't hurt thee," I said in English. After lifting him to his feet, I eased his hands from his face. He trembled as his teeth chattered, and the tears pooled in his bulging brown eyes slid down his cheeks. When he tried to look around, I cupped his chin and held it fast. "My name is Isaac. What is thine?"

He gulped, his face deathly pale against the darker skin of my hand. "J-Jeremiah." By the odor about him, he'd urinated on himself.

"We won't let them harm thee, Jeremiah." I doffed my buckskin frock and wrapped it around him. "Which way is thy closest neighbor?"

He turned, pointing to another trail into the wood, fortunately in the opposite direction of the road. As his gaze settled on the woman lying twenty-five paces away, he gasped. "Mama?" He pulled free and lurched toward her. "Mama!"

I caught him by the arm and stood, picking him up and pressing his face to my chest.

Behind us, wood creaked and groaned. The barn's front wall slowly caved in, sending the remainder of the roof crashing down. Out rushed a hot billow of smoke thick with embers and ash, and I turned away.

Sam shielded his face in the crook of his arm and moved toward the trail. "Nothing more we can do."

With Jeremiah still clutched to my chest, I followed. We had no choice but to pass the woman, and I couldn't look away from her. She had been shot through the back and partially scalped, with much of her light hair now matted red.

Elisabeth.

I stopped, reminded of my beloved childhood friend. From

behind, the long, wavy hair and slight frame could have been hers.

My burning throat clenched, and I moved on before I retched. The woman had lost her life, probably trying to save her boy's. Now he had no family, orphaned just as I'd been when I wasn't much younger than he.

As we tramped through the forest, Jeremiah clung to the front of my shirt. "I want Mama," he said again and again, sobbing. "I want my mama."

Tears smarted my eyes as I held him tighter. "I know thee does." And I did, for suddenly I longed for my mother as well.

~

Chinkanning Indian Village
Tunkhannock, Pennsylvania

By the time Sam and I reached our village four days later, word of our encounter with the warriors from the west had already arrived. Many of the people regarded me in silence, not even responding to my greeting as we walked between the lines of *wikwams*.

Part of me couldn't blame them. I'd traded much-needed corn for a white child's life, in their minds stealing food from their mouths and insulting our tribe by placing importance on a boy born of people who'd taken so much from them. Those who'd once esteemed my endeavors to advocate for the Lenape, both with the Six Nations who controlled us and with the province, now considered me a disgrace.

The only thing that troubled me more was the plight of young Jeremiah. The neighbor family had welcomed him with much affection, sorrowfully promising to see to the burial of his kin, but no amount of love would expunge the agony of violently losing his parents and brothers. The despair that hollowed his stare had reawakened the anguish of losing my first parents, even though I had no memory of them.

Then came my summons. Our leader wished to speak with me.

Afterward, Sam stepped into pace beside me as I left the village seeking solace. "What did Teedyuscung want?"

I slowed but didn't look at him. "He said 'tis time I leave the village."

Sam grabbed my arm, stopping me. "No."

Despite myself, I smiled. In the two years I'd known him, rarely had he shown sentiment for anyone. He'd lived alone in the wilderness for years until our tribe had come north to our former village in Wyomink and met him nearby. He made no secret of how he often preferred solitude. "Thee will miss me, then?"

He crossed his arms. "After everything you've done for them, they now want you to leave because you confronted a bunch of boys playing warrior and called one a coward?"

I shook my head. The fault was mine alone. "The wrath I showed has undermined the gentleness and reconciliation I've always encouraged. They think I've sided with the settlers. Teedyuscung also believes I must leave for my own safety. The warrior I shamed vows revenge, and I will not retaliate. Teedyuscung fears my life will be quickly taken."

Sam clapped a hand on my shoulder. "Not while I'm around, my friend."

I matched his gesture, obliged. Despite our ten-year age difference and how he dismissed the nonviolence I embraced, his loyalty was unparalleled. "I thank thee, but Teedyuscung is right." Releasing his shoulder, I started to walk again. To where, I didn't know, but I could not remain still. "I cannot stay here any longer. Too many now forsake peace, and my strivings for harmony are no longer welcome, even amongst my own Turtle Clan."

Even Teedyuscung, a fellow Turtle and once a close companion in building the chain of friendship between the Lenape and the province, had turned to retaliation of the most vile kind. "Despite our differences now, he wishes no harm come to me. 'Tis time I returned to Horsham."

"No." He seized my arm again.

"Sam, I'd decided even before he summoned me. More than two years have passed since I've seen my family. Never did I intend to stay away so long. The tribe will be moving to Diahoga when the cold spell ends, and I cannot travel any farther from home." I sighed and clasped his shoulder again. "Lord willing, I leave tomorrow."

Clenching his jaw, he stalked away. "Or maybe you're a coward as well, Isaac Lukens."

Maybe I was.

~

Lecha River Valley (Lehigh Valley), Pennsylvania

I didn't know what I loathed more, the biting cold that stung my face or the gnawing hunger that consumed my belly. After four days of travel by night, both made me yearn for a place to tarry, for the warmth of a blazing fire and a hot meal. But where?

I'd traveled the Nescopeck Path many times, but the blue-black veil of early morn and the newest blanket of snow obscured any familiarity with the landscape. Considering the moon's change in position since I'd passed Gnadenhutten—or the burned remains of the Moravian mission—surely I neared Bethlehem.

Or perhaps my disorientation came from exhaustion. Never had I longed for home more, and that pushed me on despite the ache of my limbs from plodding through snow since nightfall. With the mountainous terrain now miles behind me, the promise of easier travel over rolling hills kept me moving.

Wind clicked the bare branches high above me, and an owl hooted in the distance, breaking the hushed stillness of the snow. Something rustled within the wood, heightening my senses. I glanced through the trees on either side, searching for the glow of eyes. 'Twasn't the first time I'd sensed animal presence along the path, and hopefully, whatever it was didn't share my level of hunger.

Just as my fingers found the bone haft of the knife sheathed at my waist, the sound of movement through the snow spun me around.

Nothing there. I listened for several moments, and at hearing only silence, turned to continue. Fifteen paces ahead, a silhouette stepped from behind a tree at the road's edge, a hunting gun pointed at me. A shorter shadow emerged onto the path behind him, his gun also at the ready.

"Vhat's your name and vher are you going?" the taller one asked.

I held out my hands. "Please. I—"

"He has a knife," the other yelled.

Footsteps crunched behind me, turning me around again. A thunderous sound echoed, and a blow to my back staggered me. I tried to face my attacker, but the fire that seared through my side spun the world atilt.

When I opened my eyes, four men stood above me, two with guns trained on my face. The beating of my heart thudded in my ears. "Please," I rasped. Every breath intensified the agony that sliced through me. "I mean thee . . . no harm."

"Vhat?" One of them knelt beside me and leaned closer.

"*Ach*, I know dis man." He huffed. "You shot da Quaker peace-maker who lives vith da Lenape."

Shot?

"How was I supposed to know that, him travelin' by night an' dressed like a savage?" a gruff voice said. "He coulda been traveling with others, looking to ambush like the ones that massacred Hayes' militia."

"Looks a whole lot more Indian than Quaker to me," another voice said, followed by guffaws from at least two of them.

"*Ruhe!*" A hand clutched my arm as they provided the silence he demanded. "Vhat's your name again?"

I swallowed, gritting my teeth. "Isaac . . . Lukens."

"*Ja.*" He stood. "Shtand him up."

"What'll we do with him?"

"I vill take him to Tom McCue's. Now help me shtand him up."

Hands gripped my arms and heaved me to my feet.

The pain exploded into engulfing blackness.

The brightening deep-blue sky of dawn stretched above me. My side throbbed, the pain sharpening to a torment that stole my breath with every jostle. I lifted my head but then dropped it back onto the hay beneath me. Wooden wagon sides rose around me, and a thick blanket that smelled of damp wool and livestock covered my body.

So tired. My eyes closed, but I forced them open. Where was I, and where was I being taken?

The wagon jolted through a rut, forcing a groan from deep in my throat. I held my breath until the sting eased, then moved my hand to where it hurt most. Sticky warmth soaked my shirt.

When I pulled my arm from beneath the blanket, blood stained my hand.

Aye. The men on the Nescopeck Path, the crack of the hunting gun, the insufferable pain. A destination mentioned, but what was it? I couldn't remember.

Another jar of the wagon brought a grunt through clenched teeth.

"Ve're halfvay der." The booming voice came from somewhere above my head. "My name is Dieter Kolb. Vher ver you going?"

"Horsham. North of Philadelphia." Despair flooded me. With a bullet wound, 'twould be days before I could finish my journey.

"*Gut.* You vill be safe vher I take you—and safer yet when you get to your Horsham."

Safe? I desired not safety but peace. Peace between the people of my father, white settlers seeking religious freedom in America, and those of my mother, the Lenape who'd long inhabited the lands but had them stripped away. Reconciliation now seemed hopeless.

I closed my eyes, my heart rent. For the second time in less than three years, I was taking leave of a place where I didn't belong. I hadn't found my mother's or father's family, and I could only hope the Friends who'd reared me would extend love and grace despite the selfishness I'd displayed in departing from them.

Chapter 2

Elisabeth

Second Day, Third Month 8th, 1756
Horsham, Pennsylvania

Eventide often proved the most lonesome time of day for me. This night was no exception. As much as the care of my young siblings added to my other responsibilities tired me, I often preferred their unrelenting needs to the taunting silence that filled the house once they were abed.

Now, in the quietness save for the crackle of the fire, I had turned to the reading of Scripture to comfort me.

"What is the Almighty impressing upon thy heart tonight, daughter?"

I looked up from my Bible. Papa watched me from his usual place in the wingback chair, the *Pennsylvania Gazette* he'd been reading now folded on his lap.

Jon-Isaac stirred in the cradle beside my rocker, and I reached down and patted him. When he calmed, I returned my attention to Papa. "The book of Luke, chapter eight. The parable of the candle."

"Does any verse speak to thee particularly?"

Indeed one did, and I made the brazen decision to share it. "'For nothing is secret, that shall not be evident: neither anything hid, that shall not be known, and come to light.'" Swallowing, I met his gaze.

His dark eyebrows knit as he shook his head. "We have discussed this. As thy father, 'tis my charge to protect thee."

I sighed. There he sat in his black breeches and waistcoat, white shirt, and cravat—as plain a Friend as I'd ever seen—yet he disregarded one of our steadfast Quaker tenets. "As Friends we embrace truth. According to Christ, it sets us free."

"'Tis Christ's truth that sets us free. Not all truth. And some truth is—" He canted his head, then stood.

A horse's muffled neigh came from outside, and I rose when Papa started for the door.

He opened it enough to step into the gap. "Hello?"

"Inside. Make haste," a familiar voice said. I couldn't immediately place it.

Papa backed up, swinging the door wide, and quick footfall sounded on the porch. A man in a dark woolen coat and hat ushered in two women fully shrouded in hooded cloaks.

Papa shut the door behind them.

The man looked up, and the glow of the candles and hearth fire illuminated his weathered face. Abner Jones, a Friend who lived a few miles to the north. "Please forgive the late intrusion, Jonathan. These two are in need of Friends' assistance." He turned to me. "Thy help especially."

Mine? The women huddled close together, one much taller than the other and both with their heads lowered to conceal their faces. "In any way I can."

Abner drew back the hoods. "This is Samson and Ruthie."

My breath caught. Before me stood a young man, about seventeen years, with thick black hair and the darkest skin I'd ever seen. His emotionless eyes, their whites yellowed, met mine momentarily before he averted them. Ruthie, with lighter skin, finer features, and a mass of long curly hair, lifted her head only slightly before crying out and clutching her middle.

Samson and Abner grabbed her arms as I moved closer. By the way she moaned, and Abner's comment to me, I suspected not illness but labor of childbirth.

"Breathe, Ruthie." I leaned over beside her and rubbed her lower back. "Breathe until it eases."

Her groans finally ceased. Straightening, she leaned against Samson.

She was but a child herself, fifteen years at most. Though likely five years younger than I, she would soon be a mother.

I disregarded that thought to attend what mattered most. "How close together are thy pains?"

She shook her head. "Don't know."

"I found them hiding in our barn tonight," Abner said. "Their master has men chasing them. Ruthie said her bag of waters broke this forenoon, and her labor started a few hours afterward." He looked to Papa. "I took them to Susannah Lukens, but no one was at home. I know she has been training Elisabeth in midwifery, and word is you both have helped the enslaved before. I hope you do not mind—"

"Of course not." I untied the strings at Ruthie's neck, and Abner slipped the cloak from her shoulders. "Come. We shall get thee more comfortable."

Samson removed his own cloak, then loosed the ties of the petticoat fastened low about his hips. He stepped out of it and handed it to Abner.

"These men pursuing you," Papa said to Samson, "are they close behind?"

Samson nodded once. "Near caught us last night."

Papa picked up the candle on the table beside his chair, then crossed the room to the kitchen area. After tossing back the braided rug, he lifted the door to the root cellar. "Down here."

Samson and I helped Ruthie, and Abner followed. Soon we were all in the cool, damp room that smelled of dirt, potatoes, and parsnips. By the flickering light of the candle, Papa and Abner unstacked the wooden crates behind the ladder, revealing the narrow opening in the dirt-and-stone wall. Papa slipped through first and had lit all the lanterns in the hidden room by the time the rest of us followed.

Abner looked around, taking in the sleeping pallets, basin and pitcher on a washstand, two chairs, and chamber pot. "Thee built this, Jonathan?"

"The root cellar I did." Even in the dim light, I could see Papa's expression darken. "Isaac walled in this room while he was living with us."

"I had no idea."

"'Tis safest that way." Papa glanced at me. "I shall get water and blankets. Abner, thee should go."

"Clean rags as well," I said. "And my bag."

With the two men gone, I faced Samson and Ruthie. Their clothing was filthy and tattered, even threadbare in places, and Ruthie shivered continuously, though that could have been from her labor. "Come rest." I led her to one of the pallets and knelt to help her sit.

"What can I do, mistress?" Samson asked.

"First, thee may call me Elisabeth. In the Almighty's eyes, I am no more valuable than thee. Therefore I deserve—and desire—no fancy title. And second, thee may sit behind her for support."

He did as instructed, not even hesitating at the impropriety of a man assisting, and I eased Ruthie against him.

His impassive expression softened. "You helped slaves before?"

"A few times, when the opportunity arose."

"And you birthed babies before?"

I pulled my handkerchief from my apron pocket and patted the perspiration from Ruthie's forehead. "Aye."

Just not by myself, not in a root cellar, and not when the baby's mother was a child herself and its parents were pursued by slave catchers.

Between the pains that gripped her, I helped Ruthie get undressed, washed down, into a clean shift, and settled on the blanket we placed over the pallet's straw tick. She turned onto her side, and I covered her with another blanket to ward off the chill.

The floor creaked above us as Papa, having brought down everything I needed as well as clean clothing for Samson, now moved about in the common room.

I knelt by Ruthie and drew the blanket partly aside. "Is the time right for thy confinement?"

She opened her eyes and rolled onto her back. "I reckoned it not for another month."

I felt around on her belly to determine the baby's position. Praise be to God, its head was downward and I felt quickening. "How old is thee?"

"Almost seventeen." Her face twisted, and she gritted her teeth as her belly contracted.

I let her squeeze my hand till the pain eased, then dabbed

her forehead with a dampened cloth. "Is Samson thy husband?"

She smiled, albeit faintly. "He ain't, but he loves me. He will be someday."

"The baby isn't mine." Samson's quiet words startled me, and I looked over my shoulder. He now stood behind me, having finished using the cellar's main room to wash and dress in Papa's old work clothing. "I wouldn't never compromise her. Our master, he did this to her."

Inconceivable. How any human could condone such an evil as slavery confounded me. Then I realized his narrowed eyes reflected affront toward me, not the situation. "Of course. I didn't think—" I searched for apposite words. "'Tisn't my intention to judge, only to understand so I can best help to birth this baby and keep you safe."

His expression eased.

"Please, come and sit behind her. Thy support will be a comfort."

He resumed his previous position, cradling her, and she looked up at him. With a sigh, she shifted her gaze to me. "We knew we were taking a chance, running with my time of confinement nearing, but our master found out about us—about our feelings for each other. He was gonna sell Samson. We couldn't wait."

I nodded, my heart convicted. I had spent much of the day lamenting to God about my life, and now its conditions seemed so trifling. Surely Samson and Ruthie would have traded places with me without a moment's thought. "You were brave to run, and we will do all we can to assist you."

Another pain seized her, this one so intense that she struggled to stay quiet and take the shallow breaths I demonstrated. When it ended, she relaxed against Samson but then clapped a hand over her mouth and pointed to the washstand.

I grabbed the basin, caught her grimy hair back from her face, and held the bowl as she vomited what little was in her stomach. She dry heaved a few last times, then leaned back, panting, and ran the back of her hand across her chin. "Sorry."

I set the basin aside. "No need to apologize. 'Tisn't uncommon during labor. Often, it means that birth is nearing." After re-dampening the cloth, I wiped her face again. "Does thee want to rinse thy mouth?"

She nodded.

I lowered my cupped hand into the bucket of water, then tipped it against her lower lip until a small amount of water flowed into her mouth. "Try to rest now."

She swallowed and closed her eyes.

Samson kissed the top of her head. When he rested his cheek on it, his eyes shone.

My heart went out to him. "She is doing well."

He nodded. "I love her more than anything. Despise to see her hurting. Wish I could bear the pain for her."

"You've already beared enough pain for me," she whispered. "Got the scars on your back to prove it."

He scowled. "And I'll do it again if I have to."

Tears welled in my own eyes as contradictory emotions overwhelmed me. My mind filled with fury toward an abhorrent system that treated humans as property to be used for selfish gain, yet my heart swelled with admiration—and a twinge of longing—for the bond they shared.

Sadness followed, for until a few years before, I had enjoyed such a sweet companionship with Isaac, my friend and protector from a tender age. Despite how his abrupt departure from our community still stewed bitterness deep within me, betimes I follishly allowed myself to imagine, even hope, for his return. Especially when trials came, and there had been no shortage of them since he had left.

For three more hours Ruthie labored. I tended her needs, recited the Scriptures Susannah Lukens used to comfort the women she attended, and prayed aloud for Ruthie, her baby, and our safety.

Another strong pain racked her, and this time she tried to sit up. "Need to use the chamber pot."

I stayed her with a hand on her forearm. "That's the baby thee is feeling. 'Tis time."

She nodded wildly, clenching her teeth.

How I wished we had Susannah's birthing chair—and her reassuring composure and knowledge. My legs, fortunately hidden beneath my petticoats and apron, quivered as I stood. "Samson, help her up so she can squat. Then kneel behind her, loop thy arms up under her shoulders, and steady her."

He did, and I placed a clean blanket on the floor beneath her, then lifted her shift to the tops of her legs. "Grab the fronts of thy legs now, Ruthie. Then with the next pain, bear down no matter how much it hurts."

The next contraction soon came, and with venerable strength and resolve, she bore down hard. The baby's head, covered with sodden black hair, appeared. It slipped back in when she stopped pushing but reappeared and then fully emerged with her next strain. I supported it with my hand. "Good. Now take another breath and bear down again."

She did, and after three more pushes, the baby slid out into my hands.

I turned the little girl over, lowering her head and patting her back to clear her mouth and nose. Her color looked good, but . . .

Breathe, baby. Please breathe.

Placing the infant on the blanket, I rubbed her with it to stimulate breathing and clean off the blood and pasty covering.

She squeaked, coughed a few times, and then kicked her legs and wailed.

Relief flooded me. *Oh, thank thee, Father.*

I looked up at Ruthie, whose tears now reflected not misery but joy. "Thy daughter is beautiful and has a fine set of lungs."

"My daughter," she choked out, then looked back at Samson. "Our daughter."

He nodded, smiling, and kissed her cheek. "Our *free* daughter."

~

Third Day, Third Month 9th

As soon as the sun rose the next morning, Papa sent my young stepsister, Abigail, through the wood to fetch our neighbor. Both Susannah Lukens and her elderly mother returned, and Abigail was then sent off to school, aware even at seven years of age that she mustn't mention those who hid in our root cellar. Mary Lukens stayed in the common room to care for Ethan and Jon-Isaac while Susannah and I took porridge and milk below.

Susannah examined the baby girl as Samson and Ruthie ate heartily, then handed her over to me so she could examine Ruthie.

I cradled the tiny infant close and swayed back and forth to quiet her fussing. "There, there, sweet girl." Taking in her pinched, reddening face, I considered the life she would live had her parents not fled. How I hoped she would never know such hardship.

"Thee did a fine job." Susannah's compliment came from behind, and she rested a hand on my back. "I knew thee would, when the time came."

I stroked the baby's soft cheek. "Her parents deserve the commendation, as does the Lord for his favor."

Rapid steps crossed the floor over our heads. "Elisabeth! Susannah!" Papa's voice carried into the cellar from above. "Men are riding in!"

My stomach constricted. Men? The slave catchers?

Ruthie's eyes bulged as she shook her head. "Oh, have mercy, Jesus. Have mercy on us."

Susannah took the baby. "Go back up. Close the cellar door and replace the rug." She laid the baby in Ruthie's arms. "Put her to thy breast to nurse. We must keep her quiet." She glanced back at me. "Make haste."

My heart fluttered as I left the hidden room and then climbed the ladder. My feet stumbled just as I grasped Papa's hand, and he yanked me up by one arm, then closed the door. I drew the rug overtop before hurrying to the table with him.

Sitting on the bench beside four-year-old Ethan, I cautioned, "Say not a word."

Within a minute, pounding shook the door, startling me despite how I'd expected it.

Papa calmly walked to the door and opened it.

Two men, both taller than Papa and dressed like frontiersmen, stood there. "We're lookin' for runaway slaves. Boy's eighteen, tall, black as tar. Girl's sixteen, thin but carryin' a child, brown skin, unkempt hair. You seen 'em?" The one speaking peered around Papa into the house.

Papa stepped back. "Look around if you must. You may look in the forge and barn as well."

They pushed past him, and Papa remained by the door as they entered each of the bedchambers and then returned to the common room. The one wearing a fox-fur cap started toward the table, eyeing me with a repulsive rotten-toothed grin as he crossed the braided rug. The root-cellar door creaked differently when he stepped on it, and he stopped and scowled down at it.

The crates! In my rush to leave the cellar, I'd forgotten to stack them.

Jon-Isaac fussed and reached for me, and I rose on unsteady legs and lifted him from his high chair.

Both men glanced around the common room, taking in the kitchen and sitting areas, then moved toward the front door. As they neared Papa, a whimper carried from below.

The other man spun around so quickly that his cap nearly fell off. "What was that?"

I slipped my hand beneath Jon-Isaac's petticoat and pinched his chubby leg as hard as I could.

He let out a screech, then started to wail.

"My apologies. Strangers frighten him." I held him closer and kissed his forehead.

The man beside Papa grunted. "C'mon. It's just the baby squallin'. They ain't here, and I can't stand babies cryin'. Check the forge and barn, but didn't I tell ya they're gone? This area's teemin' with these Quaker sort. The way some of them are against slavery, one o' them probably got 'em outta here durin' the night."

The other stared me down, then clomped toward the open doorway.

Papa closed the door after them. The rest of us stayed motionless for several moments, till Papa edged to the front window, staying out of sight.

I turned toward the table and handed Jon-Isaac his coral teething ring, but he pushed it away. "I'm sorry, sweet boy," I whispered and kissed his cheek.

Ethan tugged at my petticoat. "What's wrong with Jon-Isaac?"

"He's fine now." I sat next to him, holding Jon-Isaac close, and offered the ring again. This time he grabbed it with a chubby hand. He held the ring as his sobs abated, then leaned against me and gummed it.

Across the table, Mary smiled, nodding slightly.

Papa rejoined us several minutes later. "They are taking leave." He lowered himself to the bench beside me and used one finger to stroke Jon-Isaac's blond hair to the side of his forehead. "To everything there is a season, daughter." His blue eyes peered into mine. "Seasons to speak truth, and seasons when truth must be concealed. Thee understands this?"

I swallowed, still too shaken to protest. "Aye, Papa."

Sixth Day, Third Month 12th

"Does thee think Papa will return tonight?"

At Abigail's question, I looked up from watching Jon-Isaac in my arms. He slumbered deeply now, and I tucked him into his cradle, then joined her at the window. A mixture of snow and sleet pelted the glass, at times so fiercely that Abigail cringed.

When Papa had left with Abner Jones, Samson, Ruthie, and the baby early that morning, he'd told us he would be home by eventide. But that had been before the northeast snowstorm blew in. "He and Abner may have felt it safer to stay the night in Philadelphia."

She looked up at me, concern drawing her light brows together and filling her large green eyes. "Thee doesn't think danger befell them, does thee?"

I placed my hand on her shoulder. While I'd kept my temperament cheerful all day, hoping she wouldn't fret, even at her tender age she understood the risks of their trip. If Papa and

Abner were discovered to be aiding runaways, they would be heavily fined—and 'twasn't uncommon for slave catchers, in their pursuit, to harm those who assisted slaves. "I think 'tis more likely they stayed in Philadelphia to weather the storm." I glanced at the wall clock. "'Tis nearly eight. Time for bed."

"Can thee ready Ethan first? I want to watch for a while longer."

I smiled lightly. She wished for Papa's return as much as I did. "Aye. Come, Ethan." I started toward where he sat playing with his toys.

"Wait, he's coming." She rushed to the front door.

Praise be to God.

I met her there and cracked it open enough to look out. Amidst the driving snow, the wagon neared the house, then the horses halted ten paces from the porch.

"Elisabeth, help me!" 'Twas Abner Jones's voice that called out as the driver jumped down.

My stomach soured. Something was wrong. "Stay here," I bid the children, then trod across the porch and through the snow to the wagon. "Abner?"

He pulled a limp figure from the back of the wagon. "Help me get him inside."

Papa!

"What—"

"Get his legs."

I did, struggling with their weight, and we carried him into the house. "Abigail, bring a candle. Let's take him into his bedchamber." There we laid him on the bed, and Abigail set the candle on the table beside it. Even in the dimness, blood clearly covered the left side of his head and face and discolored his coat.

Abigail started to cry.

I opened the coat and placed my hand on his chest. At least

he still breathed. If he had other injuries, they weren't visible. "Hush now. Take Ethan and get some water and clean rags."

"The wagon got stuck in a rut about a mile from here," Abner said, huffing to catch his breath. "He gave me the reins and climbed down to lead the horses. The wind gusted, and a limb overhanging the road cracked. I yelled to him, but he couldn't get out of the way quickly enough. It came down right on him."

My throat threatened to close as my mind swam. I'd treated wounds before but never one so serious—and not Papa's.

He grasped my shoulder. "Staunch the bleeding. I shall go for Dr. Crossley."

I swallowed. "Take Midnight, the black stallion. He's faster. And stop to summon Susannah Lukens on thy way." Susannah knew almost as much about treating injuries as she did about midwifery. She also could be here in minutes, long before Abner could ride the two and a half miles to Hatborough to fetch the doctor and then return.

Abner squeezed my shoulder, then left.

Abigail and Ethan came back into the room, she carrying a bucket of water and he with arms full of linen rags. "Will Papa be all right?" she whispered.

My heart nearly broke at the tears in their frightened eyes. Only eight months ago, they had asked the same question about their mother. Within a day she had drawn her last breath.

But I mustn't dwell on such. "Lord willing. Now bring another candle and then watch for Susannah."

They obeyed without another word, and I used a dampened rag to start cleaning the blood from Papa's head. *Father, spare him,* I begged.

Papa and I might not have always agreed, but without him I'd be lost.